FINAL
DIAGNOSIS

A SECTOR GENERAL NOVEL

JAMES WHITE

TOR®

A TOM DOHERTY ASSOCIATES BOOK
NEW YORK

FINAL DIAGNOSIS

Copyright © 1997 by James White

Edited by Teresa Nielsen Hayden

A Tor Book
Published by Tom Doherty Associates, Inc.
175 Fifth Avenue
New York, NY 10010

Tor Books on the World Wide Web:
http://www.tor.com

Tor® is a registered trademark of Tom Doherty Associates, Inc.

ISBN: 0-812-56268-2
Library of Congress Card Catalog Number: 96-53877

First edition: May 1997
First mass market edition: July 1998

Printed in the United States of America

0 9 8 7 6 5 4 3 2 1

FOR MY LOVING WIFE PEGGY

42 YEARS ISN'T TOO LONG

CHAPTER 1

The ship's Orligian medical officer did not speak as it escorted him into and along the boarding tube to the hospital entry point, and that was the way Hewlitt wanted it. He did not like extraterrestrials and, on the few occasions when it was necessary, he preferred to discuss his business with them on a long-range communicator that was not fitted with a viewscreen. He did not like this one because the brownish-grey spikes of fur projecting through the gaps in its body covering twitched from time to time, making him itch at the thought of the parasites that might be infesting the creature. He felt a great relief when they left the narrow tube and entered the reception area beyond, because he was able to move farther away from the hairy, unprepossessing entity.

Another extraterrestrial of a type he had never seen before was standing beside an antigravity litter and obviously awaiting their arrival. This one was very large, heavily built, and supported by six thick tentacles, one of which was encircled by a band bearing what was presumably the insignia of rank or identity of the wearer. It wore no other body covering and he was relieved to see that it was hairless, although its personal hygiene was suspect since there were several patches of what looked like dry, flaking paint on the smooth skin of its flanks. He could see two lidless, recessed eyes covered by a hard, transparent material, but no other features apart from a fleshy membrane growing like a cock's comb from the top of its head, and whose purpose was revealed as an organ of speech when the creature moved closer and vibrated it at him.

"I am awaiting the arrival of a DBDG patient," it said. "You are plainly an Earth-human of the DBDG physiological classification, but you do not appear to be traumatized or displaying any lesser form of distress. Perhaps I have made a mistake and you are not—"

"No mistake, Nurse," said the Orligian, breaking in. "I am Surgeon-Lieutenant Turragh-Mar, of the Monitor Corps supply vessel *Treevendar,* which was requested to convey this patient from its home world to Sector General. But now I must return to my ship without delay. This is Patient Hewlitt, and these are its case notes."

"Thank you, Doctor," said the nurse, accepting the tape and slipping it into a recess on the litter's control panel. "Is there any more recent clinical information that the physician-in-charge should know about?"

Turragh-Mar hesitated, then said, "There has been no change in the patient's clinical condition since it was transferred from the planetary hospital to *Treevendar* six days ago. It remained as you see it now, apparently in good health. During that time I formed the opinion that, in spite of its long and complicated case history, there is a psychological component to the patient's problem."

"I understand, Doctor," said the nurse. "But Patient

Hewlitt can be assured that, however complicated its problem may turn out to be, we will do our best to solve it."

Turragh-Mar gave a short bark that came through its translator only as a short bark. It added, "I wish you luck."

"Patient Hewlitt," said the nurse as the Orligian disappeared into the boarding tube, "please climb onto the litter and make yourself comfortable. I am taking you to Ward Seven on the twenty-ninth level, where you will—"

"I am not climbing into anything!" said Hewlitt, anger and uncertainty and an instinctive dislike of this monstrous creature making his voice louder than he had intended. "There is nothing wrong with me right now, especially with my legs. I shall walk."

"Please believe me, sir," said the nurse, "you will feel much more comfortable in the litter."

"I would be much more comfortable," he replied, "if you would not talk about me as if I was a, a *thing*. On the way here that hairy Orligian apology for a doctor did it when speaking to other ship's officers, and within seconds of my arrival you were doing it, too. I am a human being, a 'he' or a 'him,' not an 'it.' You will kindly remember that in the future, Nurse."

For a long moment the other neither moved nor spoke. Then it said, "I know that you are human, just as all members of intelligent species think of themselves as being human. From my lectures on other-species anatomy I recognize you as an adult male of the DBDG Earth-human classification, but I must continue to refer to you as an 'it' unless some future clinical condition involving the reproductive organs or associated endocrinology requires me to be specific regarding your gender.

"Unfortunately," the nurse went on, "the identification of an entity's sex is not always as easy as it is in your case, especially among beings like myself, who are able to change sex several times within a life span, or with species who require more than two sexes for procreation. But it is a sensitive area, Patient Hewlitt, and often a wrong identification can be irritating or even, among some species, grossly insulting to the being wrongly identified. I believe that it will feel more comfortable and natural for you to think of me and any other being who is not of your own species as an 'it,' just as we do with you. Now will you please board the litter."

"Is your species hard of hearing, Nurse?" he said very loudly. "I said that I would walk."

The other did not speak, but it leaned backward slightly so that its enormous weight was balanced on the middle and rear tentacles. The two forelimbs uncurled suddenly, and before he could react, one had wrapped itself around his waist while the other pinioned his legs together at knee level while he was swung high into the air and deposited gently onto the litter. Their grip was firm but not uncomfortable, and he did not try to break free, because the tentacles felt hard, like warm, flexible metal, and immensely strong.

During the brief moment that he was airborne, Hewlitt saw that the limbs encircling him could act as both arms or legs. On the back of each one there was a roughened knuckle on which the creature walked while the more delicate extremity that divided into fingers was curled upward and inward away from the ground. Then the litter's padded body restraints swung inward to immobilize his upper legs, the vehicle's transparent canopy rose from each side but did not close at the top, and a hinged backrest unfolded until he was sitting upright. At least he was being allowed to hear as well as see whatever was going on around him.

Remembering the many previous litter rides in Earth hospitals, when there had been nothing to look at but a boring succession of white corridor ceilings and strip lighting fixtures, he appreciated that.

"Whether they are patients or staff," said the nurse, making no mention of the way it had just manhandled, or something-handled, him, "newcomers usually find traveling the corridors of Sector General on foot to be an intimidating experience at first. You may consider yourself fortunate that as a patient you are not allowed to walk."

"But I am *able* to walk!" Hewlitt protested as the litter was guided smoothly toward the corridor exit.

"Most of our incoming patients," said the other, "are in no condition to walk, talk, look around them, or argue with their nurse. It is a general rule that cannot be changed because of one exceptional case."

The door opened at their approach. Hewlitt immediately closed his eyes, and it was several seconds before he could force himself to open them again. All at once he was very glad of the thick, transparent canopy surrounding him.

Creatures out of the worst nightmares he had ever experienced, and a few new ones that he would probably have whenever he next went to sleep, were passing in both directions along the wide corridor, and the occasional human being among them only made the others look worse. Some of them were separated by a few yards, but more often they were clumped together into groups moving at different speeds who jostled past each other. There were massive, multitentacled beings terrifying in their great size and obvious physical strength; others who were horrifying and repugnant in the nauseous growths and slime sheen covering their dreadful, misshapen bodies. Some of the shapes were so ridiculous that he had trouble believing his eyes. One of the creatures was covered with silver fur that rippled and tufted continually as it undulated past the litter on about twenty legs. He remembered seeing a picture of one somewhere, and that their home world was called Kelgia. Gradually he was able to identify a few other familiar shapes from the extraterrestrial menagerie that was passing by.

The large, six-legged elephantine being with the four tentacles and immobile dome of a head was a Tralthan; a large, low-slung crustacean with the beautifully marked carapace that clicked past on thin, bony multijointed legs was, he recalled, a Melfan; and the small biped who looked like a half-size Earth-human covered in tightly curled red fur came from the planet Nidia.

The Nidian bumped gently against the side of the litter as it went past. It barked something at his nurse, possibly a reproof for bad driving, which was ignored. Like the cacophony of hooting, chirping, barking, or gobbling conversations going on all around him, it was just so much irritating, organic noise. This meant that the litter's translation device must have been programmed only for the languages of the nurse and himself.

Hewlitt disliked being kept in ignorance of anything that was being said around him. He wondered if he would be allowed a personal multitranslator during his stay in hospital. Probably not. If the medics here were anything like some of the ones he had met on Earth, they would not want their patient to know what was going on.

Especially if they were not sure themselves.

His unpleasant memories of many unsuccessful treatments on his home world were driven from his mind by the sight of a great, hissing metal juggernaut that was heading rapidly toward them on a collision course. He pointed and yelled, "Nurse, look out! Slow down, dammit, and move aside."

The nurse did none of those things, and the metal monster veered aside at the last moment and passed with a few inches to spare. Through the partly open canopy came the hot, odorless smell of escaping steam.

"That was the environmental protection vehicle of an SNLU," said the nurse. "It belongs to a heavy-gravity lifeform that evolved in an atmosphere of high-pressure superheated steam. We were in no danger from it."

The nurse removed one of its tentacles from the litter controls to point along the corridor before going on. "You will already have noticed that the beings you can see fall into two distinct types: those who avoid others, and those who are avoided by others. This is due to differences in medical rank, the insignia of which is displayed on a band worn around a limb or some other prominent bodily extremity. I am giving you this information now because it will also serve as a guide to establishing the relative seniority of the various doctors and nursing staff you will meet during treatment. You will soon be able to tell the difference between the band markings that I wear, which are those of a nurse-in-training, and a charge nurse, an intern, a member of the Psychology Department, a senior physician, or one of the diagnosticians.

"Theoretically," it went on, "the staff member possessing the greater medical seniority has right of way. But there are many who believe that it is stupid to suffer contusions or some lesser bodily discomfort by holding too strictly to this rule and, if the other being is more massive and well muscled than they are, simply get out of its way regardless of differences in rank. That is why nearly everyone gets out of my way. But in the case of a patient like yourself who is presumably in urgent need of treatment, the litter bearing you has priority of passage regardless of the low rank, very low in my case, of the nurse guiding it."

Feeling reassured, Hewlitt looked more closely at the beings around him instead of cowering and closing his eyes at their approach. *A person can get used to anything,* he was thinking, but a few minutes later he was not so sure.

"What . . . *what* was that disgusting, horrible thing that just went past?"

The nurse did not reply until they had turned in to an intersection and the creature was out of sight. Then it said, "That is a physiological classification PVSJ, an Illensan chlorine-breather, wearing the protective envelope necessary in an oxygen-rich environment. They have very sensitive hearing. You would do well to remember that."

Hewlitt could not remember seeing anything that looked like an ear, or an eye or a nose or mouth for that matter; just a spiny, membranous body that looked like a haphazard collection of oily, rotting vegetation writhing within the yellow fog inside the loose, transparent body cover.

"Nurse," he said with great vehemence, "no matter what my future treatment is to be, I do not want a thing like that anywhere near me!"

The nurse's speaking membrane vibrated, but no speech came through its translator. Then it said, "We will arrive in Ward Seven within a few minutes. I expect to be allowed to assist with your nursing care, Patient Hewlitt, and if there is any other way that I can help with nonmedical advice or information you have only to—"

"Aren't there any *human* doctors and nurses in this place?" he broke in sharply. "I want to be treated by people of my own species."

"There are many Earth-human DBDGs on the medical staff," the nurse replied, "but they might not want to treat you."

For a moment surprise and disbelief rendered him speechless, and not until his litter swung into a narrower and less populated corridor did the nurse answer the question that he had been too angry to ask.

"You are forgetting that this is a multispecies hospital," it said, "and recognized throughout the Galactic Federation to be the biggest and best of its kind. The people who are accepted for positions or advanced training here are selected from the best that their home planets' medical establishments can provide, and their purpose in coming here is to practice other-species medicine and surgery. So you will understand that one of them would not take your case unless specifically ordered to do so for a particular clinical reason. A DBDG Earth-human doctor would not feel that it had come all the way to Sector General just to treat another Earth-human when there are countless millions of those on Earth and the Earth-seeded worlds.

"Your Earth-human doctors and nurses want to work on the juicy ET cases," it went on. "You will come to understand that this is a very good thing, because much more care and attention, as well as a higher degree of personal and professional interest, is given to other-species patients. When a same-species doctor is treating its patient, certain clinical shortcuts may sometimes be taken, or incorrect assumptions made, or important symptoms cloaked by overfamiliarity with the patient's physiology. The occasions when mistakes like this occur are rare. But when an other-species medic is in charge of treatment, it takes nothing about its patient for granted. It is forced by the physiological differences to be very careful indeed, so that the incidence of clinical error is even rarer. Please believe me: you will be in very good hands, or whatever other appendages are appropriate.

"And remember, Patient Hewlitt," it added as the litter made another sudden change in direction, into a wide doorway, "to me, *you* are an ET case—with all that that implies. We've arrived."

Ward Seven was a large, brightly lit room about five times longer than it was wide, Hewlitt saw, with a clear area of floor running between two facing rows of beds. He felt pretty sure that they were beds because, in spite of their weird shapes and sizes and the strange equipment hanging above some of them, there was one at the other end of the room that was suitable for the use of an Earth-human. Just inside the entrance on his left there was a nurses' station and food-service facility enclosed by transparent walls, but the litter moved past it too quickly for him to see who or what was working there.

The space taken up by the combined station and kitchen allowed only eight bed spaces on that side, while there were twelve along the opposite wall. A few of them were enclosed by screens, and the quiet gobbling and barking of alien voices was coming from one of them, but without a translator he could not tell whether it was a medical consultation, friendly gossip, or the sound of an other-species patient in pain. Before he could ask, the litter stopped and he was lifted smoothly and deposited in a sitting position on the chair by his bedside.

The nurse pointed in turn to the three doors in the end wall that paralleled his bed and said, "The first one is the multispecies waste-elimination facility for mobile patients, the second is the bathroom, also multispecies, and the other one is for patients who require assistance to perform these operations. Your bedside cabinet is similar to the one you used on *Treevendar,* and the few personal effects you were allowed to bring with you will be moved to it later today. You have a call button in case you need attention, and there is a ceiling-mounted sound and vision pickup linked to monitors in the nurses' station in case you need urgent attention but are unable to call for it yourself. Your reading light is directional so that you will not inconvenience other patients during rest periods, and you have an audio plug, an earpiece, and a small viewscreen tuned to the in-hospital entertainment channels. The programs were recorded a long time ago, so you may not want to view them unless you are trying to put yourself to sleep without sedative medication.

"You are in bed eighteen," it continued. "As well as being the most convenient position to the toilet facilities, it is farthest from the ward entrance and the nurses' station. There is a generally held belief within the hospital, which has never been officially denied, that the closer a patient is to the ward entrance, where the doctor on call and the ward nurses can reach it with minimum delay, the more serious is its clinical condition and prognosis. You may like to take some comfort from that knowledge.

"And now, Patient Hewlitt," it went on briskly, "please undress, put on the hospital garment lying across your chair, and get into bed quickly before Charge Nurse arrives. I will remain outside the screen. If you need help, call me."

The nurse and its litter moved aside and the bed screens unrolled silently from their recess in the ceiling.

For what seemed like a long time Hewlitt held the hospital garment in his hands without moving. It was smooth, white, shapeless, and, like all the others he had known, at least two sizes too small. He did not want to lie in bed dressed in this thing; he wanted to sit in the chair and maintain some feeling of independence by wearing his own impeccably styled clothing. But then he remembered the nurse's vast strength and its closing remark that, if he needed help, he should call it. Had that been a politely worded threat to the effect that if he did not undress himself he would be undressed by force?

He would not give that tentacled monster the satisfaction, or perhaps the pleasure, of undressing one of its juicy ETs.

While he was climbing into bed, Hewlitt heard someone else approaching his bed, someone who made a soft, slithering noise rather than the sound of walking feet as it came. There was an unpleasant background sibilance to the translated words when it spoke.

"Nurse," it said sharply, "your paint is flaking. Give me the patient's case notes and your report, quickly, then go to your dining area without delay."

"Yes, Charge Nurse," the other replied. "When *Treevendar*'s medical officer, a Monitor Corps surgeon-lieutenant called Turragh-Mar, gave me the case notes, it said that there had been no observable symptoms or change in Patient Hewlitt's physical condition, but suggested the presence of a psychological component. The only evidence of this was its marked xenophobic reaction displayed during the ride here. I assumed from our earlier conversation that the patient has had very limited—if any—contact with other-species beings, and was likely to be disturbed by the sight of the hospital staff using the intervening corridors; and that my instructions to allow it to see them was intended to prepare it for the closer, in-ward contacts that it would experience later. By the time we reached the ward, the patient seemed to have its xenophobia under partial control, except for one species that it still finds visually distressing. . . ."

"Thank you, Nurse," the other voice broke in. "Now go at once for a respray before you collapse from hunger at my feet. I will take over from here."

The screens rose and disappeared into the ceiling to reveal the ghastly thing standing at the foot of his bed. Instinctively he pressed himself against the backrest in a vain effort to put more space between them.

"How are we feeling today, Patient Hewlitt?" it said. "I am Charge Nurse Leethveeschi and, as you have already noticed, I am an Illensan. . . ."

CHAPTER 2

Inside its chlorine envelope the thick, fleshy, yellow-green leaves twitched and slid open to reveal two stubby legs covered by what looked like oily blisters as the creature moved back from the foot of the bed.

"Do not be afraid, Patient Hewlitt," Leethveeschi said. "I have no intention of coming closer, much less of touching you, unless some future clinical emergency requires it. It may be helpful to consider the visual effect of your flabby, pink, smooth-skinned body on my aesthetic sensibilities. So please stop trying to push yourself backward through the wall and listen to me. You may close your eyes, if it helps. First, have you eaten recently? Second, do you have an urgent need to eliminate body wastes?"

"Y-yes," Hewlitt replied. Just to be contrary he kept his eyes open, trying to stare the disgusting creature down. But there were too many dark, wet swellings showing between its oily fronds and membranes for him to know which of them were eyes. He added, "Just before I left the ship. And no, I don't have to go to the toilet."

"Then you have no reason to leave your bed," said the charge nurse, "so please remain in it until Senior Physician Medalont has examined you and officially pronounced you capable of moving about the ward without nursing assistance. The next meal will be served in a little over three hours and your examination will take place before then. But there is no cause for alarm, Patient Hewlitt, because the procedure will be noninvasive and predominantly verbal.

"When you are allowed out of bed," Leethveeschi went on, "you will be given a translator programmed for the languages used by the ward patients and medical staff. It seems that you have had limited opportunities for other-species contact, and here you will be able to remedy that. Talk to the other patients as soon as you feel comfortable doing so and you are not getting in the way of the medical staff. Patients who have screens around their beds are either undergoing treatment, resting, or being isolated for other reasons, and those you must not disturb. Most of the patients will talk to you, if they are feeling sociable, and you need not worry about their outward appearance, because *all* of the patients here are ugly, gross, and visually repellent.

"Without exception."

He wondered if there had been a glint of humor in a few of the dark, wet blisters that might have been looking at him as it spoke the words, but dismissed the idea as ridiculous.

"In the bed opposite is Patient Henredth, a Kelgian," it continued. "Diagonally on your left is Patient Kletilt, from Melf, and beside you is an Ian named Makolli who is being transferred to Level Forty-Seven later today, so you may not get the chance to talk to it. I don't know who or what we will be sent in its place. But for now, Patient Hewlitt, you should try to relax, or sleep if you can, until the doctor sees you."

Leethveeschi's body parts slithered and writhed together

in a revolting fashion, and he realized that it was turning to go. He was pleased that the disgusting thing was leaving and wondered why he stopped it. After all, his question could have waited.

"Charge Nurse," he said firmly, "I have no wish to talk to anyone in this place unless it is absolutely necessary for my treatment. But there is one person I might be able to talk to with, well, less discomfort. That is the nurse who brought me here. I would not mind if it took part in my treatment, and I would prefer to call for it if there was something I needed. Please tell me its name?"

"No," said Leethveeschi with equal firmness. "Since it is the only Hudlar nurse attached to my ward, you will have no trouble identifying it. Just point a manipulatory appendage at it and call 'Nurse' loudly."

"Where I come from," said Hewlitt, trying not to lose his temper, "that would be considered the height of bad manners. Are you being deliberately unhelpful? You told me your name and those of the patients around me, so why not tell me the Hudlar's name?"

"Because," said Leethveeschi, "I don't know it."

"That is ridiculous!" Hewlitt burst out, no longer able to hold his temper with this loathsome and obviously petty-minded creature. "You are in charge of the nurses on the ward and you expect me to believe that you don't know all their names? Do you think I'm stupid? Oh, just forget it. I will ask the next time I see it and it will give me its name itself."

"I hope not!" said the charge nurse. It did something with its body that made it turn and move back until it was disconcertingly close to his bedside again.

"Regarding your degree of stupidity, Patient Hewlitt," it said, "I am constrained by politeness not to comment. But it is possible that you are ignorant rather than stupid, and I am allowed to reduce your level of ignorance.

"Our Hudlar nurse wears a band around one limb that shows its rank and hospital staff number," Leethveeschi went on. "The number is used for administrative purposes and is the only identity known to us. Since other species find Hudlars impossible to tell apart, if one of them has to be picked out of a group this is done by calling out the last few digits of its staff number. It is not called by name because the Hudlars consider their names to be their most private and personal possession. Among their species the name is used only by close members of the family, or among those who are intending to become life-mates immediately prior to conjugation.

"It seems that you may have formed a liking for our Hudlar nurse," it added, "but in the circumstances it is better that the relationship stops short of a personal exchange of names."

Leethveeschi returned to the nurses' station, making disgusting, untranslatable noises that sounded like someone in the last stages of pulmonary failure but were probably the sound of Illensan laughter. He felt sure that the heat of his embarrassment was warming the whole ward. Then he flung himself back against the pillows to glare at the monitor lens in the ceiling, wondering if the sudden reddening of his face would worry an observer and some other horrible medical creature would come hurrying to investigate.

Apparently not. Several minutes passed and there were no further visitations. But his relief was mixed with irritation as he wondered if he would have to do something melodramatic like falling out of bed and breaking an arm to attract attention. His embarrassment had faded, but it was being replaced by the old, familiar feelings of helpless anger and despair.

I should not have come here.

He looked along both sides of the ward at the large, complicated beds, several of whose occupants were not, unfortunately, screened from view, and beyond to the nurses' station, where the alien shapes were rendered a little less frightening by distance, and listened to the quiet barking and moaning and gobbling sounds of other-species' conversations. He had always felt distrustful of strangers, and even of relatives he had not met for a long time, because they usually represented varying degrees of change and disruption to the comfortable, organized, lonely, and moderately happy life he had made for himself. But now he was among the strangers who were stranger than he could ever have imagined, and it was his own stupid fault.

Hewlitt had been advised not to go to Sector General, by a succession of Earth doctors who had studied his psych profile and decided that it would not be a comfortable place for him. They had not, however, been able to do anything about his illness beyond stating the obvious, that his symptoms were unusually varied, nonspecific, and, at times, violently nonresponsive to the indicated medication. It was suggested that his trouble might lie in an overactive mind that was having a disproportionately large influence on the body containing it.

Being a solitary person out of necessity rather than choice, Hewlitt had had to take responsibility for looking after his own well-being, which included guarding himself against accident, illness, and infection. But he was not, or at least not entirely, a hypochondriac. He knew that there was something seriously wrong with him and that, in these days of advanced medical science, it was his right as a Galactic Federation citizen to demand that it be put right by somebody, somewhere.

He did not like being among strangers, but neither did he like the prospect of being intermittently and inexplicably sick for the rest of his life, so he had insisted on his rights. Now he was wondering if it would not have been better for him to stay and die comfortably on Earth. Here the treatment, and certainly the doctors prescribing it, were likely to cause him more mental anguish than the disease.

All at once Hewlitt wanted to be back home.

His attention was drawn to the nurses' station entrance, where two creatures had emerged and were moving down the ward toward him. The first one was a long, fat, silver-furred being who undulated along the floor on more legs than he was able count and who belonged to the same species as Patient Henredth in the bed opposite. It was accompanied by the Hudlar nurse—for some reason he had begun to think of it as his nurse, possibly because it was both familiar and polite—whose flanks appeared to have been repainted since he had seen it last. In the Earth hospitals quite a few of the nurses had used cosmetics, although only on their faces.

For a moment he wondered if his nurse was considered beautiful by other Hudlars; then he sat up straight in the bed and steeled himself for his first medical examination by a giant extraterrestrial caterpillar. But they stopped at the bed beside his, the one containing Patient Kletilt, moved inside its screens, and completely ignored his existence.

He could hear three different voices talking quietly. There was the Kelgian modulated moaning sound that must have been coming from the doctor, an erratic scraping and clicking noise that he had never heard before but that had to belong to the Melfan patient, and—with lesser frequency, suggesting that it was in response to questions or instructions—the remembered sound of the Hudlar nurse's speaking membrane. But none of their translators were set for human speech, so he did not know what they were saying.

That irritated him, because every few minutes the fabric of the screen bulged outward as if something large and round, like the Hudlar's flanks, or small and sharp, like something else, moved behind it. In spite of the fact that it would probably have horrified him, Hewlitt wanted to know what was going on.

Whatever it was lasted for about twenty minutes; then the Kelgian doctor emerged from behind the screens and undulated toward the nurses' station without even a side glance at him. He could hear the Hudlar nurse moving around Kletilt's bed, apparently doing something to or for the patient; then it, too, appeared and began following the doctor. He did not point and shout "Nurse" as Leethveeschi had advised; he waved to attract its attention.

The nurse paused to make an adjustment to its translator, then said, "Is there anything wrong, Patient Hewlitt?"

You fool, he thought, *it should be obvious what is wrong.* But he tried to keep his tone polite as he said, "I was expecting to be examined, Nurse. What is going on? That doctor completely ignored me!"

"That doctor," the nurse replied, "was arranging for Patient Kletilt's transfer to a different ward, and I was repositioning the patient during the examination. It is Senior Physician Karthad, who is currently the hospital's specialist in other-species obstetrics and gynecology and has no interest in your case. But if you will wait for just a moment longer, Patient Hewlitt, your own doctor will be here to examine you."

CHAPTER 3

He had seen pictures of the Melfan species as well as a few life-size specimens in the corridors during his trip to the ward, but this was the first one that had been motionless and very, very close. It still looked like an outsize crab that was wearing its skeleton on the outside. But this time he barely noticed the thin, tubular legs projecting from the slits where the bony carapace and underside joined, because he was staring at the head with its big, vertically lidded eyes, enormous mandibles, and pincers projecting forward from the place where ears should have been. The two feelers growing from the sides of its mouth were so long and thin and fragile that they looked ridiculous by comparison. The creature's fearsome head moved closer and, inevitably, it said, "How are we feeling, Patient Hewlitt?"

Just as inevitably, Hewlitt replied, "Fine."

"Good," said the other. "I am Dr. Medalont, and I would like to give you a preliminary examination and ask a few questions, if you don't mind. Please fold back your blanket and lie face downward. There is no need to remove your garment; my scanner imaging will not be affected by it. I shall explain everything as we go along."

The scanner was a small, flat, rectangular object that reminded Hewlitt of an old-time book. Its "spine," Medalont told him, contained the depth-focus and enhancement controls; the matte black underside that was being moved slowly over every square inch of his body surface held the microsensors; and the top surface displayed a picture of the underlying organic structures. An enlarged scanner image was being repeated on the bedside viewscreen, possibly for the benefit of the nurse. He twisted his neck to look at it.

"Stop wriggling, Patient Hewlitt," said the doctor. "Now lie face upward. Thank you."

One of its pincers gripped him gently by the wrist and straightened his arm by his side. A feeler curled down to lie vertically along the crease inside his elbow, while the other one dropped like a soft, furry feather across his nose and mouth, making him fight a sudden urge to sneeze. A few minutes later the pincer and the feelers were withdrawn and the doctor straightened up.

"If I remember my Earth-human DBDG anatomy and vital signs correctly," said the doctor, adding a series of quiet, untranslatable clicks that might have been the Melfan equivalent of a chuckle, "I am inclined to agree with your self-diagnosis. Apart from a little general muscular tension, which is understandable in these circumstances, you are in very good physical condition."

This was how so many of the other examinations had ended, Hewlitt thought angrily, with the doctor pronouncing him fit. A few of the early ones had laughed at him, too, or accused him of wasting their time. This Medalont seemed to be a polite one, in spite of being an extraterrestrial, and would probably satisfy itself by wondering aloud what he was doing here.

Instead, it said, "I would like to ask you a few questions, Patient Hewlitt. They are questions you will have been asked many times, and your answers are in the case history. But I am hoping that those answers, because of their constant repetition, may have become inaccurate or incomplete, and I may be able to uncover information missed by my predecessors. Except as an infant and very young child on Etla, you have never traveled beyond the atmosphere of Earth, your home world. Correct?"

"Yes," said Hewlitt.

"Were there any other-species contacts on Etla?"

"I can remember seeing a few extraterrestrials," he replied, "but not well enough to describe them now. I was only four at the time and they frightened me. My parents said that I would grow out of it but kept me out of the way whenever they had other-species visitors. Obviously I didn't grow out of it."

"There is still time," said Medalont. "What do you remember of your childhood illnesses? Begin with the earliest episodes, please."

"Not much," Hewlitt replied. "I was a pretty healthy infant, I learned later. But when my parents died in the flyer accident it was decided to return me to my grandparents on Earth, and I was given the usual immunizations against Earth-human child and adult diseases. That was when the trouble started. There were very few Earth-people living on Etla at that time, and as my parents had not planned on returning to Earth, there had been no need for them to worry about giving me preventive shots."

"Do you know the reason for that?" asked the doctor.

"I think so," said Hewlitt.

"Then tell me," said the other. "Explaining it to me aloud might give you something less to worry about while living among all us aliens."

Hewlitt disliked being humored. He was neither a simple child nor a senile oldster, and it irritated him when some medical know-it-all implied that he was dim-witted, or worse, uneducated. He said, "If you sneeze I won't be affected by your Melfan germs, and vice versa. The same situation applies to all the other life-forms in the hospital. It is a matter of evolution and environment. Germs that evolved on one world cannot affect or infect beings who are native to another. On Earth people said that some hospitals, usually the very old or badly run ones, were places one went to catch other people's diseases as well as, hopefully, getting rid of one's own.

"Is that why there is only one patient of any given species in this ward?" he ended. "To eliminate the risk of own-species cross-infection?"

Dr. Medalont blinked its eyes hard enough for Hewlitt to hear the eyelids clicking together. Then it said, "That is not a reason the hospital would admit to officially, and there are other reasons. You seem to be well-informed medically, but would you now kindly return to the account of your early onset of symptoms?"

"Listening to the number of doctors that have discussed my case over the years," Hewlitt replied, "I couldn't help learning a few things. But all right, back to the symptoms. After the first immunization shot before moving to Earth, I was told that I'd had a bad reaction to it: high temperature, body rash, and inflamed mucous membranes, all of which cleared up within a few days; the symptoms were not entirely those of the diseases I was being vaccinated against. The same thing happened after I arrived on Earth, with different symptoms and recovery times. And I can remember other times when I just did not feel well, when I would become suddenly tired even though I hadn't been playing very hard, or get sick and vomit for no reason, or run a slight temperature or break out in spots. But the symptoms were not severe enough for me to remember them in detail or how long they lasted. My grandparents were curious but not seriously concerned. They took me to a local doctor who agreed with them that I was a sickly child who seemed to be catching every virus in the book.

"But I wasn't sickly," he went on, angry at the memory of that first, unjust accusation. "Between times I was very fit and was always picked for the school team and track events when . . ."

"Patient Hewlitt," Medalont broke in. "These episodes of nausea, minor skin eruptions, and the other symptoms that were not related, at least as far as you knew at the time, to the immunization shots. Could they have followed the administration of other forms of medication? A mild palliative for a headache, perhaps, or a painkiller given after an accident during a sporting contest that you were too excited to remember? Or did you eat something you should not have eaten, like uncooked or unripe vegetation?"

"No," said Hewlitt. "If somebody had butted me in the stomach during a game I would remember it. And if I had eaten something that made me sick, I would have remembered that, too, and especially not to eat it again. I'm not stupid now and I wasn't then."

"Just so," said the doctor. "Please continue."

Feeling angry and impatient, he continued, as he had done so many times in the past to so many medics who had made halfhearted attempts to hide their impatience while listening to him. He described the sudden onset of a wide variety of symptoms that were apparently without cause and, while inconvenient and at times embarrassing, were never serious enough to be disabling. At the age of nine, five years after he had been returned to Earth, his aunt had taken him to the family's aging general practitioner. That doctor had made the first positive, or perhaps it was a completely negative, contribution to his problem by deciding not to administer any form of medication whenever his inexplicable and relatively pain-free symptoms appeared. There was evidence, the doctor had said, that the number and variety of symptoms increased in direct proportion to the amount of medication administered, so the sensible course was to withhold all medication and observe the results. He could still come to see the doctor if or when symptoms reappeared, but henceforth they would do nothing but talk about them.

He had also been given an appointment to see a psychiatrist, who had listened to him with sympathy during the course of several weeks before telling his grandmother that Hewlitt was a physically healthy, highly intelligent, and very imaginative young man who would grow out of his problem with the approach of maturity.

". . . I realized later," Hewlitt went on, "that neither of them believed I had anything wrong with me. The psychiatrist said so in polite polysyllables, but the doctor did the right thing by not doing anything. For three years after his negative treatment, the symptoms were reduced in frequency and strength so that, unless a rash or something appeared on a visible part of my body, I didn't mention them to anyone. But when I reached puberty, the trouble began happening every few weeks and some of the symptoms were very embarrassing. Even so, the family doctor continued to withhold medication and the frequency of onset began to reduce again. From the time I was fourteen until I was twenty there were only three, well, attacks, but the symptoms and some of the things that happened between times were distressing and very embarrassing. . . ."

"Now I understand," Medalont broke in, "why your case history advises against prescribing medication without prior discussion with the patient. Your aged local doctor displayed the good sense that many of us younger and more enthusiastic medics lack, by deciding that when in doubt, and when the condition was not life-threatening, it was better to do nothing. But now that the episodes have become more distressing, you will have to trust us. If you are to be cured we cannot continue to do nothing for you."

"I know that," said Hewlitt. "Shall I go on?"

"Later," said the doctor. "The main meal is due shortly and Leethveeschi will scold me if I deliberately cause a patient to starve. Nurse, consultation mode, please."

A pincer and a digited tentacle rose to touch their respective translators briefly, and thereafter their conversation was completely unintelligible to him. Hewlitt took it for as long as he could, about three minutes, before anger and frustration got the better of him.

"What are you saying about me?" he burst out. "Talk so I can listen, dammit. You're just like the others. You think it's all in my mind and that nothing is wrong with me but an overactive imagination. Is that what you think?"

The doctor and nurse touched their translators again, and Medalont said, "You may listen to us if you wish, Patient Hewlitt. We are not hiding anything from you except, possibly, our own clinical confusion regarding your case. Is what others think important to you?"

"I don't like people thinking that I'm a liar," said Hewlitt in a quieter voice. "Or that there is nothing wrong with me."

The doctor was silent for a moment. Then it said, "During the days or weeks to come there will be many strange beings talking to you, and thinking about you in their strange fashions, in an effort to find the answer to your problem. But one thing they will not be thinking is that you are a liar. If there was nothing wrong with you, you would not be here. Excuse me.

"There can be little doubt," it went on, turning both of its large, protruding eyes toward the nurse, "that there is a psychological component to Patient Hewlitt's condition. While the clinical work is proceeding we will request a concurrent investigation by the Psychology Department. Bearing in mind that the symptoms include a measure of xenophobia, one of the Earth-humans, O'Mara or Braithwaite, would be best. . . ."

"With respect, Doctor," the nurse broke in, "Major O'Mara would not be my choice."

"You are probably right," Medalont replied. "It is of the same species, an able psychologist, but not a pleasant entity. A less abrasive personality would be best. Lieutenant Braithwaite, then.

"For the time being," it went on, "we will continue the no-medication regimen, with the exception of mild sedation if the patient itself requests it. The patient has had no experience of sharing a room with members of other species and may require assistance getting to sleep, but be watchful in case the sedative brings on another attack. The onset of symptoms can be sudden and disproportionately severe. For this reason, in addition to the bedside visual surveillance, I want it to wear a personal medical sensor at all times with priority flagging on your station monitor. The patient may leave its bed and move about the ward at will, to satisfy its curiosity or to socialize with other patients provided its presence at another bed is not clinically inconvenient at the time. There will be no restrictions regarding its diet, but for the time being it should eat meals alone by its bedside."

Dr. Medalont returned its attention to Hewlitt and said, "Many of the beings who come here have an initial aversion to watching members of other species eat. It is nothing of which you should feel ashamed. The first time I saw a Kelgian eating glunce stew it made me want to turn myself inside out."

"No!" said Hewlitt, trying to control his growing panic. "I will not eat or socialize with any of the creatures in here—now, soon, or ever. That, that big elephant thing I saw coming in, the one beside the nurses' station, looked like it could eat me."

"Patient Cossunallen is an herbivore," said the doctor, "so do not be concerned. Making social contact with the other patients is recommended but not obligatory. You should remember, however, that at present you are an unusually healthy patient who may not wish to spend all your time in bed except for an occasional trip to the washroom. Boredom, not the medical staff, may force you to socialize with the other patients."

Hewlitt made a loud, incredulous sound, which he knew did not translate.

"I will have to leave you now," Medalont said. "If you have questions that the nursing staff cannot answer, which is unlikely, I will be back to see you again before the next sleep period. Enjoy your lunch."

The light clicking of Melfan feet and the heavier but softer sound of Hudlar tentacles receded up the ward, leaving him to stare at the inside of the bed screen and worry about the dreadful things a place like this would expect him to eat. A few minutes later the Hudlar nurse pushed between the screens to place a covered tray on his bedside table.

"As yet we have no information regarding your food preferences," it said, "so we have selected a meal that is acceptable to many of the Earth-humans on the staff. It is composed of a brown, flat slab which is called steak, I think, with other lumpy vegetable objects. Before you start to eat, please wait until I attach some equipment to your body. The sensor on your chest lets the nurses' station know how you are doing from moment to moment, and the translator, which I will hang around your neck, is programmed for the languages used by the ward patients and medical staff. It will let you know what everyone is saying about you and everyone else.

"I thought that you might feel more comfortable eating in visual privacy," it went on, "at least until you settle in. That is why I have not raised your screens. I must leave now, but push the call button if you need anything. All right, Patient Hewlitt?"

"Yes, yes, thank you," he said. "But, Nurse . . ."

He broke off in confusion, not knowing why he felt so grateful to this monstrous creature and wanting to say more than a simple word of thanks. Maybe he could say something complimentary.

The nurse was backing through one of the overlapping sections of screen, and he could see that its body paint had left a large smear on the fabric. It stopped moving and said, "Yes, Patient Hewlitt?"

"Nurse," he said awkwardly, "I didn't expect something like you to be so, well, considerate toward me. I mean, you look like nothing on Earth . . ."

"I should hope so," said the Hudlar.

"I didn't mean that to be taken literally," he said. "I just wanted to say thanks and, and your body makeup looks very smart."

The nurse made a small, untranslatable sound and said, "Hudlars do not use body decoration, Patient Hewlitt. That is my lunch."

CHAPTER 4

During his first night in the ward, Hewlitt could not sleep. His bed was very comfortable, the shaded light from his bedside was subdued, and he was more than tired enough because his watch was still set to ship rather than hospital time, and it was telling him that it was early afternoon of the day following his arrival. But his heavy eyes would not stay closed and he decided that, consciously as well as subconsciously, he must be terrified of losing consciousness in this place.

For what seemed like hours he lay listening to the night noises of the ward that drifted through his screens. The continuous sighing of the ventilation system that had been inaudible during the day seemed to grow louder by the hour, as did the quiet sound of the nurses' feet, or whatever, as they attended to the patients. Occasionally he could hear the moaning or bubbling noises of patients in pain, although, considering the painkilling medication available, it was more likely to be the sound of extraterrestrial snoring.

In desperation he switched on the bedside viewscreen and, using an earpiece so as not to bring a nurse down on him for disturbing the other patients, he searched for the entertainment channels. Most of them were intended for other-species' viewers, but even though his translator reproduced the dialogue, a Tralthan or Melfan situation comedy looked more like a horror play to him. When he found one that was designed for Earth-human viewing, the plot and dialogue were close to prehistoric. It should have sent him straight to sleep, but did not.

He returned to watching a Tralthan family performing weird, incomprehensible actions and saying banal things while doing them, until his screens opened to reveal a massive Hudlar body.

"You should be asleep, Patient Hewlitt," it said in a voice so quiet that it barely reached him. "Is anything wrong?"

"Are you the nurse who brought me here today," he asked, "or another one?"

"All the other nurses, including Leethveeschi, have been relieved," it replied, "but my species is able to go for long periods without sleep and I will be completing the night duty. Tomorrow and the day after are my rest and study days so you will not see me until the day after, if you are still here. Your body sensors indicate raised levels of tension and fatigue. Why are you not sleeping?"

"I—I think I'm afraid to sleep," he said, wondering why the admission of a weakness to an extraterrestrial seemed less embarrassing than it would to a human. "If I slept in this place I would have nightmares, and wake up again feeling worse. I suppose you know what nightmares are?"

"Yes," said the nurse. It raised a forward tentacle and waved the tip in the direction of the ward beyond the screens. "You would have nightmares, about us?"

Hewlitt did not reply because he had already answered the question, and he was beginning to feel ashamed.

"If you go to sleep and have nightmares about us," the nurse went on, "and then wake up to find that your nightmares have substance and are all around you, either suffering with you as fellow patients or trying to cure you, isn't trying to stay wakeful a waste of time? Knowing that we will be here when you awaken might give your nightmare less force so that your mind might decide to dream about something more pleasant. Isn't that a logical suggestion, Patient Hewlitt, and worth trying?"

Again, Hewlitt did not reply. This time it was because he was trying to come to grips with Hudlar logic.

"Besides," said the nurse, "that Melfan quiz-forfeit show is injurious to mental health, regardless of the viewer's species. Would you like to talk to me instead?"

"Yes—I mean, no," said Hewlitt. "There are patients here who are sick and more in need of your attention. I have nothing wrong with me, at least not right now."

"Right now," the nurse replied, "all of the other patients are quiet, comfortable, and stable and are being monitored in their sleep. You are awake, and, for a young and mentally active trainee nurse, night duty can be boring. Is there anything you would like to say or ask?"

Hewlitt stared at the great, six-tentacled monster with its speaking membrane rippling like a fleshy flag and the skin that covered its limbs and body like seamless armor. Then he said, "Your paint is beginning to flake again."

"Thank you for the warning," said the Hudlar, "but there is no risk. It will last until the day staff come on duty."

"I do not understand you," said Hewlitt. "At least, not well enough to ask questions."

"From your earlier words about my use of cosmetics," said the nurse, "I thought that might be the case. Do you know why Hudlars use nutrient paint?"

He was not terribly interested in anything extraterrestrials did. But this one wanted to talk, if only to relieve its boredom, and listening to it might take his mind off the extraterrestrial menagerie around him. A case of listening to one known monster in order to forget his dread of the unknown others. And after all, it might be trying in its own way to reassure him.

"No," he said. "Why, Nurse?"

The first thing he learned was that Hudlars did not have mouths. Instead they had what they called organs of absorption, and from there one question led to another.

The species had evolved to intelligence on a heavy-gravity world with a proportionately high atmospheric pressure. The lower reaches of its atmosphere resembled a thick, semiliquid soup filled with tiny, airborne forms of animal and vegetable life which were ingested by the absorption mechanism covering the Hudlars' back and flanks; and, because they were an intensely energy-hungry species, the process was continuous. The home planet's atmosphere was very difficult to reproduce, so that in off-world environments such as the hospital it had been found more convenient to spray them at regular intervals with a concentrated nutrient paint.

"Sometimes," the nurse went on, "we concentrate too deeply on what we are doing and forget our next meal spray. When that happens we grow weak from the effects of accelerated malnutrition wherever we happen to be, and the first member of the medical or maintenance staff to come along, or even an ambulatory patient like yourself, revives us with a quick respray. There are racks of Hudlar food tanks in most of the main corridors and wards, including the one on the wall beside the nurses' station. The sprayer mechanism is very easy to use, although I hope you will never have to use one on me.

"It disrupts the routine to have a Hudlar collapsing in the middle of a ward," it continued, "and the nutrient makes a mess on the floor or nearby beds. That would severely irritate Charge Nurse Leethveeschi, and we would not want that to happen."

"No, we wouldn't," he said, unable to imagine a severely irritated chlorine-breather but agreeing anyway. "But, but meals painted on from the outside . . . that's terrible. I thought I had problems."

"I am not the patient here, Patient Hewlitt," said the nurse, "and your sensors are registering a high level of fatigue and I am being selfish by keeping you awake. Are you ready to go to sleep now?"

The thought of being left alone again, his dimly lit bed like a raft surrounded by a dark sea peopled with fearful alien monsters, with this one monstrous exception, brought the fear that had been held in check by their conversation to come rushing back. Hewlitt did *not* want to go to sleep, so he answered indirectly in the negative by asking another question.

"I don't see how it could happen," he said, "but do you people have the equivalent of stomach ache? Or do you ever take sick?"

"Never," said the nurse. "You must try to sleep, Patient Hewlitt."

"If you don't take sick," he persisted, fighting a conversational rearguard action, "why do Hudlars need doctors and nurses?"

"As very young children," the other replied, "we are subject to a wide variety of diseases, but by puberty we develop a complete immunity to them which lasts until a few years before termination, when age-related psychological and physiological degeneration takes place. Diagnostician Conway is heading a project to train Hudlar medical staff who will alleviate the more distressing aspects of the condition, which responds only to major surgery, but the work has many years to go before the aged population as a whole will benefit."

"Is this the work you are training to do?" Hewlitt asked. "To care for the Hudlar aged?"

The nurse had no features that he could read, because it had no face and the rest of its smooth, hard body was as expressionless as an inflated balloon. But when it replied it spoke quickly, giving him the feeling that it might be embarrassed or ashamed of its answer.

"No," it said. "I am studying general other-species medicine and surgery. Within the Galactic Federation we Hudlars are a unique species. Because of the nature of our body tegument we are able to live and work in a great many hostile environments. We can survive pressure variations ranging from the very dense down to the vacuum of space, and we do not need an atmosphere in order to absorb our nutrient paint. Hudlars are greatly in demand for work in conditions where other species would be severely hampered by their environmental-protection equipment, and especially on space construction projects. A Hudlar medic with Sector General qualifications, who would be able to bring medical assistance to space construction workers of many different species without the time-consuming necessity for donning protective garments, would be a valuable asset onsite.

"Ours has never been a rich planet," it added. "No mineral resources, no fabricated items to trade, no scenery to attract visitors. It has nothing that anybody wants, except its immensely strong, tireless people who can work anywhere and are very well rewarded by the other Federation species for doing so."

"And after you have achieved fame and fortune in space," said Hewlitt, "I suppose you will settle down at home and have a large family?"

The nurse still seemed to be bothered about something. He wondered if it could be feeling ashamed for leaving home and training for a well-paid job in space and thereby ducking the responsibility for looking after an aged and sick relative. He should not have asked that question.

"I will have half of a large family," it said.

"Again," he said, "I do not understand you."

"Patient Hewlitt," it said, "you are not very well informed about Hudlars. I was born and currently remain in female mode, and I intend to continue in this form until I choose to mate for the purpose of procreation rather than pleasure. That is when the gravid female, myself, because of the physiological necessity for avoiding further sexual contact with my life-mate, changes gradually into male mode and, concurrently, my mate slowly becomes female. A Hudlar year after parturition, the changes to both are complete, the offspring requires diminishing attention, and the mother-that-was is ready to become a father-to-be and the father-that-was has the opportunity of bearing the next child. The process continues until the desired number of offspring is reached, usually an even number so that the childbearing is equally divided, after which the life-mates decide together on which one will remain in male or female mode for the rest of their lives.

"It is a very simple, balanced, and emotionally satisfying arrangement," it went on. "I am surprised that the other intelligent species have not evolved this system."

"Yes, Nurse," said Hewlitt.

He could think of nothing else to say.

CHAPTER 5

Hewlitt had been lying awake or, more accurately, trying hard to stay awake because of the completely alien and unknown living nightmares sharing the ward with him as patients and medical staff. But now he was wondering if it was extreme fatigue that was dulling his emotional reactions and causing him to relax, because he could not imagine anything more alien than the spaceproof skin, weird eating habits, and routine sex changes of this friendly monstrosity, and it was no longer unknown.

"Nurse," he said, "thank you for talking to me for so long. I think I can sleep now."

"No," said the Hudlar firmly. "I would advise against that, Patient Hewlitt. The day staff will be coming on duty in twenty minutes and they will be waking everyone so that they can be washed before the first meal is served. We have three other ambulatory patients here, and you may prefer not to share the washroom facilities with them on your first morning in the ward, so it might be more comfortable for you if you get in there and finish first."

"Yes, indeed," said Hewlitt without hesitation. "But I'm *tired,* Nurse. Can I wash later?"

"Bearing in mind your uneasiness in the close proximity of other species," said the nurse, "I will not accompany you. Instead I will remain close by the washroom in case your personal monitor, which you must not remove while cleansing yourself, should signal an emergency condition or you request help because of unfamiliarity with the equipment.

"If a very high level of mental and physical fatigue is present," it went on, "you have the option of taking a blanket bath. This operation would be carried out by our three junior trainees, a Melfan and two Kelgians, who would be pleased at the chance to gain more experience in handling and bathing a nontraumatized Earth-human like yourself. I know that they are particularly anxious to master the technique of scraping away the fur bristles that grow overnight on DBDG faces, and they would be pleased to perform this service for you."

Before it had finished speaking, Hewlitt had thrown back the covers and swung his feet onto the floor, where a pair of soft ward shoes were waiting for them. Then he stood up quickly and said, "I like your first suggestion better, Nurse."

The Hudlar moved aside to allow him to leave.

About twenty minutes later he was climbing back into bed, feeling clean and fresh and less tired, when the ceiling lights brightened to full strength and the day staff came bustling along the ward. A Kelgian pushing a small trolley loaded with basins and towels poked its furry head and shoulders between the screens and said, "Good morning, Patient Hewlitt. You look clean. Are you?"

"Yes," he said, and it disappeared.

A few minutes later he heard two patients approaching and then passing his bed on their way to the washroom. One seemed to be large and heavy and walking on more than four feet, while the other one moved with an irregular, tapping sound. He knew they were patients because one was complaining about being wakened when it had only just succeeded in getting to sleep, and the other was insisting that Leethveeschi was conducting illegal sleep-deprivation research and it was being brainwashed as well as waiting to have the croamsteti on its kuld duct replaced. His translator reproduced the original word sounds, so presumably there was no equivalent part of an Earth-human body. He sympathized with them, whatever they were, over their missed sleep.

He had just settled back in the bed and closed his eyes, and the sounds of the ward were beginning to fade, when the Kelgian nurse reappeared, this time carrying his breakfast on a tray. Or maybe it was another Kelgian. As yet he could not tell the difference between one outsize, furry caterpillar and another, and doubted if he ever would.

"Sit up and eat at the bedside table, Patient Hewlitt," it said. "Your particular species is subject to digestive upsets with accompanying regurgitation, I have learned, if gravity is not allowed to aid the movement of food to the stomach. Enjoy."

"I don't want to eat, Nurse," he said, trying hard to control his irritation, "I want to *sleep*. Please go away."

"Eat it, then sleep," said the nurse. "Or try to eat some of it, or Charge Nurse Leethveeschi will eat me."

"It would?" said Hewlitt, the return of his earlier fears bringing him fully awake. In this place it might not be joking.

"Of course not," said the nurse. "But only because it is a chlorine-breather and my body meat would poison it."

"All right, I'll try," he said, knowing that way out here in Sector General, as it had been on the ship, the food would be synthesized. But when he raised the tray cover to look inside and the odor wafted up, he realized how long it had been since he had eaten, and added, "It looks and smells very good, Nurse."

"It is a visually disgusting and nauseating mess," said the nurse, backing hurriedly through the screens, "and it smells even worse."

"You don't have much tact, do you, Nurse?" said Hewlitt, but its multiple footfalls were already receding up the ward. Then another voice called out to him from the bed opposite, belonging, he recalled, to a Kelgian patient called Henredth.

"What is tact?" it said.

Hewlitt ignored the question and tried to close his ears to the other questions that followed it until he had finished his breakfast, after which his eyes closed by themselves.

He wakened to the sound of quiet, alien voices and the sight of the screen that was still around his bed, which made him realize where he was. But somehow the realization was not as terrifying as it had been yesterday and, after a few minutes listening through his translator, he pressed the button that raised his bed screens.

Hewlitt saw at once that the Ian who had been in the bed beside his, Patient Makolli, had been moved while he had been asleep, because there was an Orligian lying there now. He recognized the species at once because it was the same as that of the medical officer on *Treevendar,* but this specimen seemed much older. The parts of it that were not hidden by the blankets—its head, arms, and upper chest—were covered by reddish brown fur that was streaked with grey. It was wearing a personal monitor like his own as well as a translator, but it took no notice of him. He was not sure whether it was asleep, anesthetized, or being antisocial.

In the bed opposite, Patient Kletilt had moved its viewscreen to what, for a Melfan, must have been a more convenient position for viewing in bed. Its eyes were hidden by the back of the set and it did not appear to be interested in anything or anyone but the program it was watching. Hewlitt had not known that his set could be swung over the bed like that and he made a mental note to experiment with it later.

In the bed beside Kletilt the Kelgian patient, Henredth, and a nurse belonging to a species he had never seen before, were talking together, but so quietly that his translator missed most of what they were saying. Beyond them there was a huge, elephantlike creature that he recognized as being a Tralthan. Instead of lying in a bed it stood on its six blocky legs, surrounded by a complicated framework to which was attached the harness that held it upright. He remembered reading somewhere that Tralthans did everything including sleeping on their feet, and even the healthy ones had great difficulty getting up again if they fell onto their sides.

He was still thinking about that and wondering why the creature was in hospital when Senior Physician Medalont, followed by Charge Nurse Leethveeschi, emerged from the nurses' station. They skittered and squelched respectively along the center of the aisle, speaking to nobody and looking only in Hewlitt's direction. He knew what the doctor's first words would be.

"How are we feeling today, Patient Hewlitt?"

"Fine," he replied, as it knew he would.

"Patient Hewlitt's monitor readout since its arrival," said Leethveeschi, "supports its nonclinical and subjective self-assessment. The patient appears to be in optimum health."

"Good," said the senior physician, clicking one of its pincers together in a gesture that might have signified approval but that looked threatening. "I would like to have another long talk with you, Patient Hewlitt, this time covering the episode that resulted in your first admission to an Earth hospital when you . . ."

"But you already have that information," Hewlitt broke

in. "It's in my case history, in much more detail than I could possibly remember now. There is nothing wrong with me, at least not right now. Instead of wasting time talking to me, surely you could visit patients who are more in need of attention?"

"They received attention," Leethveeschi joined in, "while you were sleeping. Now it's your turn. But Patient Hewlitt is right. I have more important things to do than listen to two healthy beings talking to each other. Do you need me here, Doctor?"

"Thank you, no, Charge Nurse," Medalont replied. It returned its attention to Hewlitt and went on, "I am not wasting my time talking to you, because I am hoping that today, or sometime soon, you will tell me something that is not in your case history, something that will enable me to solve this clinical conundrum. . . ."

The interrogation resumed at the point where it had ended the previous day, and it seemed to last forever. If Hewlitt could have read the other's bony exoskeletal features, he felt sure that they would have been registering disappointment. But they were forced to break off when the voice of the charge nurse spoke from his bedside viewer. Until then he had not known that the device included a communicator.

"Doctor," said Leethveeschi, "the midday meal is due in thirty minutes. Will you be finished with your patient by then?"

"Yes, at least for today," said Medalont. To Hewlitt it went on, "I try to do something more for our patients than bore them to death with questions. We will need to make a series of tests, which means me taking samples of your blood for path lab investigation. Don't worry about it; the process is completely painless. Please uncover your upper arm."

"You—you're not supposed to give me anything that might . . ." began Hewlitt.

"I know, I know," said the doctor, its rapid, clicking speech sounding more impatient than usual. "If you remember, it was I who told you that you are to receive no medication of any kind until we have identified the condition we are treating, which is why I require a fairly large sample. I am withdrawing blood, Patient Hewlitt, not injecting medication. You will feel nothing, but if the sight distresses you then close your eyes."

He had never been distressed by the sight of his own blood, at least not in the number of small quantities that the doctor seemed to consider a large sample. When it was over, Medalont thanked him and said that it would have to hurry if it was to make a lunch meeting on time.

As the doctor had promised, Hewlitt had not felt a thing, and a small area of nonsensation persisted inside the fold of his elbow where the samples had been withdrawn. He relaxed back into the pillows but decided to stay awake until after lunch by watching and listening to the other patients who were within range of his translator. Compared to his blind near-panic of yesterday, he was surprised by the growing curiosity he was feeling about them.

Hewlitt did not know how much time went by, because it was too much trouble to bother lifting his wrist to look at his watch. He continued to feel fine, comfortable, without pain, and very curious about the thick, grey fog that had drifted into the ward and was keeping him from seeing the other beds. The sounds of the ward, too, were fading, but he was able to see and hear the flashing red light and the strident beeping noises coming from the monitor on his chest, and Charge Nurse Leethveeschi looming over him and shouting into its communicator.

"Bed eighteen, classification DBDG Earth-human. Two-plus minutes into cardiac and respiratory arrest. Resuscitation team, *move!*"

Something like a column of oily seaweed projected from

Leethveeschi's body and pushed a bulge in the creature's protective envelope to flop onto Hewlitt's chest. He felt the steady, regular pressure of a heart massage, and the last thing he saw was the charge nurse leaning closer.

No, not mouth-to-mouth, he thought desperately, *you're a bloody chlorine-breather. . . .*

CHAPTER 6

The sight of the procession that was emerging from the nurses' station brought all other activity and conversations in the ward to a halt. It was led by Senior Physician Medalont, followed by Charge Nurse Leethveeschi, his nameless Hudlar nurse, and a Kelgian and a Nidian intern who were guiding a float containing the multispecies resuscitation equipment between them, and an Earth-human wearing a green Monitor Corps uniform who brought up the rear. Inevitably they traveled the full length of the ward to gather in a semicircle around his bed.

Coming close to death five hours earlier had not made him feel any less fearful of ETs, nor had it improved his disposition one little bit.

"What the hell are you going to do to me this time?" he said.

"Nothing that I haven't already done," the senior physician replied in a voice that might have been reassuring to another Melfan. "Do not be concerned; I am simply with-drawing another blood sample. Please bare your upper arm."

The Kelgian intern looked at its Nidian colleague, its sil-very fur tufting into spikes. It edged the resuscitation trolley closer and added, "If you do nothing, Patient Hewlitt, then neither will we."

One of the things he had learned from his few brief con-versations with the Kelgian patient in the adjoining bed was that members of that species were incapable of telling a lie. To another Kelgian, the continuous, subtle, and expressive movements of their silvery fur displayed what they were feeling and thinking from moment to moment, like a form of visual telepathy, so they did not know or understand the meaning of the word. They had the same difficulty with con-cepts like tact, politeness, diplomacy, and bedside manners.

Once again Hewlitt felt the tiny circle of metal pressed against his skin. Medalont said, "The instrument currently in contact with your arm contains one very fine, short, recessed needle whose entry you will not feel, and another that is longer and slightly thicker. The first one injects a local anesthetic which desensitizes the underlying nerve endings, and the second withdraws the blood. Good, here it comes. Thank you, Patient Hewlitt. How do you feel?"

"Fine," Hewlitt replied. "How am I supposed to feel?"

Medalont ignored the question and said, "Are you aware of any changes of sensation, however small, anywhere within your body?"

"No," he said.

"Any feeling of discomfort in the chest or arms," it went on, "or difficulty with breathing? Tingling or loss of sensa-tion in the extremities? Headache?"

"No," said Hewlitt. "There is a numb patch where you took the blood. It feels the same as last time."

"If present," said Medalont, "the symptoms would be minor, an early warning of possible trouble to come. They could be so minor, in fact, that you may be unsure whether or not you are imagining them."

"So far as I know," said Hewlitt, making an effort to control his temper, "I have no minor, imaginary symptoms."

The Earth-human in the green uniform smiled briefly and resumed doing and saying nothing.

"Have you any nonphysical symptoms?" Medalont persisted. "An anxiety or fear, perhaps, that could intensify to the point where it might cause stress on the physical level? I realize that I am moving into Lieutenant Braithwaite's territory, but . . ."

"You are," said the uniformed man, speaking for the first time. "But feel free, everyone else does."

Before the senior physician could reply, Hewlitt said, "If you mean am I worried then yes, I feel worried, very worried. Until I came to this place I never had a heart attack, but I don't think I feel bad enough to frighten myself into another one."

"Were you feeling frightened before the first one?" asked Medalont.

"No, just sleepy and relaxed," said Hewlitt. "But right now I'm scared."

"We won't allow anything to happen to you this time," said Medalont, "so try not to worry."

For what seemed like a very long time there was silence from everyone. Leethveeschi's body pulsed slowly inside its chlorine envelope, the Hudlar's speaking membrane remained still, the Kelgian's fur was rippling along its body as if blown by an unfelt wind while its Nidian partner checked the equipment on the resuscitation float, and Medalont opened and closed its pincers once every few seconds like some kind of silent, organic metronome. It was the senior physician who spoke first.

"Charge Nurse, give me your estimate again of the elapsed time between my first withdrawal of blood sample, the monitor's signaling the patient's distress, and the sequence of events which followed."

"Out of consideration for the feelings of the patient," said Leethveeschi, "who appears to have some understanding of medical nomenclature, it might be better if that information were withheld."

"And I," said Medalont, "am hoping that with full information available the patient may be able to shed some light on its own condition. Go on, Charge Nurse."

"Approximately twelve and a half minutes after you withdrew the blood sample and left," said Leethveeschi, in a tone as corrosive as the chlorine it was breathing, "the patient's monitor signaled an emergency condition. Ten seconds later the life signs went flat, completely flat, and sensory response and cerebration began the shutdown characteristic of approaching termination. The nursing staff were outside the station and busy preparing to serve a meal so I responded, preferring not to waste an additional few seconds needed to relay the information to another. Considering the stability of the patient's condition until then, I suspected that equipment rather than cardiac failure had occurred. When I reached the patient and initiated chest massage forty seconds later it had lost consciousness, and it remained in that condition until the resuscitation team arrived six and one-quarter minutes later—"

"Are you sure about that, Nurse?" Medalont broke in. "In the excitement could subjective factors have caused you to exaggerate? Six minutes is not a good response time."

"Patient Hewlitt was not responding either," said Leethveeschi, "and I was watching the clock while I worked. The ward clock is not subject to exaggeration."

"The charge nurse is right," said the Nidian medic with a side glance at its partner, "and so are you, Doctor. Normally it would be considered an inexcusably slow response time. But we had an accident on the way, a collision with a food delivery float whose servers moved clear when they saw our flashing lights but left their vehicle in the middle of the ward. There were no casualties—just a mess of other-species meals spread all over the ward floor and nearby beds . . ."

"Patient Hewlitt," the Kelgian doctor broke in, "chose an inconvenient time to arrest."

"We had to spend a few minutes checking for equipment damage," the Nidian doctor went on. "A jolt that would restart a Tralthan's heart would cook an Earth-human's in its own . . ."

"Yes, yes," said Medalont. "After six-plus minutes you revived the patient. What degree of mental or verbal confusion did you observe while it was returning to full consciousness?"

"No, and none," the other replied. "We did not revive the patient; Charge Nurse Leethveeschi must have done that before we could attach the lines. The patient did not appear to be confused at all. Its first words were to tell the charge nurse to stop hitting it in the chest or it would damage its rib cage. Its words were coherent, well organized, and distinct, if not very respectful."

"I'm sorry," said the senior physician. "I had assumed your equipment brought the patient back. Well done, Charge Nurse. I hope the patient was not too disrespectful."

"I have been called worse names," said Leethveeschi, "and I was relieved rather than insulted by its response."

"Indeed, yes," said Medalont. To the Kelgian it went on, "Continue, please."

"When it was clear that Patient Hewlitt was fully conscious," it replied, "we joined the charge nurse in asking it questions aimed at discovering whether or not there had been a loss of cerebration. We were still doing that when you returned to ask it more of the same questions. The rest you know."

"Yes," said the senior physician. "And after two hours of

questioning there was no detectable memory or speech dysfunction or loss of physical coordination. Patient Hewlitt's monitor registered optimum levels on all life signs, just as it is doing now."

"But now," Leethveeschi said, with a wet, floppy gesture toward the ward clock, "it is four and a half minutes beyond the time that elapsed between the original blood withdrawal and the onset of the first cardiac episode."

While the medics were talking, Hewlitt had been trying to think of a way of both apologizing to the charge nurse and thanking it for saving his life, but the meaning of what the loathsome creature had just said drove all thoughts of gratitude from his mind.

"What's going *on* here?" he burst out. "Are you just standing around waiting for me to have another bloody heart attack? Or are you disappointed it didn't happen?"

For a moment there was silence, and stillness except for the Hudlar nurse who moved a tentacle toward him and lowered it again. Then the Medalont said, "We are not disappointed, Patient Hewlitt, but otherwise your assessment of the situation is accurate. The first cardiac incident had to be caused by something, and there was a possibility, admittedly a very slim one, that my extraction of the blood specimen was responsible. Although you were not to receive any medication, I overlooked the fact that a trace quantity of local anesthetic is injected routinely prior to blood withdrawal so as to render the procedure pain-free. The timing and circumstances have now been reproduced, so far without results, which means that we must look elsewhere for the cause. Unless . . . Your facial skin coloration is darkening, Patient Hewlitt. How do you feel now?"

I feel like strangling you, he thought. Aloud, he said, "Fine, Doctor."

"The monitor confirms," said Leethveeschi.

"In that case," said Medalont, looking at the others in

turn, "you will maintain monitor surveillance, station the resuscitation team within a two-minute response distance, and allow the patient to compose itself before lunch. Never fear, Patient Hewlitt, we will find out and cure whatever it is that is troubling you. But for the present we will leave you alone."

"Not entirely alone," said Braithwaite. "I would like to have a few words with him."

"As you wish, Lieutenant," said the senior physician as it and the other two doctors withdrew. Leethveeschi and the Hudlar nurse held back.

"You are not to do anything that will disturb my patient," said the Illensan in its most authoritative charge-nurse voice. "Nor will you ask or say anything that is likely to precipitate another medical emergency."

Lieutenant Braithwaite looked from the irate chlorine-breather to the hulking, massively strong body of the Hudlar and back again. "Nurses," he said, smiling, "I wouldn't dare."

When they were alone he sat down on the edge of Hewlitt's bed and said, "I'm Braithwaite, Other-Species Psychology Department. It makes a nice change to talk to someone who has the right number of limbs and things."

Hewlitt still felt like strangling or at least verbally assaulting someone, but this Braithwaite character had not said or done anything to make himself a candidate. Not yet. Instead he looked along the ward in the direction of the nurses' station and the figure of Leethveeschi and ignored the psychologist.

"What are you thinking about?" Braithwaite said when the silence began to drag. He smiled and added, "Is that the kind of question you are expecting me to ask?"

"You didn't call me Patient Hewlitt like the others," he replied, turning to face the psychologist. "Was that intentional, or because you don't think there is anything wrong with me so I'm not a real patient? Or did you forget my name?"

"You need not call me Lieutenant or Braithwaite," said the other, and the silence returned.

Finally Hewlitt said, "All right, I'll answer your question. I am thinking about that ghastly charge nurse, and wondering how I can say that I'm sorry for misjudging it and thank it for saving my life."

Braithwaite nodded. "I'd say that you have the words about right, and all you have to do is say them to Leethveeschi rather than me."

For some reason Hewlitt was finding it difficult to maintain his anger toward this man. He said, "You are here to tell me, or to try to convince me, that my problems are all in my mind. This has happened to me many times, man and boy, so let's not waste our time being friendly. Yes?"

"No," said Braithwaite firmly. "I intend to waste time being friendly."

The lieutenant changed his position on the side of the bed, moving so close that he had to support his weight with one arm stretched across Hewlitt's thighs. Hewlitt could feel the other's breath on his face as he said, "Do you mind me sitting here? Would you prefer me to move back, or stand?"

"It's the extraterrestrials I worry about when they come too close," he replied. "Just don't sit on my legs."

Braithwaite nodded. The polite and seemingly innocent question-and-answer had established the fact that he was not emotionally distressed by the close proximity of another human being, which was a useful psychological datum that eliminated one potential area of trouble. From long experience Hewlitt knew what the other was doing, and the lieutenant was probably intelligent enough to know that Hewlitt knew.

"We both know that yours is not a simple case," Braithwaite went on, with a glance toward his monitor. "You appear to be completely healthy, while suffering from an intermittent and nonspecific condition which, if the recent cardiac arrest was a symptom, is life-threatening. We also know that a serious problem in the body can have a proportionate effect on the mind, and vice versa, even when there appears, as now, to be no apparent connection between the two. I would like to find and identify that connection, but only if there is one.".

He waited until Hewlitt gave a wary nod, then continued, "Normally a patient is admitted to this hospital because he, she, or it is sick or injured. The problem and clinical solution are usually obvious from the start, and the medics can use the facilities of the Federation's leading hospital to treat or remove or repair the condition and, in most cases, to send the patient home good as new. But when the problem has or appears to have a psychological component . . ."

"You use your tongue," Hewlitt finished for him.

"My ears, mostly," said Braithwaite, ignoring the sarcasm. "Very soon, I hope, you will be doing all the talking. You should begin by describing any unusual events or circumstances that you can remember prior to the first onset of symptoms. Tell me what you as a child were thinking about the situation at the time, not what your doctors and relatives thought later. Go ahead, you talk and I'll listen."

"You want me to tell you all about the times when I *wasn't* sick?" said Hewlitt. He inclined his head in the direction of the diet kitchen, where the ward serving floats loaded with meal trays were emerging, and added, "But there isn't enough . . . It's lunchtime."

Braithwaite sighed and said, "I would like to finish this talk with you as soon as possible, in case Medalont, who has the rank, thinks of doing something more urgent and positive for you. Would you do me a favor by ordering a meal for me? Nothing special, whatever they are giving you will do nicely."

"But you're not a patient," said Hewlitt. "Yesterday I heard Leethveeschi telling an intern not to be a lazy scrassug, whatever that is, and to go to the staff dining hall instead of sneaking food from the ward kitchen. I don't think the charge nurse will allow it."

"The charge nurse will allow it," said the lieutenant, "if you ask to speak to it about a personal matter which you feel is important. After the medical melodrama of five hours ago it will not want to risk a refusal. When it comes, say what you told me you wanted to say to it, that you are sorry for misjudging its actions and are grateful for it saving your life. Then you can say that you feel our talk could be important to your case, and would it be possible for it to order up another DBDG meal for me so that the conversation can continue without interruption.

"Illensans receive a lot of professional compliments from the staff," Braithwaite went on, "because they are very good at what they do. But not from the patients, who are rarely here long enough to appreciate their good points. It comes of being the only chlorine-breathing, as well as the ugliest, species in the Federation. But if you do as I say, it will be too surprised and pleased to refuse you anything."

Hewlitt was silent for a moment; then he said, "Lieutenant, you are a selfish, devious, calculating son of a . . . of a scrassug."

"Of course," said Braithwaite. "I'm a psychologist."

He was beginning to sweat at the idea of actually calling the loathsome Leethveeschi to his bedside. He said, "I was thinking of saying those things to it, but later," he said. "I need more time to work up the nerve."

Braithwaite smiled and pointed at the communicator.

CHAPTER 7

The first and best-remembered early unusual incident had happened when he was a few days past his fourth birthday. His parents had been working at their separate home terminals, safe in the knowledge that they would be free from interruptions, because each was sure that the other was watching out for him, and doubly sure in that he was unable to leave his room without being seen.

Normally there would not have been a problem, because he would have been busy at his own, scaled-down terminal with its garish paint job and the extra flashing lights, playing with the latest educational adventure game that had been his birthday present. But that day he was feeling restless and bored because the educational content of the game was getting in the way of the adventures, and the room's high, open window was offering the promise of more enjoyable things to do in the garden.

His parents had made two further wrong assumptions:

that he would not climb out of the window because he had never done so before; and that their garden, when eventually he grew bored with it, too, had a childproof fence.

Beyond the garden fence the world was a very exciting and, although he did not know it at the time, a dangerous place. The whole area had been devastated by a major battle in the civil war that had resulted when the planetary population had risen to overthrow an interstellar government that had fought and lost an interstellar war that the deliberately misguided population had never wanted, even though a great many of them had suffered and died to support it. A few of the ruined houses had been repaired and occupied by off-planet advisors and reconstruction specialists like his parents after the area had been sensor-scanned and any live ordnance or vehicle power packs removed. The broken and rusting remains had been left where they were. Like the ruined houses, they were being overrun by the wild vegetation that was the ultimate winner of every battle and, on this occasion, by one small boy.

He waded through the long grass that seemed to be everywhere, and wandered happily between the trees and bushes, climbed over broken sections of road paving, and explored one of the ruined buildings. Inside were small, furry animals that ran away from him, and one with a long, thick tail that climbed into the roof beams and scolded him until he went away. He was careful to avoid the occupied houses, because they might not contain people like himself. On the single occasion that his parents had taken him for a walk beyond the garden, they had told him that there were other-species families in the neighborhood, and that while they would not deliberately harm him, their young could do unpredictable and possibly dangerous things while playing with other-species children.

There had been no need to remind him of the time when he was learning to swim in the communal pool and a Melfan kid of his own age, thinking that he was an amphibian too, had pulled him to the bottom to play. Since then he had been scared of extraterrestrials, regardless of their shape, size, or age, and tried not to go anywhere near them.

But there were much better places to explore than other people's gardens, which might have nasty, other-species kids playing in them. Everywhere he looked there were the scattered shapes of armored vehicles showing dark rust-red amid the sunlit greenery. Some of them looked as if they were not broken and were ready to move any minute; others were lying on their sides, and one had been knocked upside down. Most of them had their doors hanging open, and a few had holes in them that were bigger than the doors, but the edges were sharp and tore his shirt when he tried to crawl inside. He found one that had a gun barrel hanging low enough for him to swing on it. One of its tracks had come off and was lying along the ground like a narrow, rusting carpet with grass and flowers pushing through it. Small animals were hiding in some of the vehicles, but they ran away whenever he climbed in. One of them was filled with the sound of insects, and he knew that he might be stung if he tried to explore that one.

Then he found one that had no insects or animals inside, and with enough sunlight shining through the open hatches to show a bucket seat facing the vehicle's control console and screens. The seat was soft and dirty and so big that he had to sit on the edge to reach the control keys. Everything was rusty except for the plastic bits, which were covered with thick, sticky dust. He had to rub the keys with his fingers to see what color they were. Neither the dust nor the rust, which was all over his shirt and trousers by then, nor the dead master screen facing him, made any difference to the battles he was fighting.

This had been a real fighting machine with a real soldier in it, and in his imagination the screen was filled with bright images of enemy tanks and aircraft that exploded even more brightly as soon as they attacked him, because his was a very special, secret tank and he was invincible. He had heard his father and mother talking about the times when such battles had really happened, but they never thought them exciting or interesting and they acted as if everyone concerned in them were sick or something.

But now he was shooting at anything he wanted to imagine—dive bombers, attacking spaceships, horrible other-species soldiers coming at him through the trees—and shouting out loud with excitement when he blew them out of the sky or wiped them out as he always did at the last moment. His parents were not there to stop him yelling, or to remind him that the pretend targets he was shooting down had imaginary people inside them, and that it did not matter what kind of horrible monsters he was pretending to shoot at because they were still people.

Some of their other-species neighbors really were horrible monsters, at least to him, and if any of them had visited the house and found him shooting down things that looked like the visitors, his parents had said, they might take offense and consider the whole Hewlitt family to be less than civilized and not call again. Big people never seemed to have any fun.

Gradually he was running out of imaginary enemies to destroy. The sun was no longer shining into the vehicle, and the rusty metal looked almost black instead of red. It was silly, but he started thinking about the being who had driven the tank, and what would happen to him if it came back and found him playing inside. He climbed out so quickly that he tore his trousers again.

The sun had gone down below the trees, but the sky was blue and clear and there was still plenty of light. He could not see anything nearby that he wanted to explore, and he was beginning to feel hungry. It was time to go home, sneak back through the window, and ask his mother for something to eat. But he could see nothing but trees and long grass in every direction.

When he climbed onto the top of the largest vehicle he could find, the view was better. Not far away there was a tall tree standing on the edge of a deep ravine. It had lots of thick, twisting, leafy branches growing close to the ground and nearly all the way to the top, where there was a cluster of bare, thinner branches with fruit hanging from them. From the top he should be able to see his house.

It was another adventure, he told himself as he began to climb, but this time it was real instead of a pretend one. He was not feeling scared, just hungry and all alone, and he wanted to see where his house was so that he could return and eat and end this game. As he climbed higher he could look down through the branches onto the floor of the ravine, where there were more rusting shapes, including a fat, round one directly below him. Then he climbed up into sunlight and was dazzled so that the inside of the ravine became dark and blurred.

Still he could not see any houses, because smaller trees instead of long grass were in the way, so he climbed higher. Then two things happened at once: he reached the top of the tree where the clusters of fruit were and he saw his house. The house was closer than he had expected, and between him and it there was a signpost in the shape of a small tree with funny branches on it. But his arms and legs were very tired, he felt hot and thirsty as well as hungry, and the clusters of fruit were hanging just above him, bobbing gently in the wind that was beginning to blow through the high branches.

At the end of a great adventure, he thought, there should be a reward. The fruit had to be it.

The branch he was sitting on was thick and strong, and one of its twists took it within reach of a fruit cluster. No longer feeling tired, he crawled along it, gripping the twigs growing from it to hold himself steady. The sun was beginning to go down behind the trees, and below him the lower branches were getting harder to see and the ravine was just a dark green blur. He stopped looking down, because the cluster of fruit above him was almost touching his head.

When he tried to pull off the first one, it squashed in his hand. With the second one he was more careful and it came away in one piece.

It looked like a big pear, but none of the pears he had seen in the Earth vegetation tapes had dark green-and-yellow stripes running vertically from the stem to the heavy end. He already knew from the way the first one had squashed that it was full of juice, and this one was so heavy and squishy that it felt like a small balloon filled with water. The juice that had spilled over his hand was drying already and was making it feel nice and cool. He watched the last damp patch on his wrist steaming as it dried off.

He still felt hungry and wanted to eat something solid, but he was hot as well after his climb and a drink of cold juice would be nice, too, so he held on to the branch with only his legs and took the fruit in both cupped hands.

The juice had a funny taste, not nice but not nasty, either. Not wanting to make a mess, he bit out a tiny hole with his teeth and sucked the fruit empty. When he used his fingers to widen the hole, the skin split open along one of the green-and-yellow lines and he discovered that it was not empty. As well as the juice there was a soft, yellow spongy mass with black seeds in the center. He spat out the seeds because they burned his tongue, and the rest of it had the same taste as the juice but it helped fill his stomach better.

He was still not sure whether he liked the fruit or not. While he was trying to make up his mind about eating another one, he felt a pain in his stomach that came and went and grew steadily worse every time.

For the first time since leaving the house he felt scared and wanted to go home. He began bumping himself backward along the branch toward the main trunk, where he could climb down again, but the stomach pains were so bad that they made him yell out loud, and tears were making it hard for him to see what he was doing. Then one very bad pain made him grab his stomach with both hands, and he felt himself falling sideways. For a moment he hung upside down with his legs still wrapped tightly around the branch, but when he tried to pull himself upright again the pains got so bad that he could think about nothing else. He felt himself falling.

He saw sunlit leaves whipping past him, then others that were in shadow, and felt branches hitting his back, arms, and legs; then it was dark for a moment and nothing was hitting him. He knew where he was when he hit the steep slope of the ravine and began rolling to the bottom, then all at once his arms, legs, and back were feeling as sore as his stomach. The side of his head and body hit something that broke under his weight, and the pain in his stomach and everything else faded away.

He wakened to the sound of many voices, two of them belonging to his parents, and with a spotlight shining down onto the floor of the ravine around him. In the beam he could see an adult wearing Monitor Corps uniform and an anti-gravity belt floating down to him. His parents and some other-species people were scrambling down the slopes using their hands, feet, or whatever. The monitor landed beside him and knelt down.

"So you're awake, young man," he said. "What have you been doing to yourself. But first, where does it hurt?"

"It doesn't hurt now," he replied, pushing a hand against his stomach and then feeling the side of his head. "It doesn't hurt anywhere."

"Good," said the man. From a satchel hanging from his

shoulder he produced a flat instrument with a tiny lighted screen on one side and began moving it slowly across the surface of Hewlitt's head, limbs, and body.

"I ate some fruit from that tree up there," he went on. "It gave me a bad tummy ache and I fell off."

"That is a very tall tree," said the other, in the same tone of voice Hewlitt's father used when he thought he was being told a very tall story. "Put your hand down again and don't move until I've finished scanning you. Did you fall asleep at any time since the fall?"

"Yes," he replied, "but I don't know how long. The sun was going down when I fell. You woke me up."

"Out for four, maybe five hours," said the man in a quiet, worried voice. "When I help you to sit up, tell me if anything hurts, right? I want to do a head scan."

This time the scanner was moved very slowly over the front, top, and sides of his head and down to the back of his neck; then the monitor put the instrument back in his satchel and stood up. Before he could speak, Hewlitt's parents arrived. His mother knelt down and grabbed him so tightly in both arms that he could hardly breathe, and she cried while his dad asked questions.

"He is a very fortunate young man," he heard the medic say in a quiet voice. "As you can see, his clothes are cut to ribbons, probably from playing among the war relics and from a long slide down into the ravine, but there isn't a scratch on him. He told me that he had eaten some fruit from that Pessinith tree up there. He says it gave him stomach cramps and that he fell from it and has been unconscious since before sunset. Now it isn't my job to argue with an overimaginative child, but look at the facts. The stomach disorder has disappeared; a fall from the top of that tree should have resulted in cuts, abrasions, fractures, and concussion, but his skin isn't even broken. A four-hour period of unconsciousness should be accompanied by some form of traumatic wounding that I could not have missed.

"From the state of his clothing," the monitor went on, "I would guess that he overtired himself playing among the wreckage, and when he climbed down here he simply fell asleep. The stomach ache and his alleged fall could be an appeal for sympathy and an attempt to divert parental wrath."

His mother had stopped crying and was asking him if he was really all right, but between her words he could hear his father saying that the wrath would be minimal because they were so glad to find him safe and sound.

"Children wander off and get lost sometimes," said the monitor, "and sometimes it doesn't end so well. We'll give him a ride home in our gravity sled, but only because he may still be overtired. I'll call in and check on him again tomorrow, although it really isn't necessary—he is in fine shape. You have a very healthy young man there, and there isn't a thing wrong with him. . . ."

The warm feeling of his mother's arms around him and the sight of the floodlit ravine and the overtalkative monitor medic faded, to be replaced by the familiar surroundings of Ward Seven and another monitor officer who was watching him and saying nothing.

CHAPTER 8

He thought I was lying," said Hewlitt, trying to hide his anger. "So did my parents, the few times I tried to tell them about it, and so do you."

Lieutenant Braithwaite studied him in silence for a moment before he said, "The way you have just told it, I can understand why. He had good medical and anatomical reasons for thinking you were lying and, because most people trust the members of the medical profession, your parents believed him rather than their, well, imaginative four-year-old son. I don't know what or who to believe, because I wasn't there and the truth can be a very subjective thing. I believe that you believe you are telling the truth, but that is not the same as me believing you are a liar."

"You're confusing me," said Hewlitt. "Do you think I'm a liar but don't want to come straight out and say it?"

Braithwaite ignored the question and said, "Did you tell your other doctors about the ravine incident?"

"Yes," he replied, "but I stopped doing so. None of them were interested in hearing about my lucky escapes. The psychologists thought that it was all my imagination, just like you."

"I suppose," said Braithwaite, smiling, "they asked you whether or not you disliked your parents, and if so, how much? Sorry, but I have to ask, too."

"You suppose right," said Hewlitt, "and you're wasting your time. Sure there were times when I disliked my parents, when they didn't do or give me what I wanted or they were too busy to play with me and made me work on school stuff instead. This didn't happen very often, only when something urgent came up and they were both busy. They were attached to the cultural-contact department in the nearby base, and both of them were in the Monitor Corps but didn't wear the uniform often because they worked mostly from home. But I wasn't neglected. My mother was nice and could be coaxed into doing things for me, and my father was harder to fool but was more fun. One or the other was usually at home, and they spent plenty of time with me once I'd done the schoolwork. But I always wanted more time with them. Maybe that was because I knew, somehow, that I was going to lose them and there wasn't much time left. I really missed them. I still do.

"Anyway," he went on, shaking his head in a vain attempt to lose those memories, "your psychological colleagues decided that I had been behaving like a selfish, scheming, and normal four-year-old."

Braithwaite nodded and said, "The psychological trauma of losing both parents at the age of four can have long-lasting emotional effects. They were killed in a flyer crash and you survived it. How much can you remember about the accident, and your feelings about it then and now?"

"I can remember everything," he replied, wishing that the other would change to a less painful subject. "At the time I didn't know what was happening, but I found out later that we were flying over a forested area on the way to a weeklong conference in a city on the other side of Etla when there was a major malfunction. We were using the small aircraft flight level, five thousand feet, and there must have been a few minutes before we hit the trees. My mother climbed into the backseat where I was strapped and wrapped herself around me while my father tried to regain control. We hit hard and tree branches pushed through the floor and one side of the fuselage and I passed out. When they found us next day my parents were dead and I was completely unhurt."

"You were very lucky," said the psychologist quietly. "That is, if a kid who had just lost both parents could be considered lucky."

Hewlitt did not reply, and after a moment Braithwaite went on, "Let's go back to the tree you climbed, or believed that you climbed, and the fruit you are supposed to have eaten that gave you the severe stomach cramps. Was there ever a recurrence of those symptoms later, before or after the flyer accident?"

"Why should I tell you," said Hewlitt, "when you are thinking that I imagined everything?"

"If it is any consolation to you," said Braithwaite, "I haven't decided what to think."

"All right, then," Hewlitt said, feeling that this was going to be another waste of time. "For the first few days after I fell into the ravine I felt nauseated every time I ate something, but not badly enough to upchuck, and after that with reducing frequency until it went away altogether. It came back for a short time after I moved to my grandparents' place on Earth, but I suppose that could have been due to the change of food and cooking. On Etla and on Earth, no medical cause could be found for these mild attacks of nausea, and I first began to hear the phrase 'the condition has a psychological component.' It hadn't happened for years until I tasted my first synthesized meal on *Treevendar,* and then it was mild and happened only once. Obviously it was my imagination."

Braithwaite ignored the sarcasm and said, "Would you really like to know that it was your imagination, or would you rather not be sure? Think very carefully before you answer."

"If I'm imagining things," said Hewlitt sharply, "I don't want to be the only one who doesn't know it."

"Fair enough," Braithwaite replied. "How well do you remember that tree you say you climbed on Etla, and the appearance of the fruit you may have eaten?"

"Well enough to draw a picture of it," said Hewlitt, "if I could draw. Do you want me to try?"

"No," the psychologist replied. He leaned sideways until he could reach the communicator keyboard with one hand and tapped briefly. When the screen lit up with the Sector General emblem, he said, "Library, nonmedical, vocal input, visual and translated vocal output, subject former Etlan Empire, planet Etla the Sick."

"Please wait," said the cool, impersonal voice of the library computer.

Surprised, Hewlitt said, "I didn't know I could get the library on that thing, just the nurses' station and the so-called entertainment channels."

"Without the correct access codes, you can't," said Braithwaite. "But if you ever feel so bored that you want to browse, I could probably get you authorization. You won't be given the codes for the medical library, though. When a case is thought to include a degree of hypochondria, the patient concerned should not be allowed access to a virtually unlimited number of symptoms."

Hewlitt laughed suddenly in spite of himself and said, "I can understand why."

Before Braithwaite could respond, the library voice said, "Caution. The Etla data is accurate but not yet complete. Following the large-scale police action taken against the then-Etlan Empire by the Monitor Corps, and the subsequent acceptance of its planets as members of the Galactic Federation twenty-seven standard years ago, the required transfer of Etlan botanical information to Central Records has been given a low order of priority owing to an intervening period of social unrest. The current situation is stable, the native intelligent life-form is physiological classification DBDG and nonhostile, and visits by other Federation citizens are encouraged. Please state your area of interest."

A large-scale police action, Hewlitt thought. There had been a savage and mercifully short interstellar war fought between the Etlan Empire and the Federation, brought about by the need of the ruling group to maintain itself in power while diverting the attention of its citizens from its own shortcomings. But the function of the Monitor Corps was to maintain the Federation's peace and not fight wars, so the response to the Etlan invasion of a whole galactic sector was a police action rather than a war. The fact that peace and stability had returned to the Etlan worlds meant that the Federation had won it.

"Etlan native flora," said Braithwaite, interrupting Hewlitt's cynical train of thought. "Specifically, a listing of all large fruit-bearing trees, ten meters tall or higher, found in the south temperate zone. Display for twenty seconds' duration unless requested otherwise."

For some reason Hewlitt was beginning to feel uneasy. He looked at Braithwaite and opened his mouth to speak, but the lieutenant shook his head, pointed at the viewscreen, and said, "You described your tree as being very tall, but it may have looked tall because at the time you were a very small child. I thought it better to start with ten meters."

It was like one of his childhood botany lessons, Hewlitt thought, a steady succession of tree pictures which in the present situation he found anything but boring. Most of them were strange to him, both in shape and foliage and in the fruit they bore, while others resembled the large bushes he had seen growing outside the garden fence. But one of them . . .

"That's it!" he said.

"Hold: replay and expand data on the Pessinith tree," said Braithwaite into the communicator. Then he said to Hewlitt, "It certainly looks like the tree you described: thick, twisted branches, with four thinner ones without bark at the top bearing the fruit clusters. And the color of the foliage is right for late summer when you climbed it. Library, run and repeat close-ups of the fruit showing seasonal growth and color changes."

For several minutes he watched while the screen showed the fruit going through its cycle of green bud to small, dark brown sphere to the fully ripe, green-and-yellow-striped pear shape. It was so familiar that he had a twinge of remembered stomach cramps, and the feeling was so strong that he missed hearing the library computer's boring recitation of the relevant nonvisual information.

"That is it," he said again. "Definitely. Now do you believe me?"

"Well," said Braithwaite, shaking his head in a way that suggested confusion as much as negation, "I now have another reason why that monitor medic didn't believe you. And you haven't been listening. That tree doesn't reach the fruit-bearing stage until it is fifteen to twenty meters tall, and the fruit hangs from the topmost branches. If the tree was overhanging a ravine, and you fell from the top, you should have broken your stupid little four-year-old neck. Instead you escaped without a scratch.

"I suppose it is possible that intervening branches slowed

your fall," he went on, "or you fell into a thick bush before hitting the side of the ravine and rolling down. Stranger accidents have happened before now, and it would explain why you, an intelligent and seemingly well balanced person, are sticking to this incredible story. But that isn't all you say you did. Don't talk, Patient Hewlitt, just listen."

In the silence the calm, impersonal voice of the library computer sounded clear and almost loud.

". . . While the fruit is ripening," it was saying, "the spongy internal mass absorbs all of the juice and grows to fill the striped envelope which, before parturition, becomes tough and flexible. When the semiliquid, sponged-filled fruit strikes the ground, it bounces or rolls a short distance until chemical sensors in the skin indicate an underlying soil type suitable for germination, whereupon the area of skin in contact with the ground decomposes, enabling the sponge to release its liquid content and seeds into the soil and begin its own slower process of decomposition. This has a twofold purpose, in that the rotting spongy material promotes initial growth in the seeds, while the juice permeates the surrounding soil and inhibits or kills off competing growths.

"Warning," it went on. "The fruit of the Pessinith tree is highly toxic to all known warm-blooded oxygen-breathing physiological classifications as well as the native Etlan lifeforms of all species. It has been investigated for possible medicinal use in trace quantities without success. Two cubic centimeters of the juice ingested by an entity of average body mass, such as an adult Orligian, Kelgian, or Earth-human, causes a rapid loss of consciousness and termination within one standard hour, and three cubic centimeters would have the same effect on a Hudlar or Tralthan. The effect is irreversible and there is no known antidote. . . ."

"Thank you, Library," said Braithwaite. His voice was calm, his face expressionless, but he hit the communicator's cutoff key so hard that it might have been a mortal enemy. For a long moment the lieutenant stared at him without blinking. Hewlitt told himself that it was going to happen again, that another medical person was about to tell him that he had imagined everything. But when the psychologist spoke there was curiosity rather than disbelief in his voice.

"A few drops of Pessinith fruit juice will kill a fully-grown man," he said calmly, "and you were a four-year-old child who sucked dry the contents of a whole fruit. Can you explain that, Patient Hewlitt?"

"You know I can't."

"Neither can I," said the lieutenant.

Hewlitt took a deep breath and let it out slowly before he trusted himself to speak. He said, "I have been talking to you for over four hours, Lieutenant. Surely that is long enough for you to establish whether or not I am a hypochondriac. Tell me—and be truthful, not polite."

"I'll try to be both," said the psychologist. He sighed, then went on, "You are not a simple case. There are episodes in your childhood that could have led to severe emotional disturbance in later life, but so far I have found nothing to indicate that any lasting psychological damage was done. Your personality is well integrated, your intelligence is above average, and you appear to be coming to terms with your initial xenophobia. Apart from being hypersensitive and constantly on the defensive because up to now nobody has believed that there is anything wrong with you . . ."

"Up to now?" Hewlitt broke in. "Does that mean you are beginning to believe me?"

Braithwaite ignored the question and went on, "Your behavior is not characteristic of a hypochondriac who, as we know, produces imaginary medical symptoms for psychological reasons, such as a need to attract attention or gain sympathy, or to escape some deeply concealed, nonphysical problem or event that the hypochondriac refuses to face and where illness is the only perceived defense. If the latter, and you were able to hide it from yourself for most of your life, and from me during a four-hour interview, then it must be something pretty terrible that you have made yourself forget. But I cannot believe that you are hiding anything like that from me. But neither can I believe that you ate Pessinith fruit or fell from that tree. That escape was not just incredibly lucky, it was downright miraculous!"

Braithwaite stared at him without blinking for what seemed a long time. Then he said, "The medical profession is not comfortable with miraculous occurrences, and neither am I. That is Lioren's area of expertise. But even the Padre is unhappy with them, because it believes that the advances in medicinal science have rendered them obsolete. Do you believe in miracles?"

"No," said Hewlitt firmly. "I have never been a believer in anything."

"Right," said Braithwaite. "At least that gets one non-physical factor out of the way. But there is another that we should eliminate as well—specifically your early xenophobia. That may have been caused by an incident involving an off-worlder so frightening that you now refuse to remember it. I would like to conduct a test."

"Can I refuse to take it?" said Hewlitt.

"You must understand," said Braithwaite, again ignoring his question, "that this is not a psychiatric hospital. My department is responsible for maintaining the mental health of a staff comprising sixty-odd different life-forms, and keeping that bunch happy and out of each other's hair, or whatever, is more than enough for us. The test will help me to decide whether to hand you back to Medalont for further medical investigation or recommend your transfer to a planetary psychiatric facility."

Hewlitt felt the old anger and embarrassment and despair

welling up in him again. From the Galactic Federation's leading hospital he had expected something better. Bitterly, he said, "What are you going to do to me?"

"I can't tell you," said Braithwaite, smiling again. "It will be uncomfortable for you, not life-threatening but with a high level of stress, and I'll try not to allow things to get out of control."

CHAPTER 9

A nightmare, Hewlitt told himself as he fought a sudden urge to hide his head under the blanket, was a nonphysical event from which he could expect to wake up. His problem was that he was not asleep.

There were fifteen of them walking and tapping and slithering in procession down the ward and, he knew with a dreadful inevitability, they were heading for his bedside. Three members of the group were familiar, he saw as they halted in a semicircle around him: his Hudlar nurse, Lieutenant Braithwaite, and Senior Physician Medalont. The nurse's speaking membrane remained still, the psychologist smiled in silent reassurance, and everyone else joined in maintaining the silence until Medalont broke it.

"As you may already know, Patient Hewlitt," said the senior physician, "Sector General is a teaching hospital. This means that at any given time a proportion of its medical staff is composed of trainees who hope one day to qualify as multispecies doctors and nurses who may choose to practice here, or as medical officers attached to one of the Federation's space construction projects. Long before that stage is reached the trainees must gain basic experience of other-species' physiology, which is where you come in. You are not obliged to submit to physical examination by trainees, but most of our patients do so willingly because they know that we have their best interests at heart."

Hewlitt forced himself to look at the trainees one by one. He identified two Kelgians, another Melfan, who differed from Medalont only in the markings on its carapace, three Nidians, and a six-legged elephantine Tralthan similar to one of the patients in the ward, but the rest of them were strange and therefore frightening. He wanted to shake his head but it would not move and his mouth was too dry to say "No."

"To be accepted for training here," the senior physician went on, "the entities around you must first have demonstrated a particular aptitude for advanced surgical and medical work and possess wide experience in their former planetary hospitals. I mention this so that you will know that they are not complete medical idiots in spite of what some of their tutors may say about them."

A quiet cacophony of alien sounds that did not translate emanated from the members of the group. Probably, Hewlitt thought, it was a dutiful response to their superior's little joke.

Medalont ignored them and said, "You have already been examined and had physical contact with your other-species nurse and myself without any accompanying physical discomfort. I can further assure you that if any of the trainees do or say anything to cause you distress, I shall have very harsh words to say to them afterward. May we proceed, Patient Hewlitt?"

They were all staring at him with far too many eyes.

Braithwaite and the nurse moved closer. The lieutenant was frowning and smiling at the same time in a strange expression that combined worry with reassurance, Hewlitt thought, and all the other expressions were unreadable. He opened his mouth, but the sound that came out was not even translatable by himself.

"Thank you," said Medalont; then, to the others, "Well, who wants first crack?"

Inevitably it was the biggest one present, the Tralthan, who lumbered forward to stand by his bedside. One of the eyes projecting from its domelike, immobile head curved down to regard his face; another was directed at Medalont and the other two somewhere behind it. Two of the four tentacles growing from its massive shoulders were lowered to within a few inches of his chest, one of them holding a scanner, and he did not know where the surprisingly quiet voice was coming from when it spoke.

"Please do not be alarmed, Patient Hewlitt," it said as he tried vainly to burrow backward into his bed. "The examination will be verbal or physically noninvasive, unless my questions should invade your privacy, in which case I shall not expect an answer. My intended specialty is other-species intercranial surgery, so I shall be concentrating the scanner examination in that area. I would like to begin at the rear base of the cranium where the nerve trunks enter the upper vertebrae.

"Could you please sit up," it went on, "and rest the front of your head on the joints midway along your ambulatory appendages? I think the nonmedical words for them is knees. Is this so?"

"Yes," said Hewlitt and Medalont together.

"Thank you," it said. With one eye still fixed on the senior physician it continued, "The Earth-human DBDG classification is fortunate in that the length of the nerve connections between the visual, aural, olfactory, and tactual sensors and the brain proper are shorter than in the majority of other intelligent life-forms, including my own, and the advantage in reaction times during the pre-sapient stage of their evolution undoubtedly led to species dominance. But the cranial contents are densely packed so that the charting of neural pathways is difficult, and precise work is required if a surgical intervention becomes necessary. When you open and close your upper and lower mandibles, Patient Hewlitt, is there subjective evidence of compression effects on the brain stem?"

"No," said Hewlitt and the senior physician together. Medalont gave the impression that it considered the question a stupid one, and added, "Enough. Who's next?"

The creature who came forward had a narrow, tubular body covered by brown and yellow stripes and supported by six long, very thin limbs. Two sets of wings sprouted from the sides of its body, but they were so tightly folded that he could not be sure which color predominated, and two long, black, furry antennae projected from the top of its insectile head. It raised itself almost upright by placing its middle limbs on the edge of his bed and looked down at him with enormous, lidless eyes.

His first impulse was to swat it the way he swatted all large insects that came too close, but he stopped himself. To a creature as fragile as this one, any kind of blow would be sure to inflict serious injury, which meant that he had nothing to fear from it. Besides, he had never ever swatted a butterfly, even though he had never been faced with a specimen as big as this one.

"I am a Dwerlan, Patient Hewlitt," it said, taking a scanner from the equipment pouch strapped to its body. "Since I am the only member of my species currently attached to the hospital and we are not a well-traveled race, I hope this first meeting with one of us will cause you the minimum of emotional distress. My interest is in other-species general surgery and so, with your permission, I shall examine you from the head to the nonmanipulatory digits on your feet. . . ."

A big butterfly, Hewlitt thought, *with an impeccable bedside manner.*

". . . You are not the first Earth-human DBDG that I have examined and recorded for later study," it went on. "But the others, as is usual in a hospital, were in a diseased or damaged condition. You are an apparently perfect physical specimen and as such are of particular interest to me for purposes of clinical comparison. I will begin by taking your pulse at the temporal and carotid arteries and at the wrist, since emergencies can arise when a scanner is not available."

Its head tilted forward and inclined to one side so that one of its antennae touched the side of his head and throat, so lightly that if his eyes had been closed he might not have felt it.

"As well," it continued, "with the equipment I am using, it will not be necessary for you to uncover your body completely, particularly in the area containing the genitalia. From my nonmedical behavioral studies I know that Earthhumans subscribe to a nudity taboo which makes them sensitive about openly displaying this area. As I have no intention of causing you embarrassment, Patient Hewlitt, whether you are male or female—"

"Can't you see it's a male, stupid?" one of the Kelgians broke in. "Look at the flat, vestigial mammaries. Even through the bed garment you can see, or more accurately you cannot see, the contours on its chest. In females they are fully developed, which gives the female DBDG its characteristically top-heavy appearance—"

It broke off as Medalont raised one pincer, clicked twice, and said, "Enough. The time for clinical argument is not now, when the patient can overhear and, perhaps, draw its own conclusions regarding your medical ability."

The next one to come forward was the Kelgian responsible for the interruption. It stood on its three rearmost sets of tiny, caterpillar-like legs and curled over the bed like a furry question mark. Being a Kelgian, it would not have a bedside manner.

"My examination will be similar to that of my Dwerlan colleague," it said, "but I would also like to ask questions. The first one is, What is an apparently healthy patient like yourself doing in hospital? According to the senior physician's case notes, there is nothing clinically wrong with you, except that you have displayed life-threatening cardiac symptoms for no apparent reason. What is wrong with you, Patient Hewlitt? Or what do you think may be wrong with you?"

"I don't know," said Hewlitt, "twice."

.Like all Kelgians', this one's manner was impolite, honest, and completely forthright because that was the only way it knew how to behave. If his reaction was the same it would not be offended, because politeness and diplomacy were alien concepts to it. That was one of the things he had learned since coming to this medical madhouse, and he might be able to put that knowledge to use now by asking the right questions. Kelgians did not know how to lie.

"The condition is intermittent," Hewlitt went on, "with no detectable cause or advance warning symptoms. But my case notes must have told you that, too. What else did they tell you?"

"The notes also discussed the possibility that you yourself are the primary cause," said the other, "and that the condition is due to an intense hysterical reaction triggered by a deep-seated psychosis which manifests itself on the physical level, and that a rigorous psychological investigation has been undertaken to prove or disprove this theory. Turn onto your left side."

"So far," said Hewlitt, looking at Braithwaite, who

smiled and looked at the ceiling, "there has been no evidence of a psychosis, deep-rooted or otherwise, because there isn't any to be found. If there was some past childhood experience or event or crime buried in my subconscious, so terrible and heinous that I have forced myself to forget it, surely there would be gaps in my memory or bad dreams or some indication other than the sudden onset of a cardiac arrest?"

The Kelgian's fur was moving in fast, erratic waves from its nose to the section of the body hidden by the bedside. It said, "I am not an ET psychologist, not even a Kelgian psychologist, but I disagree with you. It is generally accepted that a memory deeply buried is likely to have effects in direct proportion to the depth of its burial when it is uncovered. There is something hiding inside your mind that does not want to come out. If the threat of its discovery can cause a cardiac arrest as well as the other symptoms listed during similar episodes in the past, then it must be located, identified, and uncovered very carefully if you are to survive the experience."

This time it was the Kelgian who looked at Braithwaite, who nodded in agreement. So once again everyone was thinking that it was all in his mind. Trying to control his anger, which was unnecessary when talking to a Kelgian, Hewlitt said, "And how would you locate and identify this thing?"

There was a moment's silence, broken by Medalont, who said, "The patient seems to be examining its doctor now. But I, too, am interested in the answer."

The Kelgian's fur rose into spikes and subsided before it said, "As yet Senior Physician Medalont has been unable to discover a clinical reason for your condition, Patient Hewlitt, and Lieutenant Braithwaite has found no evidence of major psychological disturbance. But if there is something there you must be aware of it, you must feel that something is wrong however tenuous the feeling might be. I suggest that an even closer investigation be made of your feelings, a more thorough one than is possible using the lieutenant's verbal examination techniques.

"An examination by a Cinrusskin empath like Prilicla," it ended, "might be able to detect feelings that you were unaware of having, and probably the reasons for them."

"But I feel well, usually," Hewlitt protested. "And wouldn't I be the first to know if I didn't? Anyway, I have met some pretty horrible-looking people since I came here, but I don't remember if one of them was a Cinrusskin."

"If you had seen Prilicla," said the Kelgian, "you would remember it."

Before he could reply, Medalont clicked a pincer for silence and said, "And you must also remember that Cinrusskins are empaths, not telepaths, who can detect and isolate the most subtle feelings, but not the reasons for them. The suggestion of exposing Patient Hewlitt to an emotion-sensitive is a good one, so good that it has already been suggested by Psychology Department and myself. Regrettably, it cannot be adopted until Senior Physician Prilicla returns from Wemar, two weeks hence. In the meantime, Patient Hewlitt has kindly agreed to assist your training by submitting to a multispecies examination by all of you. You have lectures to attend and your time here is limited. Let us proceed."

Some of the examinations were less gentle than others, but none so uncomfortable that he felt it necessary to complain, and he had to answer the questions instead of trying to ask them. Finally it was over. Medalont and the trainees thanked him individually and departed, leaving him alone with Braithwaite.

"You survived that very well, Patient Hewlitt," said the lieutenant. "I'm impressed."

"And what about your special, uncomfortable, and stressful test that you won't allow to get out of hand?" said Hewlitt, "Will I survive that as well?"

Braithwaite laughed. "You just did."

"I see," said Hewlitt. "You were seeing how my nonexistent psychosis would react to a mass attack by aliens, right? Well, I still don't feel comfortable with them around me, but for some reason I seem to be feeling more curious, I mean really curious about them, rather than frightened. Why should that be?"

"Curious, that's good," said the psychologist. Without answering the question, he went on, "You have another problem. The amount of time that a hospital doctor can spend with any patient, especially a non-urgent patient undergoing negative treatment like yourself, is very small. Have you any ideas for keeping yourself amused during the next few weeks?"

"Are you trying to tell me," said Hewlitt angrily, "that nothing will be done about me, apart from using my body as a kind of healthy benchmark for trainees, until this Prilicla character arrives to read my emotions? Then, I suppose it, too, will tell me that there is nothing wrong with me, that it is all in my mind, and that I should get a grip on myself, go home and stop wasting everybody's time. And until then you are going to do nothing at all?"

Braithwaite laughed again and shook his head.

"It isn't funny, dammit," said Hewlitt. "At least, not to me."

"It will be," said the lieutenant, "after you meet your first Cinrusskin. Prilicla doesn't talk that way to people. And we are trying to do something other than keeping you under close medical surveillance. It isn't much, I admit, but a suggestion has been made that there could be some truth in your story about eating the poisonous fruit if— and this is a pretty tenuous theory—the juice that is lethal in small quantities has curative properties when taken in bulk. I can't give you the medical reasons why that should happen, but there is one known precedent. In that particular case there were long-term aftereffects which might explain, although again I don't know how, the intermittent nature of your symptoms. That is why we are sending to Etla the Sick for samples of the fruit so that Pathology can make an independent investigation of its degree of toxicity.

"The two-way hyperjump between here and Etla," he went on, "and a couple of days to find, gather, and pack the fruit, plus the time needed for the analysis, means a wait of two weeks minimum. During that time nothing much will be happening to you, unless Prilicla returns early or Medalont comes up with another form of treatment. That's why I wanted to know how you plan to pass the time."

"I don't know," said Hewlitt. "Reading and viewing, I suppose, when you give me the library codes. Was it your idea about the Pessinith fruit?"

Braithwaite shook his head again. "I wouldn't want to be associated with a weird idea like that. It was Padre Lioren's. It is a Tarlan BRLH attached to Psychology Department, who will probably visit you within the next few days. Visually it is a pretty fierce-looking character, but it might be able to help you, and after the way you behaved during the trainees' examination its appearance shouldn't cause you any problems."

"I suppose not," said Hewlitt, refusing to feel pleased at the compliment. "But . . . does what you have been saying mean that you are beginning to believe me?"

"Sorry, no," Braithwaite replied. "As I told you earlier, we believe that you believe yourself, which is different from us believing that what you tell us is completely true. The Pessinith fruit incident is evidence, the only piece of hard evidence you have given us, that can be checked. We must try to prove or disprove it and move on from there."

"And how exactly do you plan to do that?" said Hewlitt. "By feeding me with Pessinith fruit and seeing if I die?"

"As a nonmedic I cannot answer that," Braithwaite replied with another smile. "There would be safeguards, of course, but you are probably right."

CHAPTER 10

Hewlitt knew that it was not a symptom which would register on his medical monitor, but he was beginning to wonder whether there was such a condition as terminal boredom allied to atrophication of the tongue.

Apart from asking how he was feeling and saying "That's good," Medalont said nothing to him. His Hudlar nurse, although friendly enough and helpful when it did speak, was absent for most of the day on lectures and busy at other times. Braithwaite called for a few minutes every day on his way to the dining hall and insisted that, because they were on his own rather than the department's time, they were social rather than professional visits. He gave Hewlitt a few useful library access codes and talked a lot without saying anything. Charge Nurse Leethveeschi had time for him only if his monitor signaled a medical emergency; the lieutenant's Tarlan colleague, Padre Lioren, had yet to appear.

The ambulatory patients who passed his bed on the way

to the bathroom—a couple of Melfans, a newly arrived Dwerlan, a Kelgian, and one slow-moving Tralthan—sometimes talked among themselves but never to him, and the few conversations he could overhear from farther up the ward were never widened to include Patient Hewlitt. He could not talk to the patients in the beds beside and opposite him because they had been transferred somewhere else.

He was growing heartily sick and tired of listening to the condescending voice of the library computer for hours on end. It was beginning to make him feel as he had done as a boy when confronted with an unending succession of thinly disguised school lessons. Then as now he had felt bored and restless, but then there had been an open window beckoning and beyond it a landscape filled with interesting things to play with. Here there were no windows that opened and nothing but space outside them if they had. In a desperate attempt to relieve his restlessness he decided to walk up and down the ward.

He had walked the length of the ward twice and was on his third lap when Leethveeschi waddled out of the nurses' station to bar his path.

"Patient Hewlitt," it said, "please do not walk so fast. You could collide with one of my nurses and injure them, or they you. As well, and I realize that the thought may not have occurred to you, it shows great insensitivity on your part to parade your obvious physical fitness in this fashion before the other patients, some of whom are seriously ill, injured, or bedridden. You may continue with your exercise, slowly."

"Sorry, Charge Nurse," said Hewlitt.

Moving at the slower pace, Hewlitt felt awkward just staring straight in front of him or down at the floor ahead, so he began to sneak quick looks at the patients he was passing. The majority of them did not look at him, probably because they were sleeping, they were too ill, or they thought him as ugly as he did them. The other patients followed him with their eyes, too many eyes in some cases, and it came as no surprise that the only one who spoke to him was a Kelgian.

"You look all right to me, for an Earth-human," it said, rippling the fur that was not concealed by a large rectangle of silvery grey fabric taped to its side. "What's wrong with you?"

"I don't know what's wrong with me," said Hewlitt, stopping and turning to face it. "The hospital is trying to find out."

"Leethveeschi called out the resuscitation team for you the day you arrived," it said. "It must be serious. Are you going to die?"

"I don't know," Hewlitt replied, "and I hope not."

The Kelgian was lying on its side in a large, square bed on top of the blanket and with its furry body curved into the shape of a flattened S. It drew itself up, flattening the S even more, and said, "Seeing you Earth-humans balancing like that on just two legs makes me uneasy. If you want to talk, sit on the bed. I won't break. I won't bite, either; I'm herbivorous."

Hewlitt sat sideways on the edge of the bed, taking care that his hip did not touch the other's furry body or stubby, caterpillar legs. He had always liked talking to people, and provided he closed his eyes or looked away from time to time, he might be able to fool himself into thinking that the creatures in this place fell into that category.

Now that the Kelgian had mentioned it, he realized that a creature who moved on twenty feet would feel a little strange about someone who used only two. The feeling was mutual.

He cleared his throat and prepared to make polite conversation, if it was possible to do that with a Kelgian.

"My name is Hewlitt," he said. "I noticed you passing my bed a few times, usually with a Tralthan or a Dwerlan and once, I think, with a Duthan. I've been keying into the

library to learn and identify the different physiological classifications so that I'll know what as well as who is doing
things to me, but some of them I'm still not sure about."

"I am Morredeth," said the Kelgian. "You are right about
the Duthan and the other two. When we passed your bed you
did not speak. We decided that you were either very ill or
very antisocial."

"I did not speak because you were always talking to your
companions," he said, "and interrupting you would not have
been polite."

" 'Polite,' that word again!" said the other, its fur rising
into spikes. "There is no equivalent meaning in our language. If you wanted to speak to me you should have done
so, and if I had not wanted to listen to you I would have told
you to be quiet. Why must non-Kelgians make everything so
complicated?"

He decided to treat it as a rhetorical question and asked,
"What is wrong with you, Morredeth? Is it serious?"

The silence began to lengthen and still the other did not
reply. Kelgians were psychologically incapable of telling a
lie, Hewlitt reminded himself, but there was nothing to keep
them from remaining silent if they did not want to answer.
He was about to apologize for asking the question when the
other spoke.

"The original injury was not disabling," said Morredeth,
"but the resulting condition is very serious, and incurable.
Unfortunately, it will not kill me. I do not wish to talk about
it."

Hewlitt hesitated, then said, "Do you wish to talk about
something else, or would you prefer me to leave?"

Morredeth ignored him and went on, "I should try to talk
about it, Lioren says, and think about it instead of trying to
push it out of my mind. Right now I want to talk about the
other patients, the medical staff, and anybody or anything
else so that I will not have to think about it. But I can't talk

and think about other things all the time, not when the patients are sleeping, or when the night nurse stops talking to me because it has other things to do, or when I fall asleep myself. I don't know about your kind, but Kelgians have no voluntary control over the subject of their dreams."

"Nor have we," said Hewlitt, looking at the rectangle of silvery fabric attached to the other's body and wondering what terrible injury it concealed.

Morredeth saw where he was looking. It ruffled its fur and said, "I will not talk about it."

But you have been not-talking about it, or talking all around it, since I sat down on your bed. A psychologist would be able to make something of that, Hewlitt thought. Aloud, he said, "You mentioned a person called Lioren. I have been told that a Tarlan with that name might be calling on me soon."

"Not too soon, I hope," said Morredeth.

"Why do you say that?" Hewlitt asked, beginning to feel uneasy. "Is it a particularly unpleasant creature?"

"No," the other replied. "I have found it to be a pleasant entity, at least for a non-Kelgian. I have not been here long enough to know what exactly it does, but Horrantor tells me that it is usually sent to patients that the medics are no longer able to help. You know, the hopeless cases."

Hewlitt did not like the sound of that, and wondered if Braithwaite's earlier reference to Lioren had been entirely factual. Not everyone, in fact not anyone, was as forthright as a Kelgian.

"Who is Horrantor?" he asked. "One of the medics?"

"One of the patients," said Morredeth, pointing. "That one. It is coming to find out what we are talking about. You can feel the floor shaking."

"What is wrong with it?" said Hewlitt. He kept his voice low in case the Tralthan patient, too, was reticent about its medical problems.

"Surely that is obvious," the Kelgian snapped at him, "when it is walking on only five legs. The strapped-up leg was crushed in an industrial accident, rebuilt with microsurgery, and will be good as new. There was damage to the reproductive system and birth canal which still require treatment, but don't ask it for the gory details. At least, not while I'm with you. I have heard more than enough about its reproductive plumbing, and anyway, it reminds me of my own problems. Oh, Bowab is heading this way, too. We usually play cards, bellas or scremman, to pass the time. Do you play any card games?"

"Yes, no," said Hewlitt. "What I mean is, I know the rules of a few Earth games, but I don't play them well. Is Bowab the Duthan who is walking behind Horrantor? What is wrong with it?"

"You are very indecisive, Hewlitt," said Morredeth. "Either you can play or you cannot. Bellas is a Tralthan game of skill similar to Earth whist. Scremman is from Nidia originally and, according to Bowab, who considers itself an expert, is a game of chance played by skillful, passive liars and cheats. I don't know what is wrong with the Duthan except that the problem is uncommon, and medical rather than surgical. This is the hospital's main observation, transition, and sometimes recuperation ward for patients lucky enough to survive—which, Leethveeschi tells us, is most of them. They send some pretty weird patients here sometimes."

"Yes," said Hewlitt, watching the two who were approaching and wondering whether, in the present company, the remark was aimed at him.

Horrantor came to a stop at the bottom of the bed, its injured leg barely touching the floor. One each of the four, extensible eyes projecting from around the immobile dome of its head were directed at Morredeth, Bowab, Hewlitt, and, for some reason, the distant nurses' station. The Duthan moved to the side of the bed opposite Hewlitt. He wondered whether the irregular brown patches of fur on its otherwise dark green, centaurlike body were a symptom of its medical condition, or a natural feature like the thick, white line that began in the center of its forehead then widened along the upper and lower spine to disappear into the long bushy tail, but decided not to ask. It folded its rear legs, stood on the forward set, and leaned its elbows and forearms on the bed. Both of its eyes, which were capable of looking in only one direction at a time, were staring at him.

Hewlitt hesitated, then introduced himself and followed with a brief description of his problem. He could think of nothing else to talk about, because all they had in common was a collection of symptoms.

Horrantor made a low, moaning sound that might have indicated sympathy and said, "At least we know what is wrong with us. If they don't know what is wrong with you and you feel physically fit, it might take a long time before they find a cure."

"Yes, indeed," said Bowab, "more than enough time to become terminally bored. Unless, of course, you can find an amusing way of passing the time. Are you a gambling person, Patient Hewlitt?"

Before he could reply, Morredeth said, "Even a Kelgian could change the subject more gradually than that. Hewlitt knows how to play cards, but not bellas or scremman. We might be able to teach it, or it might prefer to teach us one of its games."

"That would give you initial advantages, Patient Hewlitt," said Horrantor, turning another eye in his direction. "With us as opponents, you would need them."

It was obvious that these people had a high opinion of themselves as cardplayers, and he was tempted to try confusing them with the rules of a complicated and partnered game like whist—or better still, bridge. But if their self-assessment was accurate, they might not be confused for long.

"I would prefer to learn than teach," he said. "Besides, I didn't think that I would need to bring Earth playing cards with me."

"You don't," said Bowab, as it reached into the pocket of its abbreviated apron, the only item of clothing that it was wearing, and drew out a very thick pack of cards. "If anyone needs them, Leethveeschi can request a pack from the staff recreation level. That's how we got ours. We'll play a few practice games with the cards faceup to let you know what is going on. But let's not waste time, Morredeth. Squeeze up the bed and give us some playing space."

The Kelgian coiled itself into a flatter S so that the bottom of its bed was left clear, then twisted its conical head and upper body sideways until its short arms hung over the playing area. Bowab, Horrantor, and Hewlitt were already in position when the Tralthan said, "Leethveeschi is heading this way. What can it want with us at this time of the day? Is anybody due medication?"

"Patient Hewlitt," said the charge nurse, stopping so that it could look at him through the clear space between Horrantor and Bowab. "I am glad to see that you have begun socializing and indulging in a group activity with other patients, and Lieutenant Braithwaite will also be pleased when he hears about it.

"But there is a hospital regulation governing the group activity in which you are about to engage," it went on. "The game must be played for mental exercise only. No personal property, negotiable Federation currency, or promissory notes of any kind may be exchanged as a result of playing it. You find yourself among a group of civilized predators, Patient Hewlitt, and the thought that comes most readily to my mind is best described by the Earth-human phrase 'a sheep among wolves.' Please try not to become too excited in case your medical monitor reports it as a clinical emergency. Also . . ."

One green, shapeless hand dug into a pocket attached to the outer surface of Leethveeschi's protective envelope and withdrew a small, plastic box, which it tossed onto the bed beside him.

". . . These are used by your species, among others," it continued, "to remove food scraps adhering to the spaces between their teeth. Doubtless you will find another use for them. Good luck."

After the charge nurse left them it was Bowab who was the first to find its voice.

"Toothpicks, a full box!" it said. "We had to divide half a box among us. Hewlitt, you are a millionaire!"

CHAPTER 11

The game was not as complicated as Hewlitt had first thought, even though it was played with a pack containing seventy-five cards in five fifteen-card suits, each with its own individual symbol and color: blue crescents, red spears, yellow shields, black serpents, and green trees. The highest-value cards were the Ruler, his-her-or-its Mate, and the Heir, followed in descending order by the values twelve to one. Unlike the Earth games he knew, where the ace had the highest value, the Poor One, as it was called, was the lowest card—except when a hand contained a twelve of the same suit, in which case the combination could depose one of the three ruling cards.

There were historic and sociopolitical implications to the game, the others explained, in that the merging of the lowest and the highest non-Ruler cards signified a popular uprising, a palace revolution, or, in present times, a successful corporate takeover. Three, four, or five cards of the same number in different suits had particular values, and if the hand also contained a ten it could depose two of an opponent's Rulers. There were other combinations of numbers and symbols of lesser power which were capable of reducing the value of an opponents' single cards or combinations, but Hewlitt thought that it would take a little time to learn them all.

The players could request an extra card free during the first three rounds of the game, but were required to discard it or another from their hands each time, and after that they had to buy the cards from the dealer, called the Ruler of the Game, by raising the stake. Players who did not buy extra cards either had bad hands and were unwilling to waste money, or very good ones and were sitting tight.

A further complication was that each player had two discard piles of up to three cards placed faceup, but only he, she, or it knew which pile was for permanent discard and which was for returning to the hand, if required, before the end of the game. It was possible to discover which was the true discard pile by studying the body language of an opponent, always bearing in mind the possibility that it was probably generating false signals.

"During the first few games we will go easy on you," said Horrantor, with an untranslatable sound that might have been the Tralthan equivalent of laughter, "and point out your mistakes as we go. I think you now understand the rules well enough for us to begin."

"But not well enough," said Bowab, hunching closer to the bed, "to begin cheating."

"Cheating, yes," the Tralthan went on. "You must always remember, Patient Hewlitt, that your opponents will try to cheat; that is, to take unfair advantage of you in any way possible to them. This includes using their physiological differences against you. For example, it may not have occurred to you that, with me standing as I am next to you, one of my eyes can be extended laterally so as to see across your hand. There is also the fact that Duthans have the ability to sharpen the focus of their eyes when the object, in this case your own eyes, are remaining at a fixed distance. The reflection of your cards in your eyes is clear, especially the card you are lifting into your hand, so you should obscure your opponent's view by slitting your eyes and looking through the unsightly fringes of hair on the edges of your upper and lower eyelids. More subtle methods of cheating will be used against you which, in the beginning, we will allow you to detect and counter for yourself."

"Th-thank you," said Hewlitt.

"Stop talking and deal," said Morredeth.

The next two hours passed very quickly until the arrival of the Hudlar nurse with the announcement that the evening meal was about to be served.

"If you wish to continue with your conversation and group activity," it said, "you may eat together at the table outside the nurses' station; otherwise the meal must be delivered to your individual beds. Well?"

Horrantor, Bowab, and Morredeth said "the table" in unison, and Hewlitt said the same a moment later.

"Are you sure, Patient Hewlitt?" asked the nurse. "You have limited other-species' social experience, and seeing some of them at table for the first time may be psychologically disquieting. Or have you dined with off-worlders before now?"

"Well, no," he replied, "but I don't want to interrupt our conversation. I'm sure it will be all right, Nurse."

"The trick," said Horrantor, "is to look at nobody's platter but your own."

But when the trays arrived he could not help sneaking a glance at the others' platters, and decided that their food looked unappetizing but not revolting. It was the sight of Horrantor pushing enormous quantities of cooked vegetation—it had at least six times the body mass of an Earth-human and no doubt needed generous helpings—into an opening that he had not suspected was a mouth that he found most disconcerting. Morredeth was an herbivore also, and made a lot of noise while demolishing a selection of crisp, uncooked, and unidentifiable vegetables. He could not tell what Bowab was eating, although it had a strange, spicy smell, and he noticed that none of them was looking at his platter.

Was it simple good manners, he wondered, or was the sight of his synthetic steak and mushrooms having an even worse effect on them?

As soon as they were finished the other three returned their trays to the delivery float, so Hewlitt did the same. He did not know whether this was to save time and effort for the nursing staff or to clear the table quickly for another game. Either way he thought it was a good idea.

While Bowab, the overall winner of the previous game, was dealing he said, "You people are really devious and nasty and vicious as players. I wouldn't call those last three games going easy on me. It isn't fair. I've lost half of my toothpicks already."

"Think of it as the involuntary payment of tuition fees," said Bowab. "Besides, scremman isn't a fair game, it is you who are fair game."

A furry centaur who makes jokes, Hewlitt thought. He laughed politely and said, "It is a most unfair game, so far as I am concerned, because winning depends not only on a player's capacity for misdirection, concealment, and bluff, but on the accurate reading of an opponent's expression. Under all that Kelgian and Duthan fur I don't even know if there are expressions to read, and Horrantor's head skin is about as expressive as Hudlar hide. Until I came to this place I spoke to off-worlders only by communicator. You people are so completely strange to me that I wouldn't know a revealing expression if I saw one."

"Since coming here," said Bowab, "we have seen you studying the library's physiological classification system used to describe and identify Federation citizens, which includes basic information on their sociopsychological behavior. During the last game you were quick to discover my true discard pile. Either you are being too modest, Patient Hewlitt, or you are not as ignorant as you are leading us to believe."

"In which case," said Horrantor, joining in, "you have learned that there is a psychological extension to scremman which operates during the breaks between play. You are indeed progressing well."

"And should I also learn," said Hewlitt, "not to be disarmed by compliments?"

"Of course," said Bowab.

He laughed again and said, "Then if I admit to ignorance on any subject, it would not weaken my position because the admission would be treated as a possible misdirection aimed at concealing a strength. But what do you do with a person like Morredeth? Surely it must be at a disadvantage because it cannot tell a lie?"

"Kelgian misdirection," said Horrantor, "involves concealing the intentions by not saying anything. We must try to discover what it is thinking by observing its fur movements. They are subtle and very difficult for a non-Kelgian to identify."

Bowab looked at Horrantor and back to Hewlitt, making a growling sound that did not translate. He could not be sure, but he thought that the Duthan was trying to warn him about something.

"When I was a child," Hewlitt went on, "I knew one furry creature well enough to guess at what it was thinking, or at least feeling. Sometimes I could make it change its mind and play when it wanted to sleep, and at other times it was able to make me do what it wanted. It was called a kitten, that is an immature cat, which is a nonsapient Earth-evolved pet that was technically the property of my parents although its behavior suggested that the opposite held true. It was a handsome female which, because of the peculiar mottled, brown color, was given the name of a sugary home-made candy Earth-people call Fudge. When it was angry or frightened its fur rose, which was an instinctive response from predomesticated times which made it look larger and more fearsome, but it soon learned more subtle methods of communication.

"If it wanted food," he continued, "it would rub its head against my ankles or, if its needs were persistently ignored, it would unsheath its claws and try to climb up my legs. When it rolled from side to side on its back and punched at the air with its paws, that meant it wanted to play, and if it curled up on my lap with its eyes closed, limbs folded under its body and chin on its tail, it wanted to sleep. Sometimes it did not seem to know whether it wanted to sleep or play on my lap.

"But it was a very active and friendly entity," said Hewlitt, and for a moment he could almost see it walking stiff-legged and tail erect around the center of their table and pushing at the cards with a forepaw, "so it did not object when I made its mind up for it and began patting and stroking and tickling it, very gently, on its stomach and under its chin and around its ears. It liked that but pretended it didn't by striking my hand with its paws, softly and with its claws sheathed. Most of all it liked me to stroke its back, especially when I began by gently pressing my fingertips on its head between the eyes and moving them slowly between its ears and along the spine to its tail, which by then was standing up straight. When I did that it would purr, which is the noise cats make when they are feeling pleasure. . . ."

"This conversation," said Morredeth, its fur rippling in

uneven waves, "is becoming very erotic and for me unpleasant. Stop it at once."

"It is bothering me, too," Bowab agreed, "but pleasantly. Why are you talking so much about this furry pet of yours? In character or behavior did it resemble Morredeth or myself? Was it a special, nonsapient friend? What happened to it and where is the story leading?"

"I'm sorry, I didn't intend to offend anyone," said Hewlitt, "and I don't know why I am talking about that cat now when I haven't even thought about it for years. Maybe it is because it was my first nonhuman friend. It was very friendly and did not resemble anyone here, especially while you are playing scremman, but it was too adventurous for its own good. There was an accident when it ran too close to a large antigravity vehicle and was crushed by the outer edge of the repulsor field. It did not appear to be badly injured because it was still breathing and there was only a small amount of blood around its mouth and ears, but my parents said that there was no hope for it and they would send for the pet healer to have the poor thing put out of its misery. Before they could stop me I lifted it and took it to my room, and locked the door so nobody could take it away from me, then I nursed it in bed with me all night until . . ."

"Until it died," said Horrantor in a voice that seemed too soft and low for it to be coming from such a massive creature. "A sad story."

"No it isn't," said Hewlitt. "I nursed it until it was better. Next morning it was walking about good as new, and butting my ankles to be fed. My parents could not believe it, but my father said that cats had nine lives, that is an old Earth saying based on the fact that they have great agility and sense of balance and rarely fall, and that this one must have used all of them at once. I suppose it died eventually of old age."

"A sad story with a happy ending," said Bowab. "That is the kind I like best."

"Are we going to talk about furry pets," said Morredeth, its fur tufting into strange, uneven spikes and waves that might have denoted anger or impatience or something else entirely, "or play scremman?"

The question answered itself as Horrantor began to deal. Hewlitt tried to placate the Kelgian, who for some reason did not like him talking about cats. He said, "The reason I brought up the subject of my pet, and especially its fur, was that I was thinking about the unfairness of my not being able to read other-species expressions. Horrantor and Bowab do not show any changes of expression that I can detect, and Morredeth shows far too many for me to read. Perhaps I will learn to do it in time, but right now it is Morredeth who should be complaining about unfairness because you two have had longer to observe its fur movements than I have."

"Patient Hewlitt," Morredeth broke in, its fur rippling and tufting as if there were a strong wind blowing along the ward, "you will not learn to read my feelings no matter how long we are here. Even another Kelgian would have trouble doing that."

The game continued in a disapproving silence and Hewlitt knew that he had said the wrong thing again.

CHAPTER 12

The thought of what that wrong thing might have been, and how he could avoid repeating the mistake, was still in Hewlitt's mind when the game was halted by the Hudlar nurse telling them to return to their beds for the evening medication round and, hopefully, to sleep. The other three players passed his bed, Morredeth without speaking, on their way to and from the bathroom, but he did not talk to any of them about it in case he made matters worse. He was not being given any medication, which meant that he would be visited last.

The Hudlar nurse had only to check the sensor connections to his medical monitor and would have nothing more to do, barring emergencies, until its next round of observing sleeping patients in another two hours. Ahead of it stretched a long spell of night duty during which, he hoped, its boredom and his curiosity could be relieved by a few questions.

"Try not to use the viewscreen tonight," it said. "Charge

Nurse Leethveeschi tells me that you've had enough excitement for one day. Playing scremman makes the time pass quickly and I'm glad that you are making other-species' friends. But now you must sleep."

"I'll try, Nurse," he said. "But there is something worrying me."

"Is there pain?" it said, moving quickly to the bedside. "Your monitor is registering optimum life-sign levels for a healthy DBDG. Please describe the symptoms. Be as specific as you can."

"Sorry, Nurse, I misled you," he said. "It has nothing to do with my physical condition. During the day I offended another patient, the Kelgian, Morredeth, but I don't know what it was that I said or did that was offensive. We were playing scremman and the other two seemed to be trying to tell me nonverbally to stop whatever it was I was doing or saying. I would like to know what it was I was doing wrong so that I will know not to do it again and, if it was serious, to apologize."

Even though it had no features that he could identify, the nurse appeared to relax. It said, "I don't think this is anything to worry about, Patient Hewlitt. During a game of scremman that lasted for many hours, as I have been told yours did, the exchange of insulting and critical words is a common occurrence . . ."

"I noticed," he said.

". . . and such words are forgotten by the next deal," it went on. "Just forget the incident, as the others will have done by now, and go to sleep."

"But it didn't happen like that," he said. "At the time we were between games and the words were spoken while we were eating lunch."

The Hudlar was silent for a moment while it looked along the beds on both sides of the ward. Everyone but Hewlitt and itself seemed to be asleep, so that there was nothing more urgent to claim its professional attention. He felt pleased, and a little ashamed, of his newfound ability to maneuver this medical monstrosity to his will.

"Very well, Patient Hewlitt," it said, "what was the subject of conversation, and can you recall the remark that caused Patient Morredeth to take offense?"

"I already told you I couldn't," said Hewlitt. "I was simply describing and talking about a small, furry animal, a household pet . . . Do Hudlars keep pets? . . . I had played with as a child. Morredeth did not object to anything I was saying until it suddenly accused me of talking dirty, and Bowab agreed with it. At the time I thought they were joking, but now I'm not so sure."

"In its present condition," said the nurse, the speaking membrane vibrating in the Hudlar equivalent of a near whisper, "Patient Morredeth is unusually sensitive about its fur. But you were not to know that. Tell me what was said, exactly?"

Was it possible, Hewlitt wondered suddenly, that the nurse was using him instead of the other way around? Was it pleased and eager to use any excuse to ease the boredom of night duty by giving nonmedical support to a worried patient, and would that be its clinically acceptable excuse to Leethveeschi for what might turn out to be a prolonged midnight chat? He took his time and repeated everything that had been said leading up to and during the description and behavior of his cat while it was being petted. He did not think that a being whose skin was like flexible steel could have erotic fantasies about fur, but in this place one could never be sure of anything.

When he finished speaking, the nurse said, "Now I understand. Before I try to explain what happened, tell me how much you already know about the Kelgian life-form."

"Only the information given in the introductory paragraphs from the nonmedical library listing of member races of the Federation," he said, "most of which was historical material. The Kelgians are physiological classification DBLF, warm-blooded, multipedal, and possessing a cylindrical body covered overall with mobile, silvery fur which is continually in motion while the being is conscious and, to a lesser extent, when it is dreaming.

"Because of inadequacies in the Kelgian speech organ," he went on, "their spoken language lacks modulation, inflection, or any other form of emotional expression. But they are compensated for this by their fur, which acts, so far as another Kelgian is concerned, as a perfect and uncontrollable mirror of the speaker's emotional state. As a result, the concepts of lying or being diplomatic, tactful or even polite are completely alien to them. A Kelgian says exactly what it means or feels because the fur is revealing its feelings from moment to moment, and to do otherwise is considered a stupid waste of time. Am I right so far?"

"Yes," said the Hudlar. "But in this situation the medical library data would have been of more use to you. Did Morredeth discuss its condition with you?"

"No," he replied. "When I asked, it said that it didn't want to talk about it. I was curious but decided that its ailment might be embarrassing and was none of my business anyway, and dropped the subject."

"Sometimes Patient Morredeth will not talk about its troubles," said the nurse, "and at other times it will. If you ask tomorrow or the next day it will probably tell you about its accident and the long-term results, which are very serious but not life-threatening, in great detail. I am telling you this because nearly everyone in the ward knows of Morredeth's problem, so I am not breaking patient confidentiality by discussing the physiological and emotional aspects of the case with you."

"I understand," he said.

"You do not understand," said the Hudlar, moving closer

to his bed and lowering its voice in inverse proportion to the distance, "but soon you will. If any of the anatomical terms I use are unclear, which is unlikely considering your medical history and prior experience of hospital treatments, please stop me and ask for a layperson's explanation. Shall I begin?"

Hewlitt stared at the nurse's massive body balanced on its six, curling tentacles and wondered if there was any intelligent species, regardless of its size, shape, or number of limbs, whose members did not enjoy a good gossip.

Remembering the trouble that a few unthinking words had caused with Morredeth, Hewlitt decided not to ask the question aloud.

"Anatomically," the Hudlar went on in exactly the same tone as that used by Senior Physician Medalont to its trainees, "the most important fact that you should know about Kelgians is that, apart from the thin-walled, cranial casing that protects the brain, the DBLF classification has no bony structure. Their bodies are composed of an outer cylinder of musculature which, in addition to assisting with locomotion, serves as protection for the vital organs within it. To the minds of beings like ourselves, whose bodies are more generously reinforced with bone structure, this protection seems far from adequate. Another severe disadvantage in the event of injury is the complex and extremely vulnerable circulatory system. The blood supply, which has to feed the large bands of muscle encircling the body, lies just beneath the skin, as does the nerve network that controls the mobile fur. Some protection is given by the thickness of the fur, but not against deep, lacerated wounding of more than one-tenth of the body area sustained as the result of Patient Morredeth being thrown against an uneven metal obstruction during a space collision. . . ."

An injury which in many other species would be considered superficial, the nurse explained, could result in a Kelgian bleeding to death within a few minutes.

The emergency coagulant administered at the time of the accident had checked the bleeding and saved Morredeth's life, but at a price. On the ambulance ship and later in hospital the damaged major blood vessels had been repaired, but even Sector General's DBLF microsurgery team had been unable to save the capilliary and nerve networks that had served the lost or damaged fur. As a result the beautiful Kelgian fur, which played such an important tactile as well as an aesthetic visual role between them during the preliminaries to courtship and mating, would never grow properly in those areas. Or if it did grow, the fur would be stiff, yellow, lifeless, and visually repulsive to another Kelgian of either gender.

It was possible to have the damaged area covered with artificial fur, but the synthetic material lacked the mobility and the deep, rich luster of living fur and would be immediately recognized for what it was. Kelgians in Morredeth's situation were usually too proud to be seen wearing such a patch and elected instead to live and work in solitude or with minimum social contact.

"The other Kelgians on the medical staff," the Hudlar went on, "tell me that Morredeth is, or was, a particularly handsome young female who has no longer any hope of mating or living a normal life. At present its problem is emotional rather than medical."

"And I," said Hewlitt, feeling hot with embarrassment, "had to talk to it about my cat's beautiful fur. I'm surprised it didn't hit me with something. Is there nothing more that can be done for it? And should I apologize, or would that just make matters worse?"

"In the space of a few days," said the Hudlar, ignoring the question, "you appear to be at ease, or even on terms of friendship, with Horrantor, Bowab, and Morredeth. On arrival you displayed symptoms of severe xenophobia which have since disappeared. If this is a true reaction to your first multiple, other-species contacts and not just a polite pretense of accepting an emotionally disturbing situation that you could do nothing about, then I am impressed with your ability to adapt. But I find your recent behavior, well, surprising."

"It wasn't a pretense," he said without hesitation, "and I'm not as polite as all that. Maybe it was because, as the only healthy patient in the ward, I was bored and curious, and it was you who suggested that I should try talking to the other patients in the first place. They all looked like waking nightmares to me and still do. But something, I don't know what exactly, made me want to meet them. It was a surprise to me, too."

The nurse's speaking membrane vibrated, too slowly for any words to form, and Hewlitt wondered if he was seeing the Hudlar equivalent of a stammer of hesitation. Finally it said, "To answer your earlier question, there is nothing more that can be done for Morredeth other than to change its dressings, which will heal the surface wounding without regenerating the damage to the underlying nerve network, and to apply the nonmedical treatment prescribed by Senior Physician Medalont at the suggestion of Padre Lioren, who until now has been visiting Morredeth every day. Today it called but remained in the nurses' station, where it listened to the conversation picked up by your medical monitor before—"

"It listened to our private conversation?" Hewlitt broke in. "That, that was wrong! I didn't know my monitor could be used that way. I, we might have said something that others were not supposed to hear."

"You did," said the nurse, "but Leethveeschi is used to hearing derogatory remarks about itself. Your monitor is capable of picking up words spoken very faintly in case you feel something is going wrong before the instrument does and call for help. Lioren said that the scremman game with a new and untutored player was helping to take the patient's mind off its troubles, and was probably doing more good than anything it could have said or done just then, and that it would visit Morredeth tomorrow."

Before Hewlitt could reply, it went on, "Morredeth's non-medical treatment includes a reduction in night sedation, which has been massive up until now, so that it will have more time to be alone with its thoughts. Medalont and Lioren are hoping that this will enable it to come to terms with its emotional problems. During the day, you may have noticed, it does not give itself time to think. As of tonight I have been instructed not to speak more than a few words to it unless there are strong medical reasons for doing so. You Earth-people have a saying that describes the situation very well, but my own feeling is that a healer should never be cruel to be kind, especially when a patient's suffering can be reduced by engaging in a friendly conversation with it. I am not, therefore, in agreement with this proposed course of treatment."

Once again the nurse's speaking membrane twitched silently. Hewlitt clapped a hand over his monitor, hoping that he was covering the sound sensor so that no word of its mutinous feelings would reach a more senior medic who might want to listen to the conversation later.

"Earlier you asked me what you should do about your insensitive behavior toward Morredeth," the nurse said as it turned to leave. "If you see that the patient is continuously wakeful, as it will be, it would do no harm then to apologize and talk to it."

He watched as the nurse moved along the darkened ward, in complete silence despite its tremendous body weight, and thought that for a great, hulking creature with hide like flex-ible metal it had a very soft heart. He did not have to be an empath, Hewlitt thought, to know what the other expected of him.

For psychological reasons that it found objectionable, the nurse had been forbidden by its superior to engage Morredeth in extended conversation and, without actually disobeying its instructions, it was making sure that someone else did.

CHAPTER 13

Hewlitt lay propped on one elbow so that he could see across the intervening patients to Morredeth's bed, listening to a ward full of extraterrestrials making their various sleeping noises and wondering how long he should wait before approaching the Kelgian. Its bed was screened and there was a faint glow visible on the ceiling, but the light was steady as if it was coming from the bedside lamp rather than an entertainment channel on the viewscreen. It was possible that Morredeth was reading or had already fallen asleep with its light on, and one of the strange noises he could hear might be the Kelgian snoring. If so it would have harsh things to say to the stupid Earth-person who wakened it.

To be on the safe side he decided to wait until Morredeth paid its nightly visit to the bathroom and talk to it after it had returned to its bed. But tonight it seemed that nobody needed to use the bathroom and he was becoming intensely bored with nothing to look at but rows of shadowy, alien beds and the single, glowing patch of ceiling above the Kelgian's position. Even the entertainment channel would be more exciting than this, he thought, and decided to make his apology without further delay and then try to get some sleep himself.

He sat upright, swung his legs over the edge of the bed, and felt around with his feet in the darkness until they found the sandals. They were hospital-issue and much too large so that the soft, flapping sounds they made against the floor seemed much louder now than they had during the daytime bustle of the ward. If Morredeth was awake it would hear him coming, and if it was asleep he would owe it a second apology for waking it up.

Morredeth was lying like a fat, furry question mark on its uninjured side, its only covering the large rectangle of fabric that held the wound dressings in place. With all that natural insulation, Hewlitt supposed, a Kelgian would not need blankets very often. Its eyes were closed and its legs were tucked up and almost hidden by the thick, restless fur, but the small, erratic movements did not necessarily mean that Morredeth was unconscious.

"Morredeth," said Hewlitt, in a voice so quiet that he barely heard it himself, "are you awake?"

"Yes," it said without opening its eyes.

"If you can't sleep," said Hewlitt, "would you like me to talk to you for a while?"

"No," said Morredeth, then a moment later, "Yes."

"What would you like to talk about?"

"Talk about anything you like," said the Kelgian, opening its eyes, "except me."

It was going to be difficult, Hewlitt thought, talking to a being who could not lie and always said exactly what it thought, especially when there were no other normally polite liars present to keep him reminded of the social niceties. He would have to be very careful or he might end up talking honestly, like a Kelgian. The feeling that he was about to do just that was very strong and he had no explanation for it.

Why am I thinking this way? he asked himself, not for the first time. *This isn't like me at all.*

Aloud he said, "My primary reason for coming to see you is to apologize. I should not have talked about my furry pet to you in such detail. I had no intention of causing you emotional distress, and since learning of the long-term effects of your injury, I realize now that I was being thoughtless, insensitive, and stupid. Patient Morredeth, I am very sorry."

For a few seconds there was no response except for the agitated rippling of the other's fur, so marked that the edges of the fabric covering the wound dressings were twitching in sympathy. Then it said, "You had no intention of causing distress, so you were ignorant, not stupid. Sit on the bed. What is your secondary reason for coming?"

When Hewlitt did not reply at once, Morredeth said, "Why do non-Kelgians waste so much time thinking up many words for their answers when a few would do? I asked you a simple question."

And you will get a simple, Kelgian answer, Hewlitt decided. He said, "I was curious about you and your injury. But you have forbidden me to talk about you. Shall I return to my bed?"

"No," said Morredeth.

"Is there anything or anyone else you would like to talk about?"

"You," said the Kelgian.

Hewlitt hesitated and Morredeth went on, "My ears are sensitive and I have heard nearly every word that has passed between the medics and yourself. You are healthy, you receive no medication or treatment, except once when it made you pass out and the resuscitation team arrived, and nobody will say what is wrong with you. I heard you tell the

Earth-human psychologist how you survived poisoning and a fall that should have killed you. But a hospital is for the sick and injured, not for people who have already recovered. So what is wrong with you? Is it a personal or shameful thing that you do not wish to talk about, even to a member of a different species who might not understand your shame?"

"No, nothing like that," Hewlitt replied. "It is just that telling you all about it would take a long time, especially if I had to stop to explain some of the Earth-human social behavior and customs. Besides, talking about my troubles would make me remember how little the Earth medics were able to do because they refused to believe that there was anything at all wrong with me, so I would feel frustrated and angry and probably end up complaining to you all the time."

Morredeth's fur rippled into a new and visually more attractive pattern, making him wonder if it might be feeling amusement. It said, "You, too? That is the reason why I do not want to talk about myself. You would have complained about me complaining."

"You have much more to complain about than I have," said Hewlitt, and stopped because the other's fur was standing out in spikes again, and the bands of muscle encircling its body were tightening as if they were about to go into spasm. He added quickly, "Sorry, Morredeth, I'm talking about you instead of me. What would you like me to talk about first?"

The Kelgian's body relaxed, although the fur was still restive as it said, "Talk to me about incidents from your illness that you have yet to tell or, if they are unusual or shameful or depraved, you did not want to tell Medalont or the trainees. I might find your words entertaining enough to be able to forget my own problems for a while. Are you willing to do that for me?"

"Yes," said Hewlitt. "But don't expect too much entertainment or eroticism. At the time I was on Earth and living with grandparents who didn't have a furry pet that I could play with. Some of the episodes are very embarrassing. Do Kelgians experience puberty?"

"Yes," said Morredeth. "Did you think we were sexually active from birth?"

"Puberty can be an embarrassing time," said Hewlitt, treating the question as rhetorical, "even for normally healthy people."

"Then describe your embarrassment and lack of health in detail," said Morredeth, "if you have nothing more interesting to talk about."

I could have picked a less personal subject, he thought, feeling surprised at his complete lack of hesitation as he began to speak. Maybe the fact that the other belonged to a different species had something to do with it, and talking to a Kelgian patient was no different from telling his symptoms to a Melfan senior physician or a Hudlar nurse, except that Morredeth's curiosity was more intense and less clinical.

As he was describing his transition from solitary studies on his home computer into the higher education system with its increasing emphasis on group studies and team and solo athletic events, at which he did very well, and the opportunities to form friendships with the female students that his growing reputation as an athlete provided, Morredeth interrupted him.

"Are you *complaining* about this situation?" it said. "Or being boastful about your good fortune?"

"I am complaining," Hewlitt replied, his voice raised with remembered anger, "because the opportunities and advantages were lost. Nothing ever happened. Even when I was strongly attracted to a particular young female and, I believed, she to me . . . well, it was very unsatisfactory and frustrating and, and painful."

"Were you more strongly attracted to someone or something else?" asked Morredeth. "To a female who was not attracted to you? Or had you developed even stronger feelings for one of your small furry creatures?"

"No!" said Hewlitt. He looked at the sleepers in the nearby beds and lowered his voice. "What kind of person do you think I am, dammit?"

"A very sick Earth-person," Morredeth replied. "Isn't that the reason you are here?"

"I wasn't *that* sick," said Hewlitt, laughing in spite of himself. "I wasn't sick at all, according to the university medics. They said that I was a perfect physical specimen in every respect. After many embarrassing tests and experiments were carried out, they said that there was no anatomical or hormonal reason why, after I had achieved full mental and physical arousal, my seminal fluid should not have been expelled. They also said that by some involuntary or unconscious method which they did not understand I was checking the mechanism of ejaculation at the penultimate moment, and that the sudden interference with the flow caused immediate pain followed by diminishing discomfort in the genital area until the material was reabsorbed. They suggested that my problem was probably due to a deeply buried, childhood emotional trauma that was showing itself in episodes of shyness so intense that it manifested itself on the physical level."

"What is shyness?" said Morredeth. "My translator assigns no Kelgian meaning to the word."

If a being always said exactly what it thought, it could not be expected to understand shyness. Explaining shyness to such a being might be like trying to describe color to a blind person, but he would try.

"Shyness is a psychological barrier to social interaction," he said. "It is a nonphysical wall that keeps a person from saying or doing what he or she is wanting very badly to say or do; for emotional reasons, usually involving inexperience or oversensitivity or even cowardice, the words or actions are suppressed. Among Earth-humans it is very common during puberty, when the initial social contacts between the sexes are being made."

"That is ridiculous," said Morredeth. "On Kelgia the feeling of a male or female for one of the opposite sex is impossible to hide. If the attraction felt by one for the other is very strong but is not reciprocated, the first has the option of persisting in its attempt to influence the second until the feeling is returned or of transferring the affections elsewhere. The successfully persistent ones usually make the best lifemates. Did the psychological treatment enable you to break through your shyness barrier eventually and allow normal coupling?"

"No," said Hewlitt.

For the first time in his experience the Kelgian's fur almost stopped moving, but only for a moment before it became even more agitated. Morredeth said, "I'm sorry. That situation must be very frustrating for you."

"Yes," he said.

"The senior physician might be able to help you," said Morredeth, trying to mix reassurance with honesty. "If it cannot solve your problem, Medalont will take it as a personal insult. No matter how serious the disease or injury, Sector General has the reputation of curing everything and everybody. Well, nearly everybody."

For a moment Hewlitt stared at the other's fur, which was being stirred into waves and eddies as if it were an agitated pool of mercury; then he said, "The senior physician has my medical history, but as yet it hasn't asked me about my involuntary celibacy. Maybe, like the university's psychologist, it thinks the trouble is all in my mind. But the problem wasn't, isn't, painful so long as I avoid close, one-to-one female contact.

"When it became clear that the psychologist was getting

nowhere," he went on, keeping his eyes on the increasing agitation of Morredeth's fur, "he decided that I was stubbornly refusing to respond to all his attempts at psychotherapy. I was told that living out my life without female companionship, which was probably what I secretly wanted to do, was rare but not in itself unhealthy. Many highly respected people in the past had done so, and made significant contributions to philosophy and the sciences while devoting themselves to the religious celibate life as writers and teachers, or by sublimating their sexual urges in scientific research . . ."

He broke off because Morredeth's body as well as its fur was showing increasing agitation. The underlying bands of muscle were going in and out of spasm, causing it to twist and turn and bounce against the bed.

"Are you all right?" he asked anxiously. "Shall I call the nurse?"

"No," said the Kelgian, the upper part of its body threatening to roll onto the floor. "I don't want any more of your stupid interference."

Hewlitt wondered if he should raise the screens so that the bed would be visible from the nurses' station, then remembered that the other was probably on a monitor. He looked at the writhing body again and said, "I was only trying to help you."

"Why are you doing this cruel thing?" said Morredeth. "Who told you to do this to me?"

"I, I don't understand you," he said, feeling baffled. "What did I say?"

"You are not a Kelgian," said Morredeth, "so you do not fully understand the mental hurt I feel. First you talked about stroking your furry pet, and then apologized for your insensitivity. Now you are talking about yourself and the impossibility of you ever finding a mate, but it is plain that you are really talking about me and my problems. You must have been told to do this. When Lioren tried to do these things to me earlier, I closed my ears. Who told you to talk to me like this? Lioren? Braithwaite? The senior physician? And why?"

His first impulse was to deny everything, but that would have been unfair because Kelgians did not know how to tell, nor would they expect to be told, a lie. Either he should say nothing or tell the truth.

"It was the Hudlar nurse," he said, "who asked me to talk to you."

"But the Hudlar isn't a psychologist," Morredeth broke in. "Why did it do such a cruel thing? It is unqualified and it was tinkering with my feelings. I shall report its behavior to the senior physician."

Hewlitt tried to reduce the other's growing anger by saying, "Every person I ever met thought they were good, if untrained, psychologists . . ." *Including me,* he added silently. ". . . just as they believed themselves to be expert ground-car drivers and in possession of a brilliant sense of humor. The trouble is, psychologists rarely agree on their methods of treatment. Are you feeling pain?"

"No," said Morredeth, "anger."

Considering the species of the patient, he thought, the words had to be accepted as the literal truth. As he watched the increasing agitation and violence of the fur and body movements, he wondered if he was seeing the Kelgian equivalent of bad language that the other had no need to vocalize.

"Don't be angry with the Hudlar nurse," he said. "It told me that Lioren had asked and received permission from Senior Physician Medalont to reduce your night sedation so that you would have more time alone to consider your position and, they hoped, come to terms with it. To assist the process, the medical staff on night duty was forbidden to speak to you apart from the few words required while checking your life signs. The Hudlar did not agree with this form of treatment but was unable to disobey its medical superiors. Out of concern for your expected mental distress, and learning that I wanted to apologize for the furry-pet business, it asked me to talk to you.

"It did not tell me what to say," Hewlitt went on, "only that I should try to take your mind off your troubles. Unfortunately I was not able to do that, but the fault is mine and the Hudlar is not responsible for my insensitivity and your anger."

"Then I shall not report its misconduct," said Morredeth. "But I am still angry."

"I understand," said Hewlitt, "because in the beginning I felt the same anger, frustration, and bitter disappointment. The embarrassment of knowing that my friends were laughing and whispering behind my back and thinking of me as some kind of sexual cripple was . . ."

"Your crippling was not plain for all to see," Morredeth broke in, a sudden, muscular spasm bringing its body close to the edge of the bed. "My friends will not whisper or laugh, they will be kind and avoid me so that I will not be able to see their feelings of revulsion. You do *not* understand."

"Try to lie still, dammit!" said Hewlitt. "You could fall out of bed and hurt yourself. Stop rolling about like that."

"If the sight displeases you, leave me," said Morredeth. "A Kelgian can sometimes control but never conceal feelings. Strong emotion is associated with involuntary fur and body movement. Didn't you know that?"

No, but I know now, said Hewlitt under his breath. Aloud, he went on, "Even the Earth psychologists say that relieving one's feelings is often better than keeping them bottled up. But I don't want to leave, I'm supposed to be talking and helping to take your mind off your troubles. I'm not doing a very good job so far, am I?"

"You are doing a terrible job," said Morredeth, "but stay if you want to."

The violence of its body movements seemed to be diminishing, and Hewlitt decided to take a risk by not changing the subject.

"Thank you," he said. "And of course you are right. Your situation is much worse than mine because it is permanent and visible to everyone. But that doesn't mean that I cannot understand your feelings, because for many years I have shared the same kind of problem in reduced intensity. I don't think that the emotional scars, and my need to live and work alone and avoid personal social contact with females, will ever heal completely. I do know how you must feel, but I also know that you will not always feel so badly.

"Have you ever thought that Lioren may be right and the Hudlar nurse wrong?" he went on. "Or that it is better to face up to your problem here and now, in hospital where help is available, instead of at home where you say you will be all alone? Or that you will not always feel so badly as you do now? People, Kelgians as well as Earth-humans, can adapt to almost anything. . . ."

"You even talk like Lioren . . ." began Morredeth, when it happened.

The other's fur looked no more agitated than it had been a few minutes earlier and the uncontrolled body movements had begun to subside, so that the spasm which straightened Morredeth into a long, furry cylinder and rolled it over the edge of the bed farthest from him was completely unexpected. Without taking time to think, he grabbed its body with both hands to pull it back onto the bed. His fingers tightened over the cover for the wound dressings and he checked the other's fall just as the retaining tapes snapped and the fabric came away in his hands.

The Kelgian gave a long, high-pitched moan like the sound of a falsetto foghorn; then its body spasmed again and rolled back to the opposite side of the bed on top of him.

Hewlitt half fell, half slid onto the floor with Morredeth on top of him.

"Nurse!" he yelled.

"I'm here," said the Hudlar, who was already inside the screens and looming over them. "Are you injured, Patient Hewlitt?"

"N-no," he stammered. "At least, not so far."

"Good," said the nurse. "The DBLF classification have never used their feet as natural weapons so you will probably remain in an undamaged condition. I require assistance for a few moments but I am unwilling to waste time, or appear incapable of dealing with a simple emergency, by calling for a nurse from another ward. Are you willing to assist me?"

Me assist you? Hewlitt thought. The sound he made did not translate even to himself, but the Hudlar took it as an affirmative.

"Your present position on the floor is ideal for our purpose," it went on, "which is to help me hold Patient Morredeth still. Please put your arms around it and grip its back fur in both hands. Tighter than that, please, you will not cause pain. Regrettably, four of my limbs are needed to support my body mass, which leaves one to help you immobilize the patient and one to administer the sedative. Good, that's it exactly."

With both hands trying to grip the fur and the inside of his forearms pressing against its back, and helped by the one Hudlar tentacle gently but firmly encircling its neck, he strove to keep Morredeth still while the nurse located the correct injection site. The Kelgian was still making its high-pitched, moaning sound while trying its hardest to escape from between his arms by walking up his stomach, chest, and face with its twenty-odd feet. Fortunately the legs were short, thin, and not heavily muscled and the feet, which had no toenails or other bony terminations, were like small, hard sponges, so he felt as if he were being continually prodded with padded drumsticks. The experience was disconcerting rather than painful. Morredeth's exertions must have been making it perspire, because he was aware of an increasing body odor that smelled faintly of peppermint.

He was aware of a sudden feeling of weakness in every muscle of his body, as if his strength had been drained away from him, and there was a hot, tingling sensation in his hands and bare arms where the skin was in contact with fur that was curling and twisting against his palms and between his fingers. The experience was so alien, and ticklish, that he had to make an effort not to laugh. Suddenly Morredeth arched its back and tried to twist free and he almost lost his grip.

"Sorry, my hands are sweating," he said. "It nearly got away just then."

"You are doing well, Patient Hewlitt," said the nurse, replacing the hypodermic sprayer in its satchel. "In a few seconds more I will be finished. Your temporary loss of grip may have been due to your digits encountering fur that is covered by the oily medication used on the dressings in addition to the patient's perspiration. Also, I have learned that Earth-human DBDGs sweat from the palms of the hands even when the process is not accompanied by a marked rise in body activity and temperature. It can be an indication of a severe emotional reaction to a situation that is or is likely to become stressful. . . ."

"But my palms are sweating," Hewlitt broke in, in an attempt to head off another of the nurse's medical lectures, "all the way up to the elbows."

"Either way," the Hudlar went on, "you are at no risk. Kelgian pathogens cannot cross the planetary species' barrier and . . . ah, I believe Patient Morredeth is beginning to relax."

The Kelgian's leg movements had ceased and its body

was becoming a dead weight across Hewlitt's stomach and chest. With two tentacles free now, the nurse inserted them on each side of the body's center of gravity and lifted Morredeth onto the bed. By the time Hewlitt had scrambled to his feet, it had arranged the other's limp body in the flattened S shape that resting Kelgians seemed to find comfortable and was replacing the loosened dressings, but not before he caught a glimpse of the large area of uncovered skin and lank, discolored fur.

"Patient Hewlitt," the Hudlar went on, "please wash the Kelgian medication from your hands. It will not harm you but you may find the smell unpleasant. Then return to your bed and try to sleep. I will check later to see if you have sustained any minor abrasions that the excitement of the moment may have driven from your mind.

"Before you go," it went on, "I must apologize for my late arrival. Your medical monitor includes an audio pickup and recording device so that the data is available for later study. It was obvious from the way the conversation was going that something like this might happen and that a fast-acting sedative shot would be needed. The medication is new and I am required to double-check with Pathology, if a senior ward medic is not present, before administering it. That was why I did not arrive until you were calling for help."

Hewlitt laughed. "And all the time I was thinking that your response time was impressively fast. But if the conversation with Morredeth was being recorded, does this mean you will be in trouble over what you said, or rather what I said you said, about your disagreement over your instructions for withdrawing Morredeth's sedation and forbidding you to speak to it at night?

"How is it now?" he added. "Are you sure it will be all right?"

There was no way of telling what the other was thinking, but Hewlitt had the feeling that it was worried as it said,

"Several people, including Medalont, Leethveeschi, and Lioren will study your monitor's voice recording, and many words of criticism will be spoken to me. But you must have noticed that Hudlars have thicker skins than most other life-forms. Thank you for your concern, Patient Hewlitt, and now will you please return to your bed. Morredeth is well and sleeping peacefully—"

It broke off then, because the involuntary ripplings of the Kelgian's fur had slowed almost to a stop. The tip of one of the nurse's free tentacles moved quickly to a point close to the base of Morredeth's skull, the digits apparently feeling for a pulse; then it reached into the equipment pouch and came out grasping a scanner, which it moved to two separate positions on the patient's chest. The other tentacle tip stabbed at a key on the communicator, and on the ceiling above the bed a red light began a steady, urgent blinking.

"Resuscitation team," it said. "Ward Seven, bed twelve, classification Kelgian DBLF. Estimated five seconds into cardiac arrest, both hearts. . . . Patient Hewlitt, go back to bed. Now."

Hewlitt backed away from the bedside, unable to take his eyes off the still body and fur until he was outside the screens, but he did not go to bed. Instead he waited close by until the resuscitation team with its equipment float arrived, less than a minute later. The red light in the ceiling ceased its flashing and there was a sudden absence of sound as a hush field went up around Morredeth's position.

That must have been done to avoid disturbing the sleeping patients, he thought, and not just to stop him from listening to what was going on. He was not sure how long he waited in the darkness, watching the moving shadows that were being projected onto the bed screens, and straining to hear what they were saying, until the team members emerged. But his curiosity went unsatisfied and his concern unrelieved, because they left the ward without speaking to each other. The Hudlar nurse, its large shadow unmoving, remained inside the screens.

He waited for what seemed a very long time, but the Hudlar did not leave Morredeth's bedside. Feeling sad and guilty and disappointed, he turned away and walked to the bathroom to wash the traces of Kelgian medication from his hands and arms; then he went back to his bed to lie with his eyes closed.

Twice during the rest of the night he heard the Hudlar moving quietly along the ward as it checked on the sleeping patients and the one who was only pretending to sleep, but it did not have to speak to him, because his monitor was giving it all the clinical information it required. Probably the nurse was feeling responsible for what had happened, because it had been its suggestion that Hewlitt talk to Morredeth. But he felt responsible as well, and he was almost afraid to speak to it. Instead he lay still and quiet, wondering how it was possible for him to cause a person's death simply by talking to it, and feeling worse both physically and mentally than he had ever felt in his entire life.

He was still awake and wondering when the ward lights were switched on and the day staff came on duty.

CHAPTER 14

The morning medical round was both abbreviated and incomplete. Senior Physician Medalont was accompanied by Charge Nurse Leethveeschi rather than the usual group of trainees; they visited only the most seriously ill patients, and spent most of their time at Morredeth's bed, which was still surrounded by screens and a hush field.

They were still there when Horrantor and Bowab stopped by his bed on their way from the bathroom. It was the Duthan who spoke first.

"We don't feel like playing scremman today," Bowab said. "Nobody seems to know what happened to Morredeth. I tried to ask a Kelgian nurse, but you know Kelgians, they either tell you the truth about everything or say nothing at all. Do you know anything?"

Hewlitt was still feeling guilty over his part in the incident, and he would have preferred not to talk about it. But these two had been Morredeth's friends, or a least short-term, hospital acquaintances, and they had a right to know. He did not want to lie to them, but not being a Kelgian, he could edit the truth.

"There was an emergency," he said. "The nurse called the resuscitation team and said that Morredeth's hearts had stopped. When they arrived they put up a hush field around the bed. I don't know what happened after that."

"We must have slept through it," said Horrantor. "But the Hudlar is nice and likes talking. Maybe it will tell us everything when it comes on duty tonight—" It broke off to point toward the nurses' station. "Look who's coming down the ward with Padre Lioren. Thornnastor! What is it doing here?"

The creature belonged to the same species as Horrantor, but its body was larger, its hide had a great many more wrinkles, and it was, of course, walking on six rather than five feet. The question answered itself when they stopped at Morredeth's position and it disappeared with Lioren behind the screens. A Kelgian nurse guiding an antigravity stretcher with its canopy opened arrived a few minutes later and followed them inside.

"It must be pretty crowded in there by now," said Horrantor.

There was no reply and the silence lengthened. In an attempt to erase the mind-picture of Morredeth lying on the bed with its fur completely motionless, he said, "Who is Thornnastor?"

"We've never met, you understand," said Horrantor, "but it must be Thornnastor because it is the only Tralthan in Sector General who is qualified to wear diagnostician's insignia. It is the diagnostician-in-charge of Pathology. They say it rarely leaves its lab, and usually it sees people only when they are dead or in small bits."

"Horrantor!" said Bowab. "You have about as much tact as a drunken Kelgian."

"Sorry," said the Tralthan, "it was an insensitive choice of words. . . . Look, they're coming out."

The Kelgian nurse emerged first and undulated toward the ward entrance, guiding the litter, which now had its canopy closed, followed by Thornnastor, Medalont, and Leethveeschi. The screens rose into their ceiling slots to show Lioren looking at the empty bed with all four of its eyes. When the Tarlan moved a few seconds later it did not follow the others.

"It's heading this way," said Bowab, in the growling, overloud equivalent of a Duthan whisper. "Hewlitt, I think it is looking at you."

Lioren continued looking at him with two of its eyes while it approached and stopped at his bed. The other two it directed at Bowab and Horrantor as it said, "My apologies for the interruption, friends, but would this be a convenient time for me to have a private conversation with Patient Hewlitt?"

"Of course, Padre," said Horrantor. Bowab added, "We were just leaving."

It waited until the others had moved away; then it said, "I trust this is a convenient time for you. Are you willing to talk to me now?"

Hewlitt did not reply at first. This was the first time that he had seen the Padre at close range, and the information given in the library tape he had studied had not prepared him for the actuality. The Tarlan physiological classification was BRLH, an erect quadrupedal life-form with its four short legs supporting a tapering, cone-shaped body. Four long, multi-jointed, medial arms for heavy lifting and handling sprouted from waist level, and another four that were suited to more delicate work encircled the base of the neck. Spaced equally around the head were four eyes whose stalks were capable of independent motion. An adult Tarlan was supposed to stand eight feet tall, but Lioren was above average in height and body mass. Close up it was an intimidating sight and, after the events of the previous night, he was not sure that it would have kind words to say to him. Instead of answering he asked another question, the one that had been troubling his mind for the past six hours.

"What happened to Morredeth?"

The Tarlan's strange, convoluted countenance was no easier to read than a Hudlar's as it said. "We don't know what happened to Morredeth, but it is well now, and has no problems."

Considering Lioren's profession and remembering Morredeth's newly vacant bed, those were the words of consolation that a padre would be expected to use to a bereaved relative or friend. They were the words that he had been hoping not to hear.

The busy sounds of the ward faded as Lioren reached forward with a medial hand to turn on the hush-field projector. He had no idea which facial orifice it was using to speak, but the voice was quiet and gentle as it said, "There appears to be three people who carry varying degrees of responsibility for what happened to Patient Morredeth. The Hudlar nurse, myself, and you. I would like to begin by talking about your contribution."

Before Hewlitt could reply, it went on, "The Hudlar has already told you that all of your conversations since your monitor was fitted have been recorded and added to your case history for later study. This was done without your knowledge or consent because of the unusual nature of the case. Medalont felt that your words would be less inhibited and clinically more valuable, even though most of the recorded material would be extraneous and useless, if you were kept in ignorance of what was being done. Now you know that everything you say is being recorded, but I am less interested in words about yourself than in your emotional reaction to Patient Morredeth's injury. Did you have strong feelings about its disfigurement, and are you willing to talk about them?"

Hewlitt began to relax. He had been expecting criticism from Lioren and had only now realized that a hospital padre would not use harsh or critical words.

"Yes," he said. "But don't expect too much, Padre. I didn't have any strong feelings about Morredeth other than the sympathy one feels for the misfortune of someone who is not a close friend. When I discovered how badly the damaged fur was affecting it, I tried to help by talking about the problem I'd had during my teens and early twenties. I must have said the wrong things."

"In a very difficult emotional situation," said Lioren, "you tried to say the right things. Some of the things you did say were . . . Is the problem you discussed with Morredeth solved, or not? Your case history says that you have not taken a life-mate or formed any short-term partnerships."

Wondering why the conversation had veered from Morredeth's troubles to his own, he said, "The problem isn't solved. I am not comfortable in female company even though my attraction and initial physical response to them was and is normal. I am afraid of a recurrence of the embarrassment, the embarrassment of both partners, and the pain that comes instead of the intense pleasure that should follow consummation. It is a situation which I have no wish to repeat. . . . Why are you asking me about this? Are you criticizing my behavior in some fashion? Do you think it is a moral rather than a medical question?"

"It is a medical question," Lioren replied without hesitation. "But if the matter troubles you to the extent that you might be helped by spiritual guidance or reassurance, please tell me. I have a wide knowledge of the tenets and beliefs of the principal religions practiced throughout the Federation and may be able to help you. I am very interested in your own religious beliefs if you hold any. If you do not, then please rest your mind. I am not going to preach or proselytize.

"One of the reasons for asking the question," it went on, "is that I no longer practice medicine, but I have some experience in the field and sometimes enjoy trying to second-guess my former colleagues. At worst it is a venial offense, a small sin of pride. And who am I to criticize another being who prefers the celibate life?"

"Sorry, Padre," said Hewlitt, "I'm feeling antisocial this morning. What did you want to know?"

Lioren made a low, gurgling sound that did not translate and said, "Everything you are willing to tell me. But first, you still appear to be sensitive about your, ah, extended puberty, but this matter was fully covered during your conversation with Morredeth so we will ignore it for now. Instead I would like to know if there were any other episodes, physical, psychological, or religious, which also troubled you even though they were considered unimportant or of too minor a nature for your medics to record them in your case notes. Do you remember any past incidents of that nature?"

"If they didn't go into my case notes," said Hewlitt, "I may have forgotten them. Whenever I thought there was anything seriously wrong with me I had the bad habit of complaining about it, loudly and often."

Lioren was silent for a moment. When it spoke again it seemed to be uncomfortable and it was regarding him with all four of its eyes.

"You are a very strange case, Patient Hewlitt," it said. "From our study of your recorded conversations with Medalont, Braithwaite, the Hudlar nurse, and your three cardplaying friends, and especially from the sensitivity displayed during last night's dialogue with Morredeth, we have decided that there is little wrong with your mind. Making due allowance for mental effects left by your lifelong war with the medical profession, you have displayed a personality that is stable and well integrated. If there is a psychological component to your problem, which we are beginning to doubt, it is so deeply buried that we can find no trace of it."

"I kept telling everybody that it wasn't my imagination . . ." began Hewlitt.

Lioren continued as if he hadn't spoken. "As well, you are a remarkably healthy specimen of an Earth-human DBDG. Apart from the inexplicable cardiac arrest on the evening of your arrival, your monitor has shown optimum clinical readings since you were admitted. The present slight lowering of life-sign indications we attribute to your night spent without sleep while, I have no doubt, you were thinking about Morredeth."

"So I have a healthy mind in a superman's body," he said, making no attempt to hide his anger. He was about to be discharged from the hospital, as had happened so often in the past, as some nonspecific type of malingerer. "Thank you for yet another confirmation of that fact, Padre. What do you want me to tell you?"

The Tarlan leaned over his bed and opened its mouth. For the first time he saw its very large teeth and felt its breath on his face as it spoke. He felt pleased with himself that he was able to stay in bed and not run terror-stricken up the ward. One could become used to anything in this place.

"I don't know," the Padre said. "Anything. Everything. Something that will enable me, as you Earth-humans say, to get my teeth into this problem."

"Teeth?" said Hewlitt, his eyes still on the other's open mouth. He forced a laugh and went on, "As a matter of fact I did have some trouble with my teeth. It was when I was a child, on Etla, but it was a minor problem. I was seven years old and the first two of my second set of teeth were beginning to grow and the old ones were refusing to come out. My mouth was painful, but I was more worried about not getting money from the tooth fairy in exchange for the loosened teeth when I left them on my pillow during the night. Do you know about the Earth tooth fairy? I'll tell you about it later. When the third new tooth pushed up and the old one stayed in place, our dentist lost patience and pulled out all three of the old ones. After that my teeth behaved normally and the money was waiting on the pillow as expected. But I don't think the tooth business is important."

"Who knows what is important in your case," said the Padre, "but in this instance I agree with you. Are there any other unrecorded and possibly unimportant incidents you can remember?"

The longer Hewlitt talked the more he remembered. A few of the minor incidents, he was surprised to discover, had been included in his case history. The rest was a boring catalogue of the usual childhood and teenage skin eruptions and rashes, none of them serious or long-lasting, and the accidentally cut fingers, bumps on the head, and skinned knees sustained at home or in school. His cuts and abrasions had always healed quickly, even when they had looked at first to be serious enough to require sutures.

"I didn't like doctors when I was young," he went on, "because they insisted on prescribing medication that made me feel worse instead of better. At first I thought Medalont was going to do the same, but instead it took me off all medication and, apart from the arrest on the first night, there has been no trouble. Shall I go on, Padre? Is this the kind of information you're looking for?"

"I don't know what I'm looking for, Patient Hewlitt," said the Tarlan, "or if I'd recognize it if I found it. But if all you and your many doctors say is true, and taking into account the two inexplicable clinical episodes that have involved you since you came here, there is only one obvious explanation that remains. Naturally it is more obvious to me than to you even though I myself am most reluctant to accept it."

The Tarlan was leaning so far over the bed that Hewlitt wondered if its bottom-heavy, inherently stable body would overbalance and fall on him. The features were unreadable but its tension could almost be felt.

"Patient Hewlitt," it said, "are you a member of a religious sect?"

"No," he said.

"Before they died in the flyer accident," it went on, leaning even closer, "were your parents or subsequently your grandparents members of such a sect? It may have been very small, probably restricted in numbers because of its inability to proselytize among a largely materialistic population, but it would have been highly moral, intensely devout, and utterly certain in its beliefs. Even though you were very young at the time, did your parents or grandparents, or perhaps a teacher at school, instruct you in the beliefs and disciplines of such a faith?"

"No," he said again.

"You have not taken enough time to search your memory," said Lioren. "Please do so now."

Its body swayed backward until it was upright again, and Hewlitt was not sure whether the movement signified a relaxation of tension or disappointment.

"I'm sorry, Padre," he said. "When you mentioned religion to me earlier, and I refused your offer of spiritual consolation, I assumed that you would know that I was not a religious person. Why are you asking so many religious questions? I have never been a believer."

When it replied, Hewlitt was glad that a hush field was around his bed, because the Padre's voice would have carried to the other end of the ward. It said, "I am asking them because they must be asked, and because religious beliefs can often have a strong effect on a psychological or medical condition. Mostly I am asking them because of what you did last night.

"As a result of you speaking to Patient Morredeth," it continued without lowering its voice, "and even though its clinical condition was giving no cause for concern at the time, the patient became emotionally distressed, culminating in severe convulsions. You assisted the duty nurse by restraining the patient while a sedative shot was administered, but by then both of its hearts had arrested. While the activity could never be described as dignified, much less solemn, the process that is called 'the laying on of hands' took place.

"When the resuscitation team arrived they were very irritated," it went on, its voice quieter but not quiet, "because they had been called to the same ward twice in two days on emergencies that had turned out to be false alarms. Thornnastor is completely baffled, a condition rare indeed in the diagnostician-in-charge of Pathology, and has transferred Morredeth to its lab for closer investigation into an incident that is completely without precedent. And Patient Morredeth is happy because its missing and damaged areas of fur have regrown good as new."

Lioren paused, and an almost plaintive note entered its voice as it said, "To a hospital with the reputation of performing medical miracles routinely, a real one is a major embarrassment. A miraculous cure is, well, disquieting even to me.

"Do you have any other explanation, Patient Hewlitt?"

CHAPTER 15

During the week following Morredeth's transfer to Pathology, Hewlitt noticed a change in everyone's behavior toward him, but there was nothing so definite or unpleasant that it warranted a complaint. Senior Physician Medalont's words to him were few and had nothing to do with his case, Charge Nurse Leethveeschi was almost polite, his Hudlar nurse was friendly but less talkative, and, when he tried to play three-handed scremman with Patients Horrantor and Bowab, it seemed that they had both developed a speech impediment. Everyone around him, to use a phrase much favored by his grandmother, was walking on eggs.

The only being who was willing to talk to him at length was Lioren, whose visits seemed always to end in long, unresolved, and often heated religious arguments that the other, because of his often stated lack of beliefs, preferred to call philosophical debates. Whatever they were, they shortened his days and kept his mind busy far into the intervening nights, and for that he was grateful. Even so, the Padre would not have been his first choice as the most amusing of companions, especially, as now, when it was trying to steer the conversation once again onto the increasingly tiresome subject of what could have happened to Morredeth's fur.

"When I spoke to Morredeth earlier today," said the Tarlan, "it told me that Pathology could find nothing wrong with it. There were no signs of a deterioration in its newly regenerated fur and, in its opinion, Thornnastor is running out of reasons for keeping it under observation and must soon allow it to go home. In case it doesn't see you again, it sends good wishes and thanks for whatever it was you did to cure it. . . ."

"But I didn't do anything," Hewlitt broke in, "except wrestle with it. I told you to tell it that."

"I did," said the Padre, "but it said that, just in case you did do something, it is grateful. It has trouble believing in miracles, too."

"There are no miracles," said Hewlitt, not for the first time. "There are just natural laws that we don't understand or haven't discovered yet. Because we understand how this one works, it is one miracle we perform several times a day without even thinking about it. Right?"

As he spoke, Hewlitt switched on the bedside communicator and keyed in the library menu, wondering if Lioren might take the hint and go away. It had not done so on previous occasions and the Padre was nothing if not consistent.

"A few centuries ago, vision transmission would have been a miracle," Lioren agreed, and went on, "Morredeth is very pleased and proud about the overall condition of its fur. It insisted on me placing my hands along its flanks and feeling the thickness and mobility which, it claimed, has never before felt so good. On Tarla such an activity is conducted only in circumstances of intimacy and deep emotional involvement, but Morredeth wanted me to feel its fur and at such times I can be a complete moral coward. The sensation was peculiar, unexpected, and very difficult to describe. I felt . . ."

"Utterly ridiculous?" asked Hewlitt. "That was how I felt when the same thing happened with Horrantor. Medalont asked me, as a clinical experiment, to lay my hands on the Tralthan's damaged limb. According to the senior physician, Horrantor's leg injury has complications that are slow to respond to treatment. Medalont, Leethveeschi, two Orligian nurses, and the resuscitation team were standing by in case something dramatic happened. I think they were all relieved, even Horrantor, when nothing did.

"There was no second miracle. Sorry."

"No need to apologize," said Lioren. "I feel like they did. Miracles make me very uncomfortable and insecure in my beliefs and disbeliefs, and I would as soon have proof that they did not happen."

"They don't, Padre," said Hewlitt. "Can we talk about something else?"

"It must be nice to feel such certainty," said Lioren, flexing its medial arms in a gesture that would probably have meant something to another Tarlan. "But I wonder if, in all the vastness of space and time and the immutable laws of cause and effect and perfect balance of forces that is Creation, there isn't room for the occasional miracle. But why did it happen here?"

Hewlitt shook his head, seeing no chance of getting away from the interminable subject of Morredeth's fur and the inevitable religious argument, and said, "It didn't happen here. Miracles are impossible, Padre. If they were to exist in your big, complicated, well-ordered universe, or Creation as you call it, they would be out of place, a defect in the perfect Scheme of Things. There is simply no room for miracles in your universe."

"An interesting philosophical idea," said Lioren. "It suggests that our Creation is flawed because an apparently supernatural event or events took place within it. Bearing in mind the hypothetical attributes of the Supreme Being, why should He, She, or It create an imperfection of any kind?"

"I don't know," he replied. "This isn't my area of expertise. But can we suppose that this universe was created as a prototype, an early model that requires modification and a little fine-tuning from time to time. The intrusion of random supernatural events into a universe supposedly based on natural laws might be evidence of this tinkering. Thank God . . . Oops, just a figure of speech, Padre . . . it doesn't happen very often."

"If you believe that . . ." the other began.

"I am not believing anything, Padre, just talking."

The Tarlan was silent for a moment, then it said, "If this universe is imperfect, that presupposes, eternity being what it is, without beginning or end, that there was, is, will be one that is perfect. Would you like to, ah, just talk about that for a while?"

"I haven't had a chance to think it out properly," he replied, smiling, "so I am making it up as I go along. Unlike this universe, everything would be perfect. There would be no natural laws, because if they were present it would mean that it, too, had faults and was in need of tinkering. There would be no time, no space, no physical or mental restrictions so that every event that took place would be miraculous. I expect you, and the other believers living in this imperfect creation, would call it Heaven."

"Go on," said Lioren.

Hewlitt said, "The difficulty I and an awful lot of other people have with religions is that they do not adequately explain why there is so much evil, or more accurately, tragic accidents, natural disasters, and illness, gross misbehavior in individuals and groups toward each other and, in short, so much suffering in this universe. Living in an imperfect Creation would go a long way to explaining why these things happen, especially when there is the expectation of moving to the perfected universe after death.

"This is a pretty heretical theory," Hewlitt ended. "I hope my irreverence hasn't offended you, Padre?"

"I agree," said Lioren. "Heretical and irreverent, but not entirely new to me. To do my work here I need a wide knowledge of the religious beliefs and practices of many worlds, and often the many religions practiced on a single world. I am reminded of the writings of an Earth-human theologian called Augustine who was in the habit of wondering aloud, but in reality asking polite but awkward questions of its God. One of the questions was 'What were You doing before You made the universe?' There is no record of this Augustine person ever receiving an answer, at least not during its lifetime on Earth, but you have taken the idea a stage further by suggesting that the Creator of All Things has produced a prototype which we are still inhabiting.

"I am not offended or even surprised, Patient Hewlitt," it went on. "Where other-species' religious beliefs are concerned, nothing surprises me. But the VTXM Telfi single entity I have been visiting these past few days came very close to doing so. It, they, share the belief that they were created in God's image, but that their omniscient and all-powerful Creator is composed of an infinite number of small, weak, and individually stupid entities like themselves who together make up a Supreme Being which one day they hope to join.

"For a species who evolved intelligence and a civilization," the Padre went on, "by linking together into a gestalt of individually specialized beings, it is understandable why they would believe such a thing. But I found it very difficult at first to understand or talk to it about the infinite number of persons that will make up its one God, or to give the spiritual consolation it needs. Of course, there are many religions which believe that there is a small part of God in every thinking creature. . . . Do you know anything about the Telfi?"

"A little," said Hewlitt, still trying to steer the other away from the subject of theology and, by association, miracles. "There was a brief entry in the nonmedical library's listing of Federation citizens. They operate in groups as contact telepaths to pool their mental and physical abilities. They live by absorbing the combination and varying intensities of hard radiation that bathes their home world, which circles very close to the parent sun. For travel off-planet their ship life-support radiation has to be reproduced artificially. Sometimes the environmental systems malfunction and, if they are lucky, they are rescued and end up here. But they are radiation-eaters, and no ordinary person could get close enough to them to talk and hope to go on living. Did you use a communicator or wear protective armor?"

"Thank you for the implication that I might be an extraordinary person," said the Padre. It made an untranslatable, Tarlan sound and went on, "But the answer to both questions is no. There is a fallacy among nonmedics that the Telfi cannot be closely approached or touched without the use of remotely controlled manipulators. To live they must absorb the radiation normally provided by their natural environment but when, for clinical reasons, the radiation is withdrawn for several days and they are weak from their equivalent of hunger, their radioactive emissions drop to a harmless level. When one of them was withdrawn from its treatment chamber during my visit, I was close enough to be able to touch it, which I did.

"That is one patient," Lioren ended, "who really needs a miracle."

It was obvious that the Padre felt sorry for the Telfi, and Hewlitt sympathized with its feelings, but the subject had returned to miracles. He decided to go on the offensive, as inoffensively as possible, and said, "If you are suggesting that I lay my hands on a Telfi, forget it. Surely the proper method of achieving a miracle is for you or the patient to pray for one. A miracle is supposed to be a supernatural occurrence, not something that is dependent on the cooperation of an unbelieving middleman. If you don't believe that, Padre, what do you believe?"

"I cannot tell you what I believe," said Lioren. "In the interests of the patients who might be unfairly influenced if I was to speak of my own beliefs, I am obliged not to divulge that information."

"But why?" said Hewlitt. "What possible difference could your personal beliefs make to an unbeliever?"

"I don't know," Lioren replied, "that's the problem. I have detailed knowledge of more than two hundred religions that are practiced, or more often not practiced, throughout the Federation. My function here is to listen sympathetically, to give reassurance, encouragement, or consolation to the terminally ill or seriously troubled patients in whatever way seems appropriate. Because of my background, which you must be aware of by now but are too polite to mention, there are always a few patients who want more than reassurance. In their distress they come to respect and trust me and, erroneously, to think that I know best. They want religious certainties which they think that I, with my wide knowledge and experience in dealing with their kind of problems, can provide. This I cannot do, because I must not take advantage of their confused and frightened state to compare one religion with another, or to suggest one which I think is the true one. No matter how wild and incredible some of their beliefs are, influencing an entity to change or even doubt its own religion, however small or temporary that change or doubt might be, is a responsibility I will not accept. I played God only once and I shall not do so ever again."

The Padre made another untranslatable sound and said, "I

am particularly careful with unbelievers. It would be a terrible thing if some time in the future my words were to turn you toward religion."

"Now that," said Hewlitt, laughing, "would take a real miracle."

Lioren's reply was silenced by the sudden arrival of Leethveeschi, who gestured toward the ward entrance and said, "Patient Hewlitt, prepare yourself for visitors. Diagnosticians Thornnastor and Conway, Senior Physicians Medalont and Prilicla, and Pathologist Murchison are here to see you. With that collection of high-powered medical talent interesting themselves in your case, I do not foresee you remaining here as a patient for long. Padre Lioren, Prilicla apologizes for interrupting your conversation and asks if you would please distance yourself from the patient and wait with the others so that your presence will not interfere with its investigation."

"Of course," said Lioren.

He watched it move up the ward to join the group that was standing and, in one case, hovering about thirty meters away. He barely noticed Medalont and the Tralthan and Earth-human diagnosticians, Thornnastor and Conway, or even the mature but strikingly beautiful female Earth-human who had to be Pathologist Murchison, because all of his attention was focused on the enormous but incredibly fragile insect that was flying on three sets of slowly beating, iridescent wings toward him.

As it drifted to a halt above his bed and he felt the faint downdraft from its wings, Hewlitt remembered that he had always disliked insects, and the larger they were the more he wanted to swat them. But this one was the most delicate and beautiful creature he had ever seen. Even his tongue was paralyzed with wonder.

"Thank you, friend Hewlitt," it said, the quiet trilling and clicking sound of its speech forming an almost musical background to the translated words. "Your emotional radiation is pleasant and most complimentary. I am Prilicla."

"What," he said, finding both his voice and his anxiety again, "what exactly are you going to do to me?"

"I have already done all that is necessary, friend Hewlitt," it replied, "so there is no reason for your anxiety."

The others who had been waiting must have overheard it, because they were moving closer. When they had gathered around his bed, Prilicla raised its voice and went on, "At the present time there are no detectable abnormalities present in Patient Hewlitt's mind, nor were there during my earlier examination of Patient Morredeth, who should now be discharged and sent home without further delay. I feel the disappointment in all of you, naturally, and I am sorry. So far as I am concerned I can feel absolutely nothing wrong with the patient.

"Friend Hewlitt," it went on as it made a feather-light landing on the bottom of his bed, "how would you like a ride in an ambulance?"

He saw Prilicla's body begin to tremble and realized that the empath must be sharing his own feelings of anger and bitter disappointment, feelings that he had suffered so often in the past. He said, "Don't try to humor me, dammit! You think there's nothing wrong with me and you're going to send me home."

"Well, not exactly," said Prilicla. "This time the ambulance will be taking the patient from hospital to the scene of the original accident."

CHAPTER 16

Even though his stay in Ward Seven had just about oblit-
erated all traces of his xenophobia, Hewlitt was relieved
to discover that on this particular ambulance the Earth-
human DBDGs were in a majority of five to three.

During nonmedical operations, he learned, the special
ambulance ship *Rhabwar* was commanded by a very serious
young officer called Major Fletcher, while three other Monitor Corps lieutenants, Haslam, Chen, and Dodds, were
responsible for communications, engineering, and astrogation, respectively. Since Hewlitt was not allowed to leave the
casualty deck, he would have little contact with any of them
or they with the medical team unless the ship was called to
a medical emergency requiring their presence on the casulty
deck. If that happened, command transferred to the team's
senior medical officer, who turned out to be the empathic
Cinrusskin GLNO Prilicla, until the emergency was
resolved.

He had been surprised, and later, when he came to know her better, very pleased, to find that the empath's principal assistant was Pathologist Murchison. The remaining two medics were a Kelgian DBLF specialist in heavy rescue operations, Charge Nurse Naydrad, and Dr. Danalta, who was physiological classification TOBS and the most alien and, at times, familiar creature that Hewlitt had ever seen or expected to see.

Danalta was a polymorph who could make itself look like anything or anyone, and it loved to show off. But when it was the shape-changer's turn to watch over him, especially when he was expected to sleep and not talk, it sat on the deck by his bedside like a lumpy, green pear that was featureless except for the single, large eye and ear that it extruded for the purpose.

Except for the natural sleeping periods prescribed for Earth-human DBDG patients, he was not confined to bed.

During his first day on board, there was one very thorough physical examination, which included the withdrawal of tissue and blood specimens. While it was being done, the entire medical team stood and hovered around his bed, displaying a degree of readiness that was hair-raising in its implications while radiating a level of anxiety that even he could feel, in case he reacted in some clinically melodramatic fashion. Apart from that one examination nothing whatever was done for or to him and, because he had not reacted in any fashion whatever, they spent the next two days asking him endless questions while trying to avoid answering his.

Pathologist Murchison was a fellow Earth-human as well as being closer in personality and appearance to Hewlitt's idea of what a medical guardian angel should look like. The next time she was on casualty watch, he tried to start a polite argument with her in the hope that she, at least, would let something slip that would tell him what they were planning to do with him.

Hewlitt knew that he did not have to control his irritation because Prilicla was resting in its cabin and out of empathic range. He began, "Everyone seems to be asking me the same questions that Medalont and all my other doctors have already asked many times, and I am giving the same answers. I'd like to help if I can, but how? You won't answer questions or tell me anything at all about my condition. What do you think is wrong with me, and why won't you tell me what you are trying to do about it?"

The pathologist swung around in her seat at the diagnostic console and looked away from its big viewscreen, which had been displaying a succession of still images that resembled the top surfaces of slabs of pink and purple-veined marble, but were more likely to be sections of other-species tissue with something nasty wrong with them. Maybe, Hewlitt thought, she had been expecting the pictures to bore him to sleep.

She gave a long sigh, and said, "This information would have been given to you during the post-landing briefing tomorrow but, seeing that there has been no change in your clinical condition over the past three days, there is no good reason for keeping it from you until then. You will not like the answers I give you because . . ."

"Is, is it bad news?" he broke in. "I'd rather know the worst. I think."

"If you want answers," she said, "don't interrupt. This is embarrassing for me as it is."

Embarrassing for you, Hewlitt thought. He said, "I'm sorry, please go on."

She nodded, then said, "It is not good news, or bad news, it is no news. First, we kept asking the same questions in the hope that you would tell us something new, something you omitted to tell Medalont or the others, something that we can believe and act upon. According to Prilicla, your emotional radiation indicates that you are not consciously lying, but the truth you are telling us is not helpful at all. Your second question, what is wrong with you. Well, so far as we have been able to discover, you are not only well, you are an unusually fit and healthy specimen of an Earth-human male DBDG. The answer is that nothing is wrong with you."

She took a deep breath that expanded the spectacular chest inside her tight, white coveralls, further reminding him that he was a healthy male, and went on, "That being the case, Patient Hewlitt, we should declare you a healthy hypochondriac with psychological problems and tell you to go home and stop wasting our time as many of your other medics have done in the past. . . ."

She held up one small, well-formed hand and said, "No, don't elevate your blood pressure, we aren't going to do that. At least, not until we have found an explanation for your strange early case history and the more recent regeneration of Morredeth's damaged fur, which may or may not be related. We are hoping to find the relationship, if there is one, on Etla. That is where the initial strange occurrences took place, and where your help, advice, and memories of those early episodes will be much appreciated during the investigation.

"So the answer to your third question," she ended, smiling, "is that we don't know what to do with you."

"I'd be pleased to help," Hewlitt said, "but my childhood memories might not be accurate enough for your purpose. Have you thought of that?"

"According to the Psychology Department," she replied, "your memory is like everything else about you, well-nigh perfect. Now, Patient Hewlitt, will you please go to sleep and let me work."

"I'll try," he said. "What are you doing?"

She sighed again and said, "Among other things I am comparing a series of enlarged scanner visuals of DBDG and other-species brains, including your own, in the hope of finding a structural variation or abnormality that might explain how you were able to do some of the things you have done, if it was you and not another as yet unidentified agency that was responsible. I don't really expect to find evidence of a faculty that enables its possessor to perform miracles, but I have to try. Now go to sleep."

A few minutes later she went on, "Are you sure you have told us everything? Were there any incidents, so minor or trivial that you didn't think they were worth mentioning, like the episode with your teeth, for example, while you were a child or adult? How about contacts with people who were ill, either at home or in your working environment? For some reason the case notes make no mention of your profession or occupation. Did you have any contacts with animals, other than your kitten, that might have been ill or recently recovered from an illness, or were there any other . . ."

"Do you mean my sheep?" said Hewlitt.

"I might mean your sheep," said Murchison. "Tell me about it."

"Them," he corrected.

"You're a shepherd?" she said. "I didn't think they had shepherds these days. Go on."

"I'm not and they do," he said. "Sheepherding is a rare, specialized, and very well paid job, especially when they work for me. I inherited the family business from my grandparents, because my father was the only son and he preferred a career in the space service. When he died in the flyer crash, well, I was the last Hewlitt. The case notes didn't mention my job because nearly everyone on Earth knew who I was and what I did.

"I run Hewlitt the Tailor."

"And I have the feeling that I should be impressed," said Murchison. "Sorry, but I wasn't born on Earth."

"Neither were ninety-odd percent of the Federation citizens," he said, "so I'm not offended. It is a small but very exclusive company that can charge the Earth and moon for its services, which is to provide handcrafted, custom-built garments made from the original, handwoven or spun tweeds and fine worsted materials. In these days of cheap, synthesized clothing there are people who are willing and wealthy enough to pay our prices, or even to try bribing their way onto our waiting list. But in spite of the fearsome prices we charge, the profit margin isn't excessive. We have to maintain herds of sheep and other wool-bearing animals, who are classified as protected species. They still need to be shorn periodically, which is how we get the raw material for our weaving mill, but the high level and cost of health care our animals are given you wouldn't believe.

"My job requires periodic inspection visits to our herds," he went on, "which includes feeling the quality of wool on a few of the animals before shearing. But they are never, ever allowed to take sick or catch any infectious diseases. So I'm sorry. This information isn't very useful to you, is it?"

"Probably not useful," she agreed, "but interesting. We'll need to give it some serious thought."

"And I'm not a tailor," he ended, "just an impeccably dressed company figurehead, when I'm not wearing a hospital nightshirt."

Murchison smiled and nodded. "We were all wondering why an apparently non-urgent case like yours was referred to Sector General. Maybe one of your rich and influential clients might have had something to do with it, especially if he happened to be a highly placed medic anxious to get onto your waiting list."

"But surely not influential enough," said Hewlitt, "to have an ambulance ship like *Rhabwar* assisting with my case. Why am I considered that important?"

He knew at once from her sudden lack of expression that she was not going to answer. Instead she smiled again and said firmly, "No more questions, Patient Hewlitt. You can count sheep if you like, but go to sleep."

She continued to watch him until he closed his eyes; then he heard her resume the quiet, intermittent tapping on her console. In the darkness behind his closed lids, the background silence of a ship in hyperflight became diluted by the soft, metallic creaking and humming noises interspersed with the distant, muffled, and barely audible voices of the crew that drifted aft along the communications well, sounds that at other times he would not have been aware of hearing. He lay for a subjective eternity, trying not to think about anything at all while wriggling to relieve the increasing discomfort of his sinfully comfortable bed until he could take it no longer.

"I'm not sleeping," he said, opening his eyes.

"That is what your monitor has been telling me for the past two hours," said Murchison, trying to hide her irritation behind a smile. "But it is always nice to have verbal corroboration. What am I going to do with you?"

Hewlitt recognized a rhetorical question when he heard one and remained silent.

She went on, "You are forbidden all medication, which, naturally, includes sedation. *Rhabwar* doesn't have an entertainment channel to bore you to sleep because the occupants of the casualty deck are usually in no condition to be entertained. Danalta will be relieving me in an hour. Unless you want to spend the rest of the night watching it change shape, which is not a pretty sight, our closest equivalent to in-flight entertainment is the ship's log of past operations. I can run that on the main screen if you like, with the nonmedical summary. Some of the material will provide useful background information for tomorrow's briefing on Etla."

"And will it bore me to sleep?" asked Hewlitt.

"I very much doubt it," she replied. "Raise the backrest

until you can see the whole screen without dislocating your neck. Okay? Here we go. . . ."

There had been time to call up the library information on *Rhabwar* before they had moved him on board, so he already knew that he was on a special ambulance ship whose primary purpose was the deep-space rescue, retrieval, and preliminary treatment of life-forms in distress whose physiological classifications were hitherto unknown to the Federation. In the case of a distress call from a Federation vessel, whose flight plan, planet of origin, and crew species were known, it was simpler to dispatch a rescue vessel from the home planet with a team of same-species medics and life support on board.

With the retrieval of *Rhabwar*'s type of casualty, the situation was different and potentially more dangerous. In addition to being traumatized and their ability to observe and reason logically reduced by pain, shock, fear, and confusion, its casualties were more often as not thrown into a panic reaction caused by the sight of the grotesque creatures who were trying to rescue them. That was why *Rhabwar*'s crew had to include other-species technology experts and first-contact specialists as well as medics.

When it was not engaged on specialist rescue missions, the ship was expected to respond to the more general type of emergency ranging from large-scale space structural accidents to the coordination of medical disaster relief operations on-planet. But the majority of the missions, as well as being the most entertaining and hair-raising, were those which the log noted as requiring unique solutions.

The present mission, he had overheard Murchison tell Naydrad, would probably hold the all-time record for being both the weirdest and least dangerous they had ever been assigned.

Because his hearing was very good he had also overheard the medical team making obscure references to problems they had encountered on previous missions, to beings called the Dewatti, a pregnant Gogleskan called Khone, and the Blind Ones and their incredibly savage servants, the Protectors of the Unborn, among others. But now, as the images of devastated ships, drifting masses of space wreckage with the dead or dying debris it contained, and the pictures of barely living organic wreckage occupying his own and the other beds around him filled the screen, those references were no longer obscure.

Murchison had been right. The pictures that were unfolding were not conducive to sleep, and so keen was he not to miss anything that he closed his eyes only to blink. He noticed neither the arrival of Danalta or the pathologist's departure, and he grew aware of events beyond the borders of the big viewscreen only when the deck lighting came on, the screen darkened, and he felt the gentle downdraft from Prilicla's wings as the Cinrusskin hovered above his bed.

"Good morning, friend Hewlitt," it said. "We have emerged from hyperspace and will be landing in five hours' time. I feel from you the emotional radiation characteristic of a high level of fatigue, although you consciously admitted its presence. It would look bad for all of us if you yawned your way through the briefing, so relax, empty your mind, and close your eyes for ten seconds and you will find yourself asleep. Trust me."

CHAPTER 17

Rabwar possessed the delta-wing configuration and flight characteristics but not the armament of a Monitor Corps light cruiser. It was the largest class of vessel in service capable of aerodynamic maneuvering within an atmosphere as well as being able to land with minimal effect on the local environment. That was not an important consideration here because, so far as Hewlitt could see, the area where he had played and strayed in his youth remained as he remembered it, a wreckage-strewn, overgrown wilderness. While the ship was descending onto a clear area midway between his former home and the clump of tall trees with the ravine running through them, he was able to trace with his finger on the main viewscreen the path he had taken all those years ago.

Present at the briefing, which was held on the casualty deck because it was the largest compartment in the ship, were the medical team, Captain Fletcher, Hewlitt, and, onscreen, the grey, fur-covered features of Colonel Shech-Rar, commander of the local Monitor Corps base. The officer projected the image of a very busy and impatient Orligian.

"Your names and *Rhabwar*'s reputation precede you, Doctor," it broke in before Prilicla had completed its friendly, informal introductions. "Let us not waste time. Sector General has requested my full cooperation during your stay here. What is the nature of your mission, how long will it take, and what facilities will you require?"

Hewlitt, who had been introduced as a nonmedical advisor, wondered whether its service career had been spent among too many Kelgians or two few Cinrusskins or if its bad manners were an inherited characteristic.

"Regretably, Colonel," Prilicla replied, with no detectable change in its friendly manner, "I am not at liberty to divulge the precise details of our mission, other than to say that it involves the investigation of incidents which took place over twenty years ago and which may have an important bearing on a present medical research project. It is not a matter of Federation security, a Galactic Secret, or anything of a sensitive or important nature for which, I am sure, you would have full clearance. At present the information is restricted because of simple patient confidentiality. As soon as the investigation has been completed and evaluated, I have no doubt that you will be informed of the results."

"Is there a possibility that your investigation will pose a health risk," said Shech-Rar, "either to my base personnel or the native population? This was Etla the Sick, remember. We succeeded in clearing it of all its ghastly diseases many years ago, and our ongoing cultural contact mission would not be helped if the people were given an unnecessary reminder of their past. Do not try to obscure your purpose with a screen of medical polysyllables, Doctor. Can you give me this assurance?"

"Yes," said Prilicla.

Shech-Rar showed its teeth, whether in a smile or a scowl Hewlitt could not be sure, then said, "A clear, single-syllable answer. Good. But when a vessel like *Rhabwar* arrives on a confidential mission that is neither important nor sensitive, that is curious and so am I. No matter, Doctor. What do you need from me?"

It took only a few minutes for Prilicla to detail its requirements, but it was obvious from Shech-Rar's voice when it spoke that suspicion had replaced its former impatience.

"I was not assigned here until five years after these incidents took place," said the colonel, "so I have no direct responsibility in the matter. The flyer accident to the subject's parents, which to my mind is the only incident worthy of attention, was fully investigated. The findings were that the cause was a combination of adverse weather conditions, a power system malfunction that affected the control linkages, and pilot error, the error being in not waiting until the storm had passed. You are welcome to a copy of the report. But why is it that young people with long lives ahead of them take needless risks while the old ones, with much less time remaining, are so careful?"

The colonel made an untranslatable sound, as if irritated with itself for digressing into philosophy, and went on, "In spite of what you have told me, the arrival of *Rhabwar* and your team here is the true measure of the mission's importance. However, if your investigation is likely to uncover any long-past act of negligence or other misbehavior on the part of any of my officers, I will not allow you to question them until I have satisfied myself that they have Corps legal representation before answering any charges. Is that understood, Doctor?"

The empath's fragile body and limbs trembled for a moment, as if it was sensing Shech-Rar's emotional radiation at extreme range; then it said, "I assure you, Colonel, it is not that kind of investigation. We require permission to explore the locality where the incidents took place and, if they are still on Etla, interview the beings concerned. We are interested in their recollections, nothing more, and will make allowances for any lapses of memory. The approximate timing of the event is known to us, but we will need your help in identifying the people concerned. At present we do not even know their names."

"That information will be on my predecessor's file," said the colonel. "Wait."

Rather than the transmission ending, when Shech-Rar's image disappeared it was replaced by the Monitor Corps symbol on a field of deep blue, indicating that the wait was not expected to be a long one. On *Rhabwar* everyone remained silent, not wishing to start a discussion that was sure to be interrupted. Hewlitt watched the screen until the hairy features of the colonel reappeared.

"The names you require," said Shech-Rar without preamble, "are Stillman, Hamilton, and Telford. Major Stillman, who was then a surgeon-lieutenant, is now retired but still attached to the base as an Etlan cultural advisor, as is Dr. Hamilton, the civilian specialist in other-species dentistry. Should you need to interview it, Surgeon-Captain Telford, the senior base medical officer at the time, was posted to Dutha three years ago. The present encumbent, Surgeon-Lieutenant Krack-Yar, will make the hospital records available and discuss them with you on request."

"The matter is not important enough to warrant going to Dutha," said Prilicla. "In the absence of the original medical officer, a copy of its records and the flyer accident investigation report will be fine, as soon as you find it convenient, Colonel."

Shech-Rar looked at someone offscreen, nodded, then said, "Is fifteen minutes soon enough?"

"You don't believe in wasting time, Colonel," said Prili-cla. "Thank you, yes."

"Rather than send you the names, locations, and a map," said Shech-Rar, "it will waste even less of your time if Major Stillman acts as your guide and escort. He can take you over the ground and introduce you to the people concerned as well as, hopefully, telling me what you are really doing here. . . ."

Definitely, thought Hewlitt, the colonel had spent a long time among Kelgians.

"The residence you mentioned," it went on, "is no longer occupied by Earth-humans. Do you still need to visit it?"

For an instant the Cinrusskin's hover became less stable. Then it recovered and said, "Yes, Colonel. If only to apologize for landing *Rhabwar* uninvited in their backyard."

Being an emotion sensitive, Prilicla always tried to avoid doing or saying anything that would cause an unpleasant emotional reaction in others, because the other person's anger or distress would be shared by the empath. Even though the colonel was well beyond the range of its empathic faculty, the habit of always saying the right thing was strong. But there were times, Hewlitt had found, when the little entity could be very economical with the truth. He had the feeling that this was one of them.

"Major Stillman will meet you at your airlock in three hours," said the colonel. "Is there anything else you need from me, Doctor?"

Before Prilicla could finish saying no and thanking it again, the transmission ended.

"I could have taken you to the site, and the house, without Stillman's help," said Hewlitt. "Why do you want to go to the house anyway? The real reason, I mean, not the polite, socially acceptable one that you gave the colonel."

"If we refused the assistance of the local Monitor Corps, friend Hewlitt," said Prilicla, "the colonel would be sure that we were trying to hide something. We are not hiding anything, because we still don't know if there is anything to hide except, perhaps, our own future embarrassment.

"I have no good reason to visit the house," it went on, "other than to cover old ground in the hope that a useful idea will occur to us, or to you, while we are doing so. I feel you radiating disbelief combined with disappointment. Perhaps you were expecting a more substantial reason. But the truth is that we have no clear idea of what, if anything, we will find there.

"We will proceed with the briefing now. . . ."

They might not know what they were looking for, Hewlitt thought, but Captain Fletcher and the entire medical team were going out well equipped to find it. His translator was working, but the language was too specialized and technical for him to understand and make a contribution, so he listened without speaking until there was an interruption from the wall speaker.

"Communications. The material promised by Colonel Shech-Rar has come in. Instructions?"

"Put it on our repeater screen, friend Haslam, and run the accident report first," said Prilicla. It drifted closer until the downdraft from its wings stirred his hair, and went on, "You are welcome to remain, friend Hewlitt, but if at any time you find this material or our conversation distressing, please feel free to return to your bed and raise the hush field."

"It happened a long time ago," he said. "I was too young to be told all the details, but now I want to know. Thank you, but I feel sure that I'll be all right."

"I will know how you feel, friend Hewlitt," said Prilicla. "Proceed, friend Haslam."

The report began with the service ID pictures of his parents, which surprised him because they looked no older than he was now, and in his mind they had always been so much bigger and older than himself. They had been looking very serious for the camera, he thought as the other personal and physiological details unrolled, but that must have been one of the few times when they had not smiled at him. The memories came flooding back, sharp and clear and corroborating in every detail the reconstruction of the accident investigators.

At the time his father had been too busy to even to look at him, but his mother had smiled and told him not to be afraid as she climbed over the backrest of the copilot's position to squeeze down beside him. She had held him very tightly in her lap with one arm while her free hand redeployed the safety harness around both of them. Outside the canopy, the sky and the tree-covered mountains were spinning around them, with the trees coming so close that he could see individual branches. Then she had pushed his head forward, folding him in two on her lap with the back of his head pressed between her breasts. There had been a sudden shock that flung them sideways and apart, a loud, tearing crash, and the feeling of rain on his face and cold air rushing past as he fell.

He remembered an explosion of pain as he hit the ground, but nothing else until one of the rescue party that had responded to the flyer's automatic distress beacon asked him where he was hurt.

According to the report, the flyer's canopy had been speared by one of the treetops and was found still lodged in the upper branches, while the rest of the ship crashed to the ground and rolled down the mountain for a distance of forty-five meters before breaking up and catching fire. Because the local vegetation was sodden after a day of heavy rain, the flames did not travel up the slope to the point where the sole survivor, the seven-year-old Hewlitt boy, was lying. The report went on to discuss at length the technical evidence gathered by the investigators, which Prilicla passed over for later study by Captain Fletcher, and ended with brief details of the autopsy, disposal, and treatment of the victims.

His parents had sustained massive trauma, and the indications were that they had probably died, and were certainly unconscious, before the fire engulfed them. Hewlitt had been found in a state of shock and confusion but otherwise unharmed, and it was assumed that the small patches of blood on his clothing belonged to his mother. Although unhurt, he had been kept under observation in hospital for the nine days it took the next-of-kin, his grandmother, to arrive and collect him and arrange for the disposal of his parents' remains.

His grandmother had not allowed Hewlitt to see the bodies because, he now realized, the cremation had simply completed the process already started by the fire.

For a moment the old but never quite forgotten pain of loss and grief returned like a great, dark vacuum filling his chest, and he tried hard to control his feelings because Prilicla was watching him and becoming unsteady in its flight. He pushed the remembered pain out of his mind and tried to concentrate on the next report that was coming up on the screen.

"Thank you, friend Hewlitt," said the empath, and went on, "As we can see, this report relates to the medical condition, treatment, and behavior of the survivor during its nine-day stay in hospital. Even then the younger Hewlitt was presenting its doctor with problems.

"They began," Prilicla went on, "when the base medical officer, Surgeon-Captain Telford, prescribed oral sedation. Although uninjured, the patient was close to physical exhaustion and emotionally distressed by the loss of its parents and was unable to sleep. The result was a violent but nonspecific reaction that included abdominal discomfort, respiratory difficulty, and a rash covering the skin of the lower chest and back. While the surgeon-captain was still trying to discover what was happening, the symptoms subsided. A different type of sedation was prescribed and, as a precaution, only a minute initial dose was administered, by subcutaneous injection. This time the result was a cardiac arrest which lasted for two-point-six minutes, accompanied by a brief recurrence of respiratory impairment, both of which passed without any detectable aftereffects.

"As you can see," Prilicla continued, indicating the treatment summary at the bottom of the screen, "Dr. Telford diagnosed a hyperallergenic reaction, cause unknown, and forbade further medication. Instead, the emotional problems were treated with verbal tranquilization and reassurance provided by a same-species nurse who was nearing retirement age, and by allowing the child, who was apparently neither ill nor injured, to tire himself out and forget some of his grief by allowing him to visit and talk to other patients, who included serving space officers with many interesting stories to tell. . . ."

"That nurse was very nice to me," Hewlitt broke in, his voice quiet with remembered sadness that he had not felt for many years, "and I realize now that some of those stories might not have been true. But the treatment worked and . . . I'm sorry for interrupting, Doctor, I didn't mean to remember out loud."

"Don't apologize, friend Hewlitt, your memories of the time are valuable to us," said Prilicla. A moment later it went on, "There is an entry here to the effect that the then Surgeon-Lieutenant Telford was completely mystified by your atypical reaction to two simple and well-tried types of sedative medication. But it had no opportunity to discover, identify, and list what he assumed to be the allergenic substances that were causing the reaction before your relative arrived to take you to Earth. Dr. Telford had no reason, other than its unsatisfied curiosity, for keeping an otherwise healthy child in hospital.

"And now," it ended, "has anyone anything they would like to say about this report?"

There were a few things Hewlitt would have liked to say, but he knew the question was not directed at him. It was Pathologist Murchison who spoke first.

She said, "Even though the condition was atypical in that the symptoms appeared and receded with unusual rapidity, Telford's diagnosis of what appeared to be a wide-ranging and nonspecific allergy was sensible in the circumstances, as was his decision not to attempt further medical treatment until he knew exactly what was going on. Essentially, that is what the patient's medics did on Earth and later in Sector General. In a word, nothing. . . ."

"Pathologist," Naydrad broke in, its fur spiking with impatience. "You are restating the problem, not offering a solution."

"Perhaps," said Murchison, who knew her Kelgians well enough not to be irritated by the interruption. "But the point I'm trying to make is that the allergy symptoms appeared at a very early age and were repeated, with minor variations, here, on Earth, and in Sector General. This makes me wonder if the patient was born with the condition and we should be looking for a genetic rift of some kind. There are no recorded instances of anyone being allergic to the food produced by the synthesizers, which is the kind most off-planet visitors favor, and certainly not baby-formula varieties. And there would be no allergic response if . . . Hewlitt, were you breast-fed as an infant?"

"If I was," he replied after a quick search of his earliest memories, "I was too young to remember."

Murchison smiled. "Too bad, but it may not be important. If you were breast-fed and weaned onto synthesized food, that might explain why the first recorded allergic reaction was to medication. There is another possibility. The symptoms first appeared in the base hospital a few hours after the flyer crash. You were not hurt, but it is reasonable to assume that the fall through the branches onto the soft, wet ground rendered you temporarily unconscious. Certainly, your shocked and confused condition when found is symptomatic of a recent concussion. But it is possible that you sustained minor lacerations or abrasions, too minor in the circumstances for the rescuers to bother recording them, and that something was introduced into your system which caused the later allergic reaction. It might have been something living in the tree or on the ground, a spore or an insect or even a small animal that bit you, or a toxic substance with unknown properties that gained entry though a scratch from the foliage itself. I suggest a search of the crash site. If the suspect organism or material is native to Etla, it will still be there.

"And stop tying your fur in knots, Naydrad," she went on. "I know that pathogens native to one world cannot affect any being who evolved on another. I also know that physiologically the natives of Etla and Earth are almost identical, so much so that there are theories about a prehistoric colonization program by common, star-traveling ancestors. But attempts at procreation between the few base personnel who, for emotional reasons, felt impelled to widen cultural contact by marrying Etlan men or women were unsuccessful. But if there is an overlap, no matter how small, in the gene structure of the two species, then that, too, should be investigated. And if Patient Hewlitt would submit to tests, very closely monitored and using trace quantities of Etlan native medication to minimize the risks, we might find the exception that proves the rule."

"No tests, friend Murchison," said Prilicla, before Hewlitt could say the same thing in stronger language. "No medication of any kind, Etlan or otherwise, until we have a clearer idea of what we are looking for. Perhaps you have forgotten that friend Hewlitt has already been affected by Etlan native vegetation, when it ingested toxic fruit prior to falling from a tree?"

"I have not forgotten," said Murchison, "that the younger Hewlitt survived two falls without injury. That was very fortuitous and it may also be significant if we assume that something in the fruit he consumed before the first fall caused the hyperallergic reaction following the flyer accident. The record of events during and after the second fall are supported by objective clinical evidence, but the circumstances surrounding the first is subjective, uncertain, and supported only by childhood memories that may prove to be untrustworthy. For example.

"Considering the small physical size of the patient at the time," she went on, "the distance fallen may have been exaggerated. The fruit consumed, which was later identified by others as being highly toxic, may have been a visually similar but nontoxic variety, and the period of unconsciousness afterward could have been due simply to natural fatigue after a long afternoon at play. Children can tell tall stories, and sometimes in retrospect they can even believe them themselves, but until we have objective evidence . . . Patient Hewlitt, please control your emotional radiation!"

He was trying very hard to suppress the anger and bitter disappointment he was feeling, because Prilicla's fragile body was being shaken by the emotional gale of Hewlitt's making. Murchison was the only same-species medic on board. When she was not being the cool and clinical team pathologist, she had been a friendly, relaxed, competent person who instilled trust. Certainly he had liked and trusted her and had thought that she, at least, was beginning to believe him, but she had turned out to be just like all the others.

"I did not call you a liar," she said, apparently reading his mind, "only that at present I need more proof that you were telling the truth."

He was about to reply when the voice of the communications officer cut him short.

"We have a signal that the ground vehicle with Major Stillman on board is leaving the base," said Lieutenant Haslam. "He is estimating arrival in eighteen minutes."

CHAPTER 18

Hewlitt watched with a mixture of surprise and professional interest as the stout, grey-haired man who was to be their guide unfolded from his tiny ground vehicle and came forward to meet them. Stillman was not in uniform and was wearing instead the native dress of short cloak, kilt, and soft, calf-length boots. The outfit looked comfortable and not without a certain style, even though, in this instance, the flowing line of the cloak was spoiled by the wearer carrying too much junk in the concealed pockets. Unlike the coveralls worn by Murchison, Fletcher, and himself, he could tell that the garments were not the product of a synthesizer. He was considering the possibility of introducing the Etlan kilt to a few of his more sartorially adventurous clients when Prilicla drifted forward to meet the other halfway.

"Friend Stillman," said the empath, "I must begin by apologizing for meeting you at the bottom of the boarding ramp, rather than inviting you inside where you could satisfy the intense curiosity you are feeling about the ship, but I formed the impression that Colonel Shech-Rar did not want us to take up too much of your time."

It had already taken several minutes for Stillman to recover from what must have been his first meeting with a Cinrusskin empath—apart from a brief, appreciative glance at the eminently noticeable Murchison, he had barely noticed the others—and to find his voice.

"I—I've retired, Dr. Prilicla," he said, smiling. "My time is my own, not the colonel's, so take up as much of it as you like. And yes, I've heard a lot about *Rhabwar* and would dearly love a look over the ship. But if it is all right with you, I think we should do as the colonel says first so that I will have more time left to satisfy my curiosity about other things."

"As you wish," said Prilicla. "What were the colonel's instructions to you?"

"To visit the house first," Stillman replied. "The present occupants work on the base, but they have been excused duty for the rest of the day and should have returned home by the time we arrive. There may be a problem if you want to meet the dentist in person. At present Dr. Hamilton is visiting our other base, on Yunnet continent, and is not due to return for another three days, but if you only need to talk to him he has instructions to contact you as soon as possible at the house or the ship. After that you will be able to spend as much time as you require in the ravine."

They were being given full cooperation, Hewlitt thought cynically, but with such enthusiasm that they were being allowed the minimum time to think or guard their tongues.

The exterior of the house looked familiar except for the front entrance, which had been enlarged and its steps replaced with a ramp to allow easy passage to the Tralthan residents, who had seen their approach and were waiting just inside the door to welcome them. Stillman, who was obviously well known to the couple, introduced them as Crajarron and Surriltor. They exchanged names without, of course, performing the uniquely Earth-human custom of shaking hands. The interior of his once familiar home was completely unrecognizable.

Most of the room dividers he remembered had disappeared, as had all but a few chairs and relaxers needed for other-species visitors because Tralthans, who could not sit down, preferred large, unobstructed expanses of flooring. Remembering Patient Hossantir's sleeping arrangements in Ward Seven, he recognized the double-sized, padded sleeping pit in one corner as the bedroom area. In contrast to the emptiness of the floor space, the walls were almost hidden by book and tape racks, pictures and woven hangings whose subjects were unclear, and narrow, cone-shaped containers of aromatic vegetation.

While he was trying to think of something complimentary to say about the place, Prilicla apologized for the inconvenience of having an ambulance ship land with no advance warning beside their charming home.

"Apologies are unnecessary, Dr. Prilicla," said Crajarron, with a dismissive wave of one tentacle. "You are the first Cinrusskin we have met and we are grateful for this very pleasant break in our routine. Can we offer hospitality, solid or liquid sustenance, perhaps? Our food synthesizer has many other-species' programs."

"Regrettably, no," said Prilicla, "we have already eaten."

Murchison, Stillman, and Hewlitt looked at the empath, knowing that it could feel their hunger. It had not told a lie, but neither had it said how long ago they had eaten.

"We came to apologize for the intrusion of our ship," it went on, "which is engaged on an investigation into an incident that occurred when friend Hewlitt was a child living here with its parents. While we were here it wished to visit its old home and, bearing in mind its sudden departure following the flyer accident, to ask if you knew what had happened to an entity to which it was emotionally attached at that time."

Hewlitt stared at the others in turn. Stillman looked as puzzled as he himself felt, but Murchison did not look surprised at all. His cat must have died of illness, accident, or old age years ago. Why was Prilicla asking questions about it now?

Crajarron turned two of its eyes in Hewlitt's direction and said, "Do you mean the small, furry Earth-being of limited intelligence called Snarfe? It was adopted by another Earth-human household, but it refused to stay there and kept returning to its old home. When we came to live here we found it wandering about the house and garden. Later we learned that some members of its species form attachments for persons and others for places. It had a friendly disposition and, once we learned its dietary requirements and how not to step on it when it tried to attract our attention by climbing our legs, it remained with us as a house pet."

Hewlitt blinked, remembering that well-loved cat when it had been little more than a kitten, and feeling surprised by his sudden feelings of sorrow and loss. But Crajarron was making a strange, irregular hissing sound that did not translate. He realized that it was a Tralthan's attempt at making the push-wushing sound Earth-people made when trying to attract the attention of a cat only when Fudge appeared in the entrance and stalked slowly toward him.

Nobody spoke as the cat stopped, looked up at him, then began to circle his feet, butting his ankles and gently lashing his lower legs with the thick, furry tail. It was a form of non-verbal communication that had no need of translation. He stooped, picked it up with both hands, and held it against his chest and shoulder. When he ran his fingers gently from its forehead along its back, the tail stiffened and it began to purr.

"Fudge," he said, "I certainly didn't expect to see you again. How are you?"

Prilicla flew closer and said, "Its emotional radiation is characteristic of a very old and contented entity who is without physical or mental distress and is presently enjoying the stroking of its fur. If it could speak it would tell you that it is well, and to please continue what you are doing. Friend Murchison, you know what to do."

"Yes indeed," the pathologist replied, producing her scanner. "Crajarron, Surriltor, may I?" To Hewlitt she added, "This won't hurt at all, just hold it steady for a moment while I scan. I'm recording for later study, if necessary."

Fudge must have thought that she was playing a new game, because it took a double swipe at the scanner with claws sheathed, then returned to the enjoyment of the petting while she completed the examination.

"Do you wish to reclaim your property, Earth-person Hewlitt?" said Crajarron. Both Tralthans were directing all of their eyes at him, and he did not need an empathic faculty or the sight of Prilicla trembling to know that the interspecies social relations were cooling fast.

"Thank you, no," he said, returning Fudge to the floor. "Plainly the cat likes it here and would be unhappy elsewhere, but I am grateful for this opportunity to renew an old friendship."

The atmosphere thawed at once, Prilicla regained flight stability, and Fudge transferred its affections to Surriltor by jumping onto one of the Tralthan's massive feet. A few minutes later their polite exchange of farewells was interrupted by the house communicator's double chime, signaling an incoming call.

It was Dr. Hamilton.

"Sorry I won't be able to answer your questions in person, Dr. Prilicla," he said. "Stillman will have told you that I'm visiting the Vespara establishment on Yunnet right now. One of the joys of being an other-species peripetetic dentist on this world. How can I help you?"

While Prilicla was explaining what it wanted, the two Tralthans, not wanting to eavesdrop on what might be a private conversation, moved to a corner of the room and raised their hush field. Hewlitt stared hard at the screen, trying to remember the other's face and voice, but the only memory that came was of shining instruments and hands projecting from white cuffs. Perhaps he had not looked at the other's face long enough for it to register.

"I remember the incident," said the dentist, "not because it was important but because it was the first and only time I was asked to extract teeth that would have detached themselves naturally. At the time I decided that the child was overimaginative, timid, and unwilling to inflict what he believed would be serious pain on himself by pulling out the teeth with his fingers, as most children do, and his mother had taken him to me to sort out the problem. It was too minor a procedure to require an anesthetic and, I remember now, there was a note in his med file warning against the use of painkilling medication because of a then unidentified allergy."

"We are still having trouble identifying it," said Murchison. "What happened to the teeth? Did you keep or examine them following the extraction?"

"There was no reason to do that," said Hamilton, and laughed. "They were just ordinary children's first teeth. Besides, if you are unfamiliar with the tooth-fairy myth current among young Earth-children, he insisted on having them back for financial reasons."

"Is there anything else you can remember about the incident, friend Hamilton?" said Prilicla. "No matter how odd or unimportant it may have seemed at the time."

"Sorry, no," the dentist replied. "I never saw the child again, so presumably the rest of his baby teeth detached normally."

Hewlitt barely heard the end of the conversation, because he was remembering something else about those teeth, something he had almost forgotten until the dentist's words brought it back. He had not told anyone about it, then or later, because they would have said that it was all his imagination. Even as a child he had hated people telling him that he was imagining things.

"Friend Hewlitt," said Prilicla, drifting closer, "your emotional radiation, comprising minor levels of irritation, caution, and expected embarrassment, suggests that you are hiding something from us. Please tell us about it. We will not laugh or embarrass you. Any new datum on this case could turn out to be important."

"I doubt that," he said, "but here it is. . . ."

Apart from one loud, untranslatable sound from Naydrad, they watched him until he had finished speaking. It was Prilicla who broke the incredulous silence.

"Dr. Hamilton made no mention of this," said the empath. "Did you show the teeth to or discuss them with anyone?"

"He didn't examine the teeth before he gave them back to me," Hewlitt replied. "They were fine and very hard to see, anyway. There were five or six of them, pale grey in color and about an inch long, on each tooth. They were in my hand all the way home, but I didn't show it to my grandmother because she was a bit irritated with me over what she thought was an unnecessary visit to the dentist. By the time we got back to the house they were gone. They must have dropped off or been blown away by the groundcar's air-conditioning. I know, none of you believe me."

Murchison laughed, then shook her head and said, "I'm sorry. But it is difficult to believe you when you keep telling us about so many strange, unsupported, unrelated, and completely incredible symptoms. Do you blame us?"

Prilicla's spidery limbs were trembling again. It said, "I promised that we would not cause embarrassment to friend Hewlitt, who feels that it is telling the truth."

"I know he thinks he is telling the truth, dammit," said Murchison. "But I ask you, hairy teeth!"

This time it was Stillman who exercised the diplomacy characteristic of a cultural contact specialist by changing the subject.

"Dr. Prilicla," he said. "Would you like to visit the ravine now?"

Hewlitt waited until they were outside before he said, "I knew that was Fudge the instant I saw it, and I know it recognized me at the same time. I can't describe . . . It was a really strange feeling."

"Your feeling of recognition toward your nonsapient little friend was complex," said the empath. "I have never before encountered an emotional response quite like it, and I would not have been surprised if you had asked the Tralthans for the animal to be returned to you. I am pleased at your response to the situation. . . . Friend Murchison, you are feeling confused and dissatisfied about something. What is it?"

"That cat," she replied, glancing behind her at the house. "My parents liked cats and never had less than two of them at home, so I'm familiar with the species. For example, the life span of a healthy cat is twelve to fourteen Earth years, not double that period, so Snarfe has no business being alive. Dr. Stillman, how sure are you that it is an Earth cat and not a more long-lived Etlan or other-species look-alike?"

"Very sure," the surgeon-captain replied. "When the cultural-contact people came to Etla, and it was clear that they would be staying here for a long time, the Corps leaned over backward in the matter of bringing out their personal effects, including, in one case, a pet cat. A few weeks after arrival it produced a litter of six kittens who were all found foster homes. Snarfe was one of them."

"Then why," said Murchison, "should an ordinary Earth cat double its life span here?"

Stillman walked several paces before he said, "I've often wondered about that myself, ma'am. My theory is that on Etla the cat was not exposed to any of the feline diseases it would normally have encountered on Earth and, as we know, Etlan pathogens have no effect on off-world species. Here it was isolated from all life-threatening or physically debilitating diseases and should die only from accident or old age, after using up all nine of its long and very healthy lives."

Murchison smiled. "We know that Fudge had one bad accident and survived it," she said. "That is a nice theory, Doctor, but is there supporting evidence? What about the other kittens from the same litter?"

"I was afraid you would ask that," said Stillman. "One lost an argument with a log transporter. All five of the others died naturally, so far as I know from old age, about ten years ago."

"Oh," said Murchison.

CHAPTER 19

Prilicla broke the long silence that followed by saying, "Friend Hewlitt, we would like to begin retracing your path from the position of the old hole in the garden enclosure where you escaped to the tree from which you fell. If you are ready, please lead the way."

On the other side of the garden fence he began half walking, half wading through the long, thick growth that looked like Earth grass unless one looked at it more closely, ignoring the insects that were too small for the differences to show, and staring up at the hot, blue sky with its scattered cloud shapes that were too irregular and normal to look alien. Stillman kept pace with him but did not speak, and the others were lagging too far behind for him to hear what they were saying. They were probably talking about him, he thought angrily, and discussing the clinical and psychological implications of his latest flight of fancy.

"I wasn't sure at first, Dr. Stillman," he said, trying to

start a conversation that might change his mental subject, "but I recognized you, too. You seemed to be much taller then, but I suppose all adults are giants to a four-year-old. Apart from that you haven't changed much."

"I didn't recognize you at all," said Stillman. He smiled and patted his ample waistline. "You have grown up while I grew out."

"It was lucky finding you still here," Hewlitt went on. "I thought the Monitor Corps moved its people all over the galaxy."

"I am very lucky to be here," said Stillman.

They walked in silence for at least thirty paces, and he was beginning to wonder if his words had somehow given offense when the other went on, "On this Etla we have an ongoing cultural-contact situation that is, well, delicate, because in so many ways the natives are not alien. When dealing with an intelligent species that is completely alien, if a misunderstanding occurs, allowances are made on both sides. Here we are trying both to understand and gradually reeducate a culture that took a wrong turning. Or rather, they were misinformed and misguided by their emperor into mass xenophobia and defending themselves offensively against a nonexistent threat. We had to gain their trust and show them—we are still showing them—that other-species intelligent life-forms are like themselves, not necessarily bad or good, just different.

"Even in your time we had a few other-species personnel attached to the base," Stillman went on. "The idea was to dilute the Etlan xenophobia by showing aliens working beside us in harmony, and occasionally we would send them out with a covert guard on very carefully arranged visits to public places. They would be spectators at important sporting events, or go on sightseeing trips where the sightseeing was two-way or, most important, to meet and talk to children in schools. Now the base personnel and specialist civilian support comprises three Etlans for every one Earth-human or other-species being, so the cultural-contact program is progressing well.

"But the problem is complicated by the fact that, even though they are nice, friendly people, they are very proud. Even I forget sometimes how different they are; mistakes can still be made. That, as well as its natural lack of charm, is the reason Shech-Rar is not pleased to have a wildly assorted bunch of extraterrestrials conducting an unspecified investigation and blundering around in ignorance of the situation.

"Nothing personal," he added, "but you have just received a condensed and edited version of my lecture to newly arrived Corps personnel."

Hewlitt did not think it was his place to reply. He could hear the others moving closer, but apparently they were more interested in listening to the two in front than talking. The silence continued until Stillman gave a small, awkward laugh and spoke again.

"If an officer is able and dedicated and successful in gaining the natives' trust," he said, "his superiors like him to remain for as long as possible so as to give continuity to the process. Apparently I displayed unusual aptitude by insisting on marrying an Etlan and staying here after my service retirement date. She is the reason why I told you I was lucky to be here."

"I understand," said Hewlitt.

The other seemed to sense his embarrassment. He said, "Don't worry, I'm not going maudlin in my old age. We met during my second year here. She was what they call a Mother Teacher of the Young, one of the people who instruct four- to seven-year-olds, and the first Etlan to agree to introduce a Tralthan teacher equivalent and share her class with it. She had already accepted the idea that the best time to instruct children was before they had a chance to acquire their parents' prejudices. She was a widow. There were an awful lot of widows and orphaned children about at the time. We could have none of our own, naturally, but we adopted four before we became too old to . . ."

"Doctor," said Murchison, lengthening her stride until she drew level with them. "I know that the species difference is a bar to procreation, but it might answer a few puzzling clinical questions, or maybe puzzle us even more, if you knew of an exception to that rule. Do you? And if so, is it possible that one of Hewlitt's parents was an Etlan. Or that he was an Etlan fosterling?"

Stillman shook his head. "Sorry, ma'am. I knew his parents very well before he was born, and I was present when he arrived."

"It was a pretty wild idea, anyway," said Murchison, holding up her hand and clenching it into a fist. "You are looking at a hand clutching at hypothetical straws."

Hewlitt remained silent. He was aware of a strange feeling of temporal double vision. The grass was waist-high as it had been to the four-year-old Hewlitt, the trees and bushes had grown taller and thicker, but so had he, and the smell of sun-warmed vegetation and the droning and ticking sounds of insects were exactly the same. Only the distances between the landmarks had shrunk with age.

"I remember this very well," he said, and raised his hand to point. "The first bush I played around is there."

"Can you remember eating anything here?" said Murchison. "A wild berry, perhaps, or did you pull a blade of grass and chew on it? I'm thinking in terms of a possible antidote to the toxic material ingested later."

"No," said Hewlitt, and pointed again. "That ruined house was next. But I'm surprised it wasn't pulled down or rebuilt by now. The whole area is still a wilderness."

"That is deliberate," said Stillman. He looked all around him before going on. "This was the place where the battle which finally overthrew their imperial representative was fought, and the area where all the off-worlders are housed. It is intended both as a reminder of the bad old days and the promise of the new. So far it seems to have worked. On public holidays this is a nice, quiet place to picnic, except when the Etlan children find some off-world kids to play with, when the noise can be horrendous."

The house was little more than a shell with its roof open to the sky and weeds growing in the debris covering the floor. There were scorch marks on one wall, but after the passage of so many years the burnt smell was probably due to memory rather than lingering smoke. A different generation of small animals and insects scampered or crawled through the weeds, and Murchison asked if he remembered being bitten or stung by any of them. He shook his head, but she asked Naydrad to help her gather and trap a few random specimens for later analysis.

"Next," he said, pointing, "I went to that burned-out fighting vehicle, over there."

This time it was Fletcher rather than Hewlitt who was doing the exploring. They heard him crawling through the dark interior, muttering not quite under his breath that it was a tighter squeeze for a man than a child, until his head and shoulders reappeared through the entry hatch.

"It is a medium-level-technology mobile gun platform," he reported, "with control positions for a crew of three. The larger weapon is designed to fire exploding shells; the smaller used belt-fed solid projectiles. The ammunition, fuel, and most of the circuit boards have been withdrawn. There is nothing left but a few items of equipment not worth salvaging and a lot of insects. Do you want specimens?"

"Yes, please," said Murchison. "Different, if possible, to those from the house."

"To me," said Fletcher in a disgruntled voice, "one squishy insect looks much like another."

"If you need information on local insects, ma'am," said Stillman, "that is one of my wife's subjects. She would be pleased to help. What kind of information are you looking for exactly?"

"We don't know exactly, Doctor," Murchison replied. "It is possible that the younger Hewlitt was having too much fun at the time to remember being stung or bitten, and that could have a bearing on what happened to him later."

"I understand," said Stillman, "I think."

They followed him to the vehicle that lay on its side with its stripped tread lying like a metal carpet beside it, and to the other vehicles he had played in, on, and around. The others had stopped speaking, because Hewlitt was talking and remembering every detail as he walked. Finally they came to the tall tree with the twisted branches and green-and-yellow, pear-shaped fruit that overhung the steep slopes of his ravine.

"Those branches only look strong," said Stillman as Fletcher was about to start climbing. "They won't bear the weight of an adult."

"That is not a problem, friend Stillman," said Prilicla. The slow beating of its wings increased in frequency and it rose like a stately, iridescent dragonfly to hover above the fruit-bearing branches of the treetop.

"Please be careful, Doctor," Stillman called after it, in a worried voice. "The skin is thin at this time of year and the juice is deadly stuff."

The Major did not speak again, although it was obvious that he wanted to interrupt several times while Hewlitt was describing how he had picked and eaten the fruit, fallen, and wakened at the bottom of the ravine with the younger Stillman bending over him. While they were climbing down the steep slope to the bottom, he kept his lips pressed so tightly together that they might have been held closed with sutures.

"I feel you wanting to say something, friend Stillman," said Prilicla. "What is it?"

The monitor officer looked around the rock- and wreckage-strewn floor of the ravine, then up at the fruit-bearing treetop. Unlike the first time Hewlitt had seen it, the sun was bright and high and showed just how dangerous the place was and how very lucky he had been to survive the fall without serious injury.

Stillman cleared his throat and said, "On Etla that tree belongs to a rare and, in spite of its lethal fruit, protected species. This one is very old and slow-growing and at most is only a few meters taller than when the young Hewlitt fell from it, and this is a deep and dangerous ravine. If he had climbed to the topmost branches, eaten even a single mouthful of that fruit, and then fallen down here, he would have been dead. Twice.

"I have no wish to offend you," he went on, looking straight at Hewlitt. "My explanation at the time was that you had been overtired, hungry, and thirsty after playing for many hours in the sun. The sight of the fruit at the top made you try to climb the tree, but gave up the attempt and slid down the slope rather than falling to the bottom. The condition of your clothing at the time, plus the fact that there was not a single scratch or a bruise on you, supports this theory. After trying to climb the tree and seeing what you thought was a cluster of edible fruit at the top, you fell asleep so that your memory of the event was a mixture of dreams and reality.

"Sorry," he ended. "You may not be aware of lying, but neither can you be telling the truth."

For several minutes the medical team maintained a diplomatic silence while busying themselves with the collection of plant and insect specimens at Murchison's direction. Hewlitt was well used to the polite disbelief of others, and

Stillman was just another doctor who had decided that an overactive imagination was all that ailed him, so his feelings were of irritation and disappointment rather than anger. That was why he was surprised when Prilicla's flying showed signs of instability—he knew that it was not his own emotional radiation that was the cause—and less surprised when the empath answered the question before anyone could ask it.

"Friend Fletcher," it said. "You are radiating high levels of curiosity and excitement. Why?"

The captain was kneeling beside a thick, torpedo-shaped object that was almost hidden by undergrowth and soil washed down from the slopes by rain. Fletcher opened his equipment pack and withdrew what looked like a high-penetration scanner.

"There is evidence of foreign technology here," he said. "This object is structurally more sophisticated than the other wreckage hereabouts. I'll be able to tell you more after I've had a closer look at the interior."

"It might not be important," said Stillman, "but Hewlitt was found sleeping beside that thing. At the time I was too interested in his condition to bother looking at another piece of wreckage."

"Thank you, Doctor," said Murchison, moving quickly to join Fletcher. "Danalta, Naydrad, until we know what this means, forget about the bug and plant specimens."

Still trembling from the emotional radiation of the others as well as its own excitement, Prilicla alighted on the ground beside them. "All recorders are on, friend Fletcher," it said. "When you are ready."

The captain's words and actions were precise and unhurried as he described aloud what he saw, thought, and did at every stage of his examination, so much so that Hewlitt wondered if the other was talking for posterity in case the thing blew up in his face. Prilicla, with whom cowardice was a prime survival characteristic, and everyone else were standing or hovering as close to Fletcher as possible without getting in his way and seemed not to be worried. Hewlitt moved closer to join them.

According to Fletcher, the object was just a hollow cylinder under three meters long and half a meter in diameter, with two sets of four triangular stabilizers projecting from the midsection and tail. The outer surface of the casing was pitted and discolored and showed evidence of surface melting that suggested it had been subjected to a brief period of ultra-high temperature. There was also a trace of radioactivity, very faint and harmless, indicating that it might have been briefly exposed to an external source of intense radiation as well as heat. Propulsion was by a single, integral chemical booster that occupied three-quarters of the volume. From the analysis of the burnt residue and a rough estimate of the vehicle's weight, he judged the range to be about sixty to seventy miles.

There were two small, recessed compartments with opened, hinged flaps spaced about one meter apart along the longitudinal axis, equidistant from the vehicle's center of gravity. The remains of four rotted strands of cable sprouted from the openings, suggesting that the vehicle was intended to be soft-landed in the horizontal position by twin parachutes. There was no sign of the parachute fabric because, Fletcher said, it was either biodegradable or it had been torn off by branches on the way down.

"The first ten inches of the nose section hinges downward," Fletcher went on. "It probably fell open on landing and was later covered by soil and grass. Apart from the latch mechanism it seems to be filled with dense padding that has not rotted. The forward quarter of the vehicle, where normally I would expect to find the warhead, is filled with the same padding except for a cylindrical space five inches in diameter running along the longitudinal axis for a distance of three-quarters of a meter. Inside the hollow there is a five-inch circle of plastic, thickly padded on the forward face and with the other side attached to a short bar and . . . and what looks like a piston mechanism designed to expel a cylindrical container of some kind from the hollow interior. But, owing possibly to a malfunction or a rough landing, the piston traveled only halfway along its track so that the container was not completely expelled and, an unknown time later, it was shattered."

The gloves he was wearing were like a tough, transparent second skin, combining sensitivity of touch with maximum protection. Fletcher kept his eyes on the scanner display as he moved his free hand into the opening.

"As well as about a million insects nesting in the padding," he continued, "there are small pieces of glasslike material inside and, yes, I can see more of them partially buried in the grass and soil around the hinged nose cone. They appear to be highly polished on one side and covered with a dark brown, matte coating on the other. I expect you will want specimens?"

Murchison dropped onto her hands and knees beside him and said, "Yes!"

Hewlitt could not remember ever hearing a word spoken with such vehemence and suppressed excitement. Fletcher gave her one of the fragments, which she placed in the portable analyzer hanging from her equipment harness. Everyone waited for her to speak.

"Our analyzers agree," she said to Fletcher. "It is a thin, brittle, very strong glasslike plastic. The degree of curvature indicates that it is a fragment of a cylindrical flask. Apart from a few small traces of insect excrement, the outer surface is clean and highly polished. The opaque coating on the inner surface appears to be a synthetic nutrient, probably in solution, that has since dried out. I will need more specimens and a lengthy session with the ship's analyzer to tell you the form of life it was meant to feed. All I can say now is that the vehicle contained an organism or organisms that needed to be kept alive."

Fletcher was about to hand her another one of the fragments when he stopped to look at Stillman.

"Doctor," he said, "did the Etlans ever use chemical or biological weapons?"

CHAPTER 20

Hewlitt took an instinctive step backward, his body break-ing into a sweat that was not due to the warmth of the sun, but nobody else moved. Either they were all lacking in imagination, which was unlikely, or there was no danger in the situation. He took another step backward anyway.

"Not to our knowledge, Captain," Stillman replied. "There is no historical record of them ever being used in Etlan planetary wars, and they would be pretty ineffective in a space battle. Besides, this world was sick enough already. They could have been developed secretly by the emperor's scientists, and toward the end of the rebellion he might have been desperate enough to use everything he had, but I would say not. The casualty lists of the period mention traumatic injuries resulting from explosions, shrapnel, and gunshot wounds, not disease."

He paused long enough for Fletcher to pass Murchison three more fragments before going on. "In any case, chemical or biological weapons are designed to burst on impact or in the air above the target. This one was soft-landed by parachute, the expulsion mechanism malfunctioned, and it didn't break open until it was struck by something."

"Or someone," said Prilicla.

One by one they turned to stare at Hewlitt, as surprised by the empath's words as he was himself. It was Stillman who spoke first.

He said, "If you mean that it was the Hewlitt child who fell onto this thing, smashed it, and released whatever was inside, I can't help you. He was lying beside it, but it was dark and I was too busy examining him to notice whether there was any broken glass lying around. Besides, Etlan pathogens cannot affect anyone from off-planet. We all know that. And, well, he looks as if he hasn't had a day's illness in his life."

There was a faint trembling in Prilicla's limbs as it nerved itself for the effort of telling another person that he was wrong.

"Friend Hewlitt has a long history of nonspecific illnesses," it said, "all of which responded negatively to treatment. For that reason, diagnosis has been uncertain and the strange succession of symptoms displayed was initially and perhaps mistakenly thought to have a purely psychological basis. Our provisional diagnosis is that he suffers from a wide-ranging, hyperallergic reaction to all forms of medication used so far. We are fairly sure that the condition is not life-threatening, except when an attempt is made to administer medication orally, by subcutaneous injection, or by external application and massage into the dermis. It is a clinically confusing picture."

Stillman shook his head, then pointed at the torpedo. "And is this thing helping to reduce your confusion?"

A faint tremor shook the empath's body as if someone, perhaps Prilicla itself, was generating unpleasant emotional radiation. Instead of answering the question, it said, "Friend Stillman, I have been feeling your hunger and that of the others since I refused the Tralthans' offer of hospitality at the house. My reason for doing so is that *Rhabwar*'s food synthesizer was recently reprogrammed by Chief Dietitian Gurronsevas himself, and we could do a better job of satisfying it on the ship. Would you like to dine with us on board, now?"

"Yes, please," said Stillman.

"I am also detecting feelings of negation and intense curiosity from one of the team. Friend Fletcher, is there a problem?"

"The problem is this soft-landed vehicle," the captain replied. "I would like to have a closer look at the actuator mechanism controlling the piston. It seems to be unnecessarily sophisticated for the simple job it had to do, but I prefer to keep the structure intact and undisturbed. For that I need Danalta to extrude the specialized limbs and digits that will enable us to examine and disassemble the actuator from inside. I have no wish to be insubordinate, Doctor, but from me you must be feeling intense curiosity rather than hunger."

Prilicla gave a low, trilling sound that did not translate before it said, "Very well, the two of you are excused. Friend Murchison, do you wish to join the mutineers?"

The pathologist shook her head. "I can do no more here," she said. "The coating on the fragments is a synthesized nutrient material suited to the needs of a wide range of warm-blooded oxygen-breathers. There are a number of unidentified organisms present; they may belong to the original contents of the flask or they may be native to Etla, or both. A full analysis isn't possible with this portable equipment, so it will have to wait until we return to the ship, and after lunch."

With its iridescent wings catching the sunlight and seeming to reflect every color in the spectrum, Prilicla rose high above the edge of the ravine to disappear in the direction of the ship, leaving Fletcher and Danalta to complete their investigation and the others to return as they had come.

The empath seemed to be in an awful hurry, Hewlitt thought. It was the first time he had seen the Cinrusskin act in a manner verging on the impolite.

"There are times," Stillman said to Murchison, who was climbing beside him, "when I wish I could fly. Or better still, that I hadn't allowed myself to become so three-dimensional in my old age."

Murchison smiled politely but remained silent until they reached the top; then she said, "Surgeon-Captain Stillman, will you answer a question?"

"You sound very formal and serious, ma'am," the other replied, "which means the question will be the same. I will if I can."

"Thank you," said the pathologist. She took three long, swishing steps through the long grass and went on, "Something very strange must have happened here during the rebellion. I know the accounts and dispatches are not secret, but when I tried to brief myself on the subject I discovered that the Monitor Corps would make them available only to accredited historians and scholars, who, it turned out, were in no hurry to publish.

"The reason given," she went on, "was that the former worlds of the Etlan Empire were being assimilated into the Galactic Federation and it would hamper the process if all the reasons for the rebellion on this world in particular were made available to the merely curious, or worse, to those wishing to abstract the more dramatic incidents to produce shallow and insensitive treatments for the mass-entertainment channels. The natives here, I was told, are still troubled by the war crimes committed against them by their emperor and must not be reminded of them.

"But what exactly were those crimes?" she continued. "Was chemical warfare or biological experimentation on sapient beings among them? It might aid our investigation if we knew. Or are you, too, forbidden to talk?"

Stillman shook his head. "No, ma'am. I can talk to people who will not misuse the information. It will be given on a patient confidentiality basis, because the emperor, and the exclusive families who were the hereditary imperial advisors, were very sick people.

"Have you another question, ma'am?" he added, smiling. "A nice, simple one that will not need a couple of hours and a very nasty slice of history to answer properly?"

Murchison did not reply until they were about to ascend *Rhabwar*'s boarding ramp.

"Yes," she said. "Do you know if Fudge ever went exploring in Hewlitt's ravine?"

Captain Fletcher and Dr. Danalta, whose curiosity regarding the object in the ravine was still outweighing their hunger, were listening on their communicators to Stillman giving his long answer to her first question because they, like Hewlitt, had not been present during the single, epic, and only multiple-ship engagement of the war, the climactic battle for Sector General.

"For political reasons," Stillman was saying as he loosened his kilt's waistband to relieve the pressure on his recently expanded stomach, "the Monitor Corps does not refer to the Etlan conflict as a war. The idea of a fifty-world empire tucked away in a hitherto unexplored galactic sector opening undeclared hostilities on a totally unprepared Federation was, well, destabilizing to say the least, and had to be played down.

"There has been only one interstellar war," he continued, "the one between Earth and Orligia, whose cessation brought about the formation of the Galactic Federation. Since then it has been generally accepted that interstellar warfare for economic or territorial gain is logistically and economically impossible. It costs too much and there are too many uninhabited planets just waiting for colonization. If the belligerent culture or its rulers were sufficiently demented to be motivated by hatred alone rather than the expectation of gain, their victim worlds could simply be detonated or otherwise rendered uninhabitable. But a culture does not develop the technology to get into space, much less to mount successful interstellar colonization projects, without learning the basic lessons of civilization, that is the ability to understand, cooperate, and live together in peace. So it was axiomatic that any new species we discovered that had an interstellar-travel capability had to be highly civilized as well as technically advanced.

"Where the Etlan Empire was concerned," he went on, "the Monitor Corps had to consider the possibility that it was the exception to that rule. But until we were sure, everything possible was done to conceal the locations of the Federation worlds from them while we found out all we could about their culture and at the same time played down the true gravity of the threat. That is why we, as the Federation's executive and law-enforcement arm, prefer to think of it as a large-scale police action. . . ."

"Doctor," said Naydrad, its fur tufting into spikes of irritation, "with hundreds of armed ships dogfighting all around us and non-nuclear torpedoes blowing chunks out of the hospital's outer hull, it felt like a war, not a riot! Were you there?"

"Yes," said Stillman. In the quiet, serious tone of one who is recalling unpleasant memories, he went on, "I was the junior medic on *Vespasian* when she collided with that Etlan transport, and helped move the casualties into the hospital. When Conway, who was the senior surviving medic by that time, saw that I had escaped with only a few bruises, he told me that they were desperately short of staff and put me to work in an other-species ward somewhere. The hospital's translation computer had been knocked out and trying to communicate was . . . Anyway, it might have felt like a war but officially it is recorded as a police operation involving organized and heavily armed lawbreakers."

In the silence that followed, Hewlitt looked from Stillman to Murchison to Prilicla, who were all reacting in characteristic fashion to their memories of a terrible experience they had shared. He felt excluded, but for the first time in his life he was grateful for being an outsider.

Stillman gave an abrupt shake of his head and continued, "The trouble began when one of your ex-patients, a very high-powered entity called Lonvellin, discovered what it called Etla the Sick Planet. . . ."

"I am familiar with the Lonvellin case," Prilicla broke in. "It was the then Senior Physician Conway's patient and I assisted with the emotional radiation readings while it was unconscious. . . . I'm sorry. Friend Stillman, please go on."

Following its discharge from Sector General, Lonvellin had boarded its private starship and resumed the interrupted search for a world, said to be in a hitherto unexplored section of the Lesser Magellanic Cloud, about which it had heard some very disquieting rumors. In spite of its physiological classification of EPLH, its massive body and fearsome natural weaponry, Lonvellin was a highly intelligent, compulsively altruistic, extremely long-lived, and intensely independent being who made it very plain that it did not and probably never would need help from anyone in rectifying any nasty situation it might find because it had been curing ailing planetary cultures for the greater part of its very long life.

It had come as a great surprise to the Monitor Corps when Lonvellin contacted them with the news that it had found the world it had been seeking and asked them for specialized assistance.

Conditions on the world Lonvellin had found were both sociologically complex and medically barbaric. It needed advice in the medical area before it could take effective action against the many social ills afflicting this truly distressed planet. It also asked that beings of physiological classification DBDG, and specifically Earth-human entities, should be sent to act as information gatherers. It explained that the natives were of that classification and were violently hostile to all off-worlders who did not closely resemble themselves, a fact that was seriously hampering Lonvellin's activities.

From the mass of evidence gathered over many months' observation and monitoring of communications channels from orbit, Lonvellin judged the planet, called Etla by the inhabitants, to have been a thriving colony world that had regressed because of the effect of a wide variety of diseases affecting more than sixty-five percent of the population. But the presence of a small and still functioning spaceport meant that Lonvellin's first and usually most difficult problem, that of making the natives trust an alien and perhaps visually horrifying being who had dropped out of their sky, should have been simplified, because the inhabitants were already used to the idea of off-planet visitors.

Lonvellin's intention had been to play the role of a not very bright off-worlder who had been forced to land in order to make repairs to its ship. For this it would require various odd and completely worthless pieces of metal or plastic, and it would pretend great difficulty in making the Etlans understand what it needed. But for this worthless material it would exchange artifacts of great value, and soon the more enterprising inhabitants would begin to take advantage of the situation.

At that stage Lonvellin did not mind being exploited, because the situation was going to change. Rather than give items of value, it would offer to perform even more valuable services, including that of a teacher. Then it would tell them that it considered its ship to be beyond the technical resources of Etla to repair, and as had happened on many previous occasions, gradually it would be accepted as a permanent resident. After that it would have been just a matter of time before it was able to begin changing the Etlan situation for the better, and time was something with which Lonvellin was well supplied.

"To an immensely long-lived and highly intelligent being like Lonvellin," Stillman went on, "it was all an elaborate and intricate game that it had played successfully many times in its past. It was a good game in that the populations of the worlds concerned benefited as well as rewarding the player with the satisfaction of a job well done. But this time Lonvellin's game went disastrously wrong. From the moment it landed on the outskirts of a small town and revealed itself, it was kept too busy with the ship's defenses to begin to play . . ."

Unable to proceed without discovering why a race with experience of space travel should be so violently xenophobic, and not being in a position to ask questions itself, Lonvellin had called for Earth-human assistance. Because of the incredibly high incidence of disease among the population, it had also asked that the senior physician who had been in charge of its case at Sector General advise and assist as well. Shortly afterward, cultural-contact specialists of the Monitor Corps accompanied by Conway had arrived, sized up the situation for themselves, and gone in.

The Etlans were contacted simultaneously at two levels. The first was by a few trained linguists and medics who were landed covertly and concealed their translators under native dress, no other disguise being necessary because the physiological resemblance was so close. Problems with accent and pronunciation were disguised by the pretense of having a speech impediment, it being difficult to identify an accent when the speaker had a stutter or a disease affecting the mouth and tongue, a medical condition that was very common on Etla.

On the second level, a large Monitor vessel landed openly at the spaceport; the Corpsmen admitted their off-world origin and conversed normally by translator. Their story was that they had heard of the plight of the native population and had come to give what medical assistance they could. The Etlans accepted this story, revealing the fact that every ten years an imperial vessel was sent to them loaded with the newest drugs and with healers on board familiar with their use, but in spite of this their medical condition continued to deteriorate. The strangers were welcome to do what they could, but the impression given was that if the medical efforts of an empire covering nearly fifty worlds was powerless to help them then the Monitor Corps was wasting its time.

The majority of Etlans were friendly, trusting people who talked freely about themselves and their empire. The Corps' contactors were also friendly, but more reticent.

When the subject of the strange and frightful entity called Lonvellin came up, the Corps pretended complete ignorance and their opinions about it leaned heavily toward the middle of the road.

But the really important information had come from the covert investigators. They discovered that the natives were terrified of Lonvellin because they had been taught that all extraterrestrials were disease carriers. The first medical lesson that all star-traveling cultures learned, that pathogens evolved on one planet could not affect the beings of another, had been withheld from them.

Deliberately.

"At least their intense and continuing fear of contracting new infections was understandable," Stillman continued, "because Etla was a very sick planet. It was a seventh-generation colony world, widely settled but not heavily populated, that had been dogged with ill health for more than a century. At the time an incredible sixty-five percent of its men, women, and children were affected by a wide variety of diseases, most of which were accompanied by a large degree of physical disablement. Very few of the conditions were life-threatening but a high proportion were disfiguring. Many of the contagious diseases would have responded to isolation and simple medical treatment, but their medical science was primitive and there were no research facilities because the empire did all their medical thinking for them.

"The situation was driving us out of our medical minds," he went on, "because so far as we could see all of the conditions we had seen were curable. If we could have declared the planet a disaster area and moved in massive medical support, the problem would have been solved within a few years at most. But we had a delicate first-contact situation on our hands: the people were proud and independent and, at that time, still loyal and grateful to their emperor on Imperial Etla and to the people of all the other worlds called Etla that made up the empire for their continuing support. The arrival of massive medical aid from strangers would have been demeaning to them and might even have been mistaken by the on-planet imperial representative, who so far had avoided contact with the Monitor Corps, and the large military establishment he maintained, as a hostile invasion from space. . . ."

In order to reassure the Etlan authorities regarding Federation intentions, and to discover why the medical aid sent to their ailing colony world was so small and infrequent, a Monitor vessel with a senior medical officer on board was sent to Imperial Etla. It was possible that distance had diminished the urgency of the plight of their sick brothers, but when the unarmed courier vessel signaled its approach and landed openly at the planetary capital's spaceport, it was immediately surrounded by elements of the imperial guard.

The reason given for this apparently unfriendly act was that a xenophobic reaction could be expected from the less intelligent among the local population and the security of the visitors was of paramount importance. This was also why the ship's crew, with the exception of their medical officer, should remain on board and make no attempt to communicate with anyone until the authorities had prepared the psychological ground.

Their medic was given the warmest of welcomes by the imperial advisors and interrogated in a manner both thorough and friendly about all aspects of the Federation while at the same time being accorded the honors normally reserved for a visiting head of state. Meanwhile the sensors on the courier vessel were uncovering some very disquieting information regarding what the broadcast media was referring to openly as the Plague Planet as well as obvious—obvious, that was, to the Corps' political analyst on board—deficiencies in the administration and financial structure of the Etlan Empire.

Their first discovery was that the Plague Planet was out of sight but most definitely not out of mind. On every street intersection and at frequent intervals along the intercity roads there were display boards advertising the plight of their desperately ill brothers on Etla the Sick in graphic and often horrifying detail, all pleading for contributions for the relief of their suffering. Every one of the vision channels ran supporting stories at frequent intervals, and the appeal was invariably mentioned by candidates seeking political office. It was the most promoted and popular charity, not only on Imperial Etla but on every other planet of the empire, and the contributions were continuous and generous.

It was impossible to believe that the donations funded the dispatch of only one aid ship every ten years.

They already knew that the ship arrived, unloaded, and left without delay, because none of the crew would stay a moment longer than necessary on that planetary pesthole. The cargo was transferred to Imperial Representative Teltrenn's estate, a large, parklike tract of land surrounding a palace and barracks whose perimeter was guarded by a heavily armed, elite force. The reason given for the military presence among the unarmed colonists, who were required to supply them with food and low-ranking support personnel, was that they were there to guard against a possible off-world invasion. At intervals of a few months, there seemed to be no great urgency about the process, Teltrenn traveled to distant parts of the colony world to distribute the new medication, information on its administration, and news of the continuing research being done on Imperial Etla.

It would have been faster and more efficient to supply the colonist medics with the new material and instructions simultaneously, but Teltrenn insisted on bringing it to them in person so that he could pass on the personal sympathy as well as the good wishes of their emperor.

This lack of urgency aroused the suspicions of Conway and the other Corps medics, who analyzed the various plague vectors going back over several decades. They found that many of the earlier diseases were disappearing, probably because the sufferers and their families were developing a natural resistance to them. But invariably a new disease appeared to replace the old, usually one involving visually horrifying skin eruptions, multiple limb deformities, or uncontrollable palsies that were, against all the laws of medical probability, rarely fatal.

All of the evidence pointed to the incredible and horrifying conclusion that the much loved and respected Imperial Representative Teltrenn was deliberately and systematically spreading diseases, not trying to cure them, and that the reason was financial.

CHAPTER 21

Even the pennies donated by a poor but sympathetic population in response to a local disaster appeal could amount to a significant total, and the Etlans were a generous and caring people who were constantly being reminded of the dreadful plight of their brothers on Etla the Sick. Those continuing contributions from the population of fifty inhabited worlds were vast beyond belief, and with a single relief ship being dispatched every decade, it was obvious that only a tiny fraction of the total donations was going to the people for whom it was intended. Instead it was being treated as a covert form of taxation and diverted into the imperial treasury for the benefit of the emperor and the proliferating families and personal armies of his hereditary representatives.

This was not a situation that the Federation could tolerate, and when direct questions regarding the misappropriation of the funds were asked, on Etla the Sick and on

Imperial Etla, Teltrenn and his emperor panicked. Missiles with chemical warheads—plainly they wanted to avoid the destruction of their spaceports by using nuclear devices—were directed at the Monitor vessels, which deployed their meteorite shields and escaped.

The medic who had been visiting Imperial Etla was never heard from again.

On the Plague Planet there was enough advance warning from the ship on Imperial Etla for the Monitor Corps personnel to be withdrawn safely before Lonvellin, who insisted that it was safe inside its ship's screens, died in a nuclear fireball.

The emperor could not allow the truth of what he was doing to be known by the imperial citizens, so he blamed the Federation for what had happened on Etla the Sick, accusing it of the crimes he himself had been committing for over a century. He said that while the Monitor Corps personnel they had seen resembled human beings like themselves, he had discovered from one of them that the majority of their Galactic Federation was composed of visually horrifying, depraved, and sadistic monsters rendered even more terrible because of their high intelligence. For the first time in its long history the very existence of the Etlan Empire was being threatened from space, and their only defense was an all-out offensive war. The imperial propagandists and the xenophobia instilled into them from earliest childhood did the rest, and a vast, crusading war fleet was assembled.

"But we are neither stupid nor completely trusting when meeting strangers," Stillman went on. "We do not tell them where we live until we are sure that they will be friendly visitors. On both Imperial Etla and here nobody with knowledge of the coordinates of Federation worlds was allowed to meet an Etlan. That is standard first-contact procedure. But one set of coordinates is known to every spacegoing medical officer in the Corps, those for Sector General, and the imperial advisors had a Corps medic in their hands.

"That was why the Etlan war fleet attacked the hospital," he continued, "to capture rather than destroy it in the hope of finding more addresses. That information had to be concealed for as long as possible, which was the reason why Sector General's patients and all of the medical and maintenance staff with any knowledge of astrogation had been evacuated, leaving only a few hundred volunteers on duty. . . ."

An unforeseen result of the staff shortage was that the battle casualties from both sides were treated in the hospital, it being impossible to tell the difference between Earth-human and Etlan wounded, and the medics refused to make the distinction anyway. The casualties overflowed the wards and corridors not blasted open to space, so that patients who had been enemies found themselves recovering in adjacent beds with, in the Etlan case, visually horrifying monsters caring for them. The opposing sets of patients continued fighting with the only weapons left to them: words. It was a bitter, bloodless battle in which the Etlans learned the truth about what was happening on their Plague Planet. The end result was that the two highest-ranking patients, each representing one side, brought the external hostilities to an end.

The Etlan war fleet re-formed and left to visit every world in the empire to spread newly discovered truth and to offer their help in removing the emperor, his hereditary representatives, and the private armies they maintained.

"It was the biggest and most widespread rebellion in known history," Stillman went on, "but the Etlans were proud as well as angry. They told us that it was a family fight and to stay away from all of the worlds called Etla, with one exception, until they had settled the matter for themselves. And it was here, in this area, that the war on Etla the Sick began and ended. It began when Teltrenn launched a nuclear missile at Lonvellin's ship; there is a crater marking the spot about ten miles to the west. The end came when the inhabitants, supported by the locally recruited personnel who had captured some armored vehicles, fought the climactic battle that led to the surrender of Teltrenn's army. But the natives are still a little ashamed about what they did, even though they had every reason to do it. That was why Shech-Rar didn't want you blundering around on a nonspecified investigation and in your ignorance trampling on some very sensitive feelings."

He looked at one of Prilicla's delicate limbs, which was hanging within a few inches of his head, and added, "I don't think the colonel has anything to worry about."

"Thank you, friend Stillman," said the empath.

The monitor officer gave a long, satisfied sigh and went on, "Before he left Sector General, the Etlan fleet commander, who had firsthand experience of Federation medical science as practiced in Sector General, asked us to please return to Etla the Sick and complete the work interrupted by the war. We did that and, as you have seen for yourselves, the xenophobia has disappeared along with all the other diseases imported by the late emperor. This is no longer a sick planet."

There was a long silence that was broken by Murchison, who said, "I like happy endings, too, and I don't want to spoil yours. But how sure are you that this place is clean? I know cross-species infection is supposed to be impossible, but with the large number of artificially created diseases that were released here, could one of them have evolved or mutated to the stage where it was able to cross the species barrier? Or let us suppose that Teltrenn, feeling angry and frightened and spiteful, launched a biological weapon against his formerly loyal and docile charges. There was a malfunction and the weapon did no harm except possibly to infect the Hewlitt child. . . ."

She was interrupted by the humming silence of a speaker that is active but not yet in use. There was the sound of an Earth-human throat being cleared followed by the voice of Captain Fletcher.

"Doctors," he said, "I have completed the examination of your chemical weapon and I think you are all on the wrong track. The missile has many of the characteristics of a biological weapon, but our reconstruction of the course elements programmed into the guidance system, which was damaged by close proximity to a nuclear detonation, indicates that the original target was sixty miles northwest of here, which is a deserted, mountainous, and heavily wooded area that would not normally be settled for a very long time. Surely an odd place to target a biological weapon. As well, the missile is not a product of Etlan technology. It is a modified Federation device.

"There is more," he went on, anticipating the questions they were about to ask. "The payload was enclosed in a thin-walled, plastic container that was strong enough to withstand the shock of a parachute landing, but not the impact and continuing pressure of a heavy object. Pathologist Murchison has already reported that the inner surface of the container fragments was coated with nutrient, and my investigation of the shape, size, and placement of the pieces indicates an impact by a large body, soft rather than hard-edged like a rock or other solid debris, that is consistent with the mass of a small child falling from a tall tree and dropping onto it."

They were all staring at the wall speaker in complete silence, and the only movement on the casualty deck came from Naydrad's fur. Fletcher cleared his throat again and went on, "Another interesting datum is that the actuator mechanism that should have opened the payload container is a very precise atomic clock set for a little over one hundred years."

Hewlitt did not understand the implications of everything the captain had been saying, but one thing was clear. After a lifetime of being treated in error as an overimaginative hypochondriac, it was impossible for him to keep quiet.

"Now you have to believe me," he said, and laughed. "I don't know why I'm laughing about it, but I did catch something here when I was a child and nobody would . . ."

He broke off because Prilicla had dropped to the deck again, its wings and body trembling, and Murchison was directing accusing looks at everyone in turn. Hewlitt had already noticed that she often went into what Naydrad called maternal mode when someone's unguarded emotional radiation was upsetting her superior.

"Whoever is responsible for this," she burst out, "control your feelings, dammit!"

Prilicla's trembling subsided, but not entirely. It said, "Calm yourself, friend Murchison, the loss of emotional control is my own. I was thinking about Lonvellin, and friend Hewlitt's loose tooth, and feeling very, very stupid. But now, hopefully, I am recovering the use of my mind. Friend Fletcher."

"Doctor," said the captain.

"We must return to Sector General at once," it went on. "Power Room, prepare to lift off as soon as the captain and Danalta are back on board. Communications, notify the hospital of the presence of a possible cross-species infection involving a wide range of nonspecific allergic reactions and originating with Patients Hewlitt and Morredeth, who are required for further clinical examination. Advise that all medical staff or patients who had physical contact with the named patients are to quarantine themselves in lightweight environmental-protection envelopes, which they will wear at all times when on duty or they themselves are under treatment. If minor injury or work-stress-related discomfort occurs among these staff members, such as headaches or muscular fatigue, they must not self-administer or be given sedative or painkilling medication. Patients under treatment are not to be given new medication of any type or in any form. Further instructions will follow when Patient Hewlitt's test results are available.

"Dr. Stillman," the empath went on, "while you were still on the way back from the ravine I prepared a tape for you, edited to remove the sections that were not relevant to the mission, of the Meeting of Diagnosticians which took place before we left the hospital. It will answer many of the questions we have been avoiding until now. Colonel Shech-Rar and yourself may take whatever action is appropriate in the light of this information. But as nobody else, to your knowledge, has displayed the nonspecific Hewlitt symptoms after a time lapse of twenty-odd years, the risk to you is small. For the present we have nothing more to do on Etla and must leave without delay.

"Friend Naydrad," it continued. "We have a four-day hyperjump to Sector General. That should give us enough time for a full-scale clinical investigation and test of responses to the complete range of DBDG medication currently in use, including types already used on Patient Hewlitt but discontinued because of the allergic reactions. In case there is an emergency, set up for continuous level-three monitoring. . . ."

"But I don't understand," said Stillman, raising his voice above the sounds of a ship preparing for imminent departure. "Lonvellin died. Its ship was vaporized with it inside before Hewlitt was even born."

"Unless you wish to make an unscheduled visit to Sector General, friend Stillman," said Prilicla as the sound of Fletcher and Danalta climbing the boarding ramp reached them, "you must leave the ship at once. There is no time to explain now, but I shall send copies of our findings to the colonel and yourself in due course. Please excuse my bad manners, thank you for your cooperation, and good-bye."

Hewlitt waited until the Monitor Corps officer disappeared through the personnel lock, and then he said, "I don't understand what the hell is going on, either. Why do you want to test me with medication you know has nearly killed me in the past?"

"Compose yourself, friend Hewlitt," said Prilicla, beginning to tremble again. "I do not believe that you will be at serious risk. Please return to your bed and remain there until I give you permission to leave it. Your hush field will be maintained while we are discussing ideas and procedures that you might find unsettling."

CHAPTER 22

Hewlitt kept his eyes on the flickering, grey noncolor of hyperspace outside the direct-vision panel and waited for something calamitous to happen to him. He did not look at any of the others, because they were watching him, waiting for the same thing to occur while smiling or otherwise trying to radiate encouragement. The amount of monitoring equipment surrounding him and the number of sensors taped to his body were not encouraging.

"You told me that I was to be given no medication of any kind," Hewlitt said as Murchison touched another hyposprayer to his upper arm and the unfelt dose was administered. "Now you seem to be trying me on everything in stock. *Why,* dammit?"

The pathologist watched him closely for about three minutes, then said, "We changed our mind. How do you feel?"

"All right," he replied. "No change except that I feel a little drowsy. How am I supposed to feel?"

"All right, and a little drowsy," said Murchison, smiling. "It was a mild sedative I gave you. It should help you to relax."

"When Senior Physician Medalont tried to give me a sedative," said Hewlitt, "you know what happened."

"Yes," said Murchison. "But we have tested you with that particular medication, and a few others in minute quantities, without any sign of your customary hyperallergic reaction. I'm trying another, a new one that was not available to your planetside doctors. What do you feel, now?"

Hewlitt felt the downdraft from Prilicla's wings against his face and chest as the little empath flew closer, but he knew that particular sensation was of no interest to the pathologist.

"Still nothing," he replied, then, "No, wait. The whole area is going numb. What's happening?"

"Nothing you need worry about," said the pathologist, smiling again. "This time I'm testing a local anesthetic. According to the monitor your life signs are optimum. But are there any other symptoms, a mild itching of the skin, a general feeling of unease or any other symptoms, possibly subjective, which could be your subconscious giving an early warning of trouble to come?"

"No," said Hewlitt.

Prilicla made a soft trilling sound that did not translate, then said, "The patient is being polite while trying to control intense feelings of curiosity, concern, confusion, and irritation. Perhaps the relief of the first would reduce the intensity of the other three. You have questions, friend Hewlitt. I can answer some of them now."

But not all of them, Hewlitt thought. He was surprised when Murchison spoke first.

"You know that we all have questions, sir," she said, looking from Danalta to Naydrad and back to Prilicla. "Why all the fuss over an ex-patient who died a quarter of a century ago? What was the reason for that signal calling for precautions against cross-species infection when we know it is impossible anyway? Why the sudden return to Sector General and the battery of tests ordered for Patient Hewlitt?"

"Those," said Hewlitt, "would have been my questions as well."

Prilicla drifted to the deck, perhaps in preparation for a surge of emotional radiation that would make it difficult to fly, and said, "There are similarities, specifically in the manner of the early negative response and subsequent acceptance of medical treatment, in the cases of Patients Lonvellin and Hewlitt. There is a possibility that I am wrong and the similarities are coincidental, but either way I must know before we reach the hospital. Friend Hewlitt is available for investigation but, regrettably, Lonvellin is not."

Murchison shook her head. "Maybe not in person," she said. "But if you need a close comparison, why not call up its case history from Records?"

"Lonvellin's records were wiped during the Etlan bombardment," Prilicla said, "when the main computer was knocked out along with the entire other-species translator system . . ."

"I remember that," said Murchison in a voice that suggested that it was not a pleasant memory, "but I remember nothing about a patient called Lonvellin."

". . . so that the only records of the case remaining to us," it went on, "are held in the fading memories of Diagnosticians Conway and Thornnastor and myself, who were the people directly concerned with the patient's treatment. Since it was discharged cured and its subsequent death was in no way due to our treatment, no effort was made to replace the case history from our recollections. Do not blame yourself for not remembering Patient Lonvellin. At the time you were a final-year trainee, not yet specialized in other-species pathology, and still to become the then Senior Physician Conway's life-mate, although I remember that your emotional radiation when your duties brought the two of you together was quite . . ."

"Doctor," said Murchison, "surely our emotional radiation in that situation was privileged."

"Hardly," said Prilicla, "since your emotional involvement at the time was common knowledge to everyone in the hospital. Besides, every Earth-human male DBDG on the staff produced similar emotional radiation in your presence, although the feelings were diluted by envy when the two of you were formally mated. While you were alone together I should have thought it unlikely that you would have spent your time in detailed clinical discussions of your current patients."

"You are right," said Murchison. The softness in her voice suggested that her mind was distant in time and space and that the place was a very pleasant one.

Prilicla allowed a moment for her to return to the here and now before going on. "This is the same information I taped for Shech-Rar and friend Stillman, and you may scan the original record at any time. But the proceedings of a Meeting of Diagnosticians might be difficult for a layperson to comprehend, so I will summarize and simplify it for friend Hewlitt's benefit. . . ."

Lonvellin had been discovered alone and unconscious inside an undamaged ship following the release of its distress beacon. Originally it was thought that the being was a criminal guilty of murder and possibly cannibalism, because the translation of the ship's log indicated the presence on board of another entity, a personal medic of some kind who had apparently been guilty of mistreating its employer and of whom there had been no physical trace. For this reason, and because the patient was a physically massive being who was well armed with natural weapons, it had been admitted and treated under Monitor Corps guard until the truth became known.

Lonvellin had been a warm-blooded oxygen-breather of physiological classification EPLH. Its cranium was protected by an immobile, osseous dome, pierced at regular intervals for visual, aural, and olfactory sensors, set atop a pear-shaped, scaly body possessing five shoulder-level tentacles, four of which terminated in clusters of specialized digits and the other in a heavy, osseous club with which it had, presumably, battered its way to the top of its evolutionary tree. Its method of locomotion was snail-like, but not slow, using a wide apron of muscle around the lower body.

The EPLH presented what appeared to be a widespread and well-developed epithelioma covering the entire body, although a cancerous skin condition of that type did not normally render a patient deeply unconscious. A fast-acting specific suited to the patient's metabolism was administered subdermally and the early results were good. But within a few minutes the patient became physically disturbed and somehow managed to neutralize the effect of the medication so that the area under treatment returned to its previous condition. During this episode the biosensors reported that the patient had remained deeply unconscious, anesthetized and supposedly incapable of all physical movement. Since the indicated medication was ineffective, the surgical removal of the affected scales was begun but this, too, was resisted. Following the excision of the first few scales, the remainder grew deep root systems which penetrated underlying organs so that their removal was impossible without the risk of inflicting life-threatening damage.

In the hope of finding an explanation for this clinically inexplicable situation, including the fact that it reacted physically while supposedly unconscious and incapable of movement, Conway requested an examination of the patient's emotional radiation.

"That was where I came in," Prilicla went on. "We discovered that there was another thinking entity inside Lonvellin, a separate and distinct and fully conscious person who was not being affected by the medication given to the patient and whose presence did not register on their diagnostic instrumentation. Friend Conway, making one of the intuitive leaps that are the mark of future diagnosticians, said that the reason might be that it was both all-pervasive and too small for normal scanner detection. It had formulated a hypothesis based on what little was known or deduced from the examination of the patient, the references to a personal physician in the ship's log, and the psychological and behavior patterns that were common to the very aged. . . ."

Lonvellin was an aging member of an extremely long-lived species. In common with all beings of advanced age it was subject to increasing physiological deterioration in spite of its efforts to maintain itself in optimum physical and mental condition so that it could continue with the planetwide sociological projects which had become its only interest and reason for living. It would have foreseen the time when it would require the services of a skilled medic on a continuous basis, and that quality of medical assistance was unlikely to be available on the type of backward world where Lonvellin was accustomed to doing its work of healing sick planetary cultures.

But somewhere in the recent past—recent because the creature was new to the job and had made mistakes— Lonvellin discovered and Conway had deduced the presence of the ultimate healer.

It was nothing less than an intelligent, organized collection of viruses living within its host and maintaining the body it occupied in perfect health while protecting it against invading pathogens as well as stimulating and directing the natural mechanisms of healing to repair physical injury. But it was a thinking creature inside a body that was deeply unconscious and therefore incapable of thought, and its emotional radiation could not be hidden from an empath like Prilicla. Conway tested his theory by mounting a crude, physical attack on Lonvellin that its natural defenses could not cope with, a spike driven very slowly into the body where there was an underlying vital organ. This tricked the virus creature into collecting itself under the puncture to defend the area with a small, dense, organic plate composed of its own and a small amount of Lonvellin's body material.

As soon as the process was complete, Conway excised the creature, discovering that its body mass was little more than that of an Earth-human's closed fist, and placed it in a sealed container for later investigation. The patient's epithelioma and the newly inflicted surgical wound were treated routinely without any further interference from Lonvellin's resident physician.

The original problem had been caused by the ignorance of the virus creature, who had been attempting to maintain the host's physical condition by retaining the dying body scales, which, in Lonvellin's species, were shed periodically so that new ones could grow. The mistake could be excused by the fact that, in spite of the intelligence of both entities, there was no direct communication between host and symbiote, merely a weak, empathic bond which allowed the transmission of feelings rather than thought.

In spite of the mistake, Lonvellin forgave its personal physician and insisted on having it returned to its former place. Sector General would dearly have loved to investigate this unique life-form, but ethically the virus creature fell into a grey area between sapient being and disease, so the hospital acquiesced. Lonvellin and its resident physician moved to Etla the Sick, where it and its ship were vaporized. At the time everyone was sure that the virus entity had perished with its patient. That was the state of knowledge when the Meeting of Diagnosticians sent *Rhabwar* to Etla in the hope of finding an explanation for the Hewlitt-Morredeth incidents. They did not expect the medical team to succeed.

"But now we know that Lonvellin foresaw the possibility of a lethal attack," Prilicla went on, "and made preparations that would enable its intelligent symbiote to survive. There was limited communication between the two, but I should think that the warning of an imminent nuclear strike furnished by the ship's sensors, and the terrible knowledge that its immensely long life was about to end, was enough of an emotional shock to drive the virus creature out of its host's body and into the survival container carried by the escape vehicle. The container was fitted with a time-release delay of one hundred standard years in the hope that, when the contents were released, both the war and the population's xenophobia would have been long forgotten. But the nuclear strike must have occurred seconds after launch, the escape vehicle was damaged, and the virus creature was released prematurely by an Earth-human child falling out of a tree and smashing the container."

"So that's what happened to me," said Hewlitt. Sheer relief that an explanation, no matter how incredible, had been found for his lifetime of apparent hypochondria made him laugh out loud. "Are you telling me that it wasn't a disease that ailed me, it was a bloody *doctor?*"

CHAPTER 23

I was fairly sure that is what happened to you," Prilicla replied, "when I made the connection between the incident of your childhood teeth and Lonvellin's scales, which also grew rootlets and refused to come loose. If we now accept that everything you have told us was true, let us fit the facts to our new theory. Consider.

"When you climbed that tree, ate the toxic fruit, and fell into the ravine," Prilicla said, "you should have died. Probably as the result of trauma associated with a fall from that height, and certainly from the quantity of poison you ingested. Instead, the virus creature's survival pod was ruptured and it invaded your damaged body. Discovering that you were a suitable host who was terminating, it sustained you while it repaired the physical damage and stimulated the natural detoxification mechanism of your body to neutralize the poison. It was able to do so quickly, I assume, because at the time your body mass was about one-twentieth that of its previous host. How and why this was done we cannot know until we devise a method of communication more precise than empathy.

"My own feeling," it continued, "is that the virus entity cannot exist for long on its own, that its continued survival depends on it occupying the largest and potentially the most long-lived creature it can find and, by abstracting the necessary data from the genetic cell material, extending both their lifetimes by maintaining the host in optimum physical health. But the creature is not infallible. It did not realize that there are times when a host body should not be maintained without change because some of the changes are normal and healthy. Lonvellin's problem with the aging scales it could not discard and your teeth that refused to loosen, plus your long history of allergic reactions to all forms of medication, are proof of this.

"But there is also evidence that the virus creature is under the partial control of its host," said Prilicla, and paused.

For a moment Hewlitt thought that it might be a pause to allow one of the others to comment, but there was no response. He wondered whether the empath was taking time to choose the right words or simply needed to rest its speaking organ.

"For example," Prilicla resumed, "there is the incident with the injured cat. You had a strong, emotional attachment to this entity, so much so that you took it to bed with you in the childish hope of nursing it back to health. So intense was your need to make it well again that the feeling caused the virus creature to invade the kitten, repair the multiple trauma, and restore it overnight to full health before returning to what it must have known was a more long-lived host.

"And many years later," it continued, "when you became friendly with Patient Morredeth and were affected by the distress it was suffering and would continue to suffer for the rest of its life because of its damaged fur, you made close physical contact with it and the same thing happened."

"But I wasn't expecting anything to happen," Hewlitt protested. "It was accidental—I just pushed my hands against its fur."

"Even though the injury was not life-threatening," Prilicla went on, "Morredeth was restored to nominal physical condition, its disfigurement cured as completely and thoroughly as were the injuries to your cat. Unlike the case of your household pet, the virus creature did not return to your body after completing its work. Why not?"

Hewlitt took the question to be rhetorical and remained silent, as did the others.

"It is natural for any organism to evolve," Prilicla went on, "and for one with intelligence to learn and seek new experience. I feel sure now that Lonvellin's former personal physician has evolved over the past quarter of a century. Perhaps the change came about as the result of proximity to a nuclear detonation, although normally that would inhibit organic growth, or it could be a normal process of evolution, whatever that may be in a collection of viruses. Either way there is evidence of increasing sensitivity both to empathic direction and reaction to external events. It was only three child-teeth that refused to loosen. Subsequent teeth behaved normally, and many of the later conditions were temporary and did not recur. This caused your symptoms to be attributed, wrongly as we now know, to an overactive imagination. Quite rightly, none of your medics on Earth or in Ward Seven would risk readministering medication that had already produced an allergic reaction. If they had, and your symbiote had learned enough about your metabolism by then to realize that the foreign material was harmless, your response to a second dose might have been normal.

"The behavior of the virus creature during your stay in

Sector General shows a distinct change," the empath continued. "Unlike the creature I remember, whose emotional radiation was composed primarily of fear and anxiety to return to Lonvellin as quickly as possible, it now seems more willing to transfer to other bodies. Perhaps it is no longer satisfied with you as a host."

"In the circumstances," said Hewlitt dryly, "I feel grateful rather than offended."

Prilicla ignored the interruption and went on, "It may be that, after a quarter of a century of occupancy, the virus creature was growing bored with the DBDG life-form and wanted to find one that was more interesting, and Sector General was the ideal place to find interesting life-forms. But I prefer to think that, for its own continued long-term survival, it needed to seek out one with an extended life span like that of its former host, Lonvellin. That is why it vacated a short-lived, nonsapient life-form like your cat and returned to you as soon as its work was done. It did not return to you, or perhaps in the ensuing confusion it did not have the opportunity to return, after it entered Morredeth and regrew the Kelgian's fur. But neither did it remain with Morredeth. I know this because it was not in occupancy when I scanned Morredeth before leaving the hospital. The past four days of testing and my monitoring of your emotional radiation since you joined *Rhabwar* show that it is not in you. Nor was it in your aged, onetime pet.

"The most serious and urgent question facing us now," it ended, "is who it is occupying at present and what is it going to do next?"

Hewlitt was still feeling relieved and happy that he was free of the creature at last, but there was a nagging doubt in his mind about his good fortune. Everyone was watching him. Danalta had no expression that anyone could read, Murchison's smile had stopped short of her eyes, Naydrad's fur was being pulled into small, tight ripples, and Prilicla had been trembling since it had begun talking. He felt the need of further reassurance.

"Is it possible," he said, "that the virus learned how to hide its emotions from you?"

"No, friend Hewlitt," the empath replied without hesitation. "Whether or not an organic entity is sapient it has feelings, and often the smallest and least intelligent beings have the strongest and most disturbing emotions. I remember that the feelings of Lonvellin's personal physician were characteristic of a highly intelligent mind. No thinking and, therefore, feeling entity can hide its emotional radiation from me. Only a nonorganic computer could do that, because it doesn't have any.

"Try not to worry, friend Hewlitt," it went on. "In the past it made unintentional mistakes, but otherwise it maintained and left Lonvellin, your pet, and yourself a legacy of perfect health. The cat, who is extremely aged for one of its short-lived species, is proof of that. I would say that, barring accidents, you also will have a proportionately long and healthy life."

"Thank you, Doctor," said Hewlitt, and laughed. "But am I missing something? Why is the creature a serious and urgent problem when you said yourself that it means no harm and is doing good work? So you have another weird, other-species doctor loose in the hospital. What else is new?"

Murchison did not smile, Danalta's body wobbled, and Naydrad's fur twitched into even stranger patterns, and it was clear that Prilicla was not appreciating his attempt at humor either.

"The virus creature does not intend to do harm," it said. "But then, it was not trying to harm you when its good intentions resulted in twenty years of clinical confusion and psychological distress. At present it seems anxious to experiment by changing hosts as often as possible, and the unintentional harm and confusion it could cause in a multi-environment hospital, where there is a choice of sixty-odd different species among the patients and staff, doesn't bear thinking about."

For an instant Hewlitt felt the twisting sensation of an emergence from hyperspace. The direct-vision panel was showing the starry blackness of normal space and the blazing, multicolored lights of Sector General, which made the hospital look enormous even at Jump distance. Only he seemed to be looking at it.

"Our first priority is to find, isolate, and withdraw the creature from its current host," said Prilicla, speaking to the others. "Then we must learn to talk to an entity who has no direct channels of communication other than the feelings it receives and radiates. Somehow we must devise a means of two-way communication so that we can reassure it, and obtain its permission for an extended, clinical investigation, before asking questions about its evolutionary background, physiology, physical and psychological needs, and, most important of all, its method and frequency of reproduction. If all goes well, and we can only hope that it does, we must decide whether or not it or its offspring can be allowed any more hosts.

"I should explain that the personal physician of Lonvellin, Morredeth, and yourself," Prilicla went on for Hewlitt's benefit, "could render all other physicians redundant. It is the only known specimen of a truly unique life-form, and if the species can reproduce itself in sufficient numbers and be active among other species without harmful side effects, medicine throughout the Galactic Federation will be reduced to the practice of accident and emergency surgical procedures."

They were all looking at the empath so intently that the accompanying emotional radiation had forced it to land again. Hewlitt was at a loss to understand it. Surely the things the empath had been saying were good and exciting news for any truly dedicated member of the medical profession. Why did he have the distinct impression that Prilicla was trying to reassure the others as much as itself, and it had failed? Hewlitt was the first to break the silence.

"I'm sorry if you still have problems," he said, "and I don't want to appear selfish, but I have more questions. If the virus creature has left me, and your tests have shown that I am no longer allergic to medication, does that mean that I'm cured of the other problems, too? And does it mean that when I return to Earth I won't have to, well, avoid female company or . . ."

"That is exactly what it means," Murchison broke in, "when you return home."

Hewlitt gave a long, satisfied sigh. He wanted to tell these people how grateful he was for all they had done for him. Even though they had not believed him at first, they had not given up on his case as all the Earthside medics had done. But the right words would not come and all he could say was "So my troubles are over."

"Your troubles," said Naydrad, "are just beginning."

"There speaks a true misogynist . . ." Hewlitt began, when there was an interruption from the wall speaker.

"Dr. Prilicla, the hospital is transmitting a recorded message with an Emergency Three coding on all non-Service frequencies. It says that all incoming ships with noncritical casualties on board should divert to the nearest same-species hospital. Only urgent cases which have obtained diagnostician clearance are to be admitted until further notice. Incoming transport and supply vessels are requested to position themselves beyond the inner beacons and prepare for a possible mass evacuation of all patients and staff. They say it is a power-generation problem and Maintenance is dealing with it.

"I'm trying to raise someone who knows what the hell is going on. . . ."

CHAPTER 24

Hewlitt returned to Sector General, but not as a patient and not to Ward Seven. Instead he had been assigned Earth-human DBDG single accommodation. Since patients like himself were not allowed to bring many personal possessions with them, the place was bare but comfortable. He was issued with a set of medic's coveralls which, with the addition of a helmet and surgical gauntlets, doubled as a lightweight environmental protection suit. All direct physical contact with other people was forbidden, but the helmet was allowed to remain open because the intelligent virus was not transmissible by air. He was told not to go exploring within the hospital unless accompanied by one of *Rhabwar*'s medical team or a member of the Psychology Department. In the event, he was accompanied and questioned so much during the first three days that the compartment was used only for sleeping.

With great reluctance he had agreed to remain in the hospital, it being very difficult not to agree when Prilicla asked a favor, in the hope that he would be able to help find the virus creature's current host. Counting all the patients and staff, there were more than ten thousand places for it to hide. When he told the other that his contribution would be negligible and he would rather go home, Prilicla had changed the subject.

Early on the fourth day, Braithwaite called to take him to what the lieutenant thought would probably be a lack-of-progress meeting in the chief psychologist's office. As soon as they arrived it was clear that everyone had been waiting for them.

"Mr. Hewlitt, I am Diagnostician Conway," said a tall Earth-human whose features were shaded by his helmet. "For your benefit I shall outline the situation as simply as possible while hoping that you won't be offended by the simplification. Please listen carefully and feel free to interrupt if you think it necessary.

"In order to avoid unnecessary speculation and consequent mental distress among the hospital personnel," he went on, looking in turn at the people who were crowding Chief Psychologist O'Mara's office, "I suggest that all knowledge of this search and its object be limited to those present, who are the only people with some idea of what we are looking for, and, naturally, the senior staff members who are already aware of the problem . . ."

And the suggestion of a diagnostician, Hewlitt had learned, was nothing less than an entry in future history.

". . . even though it is extremely unlikely that we will find the entity in its natural state," he continued, "which the last time I saw it was a fist-sized lump of pink, translucent jelly, although the coloration may have been due to a minor loss of blood while it was being surgically excised from Lonvellin's body . . ."

Major O'Mara, Hewlitt decided, had to be the elderly,

stern-faced officer in Monitor green who was seated at the big desk with Braithwaite standing beside him and Conway and the *Rhabwar* medical team facing them. They were all wearing lightweight suits, including Prilicla, who was using a gravity nullifier pack to hover because its wings were tightly folded inside the protective envelope. Apart from Naydrad, who had found a physiologically suitable piece of furniture to occupy, everyone stood and listened in silence.

"There was no opportunity for a close study of the creature," Conway said. "Being an intelligent life-form, we required its permission for such a thorough and, for it, perhaps hazardous investigation. The only communication channel available was its emotional radiation, which provided accurate information on its feelings but no clinical facts. When Lonvellin insisted that its personal physician be returned to it without delay, reabsorption took place in eight-point-three seconds via the mucosa of an eating orifice. Except for the presence of two sources of emotional radiation and the increase of body weight, which matched exactly that of the virus creature, we could detect no physical indication of its presence within the host.

"But we must find this indetectable parasite," he continued, "and quickly. It is an intelligent organism that so far has tried to be helpful even though its attempts, in the Hewlitt case, caused long-term physical and psychological distress. But an organism that can jump the species barrier, and has absolutely no medical knowledge beyond its own limited experience, cannot be allowed to run loose inside a multi-species hospital."

Conway paused to look at everyone in the room before returning his attention to Hewlitt. When he spoke, his voice was calm and clinical, but the emotional accompaniment was causing Prilicla to wobble badly in flight.

"It is imperative that we reduce the field of search," he said, "either by eliminating certain individuals or groups who are possible hosts, or by concentrating our efforts on finding the probables. The psychology staff are already plugged into the grapevine in the hope of hearing gossip about patients whose condition has deteriorated following treatment, or who have improved suddenly for no apparent reason. They will pass their findings, if any, to us for clinical investigation. But in a hospital, patients' conditions will worsen or improve normally without the help of our intelligent virus friend.

"As an ex-host with long-term, personal experience of the organism," Conway ended, "do you have any suggestions that might help us?"

As the only nonmedic in the room, Hewlitt was surprised that a question had been directed at him first. He wondered whether Diagnostician Conway was being polite or feeling really desperate.

"I, I didn't even know it was there," he said. "I'm sorry."

Speaking for the first time, O'Mara said, "You must know something even though you may not realize you do. Were you ever aware of any thoughts or feelings that seemed foreign to you at the time, or of seeing people, objects, or events from a viewpoint that might not have been your own? Do you remember having strange dreams or nightmares, or of behaving in what seemed to be an uncharacteristic fashion? The creature's occupation of your body was complete and physically traceless but your mind, even subconsciously, should have been aware of it. In retrospect, can you remember anything of that nature?

"Think carefully."

Hewlitt shook his head. "Most of the time I felt very well, and at intervals very angry when I wasn't well and nobody would believe I was sick. Now I know the reason for what was happening to me. But that thing was inside me for most of my life, so I don't know how I would have felt if it hadn't been there. I'm not being much help."

"Neither are you taking much time to think carefully," said O'Mara dryly.

"Friend Hewlitt," said Prilicla, who was sharing his feelings of embarrassment and irritation and wishing to reduce them, "we realize that the question is unreasonable because by its very nature the creature is undetectable. But consider this. For more than twenty years you have been occupied by an entity who had the ability to read your body's genetic blueprint and, as when you accidentally poisoned yourself and suffered grave injuries in a fall and a flyer accident, restore you to optimum physical condition. This may have been simple self-preservation on its part, an evolutionary need to maintain a healthy and long-lived host. It is even possible that your friend derives pleasure and satisfaction from adapting itself to new life-forms. But maybe there is more. A highly intelligent being can be expected to have other, less selfish and more subtle feelings, like altruism, a sense of justice, or simple gratitude. It was able to share your emotions, at least those which were simple and most strongly felt, although those associated with your transition through puberty probably confused it as much as they did you. Some of them, those which led to the restoration of your dying pet and Patient Morredeth's damaged fur, it understood well enough to be able to act on them.

"Did it do this because it was sharing your grief," Prilicla went on, "or was it simply taking advantage of the chance to explore another life-form? Either way, it left that kitten in a state of health that has been maintained long past the normal life expectancy for that species. It left you, Patient Morredeth, and, presumably, an as yet unknown number of others in the same condition of perfect health. We would like to know why. If friend O'Mara can gain some idea of how this entity is motivated, we will have a better chance of finding and trapping it."

"I would help you if I could . . ." Hewlitt began, when the chief psychologist raised a hand.

"We know that," said O'Mara. "This thinking entity occupied your body. It must have used your sensory input because it was aware, however imperfectly, of your outside world and was under your emotional direction during the incidents with the cat and Morredeth. I realize that the situation was abnormal in that you had no physical or psychological baseline with which to make comparisons. But if you were sharing sensory input and feelings, it is logical to assume that the process was two-way and that you had some awareness of the creature's thought processes even though you did not recognize them for what they were.

"You probably think I am clutching at straws," the chief psychologist ended. "I am. Well?"

Hewlitt was silent for a moment as he tried to organize his thoughts. Then he said, "I want to help you, Major O'Mara. But if I were to recall the memories and feelings of twenty-odd years, they might not be clear or accurate and some of them would be influenced or distorted by my present knowledge of what was really going on. Isn't that so?"

The psychologist's steady, grey eyes had been fixed on Hewlitt's face since he had begun speaking. O'Mara said, "And the next word you say will be 'But.' "

"But," said Hewlitt obligingly, "the things that happened to me since my arrival in Sector General are clearer, and some of my feelings surprised me. To explain I have to go back to when I was a child."

O'Mara continued staring at him. He seemed to have forgotten how to blink.

Hewlitt took a deep breath and went on. "I was too young at the time to be told or even to understand the cultural-contact reasons why all the off-worlders attached to Etla base were expected to show an example to the natives by other-species socializing, which included showing them the

Tralthan, Orligian, Kelgian, or whoever's children playing together, under supervision, of course. One day the supervisor happened to be looking at another area of the swimming pool when I was dragged under by a Melfan amphibian who thought that I could breathe water, too. It was an accident and I was more frightened than hurt, but I never attended the other-species playground again. My parents told me I would grow out of my fear, but they didn't push it. That was the reason I was at home and, feeling bored, wandered off to explore and had that accident in the tree.

"From your monitoring of my conversation in the ward," he continued, "you already know that my work on Earth is interesting but not exciting and never involved meetings with off-worlders. I saw them on the Earth-vision broadcasts but did not, as my parents had promised, grow out of my childhood fear of them. There were a few extraterrestrials attached to the hospitals I attended, but I refused to allow them anywhere near me, and believing that I was really a psychiatric case, my doctors agreed to keep their other-species medics away from me."

For a moment O'Mara's eyes were hidden by a frown of impatience. He said, "Presumably this is leading us somewhere?"

"Probably nowhere," Hewlitt went on, ignoring the sarcasm. "On the way here I was in the care of a great, hairy, self-opinionated Orligian medic who also thought it could effect a cure by convincing me that my problems were due to an overactive imagination. I knew consciously if not subconsciously that, in spite of its appearance, it would not harm me. It was the first other-species person I had met since childhood. I felt curiosity as well as fear in its presence, but disliked its manner too much to ask questions.

"Then I arrived here," he continued quickly. "I was met by a Hudlar nurse, and on the way to and inside the ward I passed or lay close to creatures the like of which I had not imagined in my worst nightmares. Even though I knew they were medical staff or patients, I was still so terrified by them that for a long time I was afraid to go to sleep. But I was curious, too, and wanted to know more about them in spite of being afraid. I felt frightened by Charge Nurse Leethveeschi, but curious as well."

Naydrad made a gurgling, untranslatable sound. Hewlitt ignored it, as did O'Mara and the others.

"Within a few hours," he continued, "I was asking questions of the Hudlar, Leethveeschi, and Medalont. Next day I was talking and playing cards with other patients. The point I'm trying to make is that this was not the kind of behavior I expected of myself. The xenophobia I felt at the time was mine all right, but the intense and continuing curiosity about the other life-forms around me must have belonged to somebody else."

For a moment it seemed that the office had become a still picture in which everyone was looking at him. Motion and sound returned when O'Mara nodded and spoke.

"You are right," he said, "but not entirely. It seems that your parents were right and you did grow out of your fear of other-worlders within hours of your arrival here. Prilicla was greatly impressed by you. It tells me that when you met the medical team on *Rhabwar* for the first time, your xenophobia was minimal, well controlled, and temporary. This was at a time when the virus creature was no longer in occupation. Since the Morredeth incident when the virus left you, the curiosity and interest you felt regarding ETs was entirely your own."

"I suppose that is a compliment," said Hewlitt, smiling.

O'Mara scowled. "An observation," he said. "My job here is to shrink heads, not swell them. But we may have something useful here. Can you describe this shared curiosity and its degree of intensity, and, assuming that the virus was principally interested in other life-forms as potential hosts, were you aware of this more selfish purpose behind your feeling of curiosity? For example, did you form the impression that the virus entity was able to move to another host of its own volition? And are you completely sure the transfer was dependent on your emotional state, as was the case with your cat and Morredeth? Try to recall your feelings, all of them, and take time to think about your answer."

"I don't need time to think about it," Hewlitt protested. "On the two occasions that the virus moved out of me I was feeling deep sympathy, so I cannot be absolutely sure if those feelings were necessary for the transfer. Where the cat was concerned, I held on to it all night, but the contact with Morredeth was over in a minute, maybe a little more. I remember wanting to pull my hands away because the stuff smeared over the wound and dressings felt unpleasant, but at first I couldn't move my hands. When I did pull them away, I remember that my palms and fingers felt strange, there was a hot, tingling sensation in them that disappeared after a few seconds. It was probably subjective. I didn't mention it before because at the time nobody was believing anything I said and it was probably unimportant anyway."

"And do you remember anything else that is probably unimportant?" said O'Mara.

Hewlitt took a deep breath and tried to ignore the sarcasm for Prilicla's sake rather than the major's, then said, "If we assume that physical contact is required for the creature to transfer to a new host, and it was continually interested in the possibility of making such a move, what about my interest in Leethveeschi and that doctor who drove into the ward in a pressurized tank? I am very sure that I wanted no physical contact with either of them, especially the charge nurse, so the curiosity could not have been mine. Does that mean the creature wastes its time on feelings that are impossible for it to fulfill, or is it capable of transferring itself to any living being regardless of species?"

O'Mara gave a short, irritated sigh. He said, "There was always the chance that you would add to the problem rather than help provide the solution. If you are right and our friend is not confined to transferring into warm-blooded oxygen-breathing hosts, that will seriously complicate our search." He looked at the medics in turn. "Is such a radical, cross-species transfer possible?"

Diagnostician Conway was the first to speak. He said, "As close to impossible as makes no difference."

"Until Patient Hewlitt arrived among us," said O'Mara with the sarcastic edge returning to his voice, "we thought it impossible for a microorganism that had evolved on one world to survive in a life-form from another."

Conway did not take offense. He said, "That is why I said close to impossible, sir. However, there are major differences in the metabolism and life processes of a chlorine-breathing host, and the biochemical adaptation needed would be, again, close to impossible. . . ."

"And who would want to live inside an Illensan anyway?" said Naydrad.

"As for more exotic life-forms like the TLTUs, SNLUs, or VTXMs," he went on, ignoring the interruption and glancing toward Hewlitt to show that the explanation was for his benefit, "I would say with more confidence that they are completely unsuitable as hosts. The first breathes high-pressure, superheated steam in an environment which, in the old days, was used to sterilize infected surgical instruments. SNLUs are methane life-forms with a complex mineral and liquid crystalline structure which decomposes at temperatures in excess of eighteen degrees above absolute zero. As for the VTXMs, the Telfi are another hot life-form, not because of an elevated body temperature but because they need to absorb high levels of hard radiation to support their life processes.

"It follows that these three life-forms can be eliminated

as potential hosts," the diagnostician ended, "because a virus would be unable to survive in any of them."

Before O'Mara could reply, Prilicla made an unsteady landing on top of an unoccupied piece of furniture. Its trembling was minor and of the kind, Hewlitt had discovered, indicating that it was nerving itself to the major effort of saying something disagreeable.

"It is possible that you are wrong, friend Conway," it said. "And I, too, may be contributing to the problem rather than its solution because we cannot exclude the Telfi as possible hosts. Our virus was able to survive when its escape vehicle was in close proximity to the nuclear detonation that destroyed Lonvellin's ship. The outer casing of the creature's pod was partially melted and superficially damaged by flying wreckage, but it had also absorbed sufficient radiation for strong traces to be present after twenty-five years. At the time it took the young Hewlitt as a host, it had been occupying that pod and absorbing significantly higher, although diminishing, levels of radioactivity during the five years following the original contamination."

"Oh," said the diagnostician.

O'Mara actually smiled, although it was clear that his face muscles were unused to that form of exercise. He said, "Does anyone else want to make a fool of itself? Hewlitt, you are wanting to say something."

For a moment Hewlitt wondered if the chief psychologist had an empathic faculty like Prilicla, then decided that it was probably the result of training, observation, and long experience. He shook his head and said, "It probably isn't important."

"If it isn't," said O'Mara, "I'll be the first to let you know. Spit it out."

Hewlitt was silent for a moment, wondering how such a thoroughly unsympathetic person had been able to survive and rise to a high position in a caring profession like psychiatry; then he said, "Something has been bothering me about the meeting with my cat on Etla. It was an ordinary, black-and-white cat, and big and fat instead of being the skinny near-kitten I remembered, but I recognized it. And even though I had changed physically, grown four or five times more massive and with marked differences in face and voice, it recognized and came toward me at once. You are probably thinking that I am being sentimental about a childhood pet . . ."

"The thought had crossed my mind," said O'Mara.

". . . but I think it was more than fond memories," Hewlitt went on, "because I had almost forgotten about that cat until I was admitted to the hospital and Lieutenant Braithwaite started questioning me about my childhood. It was as if there was a bond between us, a feeling almost of pride in some kind of shared experience that seemed to go beyond the child-and-his-pet relationship. The feeling is tenuous, very difficult to describe, and, well, it is probably due to all this talk about intelligent virus invasions. This time my imagination may really be running away with me. I should not have mentioned it."

"But you did mention it," said O'Mara, "even though doing so has caused you to feel embarrassed and even ridiculous. Or are you hoping that I, or one of the other fine, incisive, clinical minds here assembled, will decide whether or not it was worth mentioning?"

The fine, clinical minds in the room joined Hewlitt in remaining silent. He returned the other's stare, wondering if O'Mara's lids had been glued permanently in the open position.

"Very well," the psychologist went on. "Think carefully about what you have just said and follow it through. The word 'impossible' has been used too loosely here, so I shall resist the temptation to use it again. Are you suggesting, however reluctantly, that this strange, tenuous, indescribable feeling that you had for your onetime pet, and which you believe it reciprocated, was a legacy that may have been left by your common viral invader? And are you also suggesting that the ex-hosts of the virus might share this peculiar, insubstantial feeling of a shared experience and be able to recognize each other? Presumably I am right because your face is becoming very red, but I would like verbal corroboration."

"Yes, dammit," said Hewlitt. "To both questions."

O'Mara nodded and said, "Which means that you could act as some kind of virus witch-finder with the ability to track down our quarry through its previous and, presumably, its present hosts. Naturally, we are grateful for any help you can give us but, well, apart from the instant recognition and the vague feelings you say you shared with the cat who, regrettably, is unable to offer corroboration, have you any other evidence, observations, or vague, indescribable feelings to support your contention?"

He looked away from O'Mara, feeling that the heat of his embarrassment must be warming the whole room.

"Friend O'Mara," said Prilicla. "At the time the incident occurred I was aware of the feelings of the cat and friend Hewlitt. They were as described."

"And as I suggested, little friend," said O'Mara, "they were vague, indescribable, subjective, and probably useless." He turned to his communicator, which was already live, and went on, "Has the Padre returned? Good, send it in." To Hewlitt he said, "We have medical matters to discuss which do not require your presence. I feel sure that I have embarrassed you more than enough for one day. Thank you for your assistance. Padre Lioren will escort you to the dining hall."

In the instant that the Tarlan entered the room it stopped dead, all four of its eyes directed at Hewlitt's reddening face. He stared back at it, wanting to speak but knowing that he was going to be ridiculed again.

"Mr. Hewlitt," said O'Mara in a voice whose sarcastic tone had been replaced by one of sympathy and concern. "You have many years' experience of having your words disbelieved by the medical and psychiatric fraternity, so I hoped that your feelings would not be seriously wounded by my own incredulity. In the circumstances your reaction seems abnormal. Please, what is it that you are not wanting to tell me?"

"The vague feeling of recognition I was trying to describe," said Hewlitt, raising a hand to point at Lioren, "is coming from the Padre."

"I can confirm that," said Prilicla.

For the first time since he had entered the office, Hewlitt saw the chief psychologist blink.

CHAPTER 25

"Padre," said O'Mara, swiveling his chair to look up at the Tarlan standing in the doorway, "have you been hiding something from us?"

Lioren bent one eye in the psychologist's direction and kept the other three trained on Hewlitt as it said, "Not intentionally. This is as much of a surprise to me as it is you. Your instructions were that the psychology staff in the outer office listen in to this meeting for later discussion. I returned early from the AUGL ward and overheard Patient Hewlitt's description of his feelings about the cat. I—I need a moment to think."

"Take it," said O'Mara. "But Padre, organize your thoughts, try not to edit them."

"Very well," said Lioren. It did not appear to be offended by the other's remark unless turning one of its eyes toward the ceiling was a derogatory gesture on Tarla. After a short pause it went on. "In the course of my duties

I am aware of many subtle and often indescribable feelings that I have for my charges, both patients and staff, and of similar feelings they have toward me. Even though we Tarlans find physical contact between strangers distasteful, very often I find it necessary when the laying on of hands or a simple handclasp is required to convey feelings that are too difficult for either of the persons concerned to articulate. Until Hewlitt described the bond that it felt existed between its pet and itself, and I realized that a similar feeling existed between the two of us and another former patient, Morredeth, I had not considered the matter of any importance. Now it has become very important because it seems that I became a host to the virus creature. I also know how and when the transfer must have taken place.

"At the time I was not aware of anything unusual about the incident," the Padre went on. "The damage to a young Kelgian's fur is a particular tragedy, since it is both an unsightly deformity which precludes mating and a severe impairment of its primary channel of communication. From the time Patient Morredeth learned that the condition was permanent it was in urgent need of nonmaterial support. In common with the majority of civilized worlds, Kelgia has several religious beliefs the precepts of which are familiar to me, but Morredeth subscribed to none of them. All that I could offer it during my daily visits was sympathy and conversation and, well, gossip about other patients and staff members in an attempt to take its mind off its own troubles. The attempt was unsuccessful and the patient remained in a condition of deep, emotional distress until, on the visit following its physical encounter with Patient Hewlitt, there was a total remission of symptoms."

Lioren paused and for a moment the tall, angular body concealed by the narrow cone of its cloak trembled, apparently at the recollection, then grew still.

"In spite of being the hospital padre," it said, "I have difficulty accepting an event, no matter how inexplicable it may seem, as miraculous. But not knowing then of the existence of this intelligent virus creature, I was almost convinced otherwise. Morredeth's behavior following its cure was abnormal in that it was almost insane with delight and relief. I had already touched, or rather stroked, the area of damaged fur in an attempt at giving nonverbal reassurance. But it insisted that I share its joy by feeling for myself the mobility of the regenerated fur with one of my medial hands. That was when it must have happened.

"The fur was indeed highly mobile," Lioren continued, "so much so that long tufts of it wrapped around and became entangled in my digits. For a moment my hand was held tightly against the skin, and I was afraid to pull it free in case I uprooted strands of the newly grown fur. I was aware of my palm being wet but was unsure whether the perspiration was the patient's or my own, and at the time I had no idea that the sudden presence of moisture was associated with the creature's mechanism of transfer. Shortly afterward I removed my hand from the fur without difficulty, congratulated Patient Morredeth on its cure, then left to visit other patients."

"But didn't you feel anything?" Hewlitt said before anyone else could speak. "Like better, healthier, or at least different? Did you feel anything at all?"

O'Mara frowned at Hewlitt before returning his attention to Lioren. He said, "They would have been my questions, too. Well, Padre?"

"I do not remember any unusual feelings," Lioren replied, "nor was I expecting them. Perhaps my present feeling of being close to another one of the virus creature's ex-hosts was obscured by my relief and pleasure over Morredeth's cure. As well, my health is excellent so it would be difficult for me to feel better physically, although I am less certain about the health of my mind. Apparently our virus creature's ability as a healer does not extend to clinical psychology."

What kind of psychological problem, Hewlitt thought, could be troubling a highly moral and altruistic being whose popularity among the patients and staff was second only to that of Prilicla? He was wondering if he dared ask when the answer was provided by the chief psychologist.

"Padre," he said, "you were exonerated of all guilt for the deaths of the Cromsaggar, and soon, I hope, your subconscious will also accept that verdict. But while we are on the subject, on Cromsag you were seriously injured and given emergency treatment by a ship's medic not fully experienced in Tarlan physiology. As a result there was some minor scarring. Are the scars still visible?"

"I don't know," said Lioren, "because I rarely look closely at my own body. Narcissism is unknown among Tarlans. Shall I remove my cloak?"

"Please," said O'Mara.

Two of Lioren's medial hands emerged from slits in its long, blue cloak and began releasing the fastenings. Feeling vaguely embarrassed, he looked at Prilicla, who was hovering close by, and whispered, "Should I turn my back?"

"No, friend Hewlitt," the empath replied. "Tarlans do not subscribe to the Earth-human nudity taboos, and the Blue Cloak of Tarla that it wears is a symbol of professional and academic eminence as well as providing a site for many concealed, internal pockets. Look closely. Friend Lioren has turned completely around and, and, and I see no scars."

"Because there are none," said Lioren. Its four eyes were turned downward and hanging from each stalk like single, heavy fruit. "The surgery was neat though hurried so that the scars were not obvious, but now they have completely disappeared."

O'Mara nodded and said, "Apparently our virus has left you its usual visitor's card, a perfectly healed and healthy body. That is all the confirmation we need that you were a host. Or maybe you still are." He looked at Prilicla. "Is the virus still in residence?"

"It is not," the empath replied. "There is only one source of emotional radiation emanating from the Padre and it is its own. At this range, if another intelligence was present I would detect it at once."

"You would detect it without any possibility of error," asked O'Mara, "regardless of the species of the host?"

"Yes, friend O'Mara," Prilicla replied. "I could not help but detect it. Emotionally its presence would be obvious, as obvious as if you were to grow a second, thinking head. . . ."

O'Mara actually smiled. "In this medical madhouse that might be an advantage."

"I am less certain with a person like friend Conway," the empath went on, "who thinks he has eight or nine minds. That confuses the emotional radiation and adds an element of doubt."

"Diagnostician Conway," said Hewlitt firmly, "is not a former host."

"I concur," said Lioren.

"And I'm glad," Murchison said, laughing. "Having a multiply absentminded husband is bad enough."

The chief psychologist gave a single, impatient tap on his desktop and said, "We digress. For reasons that are obvious we must treat the discovery of the creature's present where-abouts as a matter of extreme urgency."

The reasons are not obvious to me, Hewlitt thought, but he was not being given the chance to ask questions.

"To find it we have one empathic detector who can spot its presence provided the host is within conversational distance and is not a diagnostician, and two ex-hosts who can only identify the people who have already been inhabited if they are within visual range. In both cases the exact distance involved has yet to be established. All of these former hosts as well as the current one must be traced without delay. We are fairly sure that Hewlitt's only contact within the hospital was Patient Morredeth, from whom the Padre received the virus before it moved to another patient. . . ."

"With respect," Lioren broke in, "it might not have been to another patient."

O'Mara gave a small, irritated nod and said, "Padre, I have not forgotten that your work includes counseling members of the staff as well as patients. You must interview all of them again, identify the one who inherited the virus from you, and, if it is no longer in residence, trace and talk to all of that person's subsequent contacts until you find the present host. Report the location to this department, request Monitor security assistance and a medical quarantine, and remain with the entity concerned until Dr. Prilicla arrives to confirm the presence of the virus.

"Little friend," he went on, "if you have no objections I would like you to carry out a simultaneous search, initially of the warm-blooded, oxygen-breathing wards, main dining hall, and recreation level. You may well find the creature first. But whoever does find it, regardless of the host species, it must be physically isolated, restrained, and the necessary steps taken to prevent the virus from transferring to another host. You will then try to use you projective empathy to reassure the virus entity until we can devise a better method of communication. But on no account must you operate beyond your limits of physical endurance. We need you as a detector and communicator, not a casualty."

"I am stronger than I look, friend O'Mara," said Prilicla. "Well, a little stronger."

The Earth-humans in the room laughed, including O'Mara, who went on, "There are two reasons why I want Hewlitt and the Padre to operate as a team. One is that I do not fully understand the vague and perhaps untrustworthy feeling of recognition that you have described as existing between former hosts, so that if you act together there would be less chance of both of you missing a contact. The second is that an ex-patient running loose inside the hospital, especially one who has a limited knowledge of its geography or experience of avoiding accidental damage by other life-forms, would very soon be readmitted as a casualty unless he had a, well, guardian angel in attendance. For this reason you have been transferred to accommodation closer to the Padre. Do either of you object to this arrangement?"

Hewlitt shook his head and watched while Lioren lowered two of its eyes in a gesture which probably meant the same thing.

"Good," said O'Mara. "But you should think before agreeing so quickly to anything. I want both of you to spend every waking moment on this search. Since Prilicla is uncertain about its ability to isolate the virus from the other taped entities inhabiting their minds, your first step will be to eliminate the diagnosticians. There is a meeting in three hours' time on Level Eighty-Three, Lioren knows where, and in view of the problem with the hospital's power-generation system, they will all attend. Wait outside the entrance, take a good look at them as they go in, and report your findings to me without delay. You will have many problems, Hewlitt, but the Padre will help you with them. Unless you two have anything else to contribute, this ends the non-medical part of the discussion."

"Wait," said Hewlitt. "I'm worried about the power problem you mentioned. When *Rhabwar* was coming in we were told that the main reactor was . . ."

"Worry if you must," O'Mara broke in. "It is a technical problem to which we cannot begin to suggest a solution, and we have medical problems enough without us wasting our time trying."

He nodded toward the door.

Fear was still his predominant emotion, Hewlitt thought

as he traveled once again through the crowded, three-dimensional maze of hospital corridors on foot. He had not realized at the time how pleasant it had been to be riding in the security of a gravity litter driven by a Hudlar nurse so physically massive that everyone gave them the widest possible berth, and he knew that his present experience should have been even more terrifying. But the other-species confrontations, which could have resulted in physical and possibly life-threatening collisions, had not occurred because there was always a firm, medial Tarlan hand on his shoulder guiding him out of trouble. The reason he was so afraid but not paralyzed with fear was very difficult to understand.

He decided that his strange absence of terror must be due in part to Lioren, who kept talking about every walking, crawling, or wriggling nightmare they passed as if they were mutual acquaintances, and frequently in terms which, if the information was not already widely known as gossip, was stretching the rules of confidentiality to their elastic limits. A nightmare, he thought, should not have amusing stories told about it if it was to retain its full, terrifying effect. He wondered if he was at last beginning to see these creatures for what they were, and feeling an at times fearful curiosity about them instead of merely looking at them and wanting to react with his feet by running away.

Perhaps his uncharacteristic and continuing interest in the hospital's extraterrestrials was a form of contagious curiosity and a legacy of the virus creature. He was about to mention the idea to the Padre when they turned into a long side corridor that, apart from themselves, was silent and empty.

"Staff accommodation," Lioren explained. "It isn't always as quiet as this, but right now the occupants are either on duty or asleep. This one is yours. I won't go in because the place will be crowded enough with just you in it. But you should find it comfortable enough. Go in and look around."

The room was a little larger in area but with a lower ceiling than his cabin on the ship that had brought him to Sector General. He was relieved to see that the overhead lighting was recessed, because his hair was brushing against the ceiling.

"The beds are much too short," he protested. "My feet will hang over the end onto the floor."

"Naturally," said the Padre, bending forward so that it could move one eye and an arm into the room. "It belongs to two Nidians who are absent on a ship-rescue training course for the next few weeks. The beds are movable and can be joined end-to-end. Behind the brown door is a multispecies washroom similar to the one you used in Ward Seven. I hope the wall decorations are not distasteful to you. Both of the former occupants are male and obviously prefer Nidian female subjects to landscapes."

Hewlitt looked at the pictures of red-furred teddy bears in what must have been provocative poses and tried not to laugh. He said, "I do not find them offensive."

"Good," said Lioren. "Over there is your control console. The seat is height-adjustable, the keys are large enough for Earth-human digits, and the display screen can be fine-tuned to your visual requirements. You can call up the usual entertainment, library, and training channels, and the yellow studs enclosed by the green rectangle control the menu display and selection instructions for the food dispenser. Are you as hungry as I am? Would you like to rest or go to the dining hall?"

"Yes," said Hewlitt, "and I don't know. Squeeze inside, I want to talk. Can I order something for us, and what would you suggest?"

Lioren hesitated, "By tomorrow your dispenser will have been reprogrammed to supply basic Earth meals," it said. "The taste difference between Nidian and Earth-human food is practically indistinguishable, and equally revolting to a Tarlan. I would prefer to use the main dining hall and so, I feel sure, would you. There the own-species menu is more extensive so that you would have no trouble finding something you like."

It was Hewlitt's turn to hesitate. He said, "Will it be very crowded? Worse than the corridors, I mean? And how am I expected to, well, behave?"

"All of the warm-blooded oxygen-breathers on the staff dine there," said the Padre, "although not, you will be pleased to hear, at the same time. Everyone will be sitting, kneeling, or standing around tables and eating, not trying to avoid colliding with each other. Besides, if we can find an empty table close to the entrance—and there should be no problem there, because it is not a popular area—we will be able to work while we eat."

"Work?" said Hewlitt, feeling stupid. Too much was happening to him in too short a time. "How?"

"By exercising our newly acquired talent for detection," said the Padre, "and scanning the staff members as they arrive or leave for evidence of past occupation by the virus. Even if the results are negative, it will be an effective method of eliminating a large number of staff members from the search so that we can concentrate more of our available time on the patients and on-duty ward staff. The present host must be found, quickly. A virus entity like that loose in a multispecies hospital doesn't bear thinking about."

"But why?" asked Hewlitt. "So far as I can see the creature has done no harm to anyone, the reverse in fact. The hospital is in the business of healing people and so is the virus creature. Why is everybody so worried about it? I wanted to ask O'Mara about that earlier but he didn't give me the chance. And on *Rhabwar* they avoided the question."

Lioren backed into the corridor and waited until Hewlitt had closed the room door behind him before it said, "Regrettably, I must do the same."

"But *why*, dammit?" Hewlitt said angrily. "I'm not a

patient anymore. You don't have to keep medical secrets from me."

"Because we don't have the answer for you," Lioren replied. "Your mind will be easier if we do not burden it with the unnecessary weight of our own fears and uncertainties."

"Personally," said Hewlitt, "I prefer uneasiness to ignorance."

"Personally," said Lioren, "I prefer to expect the worst while hoping for the best, which means that I am never disappointed when a result is less than a total disaster or, as may well be the case here, our concern is unfounded. We must avoid frightening ourselves unnecessarily. And the answer to your earlier question is that there aren't any."

"Any what?" said Hewlitt.

"Table manners," said the Padre. "Nobody will care about your method of ingestion, nor will they mind if you deliberately avoid looking at a table companion to whom you are talking in order to avoid seeing the disgusting messes some of us push into our mouths.

"And now, Patient Hewlitt," it ended, "we have work to do as well as food to eat."

CHAPTER 26

On *Rhabwar* he had watched Prilicla weave strands of Earth spaghetti, its favorite non-Cinrusskin dish, into lengths of slim, yellow cable that it had drawn into its tiny mouth while hovering above its platter; and Naydrad, who did not use its hands while eating but buried half of its narrow, conical head in the shredded, oily green stuff it preferred until the bowl was empty; and even the shape-changer, Danalta, who sat on top of or leaned against anything it wished to digest until only the desiccated, inedible remains were left. And earlier he had shared Ward Seven's dining table with Bowab, Horrantor, and Morredeth. The result, he was pleased to discover, was that he was able to watch the Padre refueling without the slightest trace of abdominal discomfort.

Lioren ate using the fingers of two of its upper, manipulatory appendages, with the tiny hands encased in a pair of silvered, disposable gloves that had arrived, like Hewlitt's knife and fork, in the utensils pack on its food dispenser tray. The Padre was precise and almost dainty in its movements as the food was lifted to its eating orifice, and the lumps of brown and yellow spongy material being consumed were too strange for Hewlitt to imagine what they might be or to feel repelled by them.

He hoped that the reverse also held true, because his synthesized steak was very good. There was no way of knowing; Lioren had not spoken since they had entered the dining hall.

"We've eaten," said Hewlitt with a glance toward the nearby entrance, where a group of Kelgians intending to dine was dividing around the massive form of a Tralthan who was just leaving, "but so far we haven't been working. Or did you feel something from somebody that I missed?"

"No," Lioren replied, and resumed eating.

It sounded irritated and impatient. More than two hundred staff members had walked, slithered, wriggled, or lumbered past their table since they had begun the meal. Like himself, the other might have been beginning to wonder if their ability to detect former virus hosts was mostly imagination or self-delusion.

"Perhaps the feeling, immaterial bond, or whatever it is works only between Tarlans, Earth-humans, and cats who are already well acquainted with each other," he said, when the silence lengthened, "and we don't know any of these people well enough for the before-and-after difference to register. Do you think we're wasting our time here?"

"No," said Lioren again. It took a moment to clear its plate, then went on, "The staff duty rosters are arranged so that the dining hall will not, in spite of what your eyes and ears are telling you, be overcrowded. But at any given time there is less than five percent of the warm-blooded oxygen-breathing staff using it. The Illensan chlorine-breathers, the Hudlars, the ultra-low-temperature methane life-forms, and the other exotic types have their own arrangements, as also have the patients. You are mistaking an early absence of results for failure."

"I understand," said Hewlitt. "You are telling me, tactfully, that I must be a more patient ex-patient and we should continue as we are doing."

"No," said Lioren once again. "We are not . . ."

There was an interruption from the menu-selection unit, which was displaying a red, flashing screen while its speaker began repeating a translated message in a brisk, officious voice.

"Diners who have completed their meal should vacate the table without delay so as to free it for use by subsequent diners. Your time is up. Any unfinished professional or social conversations should be continued elsewhere. Diners who have completed . . ."

"We are not allowed to stay here without eating," Lioren went on, raising its voice. "The sound output will increase in volume the longer we delay our departure, and contacting Maintenance to disable the audio circuit would waste too much time. We could always change tables and order another meal, but speaking personally I no longer feel hungry enough to attempt that . . ."

"Nor I," said Hewlitt.

". . . so I suggest that we begin the calls on my suspect patients," the Padre continued. "The first one is in your old ward. It was admitted after you left, and Charge Nurse Leethveeschi is expecting me. Unless you are one of those beings who become comatose after eating a large meal and need to sleep?"

This time it was Hewlitt's turn to say no.

The recorded message ceased as soon as they rose from the table, which was immediately taken by two hairy Orligians wearing senior physicians' insignia, but neither of them had the indefinable feel of having been former hosts of the virus.

As they were leaving, Prilicla flew in to hover gracefully inside the entrance. The empath spoke to them but did not ask how they had fared because it was already aware of their disappointment. They stood watching it for several minutes as it drifted across to the group of mixed-species diners around the nearest table, ostensibly to talk to friends but in reality to try to discover a mind or minds that contained two sources of emotional radiation instead of one. It was likely that the fragile little empath had friends at every table in the vast room. Remembering the Cinrusskin's lack of stamina, Hewlitt wished it luck and hoped that it would find what it was looking for before it crash-landed from sheer fatigue.

Prilicla broke off its conversation to call out, "Thank you, friend Hewlitt."

A few minutes later they were in one of the crowded main corridors, but only a part of Hewlitt's mind was on collision avoidance.

"I've been thinking," he said, "and worrying."

Lioren's reply did not translate.

"And wondering about this strange ability we have to recognize each other as past hosts," he went on. "A few minutes ago, when I felt concern for Prilicla and wished it good luck without speaking, it responded to the feeling even though it was distant and its attention elsewhere. There was nothing strange in that, because the Cinrusskin empathic faculty is very sensitive even at that range. But what about our own ability? Is it, too, a low order of empathy that is enough to allow simple recognition and nothing more? And if so, how close do previous hosts have to be to recognize each other? Do they have to be in line of sight? Does a physical barrier have any effect? Would you mind helping me conduct an experiment?"

"I don't know, six times," the Padre replied, "and what kind of experiment?"

"But this is not an experiment," Lioren protested when he finished explaining what he wanted, "it is a game for very young children! It would, however, provide useful data. If I agree to cooperate you must never reveal to another person that I, a mature adult who is qualified to wear the Blue Cloak, played this game with you."

"Ease your mind, Padre," said Hewlitt. "At my age I wouldn't want people to know I played hide-and-seek, either. I suppose you should be 'it' since you know where the best hiding places are. . . ."

The long corridor they were in ended with a T-junction that housed the complex of ramps, stairs, and lifts leading to upper and lower levels. Along each wall there were many doors, which opened into wards, storage compartments, equipment bays, and the maintenance tunnel network. The idea was that Hewlitt would turn his back for ten minutes so that Lioren would have time to conceal itself, either close by or a a distance along the corridor. The only rules were that the Padre would hide itself in an empty compartment rather than in a ward, which would have caused comment and risked disrupting the medical routine, and that he would seek out its hiding place by the use of the instinct, empathy, or whatever it was that he had inherited from the virus creature and not by looking behind doors.

After twenty minutes of standing before potential hiding places, ignoring the questions and critical comments of passersby while trying to feel for the presence of Lioren with his mind, he had exhausted all the potential hiding places without success. Disappointed, he used his communicator.

"I felt absolutely nothing," he said. "Come out, wherever you are."

Lioren emerged from a door he had scanned a few minutes earlier and hurried toward him. It said, "Neither did I, even though I heard you pause outside my hiding place. The sound of Earth-human footsteps is quite distinctive. But I felt the sense of recognition again, as soon as I saw you."

"Me, too," said Hewlitt. "But why do we have to be able to *see* each other?"

The Padre made a quiet, gurgling sound that did not translate and said, "God, and possibly the virus creature, knows."

Hewlitt puzzled over the question in silence all the way to his old ward. Apart from calling O'Mara to pass on the new information, the Padre refused further discussion of the subject. It was possible that a large part of Lioren's mind was on the troubles of the patient it was about to visit.

"Patient Hewlitt," said Leethveeschi the moment he entered the nurses' station, "what are *you* doing here?"

He knew that the charge nurse was used to the Padre visiting its ward, but it did not sound pleased by the presence of a former patient and proven disruptive influence like himself. Hewlitt was still trying to find a suitable reply when Lioren answered for him. He noted that the Padre did not actually lie, but it was sparing in its use of the truth.

"With your permission, Charge Nurse," Lioren said, "it will accompany me so that it may observe and talk to the patients and, if it is able, provide me with nonmedical support. I will insure that it does not talk to anyone who is currently undergoing treatment or is in an unfit condition to hold a conversation. Ex-Patient Hewlitt will not, I assure you, cause any more trouble."

A section of Leethveeschi's body twitched inside its chlorine envelope in what was probably a nonverbal gesture of assent. It said, "I think I understand. The experience with Patient Morredeth has caused it to decide, or perhaps strengthen a decision already made, to become a trainee priest-counselor. This is very laudable, ex-Patient Hewlitt, and you have a fine mentor."

"My real reason for being here . . ." Hewlitt began.

"Would take too long to explain," Leethveeschi broke in, "and right now I haven't the time to listen to an other-species theological self-examination, interesting though it might be. You may talk to any of my patients who are able to talk back. But please, let us have no more miracles."

"That is a promise," he said as he followed the Padre into the ward.

They had already eliminated Leethveeschi and the other staff on duty in the nurses' station from their list of former hosts, as well as the patient Lioren was visiting. It was a Melfan called Kennonalt whose support sling was surrounded with a worrying profusion of biosensor and life-support equipment. He did not find out what was wrong with it because, apart from exchanging names, Lioren had made it clear that the conversation with Kennonalt was to be private and that Hewlitt should spend the time checking the other patients until the Padre rejoined him.

His slow, zigzag progress down and from side to side of the ward was a trip through familiar territory, although he could not be sure of the familiarity of the patients because he still had difficulty telling one Tralthan, Kelgian, Melfan, or whatever from another. Most of them seemed glad of the chance to talk, a few appeared to be heavily sedated or were simply ignoring him, and one was undergoing treatment that could not be interrupted. But he was able to look at them, patients and medical attendants alike, closely and for more than enough time to eliminate them as former hosts. His last visit was to a Tralthan and a Duthan who were playing two-handed scremman at the ambulatory patients' dining table. By the time he spoke, they, too, had been eliminated.

"Horrantor? Bowab?" he said. "Are you well?"

"Ah, you must be Patient Hewlitt," said the Tralthan. "My

limb is mending, thank you, and Bowab is doing very well, both medically and in this accursed game. It is pleasant to see you again. Tell us about yourself. Were they able to find out what was wrong with you?"

"Yes," he replied. Choosing his words with care, he went on, "I no longer have the complaint and feel very well indeed. But it was an unusual condition, they told me, and they asked if I would help them tie up a few medical loose ends by remaining for a while. It was difficult to refuse." ·

"So now you're a healthy lab specimen," said Bowab in a worried voice. "It doesn't sound like much of an improvement. Have they done anything nasty to you yet?"

Hewlitt laughed. "No, and it isn't like that at all. I have my own quarters in the staff accommodation area, a small room that belonged to a couple of Nidians, and I'm free to wander all over the hospital so long as the Padre is with me to see that I don't get lost or run over by somebody. All they want me to do is talk to people and answer questions."

"You always were a strange patient," said Bowab, "but your convalescence sounds even stranger."

"To be serious for a moment," said Horrantor. "If all you do is talk to people and answer questions, presumably they also talk to you, or talk among themselves in your presence. Perhaps by accident or in ignorance of your nonstaff status, do they ever tell you things that you are not supposed to know? If so, and if you are allowed to answer, would you answer one of our questions?" .

This sounded like something more serious than a patient's normal hunger for the latest hospital gossip, Hewlitt thought. It was a time for caution.

"If I can," he said,

"Horrantor has a nasty, devious mind," said Bowab, joining in again, "and an imagination to match. That is why it beats me so often at scremman. We overheard some of the nurses talking together. They stopped very quickly when they realized that we were listening. Probably it was only staff gossip, or maybe nothing but our complete misunderstanding of an incomplete conversation, or it was something more than gossip. It is really worrying us."

"Everybody enjoys a good gossip," he said, "but it isn't supposed to worry you sick. What is your question?"

There was a moment's silence while Bowab and Horrantor looked at each other. Then the Duthan said, "According to what the charge nurse told me about ten days ago, I should have been discharged by now for convalescence in a home-planet hospital. In Sector General they don't believe in wasting either their time or their unique medical resources on patients who are no longer in need of them. But yesterday when I asked Leethveeschi why I was still here and if there was anything it wasn't telling me, it said that there was no environmentally suitable transport available to take me home and that there were no medical problems for me to worry about.

"About the same time," Bowab went on, "Senior Physician Medalont held a bedside lecture on Horrantor. It told the trainees that the patient was sufficiently recovered to be discharged without delay. That should have been within a few days, because the majority of the supply and transport vessels that come here, sometimes as often as four or five in a week, are crewed by warm-blooded oxygen-breathing species who are required by Federation law to provide accommodation for most of the other warm-blooded oxygen-breathers who need to travel. Traltha and Dutha, remember, are commercial hub worlds on the way to practically everywhere. But the reason Leethveeschi gave for Horrantor still being here was the same as mine, the nonavailability of environmentally suitable transport."

"Don't forget to tell it about the emergency drill," said Horrantor.

"I won't," said Bowab. "The day before yesterday a

twenty-strong maintenance team descended on the ward to conduct what Leethveeschi said was an emergency evacuation drill. They detached the beds of the most seriously ill patients from their wall supports, fitted them with extra oxygen tanks and antigravity grids, and deployed the airtight canopies, after which they moved all of us out of the ward and along the corridor to the intersection that leads to Lock Five before bringing us all back again. Leethveeschi timed the operation and told the team that they would have to do better than that; then it apologized to us for the inconvenience and told us to return to our game and not to worry. But while the maintenance people were leaving—and complaining about the charge nurse's personality defects and the unfairly high standard of performance expected by their superiors in a major evacuation drill, the like of which had not been practiced for about twenty years—we overheard a few odd scraps of conversation that worried us very much.

"Our question," Bowab ended, "is what exactly are they hiding from us?"

"I don't know," said Hewlitt, and added under his breath, "exactly."

That was the literal truth, but he was remembering his return in *Rhabwar* and the general signal from Reception for all ships to hold beyond the approach beacons unless carrying casualties in urgent need of attention. An unspecified technical problem that Maintenance was dealing with had been given as the reason, and in any case the signal had not applied to the special ambulance ship.

Hewlitt did not feel as reassuring as he sounded when he went on, "I haven't heard any rumors about an evacuation, but I'll listen and ask around. Have you considered the possibility that you misunderstood the incomplete conversations you overheard? All large, staff-intensive organizations carry out emergency drills from time to time. When someone realized that it had not been done in Sector General for twenty years, the hospital authorities must have decided that it had to be done sooner than yesterday and, naturally, it was the junior staff who suffered the inconvenience.

"It could be that Leethveeschi is right," he added, mentally crossing his fingers, "and you have nothing to worry about."

"That's what we keep telling each other," said Horrantor, "but after playing scremman together for so long, we have difficulty believing anything we say."

"Speaking of which," said Bowab, "would you like to join the game? One of us could buy you in as a short-term political consultant and watch for indications that you are going to change sides. . . ."

On the edge of his field of vision he could see the Padre approaching slowly down the ward, moving from side to side and looking at or exchanging a few words with the patients as Hewlitt had done earlier. He said, "Sorry, not this time. I'll have to leave in a few minutes."

When they were in the corridor again, he said, "From the patients and staff I felt nothing. You?"

"Nothing," said Lioren.

"But I did hear an interesting rumor," said Hewlitt. He went on to recount the observations and suspicions of Horrantor and Bowab and the wording of the signal that had been received by *Rhabwar*. He knew that the Padre would not deliberately misinform him, and that if the other could not tell the truth it would ignore his questions. He ended, "Have you heard any rumors of an evacuation, and do you know what is going on?"

It was a few moments before Lioren replied, and then it said, "Next we go to the eighty-third level and the Meeting of Diagnosticians."

CHAPTER 27

First to arrive was a large, slow-moving, and aged Tralthan whom Lioren identified as Thornnastor, the diagnostician-in-charge of Pathology. They watched it from the moment it appeared from a side corridor that was about thirty meters distant until it drew abreast of their position opposite the the room where the meeting was to take place. Without bending an eye in their direction or saying a word, it turned in to the entrance.

"No?" asked the Padre.

"No," Hewlitt agreed. "But why did it ignore us? We're big enough to see and there's nobody else in the corridor."

"It has a lot on its minds . . ." Lioren began, then broke off to say, "Here come three more. Conway and the chief psychologist we already know are clear. The Kelgian is Diagnostician Kurrsedeth. No?"

"No," said Hewlitt again.

Conway nodded as he passed, O'Mara gave them a scowl

of impatience, and Kurrsedeth said, "Why are the Padre and that Earth-human DBDG staring at me like that?"

"Right now," said O'Mara dryly, "they have nothing better to do."

A refrigerated vehicle which Lioren identified as belonging to Diagnostician Semlic turned in to the corridor. The Vosan was an ultra-low-temperature, methane life-form whose crystalline metabolism made its unsuitability as a virus host a virtual certainty. In contrast to the cold that was radiating from Semlic's vehicle, since the passage of O'Mara Hewlett had been self-generating a lot of internal heat.

"How," he said, "did such a sarcastic, ill-mannered, thoroughly obnoxious person ever get to be the hospital's chief psychologist? Why hasn't a member of the staff committed a life-threatening act of physical violence on him long since, as I feel like doing now?"

Lioren raised a medial arm to point along the corridor and said, "This one is Colonel Skempton, another Earth-human DBDG as you can see, who is in charge of supply, maintenance, and nonmedical administration. It is the ranking Monitor Corps officer on Sector General and, I think we can agree, it has never been a host of the virus creature."

"Right," said Hewlitt. "But what I don't understand is why isn't someone like Prilicla doing O'Mara's job? It is sympathetic, reassuring, pleasant all the time, and it really feels for its patients. And on that subject of empathy, why doesn't its empathic faculty work on diagnosticians? Or do I add another three questions to the list of those you will not answer?"

The Padre did not look at him when it spoke, because its eyes were directed up and down the corridor. It said, "Your last three questions have a single answer which, subject to interruptions by arriving diagnosticians, I am free to give you because it has no bearing on the present emergency.

"First," it went on, "Prilicla is much too gentle and sensitive to hold the position of chief psychologist, while O'Mara is sensitive and caring but not gentle. . . ."

"Sensitive and caring?" said Hewlitt. "Is my translator on the blink?"

"We haven't much time," said the Padre. "Do you want to hear or talk about Major O'Mara?"

"Sorry," he said, "I'm listening."

As the hospital's chief psychologist, Lioren went on to explain, O'Mara's overall responsibility was the smooth and efficient mental operations of the ten-thousand-odd members of its medical and maintenance staff. For administrative reasons he carried the rank of major and, theoretically, this placed him among the lower links in the Monitor Corps chain of command. But keeping so many different and potentially hostile life-forms working together in harmony was a large job whose limits, like O'Mara's actual authority, were difficult to define.

Given even the highest qualities of tolerance and mutual respect among all levels of its personnel, and in spite of the careful psychological screening they were given before being accepted for training, there were still occasions when serious, interpersonal friction threatened to occur because of ignorance or misunderstandings over other-species cultural and interpersonal behavior. Or a being might develop a xenophobic neurosis which, if left untreated, would ultimately affect its mental stability and professional competence.

It was the major's duty to detect and eradicate such problems before they could become life- or sanity-threatening or, if therapy failed, to remove the potentially troublesome individuals from the hospital. This constant watch for signs of wrong, unhealthy, or intolerant thinking, which his department performed with such zeal, had made him the most disliked entity in the hospital. But the chief psychologist was doubly fortunate in that he had never sought the admiration of others and gave every appearance of enjoying his work.

"O'Mara has a particular and personal responsibility," Lioren continued, "for safeguarding the sanity of the diagnosticians, who are in simultaneous possession of . . . The one who is approaching us now is the Melfan diagnostician, Ergandhir. The last time we spoke it was carrying seven tapes. Have you any feelings of recognition for it?"

Hewlitt waited until the Melfan had clicked past on its four, exoskeletal legs and gone in to join the others, then said, "No. And it was another one who completely ignored our presence. From what you just said I thought you two knew each other."

"We know each other very well," said Lioren, "so I must assume that the forefront of Ergandhir's mind is currently occupied by one of its Educator taped entities who does not know me, and never will since the original donor is no longer alive."

"I hate to ask another question," said Hewlitt, "but will you explain that?"

"It is part of the same question," the Padre said, "and I'm trying to answer it. . . ."

Educator tapes were very much a mixed blessing, Lioren explained, but their use was necessary because no single being could hope to hold in its brain all the physiological and clinical information needed for the treatment of patients in a multispecies hospital. That was why the incredible mass of data required to care for them was furnished by means of the Educator tapes, which were the complete brain recordings of great medical specialists of the past belonging to the species concerned. If an Earth-human doctor had to treat a Kelgian patient, he took one of the DBLF physiology tapes until the treatment was complete, after which he had it erased. Senior physicians with teaching duties were often called on to retain two or three of the tapes for long periods, which was not very pleasant for them, and their only consolation from their points of view was that they were better off than the diagnosticians.

They were the hospital's medical elite. A diagnostician was one of those rare entities whose mind was considered stable enough to retain permanently and simultaneously up to ten physiology tapes. To their data-crammed minds was given the job of original research in xenological medicine and the diagnosis and treatment of new diseases in hitherto unknown life-forms.

There was a well-known saying in the hospital, reputed to have originated with O'Mara himself, that anyone sane enough to want to be a diagnostician was mad.

"You must understand that it is not only the physiological data that the tapes impart," the Padre went on. "The complete memory and personality of the donor entity who possessed that knowledge is impressed as well. In effect a diagnostician subjects itself voluntarily to a most drastic form of multiple schizophrenia, with the alien personalities sharing its mind so utterly different in motivation and character that . . . Well, geniuses in any field are rarely nice people. These donor entities have no control over the host's thinking or bodily functions, but a diagnostician who does not have a stable and well-integrated personality can sometimes fool itself into believing that the opposite is true and it is no longer in charge of itself. Getting used to walking on two feet when your mind insists that you have six is bad enough, but the food preferences, the dreams that come when the body is asleep and the mind has no conscious control, are much worse. Worst of all are the other-species sexual fantasies. They can be really disturbing.

"With some of the diagnosticians," the Padre ended, "O'Mara has its hands full."

Hewlitt thought for a moment, then said, "Now I understand the reason for Pathologist Murchison's remark about her husband being multiply absentminded, and Prilicla's uncertainty about detecting the virus's emotional radiation if its host is a diagnostician, but I find it impossible to believe that . . ."

He broke off as another diagnostician waddled and squelched into view wearing a transparent suit with the helmet open. It was a Creppelian octopoid, Lioren said, a warm-blooded amphibious life-form who could breathe air or water. Owing to a skin condition associated with advanced age, it found it more convenient to breathe air and more comfortable to keep its body immersed in water. He did not catch its name because even through his translator it sounded like nothing so much as a short sneeze. When they agreed that it, too, had never been a virus host, Lioren spoke into its communicator.

"The last one has just gone in, Major," it said. "With the exception of Semlic, who was invisible inside its environmental protection, all of the diagnosticians and Colonel Skempton are cleared."

"Right, Padre," O'Mara replied. "You two resume your search at once, and don't waste time."

The sound of other-species' voices raised in anger or argument followed them as they moved away, but the sounds were too muffled for Hewlitt's translator to make any sense of them. Lioren said, "Our next call is the AUGL ward. What is it that you find impossible to believe?"

"No offense intended," said Hewlitt, "but I think your profession has made you feel too kindly disposed toward the chief psychologist. Nobody can convince me that he is anything but a sarcastic, bad-tempered, ill-mannered, unfeeling person who is sensitive and caring about nobody but himself. Every time he opens his mouth he reinforces that belief."

The Padre made an untranslatable sound and said, "It is true that Major O'Mara has personality defects, and there are many people on the staff who will tell you that the only thing that keeps them sane is the fear of what O'Mara will do to them if they dare go mad. This is an exaggeration for humorous effect on their part. It is also completely untrue."

"If you say so, Padre," he said.

They were moving along a main corridor again. Hewlitt was avoiding other-species collisions without Lioren's guiding hand on his shoulder and holding a conversation at the same time. He felt surprised and pleased with himself.

"Believe me," said the Padre, "if a being of any species is in serious need of psychiatric help, there is no better person in the hospital, and that includes myself, to give it. O'Mara takes the bad cases, those which could lead to permanent mental damage or to otherwise well-motivated and dedicated members of the staff being expelled from the hospital, and more often than not it saves their sanity as well as their future careers. But those files are closed to the other psychology staff, and neither the major nor its patients will talk about the treatment they were given afterward."

He did not know why, but Hewlitt felt sure that one of the patients concerned had been Lioren itself.

"O'Mara will tell you that the entire hospital staff are its patients," the Padre went on. "Most of them require minimum attention or no treatment at all and with them, it says, it can relax and be its normal, bad-tempered, sarcastic self. But when it begins to show concern toward a person, as it did to you when you showed signs of psychological distress on recognizing me as a former virus host, that is the time to worry. You recovered quickly, however, so O'Mara reverted to its normal behavior pattern toward a person it again considered to be one of its mentally healthy and well-adjusted patients.

"Instead of anger," it ended, "you should be feeling relieved and complimented. And perhaps a little incredulous."

Hewlitt laughed. "Thank you for the incredible information," he said. "But seriously, I have another question, the one I asked you earlier. What are you all hiding from me?"

"My previous answer was designed to change the subject by giving you something else to think about," Lioren said. "We are approaching the AUGL ward. Can you swim?"

CHAPTER 28

In the outer robing compartment, Lioren checked the helmet seals and air supply of his protective suit, a process that was repeated by Charge Nurse Hredlichli in the water-filled nurses' station, before he was allowed into the ward. Hewlitt wondered if Illensans had a medical monopoly on the senior nursing positions; the two wards he had experienced so far had both been in the charge of chlorine-breathers. Considering the fact that they were separated by the fabric of two protective suits and a few meters of intervening water, the distinctive chlorine smell was probably due to his imagination.

"The patient I am visiting is AUGL Two-Thirty-Three," said Lioren. "That is the physiological classification for this water-breathing species, and the case number is used because they do not exchange names other than with members of their family. They are visually frightening, extroverted, and, unless you forbid it, playful in the company of smaller beings, but they will never deliberately harm another sapient creature."

The Padre began swimming toward the ward entrance, its awkward, twelve-limbed, pyramidal body looking almost graceful underwater. It went on, "Most people feel a certain trepidation at their first sight of a Chalder, and it will not be considered as a lack of emotional fortitude if you are unable to make close physical contact. This is not a dare, so take your time and go out and talk to them only when or if you feel ready."

For what seemed a long time, Hewlitt stared through the transparent wall of the nurses' station into a dim, green world whose outlines were softened by what seemed to be drifting masses of decorative vegetation although, he thought, the larger pieces might have been patients. Hredlichli and a Kelgian nurse were concentrating on their monitors and ignoring him, so without further hesitation he swam slowly into the ward.

The nurses' station was less than ten meters behind him when, at the limit of visibility, one of the indistinct, dark-green shadows lying in the angle between wall and floor detached itself and came rushing silently toward him like a great, organic torpedo, taking on a terrifying, three-dimensional solidity the closer it came. As it slowed abruptly to a stop, the pressure wave and turbulence from its close approach and the rapid beating of its many fins sent him spinning end over end.

One of the massive fins swept up to lie for an instant along his back, feeling like a soft, firm mattress as it steadied him. Then it withdrew for a short distance to begin circling him, almost nose to tail, like a gigantic, open-ended doughnut that had to be at least twenty meters long. He was free to swim up or downward, but for some reason his arms, legs, and voice refused to work.

At close range he could see that the creature resembled

an enormous, armored fish with a heavy, knife-edged tail, a seemingly haphazard arrangement of stubby fins and a collar of thick, ribbon tentacles projecting from gaps in its body armor. When it was in motion the tentacles streamed backward to lie flat along its sides, but they were long enough to reach forward beyond the thick, blunt wedge of the head when it was at rest. The nearer of its two lidless eyes, looking to be about the size and shape of an upturned soup dish, watched him as it circled closer. Suddenly the head divided to reveal a vast, pink cavern of a mouth edged with a triple row of triangular white teeth. The mouth opened even wider.

"Hello," it said. "Are you the new trainee nurse? We were expecting a Kelgian."

Hewlitt opened his own mouth, but it was a moment before he found his voice. "N-no," he said. "I'm not a medic, just a layperson visiting the Chalder ward for the first time."

"Oh," said the Chalder. "I hope my approach did not frighten you. Please accept my apologies if it did, but you did not react like a first-time visitor. I am Patient AUGL Two-Eleven. If you give me the case number of the person you wish to visit, I would be pleased to take you to it."

He was about to introduce himself when he remembered in time that the Chalders did not exchange names, and avoided serious embarrassment for them both. The other's compliment must have made him him foolhardy, because he found himself saying, "Thank you. But I do not wish to speak to one particular person. Would it be possible to meet and spend a short time with all the patients?"

Patient Two-Eleven closed and opened its mouth several times. Hewlitt wondered if it was about to object when it said, "That would be possible, even desirable, especially to the three patients like myself who are overdue for discharge and are growing bored. But time is limited. The main meal of the day will be released in less than an hour. The food is synthesized, naturally, but highly mobile and lifelike, and smaller beings like yourself are required to vacate the ward during meals in case of an accidental ingestion."

"Don't worry," said Hewlitt, "I shall certainly leave before then."

"That is sensible," said the Chalder. "May I make an observation and a suggestion that may possibly offend you?"

Hewlitt looked again at the massive, armored body and size of its teeth, then said, "No offense will be taken."

"Thank you," it said, moving closer and slightly past him so that only one enormous eye, a side view of the mouth, and a stiffly projecting fin were visible. "Earth-humans are not very efficient in water; you move slowly and must expend much energy to do so. If you would grip the base of the fin that is close to you and hold on tightly with both hands, we can move between the patients in a fraction of the time you would otherwise require."

Hewlitt hesitated. "The fin looks, well, fragile. Are you sure I won't damage you?"

"Not at all," said Two-Eleven. "Admittedly I have been unwell, but I am much stronger than I look."

Unable to think of a suitable reply, Hewlitt grasped the base of the fin whose thick, red-veined stem sprouted from a gap in the scaly armor like an enormous, translucent rhubarb leaf. He tightened his grip as he felt an invisible something trying to pull him loose, then realized that it was increasing water pressure caused by their motion and that the whole ward, its decorative foliage, the massive figures of the patients, and the diminuitive medical staff were slipping past at speed.

There were no beds in the ward, he saw at once, and realized that that should not have surprised him considering the environment. What appeared to be the equivalent of bedridden patients were tethered loosely to the insides of open-ended treatment frames that looked like uncovered box kites. One of these patients, whose entire body surface was cracked and discolored by either age or disease, was being attended by Lioren. The majority of the others were floating without restraints close to their personal, marked-out areas of wall or ceiling, their eyes fixed on illuminated viewscreens and presumably being entertained. At the far end of the ward, which was apparently their destination, two Chalders were drifting motionless nose to nose. When Two-Eleven and Hewlitt approached, their massive tails flicked and they swung into a ponderous turn to face them, their vast mouths already gaping open.

"You may dismount now," said Two-Eleven, bringing forward a ribbon tentacle to point. "These are Patients One-Ninety-Three and Two-Twenty-One. And this is an Earth-human visitor who would like to talk with us."

"I can see that it isn't one of your body parasites," said One-Ninety-Three. "What does it want to talk about? The stupid reason we are still here?"

Before Hewlitt could reply, Two-Twenty-One said, "Please excuse our friend, small air-breather. A combination of impatience, boredom, and homesickness has eroded its manners. Usually its behavior is much better, well, a little better, than this. But its question remains—why are you here and what do you want to say to us?"

Hewlitt waited while the three of them changed position until they hung side by side facing him. The sight of one Chalder jaw and triple set of teeth had almost unnerved him, but three of the enormous mouths gaping open within a few meters of his head was ridiculous rather than frightening, and he felt himself begin to relax. He decided that this was another time to be sparing and perhaps a little inventive with the truth.

"I don't know what I want to talk about," he replied. "The subject doesn't matter, I just want a few minutes' conversation. I am neither a medic nor a psychologist, just a former patient helping with some follow-up research. Until I am allowed to leave the hospital there is nothing interesting for me to do, so I asked, and was given permission, to spend the time meeting and talking to as many patients and members of the staff as possible.

"Practically every member species of the Federation is represented here," he went on, "while on Earth I would be lucky to meet five off-worlders in a lifetime. The opportunity was too good to miss."

"But there are over a hundred Chalders on Earth," said Two-Eleven. "They are advising on the repopulation and education of the semisapient ocean mammals which your ancestors nearly rendered extinct."

"Most of them are Chalder scientists and their families," said Hewlitt. "Only a few Earth-human marine biologists are given permission to meet or work with them. Nonspecialist visitors like myself were forbidden, but here visits between fellow patients are allowed."

"Even so," said One-Ninety-Three, "it seems to me that a life-form as physically fragile as yours is taking a serious risk simply to avoid the boredom of waiting to go home. The Chalder environment is friendly compared with some that you will find here. Was there a psychological component to your former illness?"

"Most of the medics at home thought there was," said Hewlitt, knowing that the irony was lost on them, "but in Sector General the cause of the trouble was removed and the Earth doctors were proved wrong. There is no serious risk, because Padre Lioren has agreed to be my guide and guardian."

"The hospital must feel an obligation to you," said the other, "to grant such an unusual request. What was wrong with you?"

He was still trying to think of a suitably unrevealing reply when One-Ninety-Three said, "Probably it was one of those disgusting reproductive problems that these non-egg-layers are prone to. You can see that it doesn't want to tell us, and anyway, I don't think I want to know."

Hewlitt wanted to protest at the implication that he was a non-egg-laying female, but if he did not know whether he was talking to male or female Chalders he could hardly object to them making the same mistake with him.

"Usually," he said, "the juiciest gossip is associated with some physical or emotional aspect of the reproductive process. You will find me less reticent when telling you about other people's embarrassments."

"We understand," said One-Ninety-Three, "but right now we would prefer to know when we are likely to be sent home. Have you heard anything on that subject?"

"Sorry, no," said Hewlitt. "But I will try to find out."

That much is true, he thought, remembering the warning to *Rhabwar* and the emergency drills that had been held in his former ward. Whether or not he would be allowed to pass on his findings was another matter, because he was beginning to suspect that the explanation was neither simple nor pleasant. But it soon became clear that all the Chalders really wanted to talk about was home.

At first he had expected that their attempts to explain the water world of Chalderescol to him would be like trying to describe a sunset to a person who was color-blind, but he was wrong. Within a few minutes he was experiencing the freedom of an ocean that, apart from two small areas at the poles, covered the planetary surface in places to a depth of over a hundred miles.

The Chalders had battled their way to the top of their evolutionary underwater tree, learned to survive and later to control and utilize the power from their undersea volcanic activity while husbanding the living, nonsapient resources of the most beautiful world in the Federation, although the small-eyed air-breathers like himself required pressure vessels and visual enhancement to appreciate it. They were already a highly civilized species before their discovery of fire and the beginnings of the technology that enabled the very few of their number to fly through the near-vacuum above their ocean and into the space beyond. But no matter how far or often they traveled or their reasons for doing so, they remained a part of Chalderescol's mother ocean and needed periodically to return to it.

Considering their enormous body mass, the size and complexity of life-support required, and the extreme danger and discomfort involved in traveling in space, Hewlitt wondered why they did not stay at home.

"Why does any otherwise sane person want to travel in space?" said Two-Eleven, making him realize that he had been wondering aloud. "That is a very large philosophical question, and much too complex for debate if you still want to speak to the other patients before the lunch hunt begins. Hold on to my fin again. . . ."

His experience with the first three Chalders meant that he was able to speak briefly to the other patients with some understanding of their feelings, or at least without making a complete fool of himself. He stopped beside but did not speak to the gravely ill patient Lioren was visiting, because they were already having a conversation and he thought it better not to intrude. But from his moment of floating beside its treatment frame he was able to establish that it, along with the rest of the ward's other patients and medical staff, had never been hosts of the virus creature.

He returned to find the food-dispenser outlet beside the nurses' station open and, drifting horizontally in the water before it, what seemed like more than a hundred flattened, ovoid shapes just under a meter in diameter. Their upper surfaces were covered by irregular patches of dull color while the underside was pale grey. A long, low dorsal fin ran fore and aft, and the rim at the stern was pierced by three circular openings. While he was moving forward for a closer look his hand touched the object, sending it into a slow roll. Suddenly Charge Nurse Hredlichli was beside him.

"What . . . ?" began Hewlitt, and broke off as a shapeless, Illensan limb shot forward, grasped the object, and pulled it level again.

"Do not alter the trajectory," it said in its usual impatient voice. "For your information, if you do not already have the knowledge, that is a container of concentrated food enclosed in an edible shell and propelled by concealed capsules of high-pressure, nontoxic gas which simulates the movement through water of a fleeing, nonsapient native crustacean. It has been found that mobile food increases the patients' appetite and has beneficial psychological effects. If the food vehicle were to crash edge-on into a wall or deck and burst, it would leave a mess that my nurses would have to filter out and remove when there are more important duties requiring their attention. Please reenter the nurses' station and stay out of my head fronds. Patients, your attention please. . . ."

Its voice was coming from the ward's wall speakers as well as his headset, and Hewlitt was being ignored.

"The main lunch release is imminent," Hredlichli went on. "It will be followed in fifteen minutes by the containers marked with concentric blue circles, which are the special diets required by Patients One-Ninety-Three, Two-Eleven, and Two-Fifteen. Kindly remember that these are not to be consumed by anyone else. Patients confined to their treatment frames will have lunch delivered to them by the nurses once the mobile patients are fed. All medical staff who are not already in the nurses' station return there at once. Padre Lioren, this includes you."

Lioren returned but did not seem disposed to speak to anyone. Perhaps its mind was still on its sick patient. Hewlitt watched as fans of bubbles jetted from the sterns of the lunch vehicles and they began to accelerate down the ward, their numbers thinned by heavy, darting shapes and clashing jaws. The shape of Hredlichli, looking like a grotesque, plastic-wrapped sickly vegetable, was still drifting close by, and for the first time since his arrival it seemed to have nothing to do.

There were times, he thought, when by pretending to have a little knowledge it was possible to obtain a lot more. He decided to risk a question.

"Charge Nurse," he said in a brisk, confident voice. "The AUGL classification are not easy to move in an off-world environment. How long would it require for an emergency evacuation of all the patients in your ward, and how would you personally assess the chances of success?"

Inside Hredlichli's protective envelope a group of oily yellow fronds twitched as it said, "Obviously you are already aware of the emergency. This surprises me because the information is restricted to the very senior medical and maintenance staff and to one charge nurse, myself, whose ward poses a particular problem. Or are you more than a mere curious visitor, and there was another reason why you wished to speak to every patient in my ward?"

The answer to both questions was yes, Hewlitt thought, but he could not say so because the knowledge of the virus creature was also restricted. He wanted to ask for more details about the emergency, but could not because he was supposed to know them, and his earlier curiosity was being diluted by a growing fear.

"Sorry, Charge Nurse," he said, "I am not at liberty to answer that question."

More parts of Hredlichli twitched grotesquely. It said, "I do not approve of the secrecy where this ward is concerned. My Chalders are overlarge but they are not stupid. Even in this hospital there are too many people who equate large size with a lack of sensitivity. If my patients were to learn that there is a malfunction in the power-generation system that threatens the entire hospital and that they, because of their great size and consequent difficulty of evacuation, would be among the last to leave or, worse, that there might not be time enough to modify enough ships to accommodate them, they would not panic or try to break out. Your poisonous, rarefied atmosphere outside this ward would be as deadly to them as my own chlorine or space itself. Those that were left behind would accept their fate, and no doubt insist that their medical attendants save themselves, because they are intelligent, sensitive, and caring monsters."

"I agree," said Hewlitt. He had recently met all of them and knew. He had also had frightening confirmation of the reason for the emergency drills that were apparently being conducted everywhere but the Chalder ward, but uppermost in his mind was a sudden and inexplicable liking for this ghastly chlorine-breather. He added reassuringly, "It might never happen, Charge Nurse. This is a problem for the maintenance engineers. No doubt they will be able to solve it in time."

"Considering the time it took for them to repair the waste extractor on One-Eighty-Seven's treatment frame," Hredlichli replied, returning to character, "I lack your confidence."

All of Lioren's eyes had been directed at him while he was talking to the charge nurse, but the Padre did not comment and it remained silent after they returned to the corridor. Hewlitt wondered if his conversation with Hredlichli had caused the other to take offense.

"Are we agreed," he said, "that there are no former virus hosts in the Chalder ward?"

"Yes," said Lioren.

The word had punched a small hole in the other's wall of silence. But Hewlitt's fear was growing and so was his impatience to know more, and he knew that his next words might close the hole again.

"Did you know the reason for the evacuation drills?" he asked. "Were you deliberately keeping it from me?"

"Yes," said the Padre.

Before Hewlitt could ask the obvious question, Lioren answered it.

"There were three reasons," it went on. "You have already been told one of them, that you are not a specialist in the relevant field so that being given complete and accurate information could not have contributed to a solution of the problem. As well, the knowledge would have worried you unnecessarily and might have had an adverse effect on your conduct of our search. And my own incomplete knowledge was gained in circumstances which preclude me passing it on. In any case, you found out as much about the emergency from Hredlichli as I did, so I now feel free to discuss the situation with you. In general terms, at least."

"Does that mean," he said, trying to control his irritation, "that there is something that you are still not telling me? For my own peace of mind, naturally."

"Yes," said Lioren.

This time it was Hewlitt who erected the wall of silence, because the words he felt like using were not those normally spoken to a Padre, and it was Lioren who was trying to demolish it.

"The next call," it said, "is to a patient in the SNLU ward. It is an ultra-frigid, methane life-form with a crystalline tissue structure that is hypersensitive to bright light and minute increases in temperature. The environmental-protection vehicle is cumbersome, heavily insulated, fitted with sensory enhancement and remote manipulator systems. Because of the patients' extreme aural sensitivity it is necessary to attenuate external sound output and amplify the input. It is a very quiet ward. You will be able to move close to my patient, and the three others who are under treatment, when I introduce you, but then you must leave the two of us alone as you did in the Chalder ward and talk to the others. You will not have to concern yourself with your vehicle's controls; one of the staff will guide it remotely from the nurses' station."

Still feeling angered by the other's implication that he could not be trusted with sensitive information without losing his emotional control, Hewlitt remained silent.

"You will find," Lioren added, "that the SNLU environment will cool even the hottest temper."

CHAPTER 29

Not only was the ward cold and dark, but heavy shielding and insulation protected it from the trace quantities of radiation and heat given off by ship traffic in the vicinity of the hospital. There were no windows, because even the light that filtered in from the distant stars could not be allowed to penetrate to this area. The images that appeared on his display had been converted from the nonvisible spectrum, giving them the ghostly, unreal quality of fantasy, so that the scales covering the patients' eight-limbed, starfish bodies shone coldly through the methane mist like multihued diamonds, making them resemble a species of wondrous, heraldic beast.

When he turned off his translator while moving between patients so as to listen to their natural voices, the sound was like nothing he had ever heard before. So clear and cold and beautiful were the sounds that he could almost imagine that he was hearing the musical, amplified chiming of colliding snowflakes. Even though there were no virus hosts in the ward, and Hewlitt doubted that anything other than an SNLU could survive for more than a few minutes in that environment, it surprised him how sorry he felt when the time came to leave.

Lioren's next visit was to the quarters of an off-duty Melfan nurse called Lontallet. Again he was introduced and, after removing it from their suspect list of former virus hosts, he waited in the corridor while the other two went inside to talk.

The wait was neither long nor boring, because the corridor was invaded by a slow-moving column of patients. He counted thirty of them comprising five different oxygen-breathing species, several of whom were being transported in gravity litters. From the overheard conversations of the nursing attendants he discovered that it was both an evacuation drill and an utter shambles. The last of them was moving away when the Padre rejoined him.

"Did they pass by slowly enough for detection?" it asked. "Did you feel anything from them?"

"Yes," said Hewlitt. "And no. Where to next?"

"To the dock airlock on Level One," Lioren replied, "and calling on the wards and scanning all the passersby in the corridors between. We will have to work much faster now. No longer may we speak at length to any of the patients. A few words or a brief visual contact is all we can allow ourselves. Are you feeling tired?"

"No, curious," said Hewlitt. "And hungry. We haven't eaten since—"

"In the short term," the Padre broke in, "our hunger is not life-threatening. I contacted the department from Nurse Lontallet's room. O'Mara is in conference, this time by communicator with the waiting ships' captains, but it left a message for us. The situation has worsened but so far the exact nature of the technical emergency has not been made public.

At present there are three separate evacuation drills in progress, but as yet there are no ships at the boarding locks. The patients are complaining about the inconvenience, the medical staff know that something serious is going on and are wanting answers, and in spite of their efforts to project clinical calm, their uncertainty is being communicated to their patients and each other. Psychologically, this is a dangerous situation which must not be allowed to continue."

"But what is the problem, exactly?" said Hewlitt. "Not enough ships for a complete evacuation, or what? Keep it a secret from me if you have to, but surely the other people here are used to emergencies, medical emergencies, at least, and would react better in conditions of full knowledge, even if the knowledge is frightening, than total ignorance."

Lioren increased its pace along a clear section of corridor as it said, "Assembling enough ships to empty the hospital should not be a major problem, considering the Federation's past response times on disaster-relief operations. It may be that they can't talk about the problem because they don't fully understand it themselves, or there is more than one problem."

"Are you trying to confuse me," said Hewlitt, "or give me some kind of clue?"

Lioren ignored the question and went on, "Prilicla reported nothing unusual from the dining hall. The virus creature was not occupying any of the diners whose emotional radiation it scanned, but due to its low stamina, it requires a lengthy period of rest before it will be able to resume the search. That leaves us as the only people who are able to detect the virus, O'Mara says, and we must find it with minimum delay. As well, from now on we are ordered to seal our helmets and use only suit air to avoid wasting time when changing environments."

"But that would save only a few minutes . . ." Hewlitt began, then ended, "Never mind."

It was a stupid order, he thought, when all but two of the wards they would be visiting belonged to warm-blooded oxygen-breathers with similar atmospheric composition and pressure requirements as themselves. Maybe the emergency could affect the thinking of even the chief psychologist.

Their next ward was one of the few in Sector General— the Chalder section they had visited was another—where only one species of patient was treated. For the first time he was able to see, at close range and in horrendous, sharp focus rather than through a semitransparent chlorine enve-lope, not only one but a whole ward full of uncovered Illen-san bodies. He was not surprised to find that none of them had harbored the virus, because he could not imagine any creature, no matter how desperate it was for a host, wanting to occupy a body like that.

Ward followed ward, as did the bewildering succession of patients and medical staff, many of them belonging to species he was meeting for the first time. There was no time to ask questions or wait for answers. None of the beings were as visually unpleasant as the Illensans and neither had any of them been former virus hosts. The speed of their vis-its aroused comment, as did the odor of chlorine emanating from their unnecessary protective suits, but the presence of the Padre insured that the remarks were polite. In the inter-vening corridors all of the people they met gave similar neg-ative results.

"I'm beginning to wonder," said Hewlitt, "if we aren't deluding ourselves with our host-recognition capability. We have an indescribable—well, I suppose you could call it a fellow feeling for each other. But the feeling might be for each other and nobody else. And there is something wrong with this whole situation. I don't know what it is exactly, but I think you know and could tell me."

Lioren stopped so suddenly that Hewlitt had to take three paces backward. They seemed to have left the medical levels, because the people who passed them were wearing Maintenance coveralls and the doors and side corridors bore the interspecies symbols for power-transmission stations, heat-exchanger systems, and, above the opening just ahead of them, a radiation warning. He wondered what kind of ward he would find up here.

"Are you tired?" asked Lioren.

"No," said Hewlitt. "Are you trying to change the subject?"

"As you may already have heard," said the Padre, "I trained here as a medic before. . . . What I'm trying to say is that I know my Earth-human physiology well enough to be aware of your physical limitations. By now you should be very tired as well as hungry. My next and final patient contact is classification VXTM. That is a radiation-eater and therefore completely unsuitable as a host entity for the virus. It is also a terminal case and is being visited for no other reason than that I visited it once and it requested as many subsequent visits as were possible. You may as well take this opportunity to eat or rest."

"I'm not tired," said Hewlitt. "Have you forgotten that the legacy left us by the virus is one of optimum health which presumably includes a body that operates at peak efficiency and is less subject to fatigue? Am I right in thinking that, following our recent high level of physical activity, you also are feeling less tired than you would normally have been?"

"I dislike arguing with you," said the Padre, "especially when, as now, you are right. I have much on my mind and this is not an important matter. But very well, we are not as tired as we should be."

It was clear that Lioren was irritated with him, probably for good and perhaps religious reasons so far as a padre making a sick call was concerned. He tried to apologize.

"I seem to have spent my whole life arguing," he said, "usually with medics who were sure they were right and I was wrong. I'm sorry, it has become a bad habit that I should curb. If you have strong personal or religious reasons for not wanting my company on this visit, just say so. But I also feel that if we have checked all of your possible virus contacts together up to now, in the interests of consistency we should finish the job that way even though we may be wasting our time."

When the Padre did not respond, he laughed and went on, "As well, if you consider the Telfi radiation-eaters as unsuitable hosts, what about that ultra-low-temperature SNLU? Could a virus exist that close to absolute zero, and if it is an *intelligent* virus, why would it want to?"

Lioren ignored his attempt at humor. It said, "I do not know enough about the virus creature's motivations to be able to speculate about why it would do anything. And if you remember your home world's natural history, there are many instances of simple forms of life surviving for extended periods under your polar ice layers, sometimes for millions of years."

"And do you remember," said Hewlitt, trying hard to control his own irritation, "my telling O'Mara that our virus creature passed through the fringes of a nuclear detonation? And that it survived the experience for more than twenty years before it infected me?"

They had to move aside quickly to avoid two Orligians in Monitor Corps uniforms who were driving their equipment litters like racing vehicles, but it was a few minutes before Lioren spoke.

"I do not remember that," it said, "because I did not overhear that part of the meeting so that information is new to me. But there is a vast difference between the short burst of radiation sustained by the virus and the intense, lifelong exposure required by the Telfi. You are arguing with me again, but again you may be right. Very well, you may accompany me into the Telfi section."

"Thank you," said Hewlitt. "After I see the patient the two of you will be left alone to speak in private."

"That will not be necessary this time," said the Padre. "The patient is close to death. Beyond its self-knowledge of that fact, it has not said that there is anything troubling its mind. As you would expect, all of the Telfi religions are based on various forms of sun worship, but it has not said whether or not it believes in any of them. All that it needs or wants at this time is contact with another intelligent creature, or creatures, who will listen to it and speak in the Language of Strangers until it is no longer capable of forming thoughts or words. While it is suffering all we can do is stay with it for a while and listen in the hope that we are doing some good."

Lioren turned without warning into a side corridor so that Hewlitt had to hurry to catch up. He said, "Wouldn't the patient feel better if one of its friends were with it at a time like this?"

"Obviously," said the Padre, "you know very little about the Telfi."

"Not much," said Hewlitt, feeling his face grow warm at the implication of ignorance. "I never expected to meet one socially, so there was no reason to learn more. I know they are radioactive, very dangerous, and, well, not approachable people."

"Their environment is hostile," said Lioren, "not the people. And very few Federation citizens need to meet or learn about the Telfi person-to-person, so your lack of knowledge is not a reason for you to feel offended. Before you meet this patient you will have to learn a little about how the Telfi live, and, more important in this case, how they die. Are you able to absorb knowledge while moving your lower limbs a little faster, I hope?"

"I'll be able to keep up with you," said Hewlitt.

Lioren ignored the deliberate ambiguity and went on. "I

have promised to touch and listen to the last thoughts, if it still has the strength to articulate them for the translator, of the dying Telfi astrogator part Cherxic. So far we have had no success with our search for the virus. I want to take a little of the time we seem to be wasting to keep my promise."

"And do you have a little time," said Hewlitt, "to listen to me?"

"Yes," said the Padre without hesitation. "For some time I have sensed in you an emotional disturbance, but whether it is anger directed at me because of unsatisfied curiosity or some more serious, personal concern that distresses you I do not know. If the latter, is the matter urgent? Either way I will listen, now or later, but you know as well as I do that now is not a good time. Can you tell me simply, and I hope briefly, what is troubling you?"

Hewlitt did not look at the other as he replied, "You are right, Padre. I am curious and angry with you for not satisfying my curiosity, and I am growing increasingly frightened by the fact that you have been forbidden to satisfy it. So I keep asking myself questions that I'm not qualified to answer, and worrying. There is something about this whole business that bothers me."

"Go on," said Lioren, stopping before a rail containing Earth-human radiation protection suits in various sizes. "Put one on without removing the garment you are wearing. It would be better if you talked while I help you to dress."

It would also waste less time, he thought, but the Padre was too polite to say that.

"Right," said Hewlitt. "So far as we know, the only beings to be infected or invaded by this virus creature were myself, my cat, Morredeth, you, and some other as yet unknown person or persons. It left us with a legacy of unusually good health and, for some reason, a strange ability to recognize former hosts. Why would it want to do that? And what exactly did it do to us?"

Without waiting for a reply he went on, "Is it telepathy, or an empathic faculty like Prilicla's? We can't receive each other's thoughts or feelings with accuracy, so probably not. I don't know enough about xenobiology or the behavior of extraterrestrial viruses, intelligent or otherwise, and nobody, yourself included, will answer questions. But am I right in thinking that the recognitive ability could only have come about as the result of a physical change of some kind within us? Was this invisible, two-way name tag that identifies us to other hosts merely a side effect and did something else happen, something the virus does to everyone it occupies? Has the long-term survival of the creature's species got anything to do with it? Have we all been seeded by the thing and are busy growing virus-creature embryos?"

He had stopped moving and was standing balanced on one foot and with the other one pushed deep into the leg section of the radiation suit. The Padre was standing behind him, supporting the upper body section and not moving or speaking, either. The lengthening silence was broken by the Padre.

"I was forbidden to answer your questions," Lioren said, "for the reasons you have already been given. It was to avoid causing you mental distress by listing our more frightening speculations. But I will not continue to withhold answers when it is plain that you are discovering them for yourself."

Hewlitt was silent. He was no longer sure that he wanted his questions answered.

"You already know that the most important factor in the treatment of multispecies patients," Lioren went on, "is that we can provide it without risk of cross-infection, because pathogens native to one world cannot be transmitted to a life-form that has evolved on another. We have derived much professional comfort from the fact that, throughout the explored galaxy, no exception has ever been found to this rule. Until now."

"But the virus isn't harmful," Hewlitt protested. "It isn't a disease. The opposite, in fact."

"Yes," said the Padre. "But it is still a virus, a form of multispecies pathogen, with all that that implies. Admittedly it seems to be an intelligent, perhaps a highly intelligent organism who intends no harm to anyone, but we cannot be sure of that. We may be mistaking a simple, selfish need to occupy and maintain a host in optimum health for altruism. Certainly that is a very comforting and reassuring thought, but in a place like Sector General we cannot afford to ignore the possibility that, whether its behavior is guided by intelligence and altruism or is the result of a highly evolved survival instinct, it is the worst medical nightmare that any of us can imagine."

"I still don't understand why you're so worried," said Hewlitt. "It only *cures* people."

"You are forgetting what it has done," said the other. "On six separate occasions that we know of it has crossed the species barrier. It has done so with ease and without triggering the host's natural defenses, although later it hyperreacted to any medication or toxic material introduced into the host body. In essence it is a superpathogen, an organized, intelligent collection of viruses which is capable of modifying its structure to adapt and survive within a wide range of temperatures and the physiologies and metabolisms of an as yet unknown number of former hosts . . ."

"Wait," said Hewlitt. "Did the medical team on *Rhabwar* know about this and deliberately keep it from me?"

"Yes," said the Padre, "as soon as they realized Lonvellin's personal healer was involved and you were no longer hyperreacting to new medication, but Prilicla didn't want you to worry."

"On the way back from Etla," he said, "I remembered Naydrad saying that my troubles were just beginning. I thought it was talking about something else."

"It wasn't," said Lioren, and went on, "potentially an organism that can do all that is very dangerous indeed. It might not intend to harm anyone, but the mechanism that enables it to transfer so easily between species could also serve as a bridge that would allow the transmission of lethal pathogens between the species of its former hosts. If such an adaptable, multispecies strain were to get loose in the hospital it is possible that the virus creature could cure the victims as it has done on previous occasions, provided we could communicate and make our needs known to it. But it is only one individual who would be trying to cure patients one at a time, and if there were a hospital-wide epidemic that would not be fast enough. Sector General and possibly the entire Galactic Federation would be in very serious trouble.

"It would mean the end of our present free and open contact between planetary cultures," Lioren ended, "and we would be forced back to inhabiting only our own home planets or, if we did go visiting, taking the most stringent decontamination precautions."

"So that," said Hewlitt, "is the reason why the evacuation ships have been forbidden to dock."

This time he was not asking a question.

CHAPTER 30

For a moment Hewlitt felt that his body was so cold that he could have been back in the SNLU ward without his protective suit, and he wondered why the sweat breaking on his forehead was not dropping off as hailstones. All of the Padre's eyes were turned on him, and he did not know whether its next words were driven by impatience or the need to administer a therapeutic change of subject.

"Try not to think about it now," it said. "You are about to meet your first Telfi, regrettably one who is dying. There is information you must have and precautions you must take, both for your own safety and to avoid further distressing Patient Cherxic. Listen carefully, if possible without asking questions. . . ."

Lioren went on to describe the conditions on Telf, a planet that orbited some thirty million miles from and presented the same face to its parent sun. It was a world whose flora occupied the grey area between vegetable and mineral, a world where the temperature and radiation levels were lethal to every other intelligent species known to the Federation. It was a truly hellish place to all but the Telfi inhabitants.

They were a quasi-animal life-form that had evolved on the dayside hemisphere and required the continuous high levels of heat and hard radiation given off by their sun in order to live. As well as a spoken language they possessed a telepathic faculty which operated between individuals, and especially the members of a family gestalt, who were in physical contact at the time.

Their civilization was very old and well established by the time they achieved space travel, life-support for the Telfi being difficult to reproduce inside a ship, and the proportion of malfunctions and crew losses among them were considered very high when measured by Federation standards. But that had not kept them from traveling between the stars and, eventually, joining and sharing in the commercial and cultural benefits of Federation membership, which included making frequent use of its medical service.

Provided a Telfi ship with space casualties on board could be brought to Sector General quickly enough, it was possible to help them. The problem was that when a Telfi casualty's radiation-absorption mechanism failed because of a sudden withdrawal or a catastrophic surfeit of its radiant food supply, or a traumatic injury producing the same effect, the hospital had a maximum of one hundred hours from the time the injuries were sustained to initiation of treatment. This included reproducing in the required intensity and duration the cocktail of radiation that would enable the casualty to recover.

The need to reproduce this variety of curative radiation was the only reason why Sector General maintained a small fission reactor, which was little more than a functioning museum piece, among its contemporary fusion equipment.

Over the years the hospital had learned how to treat a large number of the nontraumatic conditions as well, the Telfi equivalents of respiratory, intestinal, or gynecological problems, but often it was work for a physicist as much as a physician.

"The patient we are about to visit," Lioren went on, "is the last and only surviving casualty of three sustained when their ship suffered a malfunction, the nature of which neither of us would understand. Cherxic was part of the specialized gestalt entity responsible for operating the vessel and, since it is no longer a functioning member of its group, the others have closed ranks as best they can and all physical, verbal, and telepathic contact with Patient Cherxic has been severed due to . . ."

"You did say," Hewlitt broke in, "that this is a civilized species?"

"Yes," said Lioren. Its eyes and medial hands moved quickly over the seals of his suit, and then it went on, "That's fine. Leave off one of your gauntlets—and the surgical glove, too, you won't need them while visiting Cherxic—but double-check your glare shield for yourself while I dress. The visual radiation where we are going is vicious stuff."

"The suit fabric," said Hewlitt doubtfully, "seems very thin."

"The fabric and visor materials are imported from Telf," said the Padre, "where they were developed for the protection of off-planet visitors. Neither you nor any offspring you may produce need worry."

"If we were carrying virus embryos," he said, trying to hold his voice steady, "would Prilicla be able to detect them?"

"Yes," said Lioren, "provided they had developed to the stage of being aware of themselves."

Hewlitt was still trying to think of a suitable response when it continued, "Patient Cherxic does not want, nor would any other Telfi even consider asking for, the presence of a family member or friend at such a time. Dying slowly while remaining conscious is a very unpleasant experience for any life-form, and for the Telfi who retain their telepathic faculty until the end, it is not one they wish to share with others of their kind. There is severe pain even while the sensorium is closing down, accompanied by fear that cannot be controlled or concealed because a telepath is incapable of controlling either, and for a being used to close physical and mental contact with its fellows from birth, there is a strange and terrible isolation, a loneliness so intense that nontelepaths can scarcely imagine it. And it is only nontelepaths like ourselves who are able to comfort a dying Telfi, by talking to it on the translator, listening to its final thoughts, and allowing it to feel contact with another sentient being for the last time, because it knows that we are feeling sympathy but will not be able to feel its pain."

Hewlitt had yet to meet the dying Cherxic, but already he was feeling a little ashamed that his sympathy for the other was being outweighed by his own selfish fear.

"What do they look like?" he asked. "And when you said close contact, how close did you mean?"

"We'll go in now," said Lioren. "Follow me and don't worry, the radiation where we are going is all in the visible spectrum."

The airlock seal swung open to reveal a boarding tunnel whose other end blazed like a square sun. By the time they had traversed it, his eyes had grown accustomed to the intense light, but in spite of his glare shield he still had to look through slitted eyes to see the details of the compartment beyond. The equipment projecting from the walls and ceiling was a blur to him, both visually and intellectually, but in the center of the deck there was a tethered gravity litter with two long, opened metal boxes resting on it. He followed as the Padre moved across the room to stand beside them, thinking that a coffin looked much the same on any world, although putting them in their last resting place before they were clinically dead showed a certain lack of sensitivity.

"These two are dead," said Lioren in a quiet, disapproving voice, making Hewlitt realize that he had been thinking aloud. "Both of them died within a few minutes of my arrival. They were left in the lock chamber close to the boarding tube so that the physical presence of their bodies would not cause distress to the living members of their gestalt, and for the convenience of Pathology, which will be sending someone to collect them. Since the Telfi do not reverence their dead other than in memory, the bodies have been donated to the hospital for research purposes on the understanding that the remains will ultimately be consigned to the surface of a sun, any sun. It is a custom among the members of their space-traveling gestalts that this be done. Excuse me, I must ask whether it is possible to meet Cherxic again. It may already have died, but please remember that death must never be mentioned in conversation with a Telfi."

"Right," said Hewlitt. "But earlier you mentioned making contact . . ."

"Padre Lioren and Patient Hewlett, an Earth-human DBDG, wish contact with the damaged part Cherxic," it said into the communicator. "Is this possible, and convenient?"

The sound in his earpiece resembled a long, modulated burst of static which the translator reproduced as, "You are welcome, Lioren, as is the stranger Hewlitt. A short visit is possible. Please wait."

The Padre moved closer to Hewlitt and joined him in looking down at one of the dead Telfi. When Lioren spoke there was sadness in its voice as it said, "The suffering and loneliness is long and there is little we can do to ease either, but the part Cherxic still lives."

After all that he had heard about this exotic, radiation-

eating species, Hewlitt had not expected them to look so
ordinary.

Apart from the extra set of forelimbs growing from the
base of the neck, the Telfi resembled nothing so much as a
large terrestrial lizard just under five feet long from bulbous
head to vestigial tail. The body was lying on its stomach so
that the two tiny, lidless eyes and the mouth, which was
closed, were the only features visible. All four of the stubby
walking limbs were bent double to lie flat against the body
while the two, longer forward manipulators were stretched
forward and crossed so as to allow the chin to rest on the
crossover point. The skin was pale grey with a mottled and
veined effect all over that made the body resemble a sculp-
ture in unpolished marble.

Hewlitt felt the need to comment, and remembering that
one should never speak ill of the dead, he said, "The, ah, skin
color is interesting. Beautiful, in fact."

"You must not say that to Cherxic when you meet it," said
the Padre sharply. "To a Telfi the pale skin is neither interesting nor beautiful, it is a symptom of advanced radiation
starvation and a lethal failure of the absorption mechanism.
You may touch it if the act is not repugnant to you. Rest your
bare hand anywhere on the body surface."

After putting his foot in his mouth with the remark about
the cadaver's beautiful skin, Hewlitt felt obliged to touch the
body. Surprised, he said, "It's very warm."

"It is no longer absorbing energy," said the Padre, "and
has risen to room temperature. Touching the top of the head
with a slow, stroking motion worked best with Cherxic.
Physical and verbal contact is a poor substitute for gestalt
telepathy, but the patient appeared to derive some comfort
from both."

Hewlitt stopped with his hand still resting on the pale
marble, lizard skull. "Wait right there," he said. "I tried to
ask this question earlier but you . . . Are you telling me that

you actually laid your bare hand on Cherxic in the same way as you did when you felt Morredeth's fur?"

"Yes," said the Padre. "But there is no need to feel so excited about it. Physiologically the Telfi are not suitable hosts for the virus creature. It would be like trying to infect a nuclear reactor."

A great light was beginning to dawn. Hewlitt said, "I told you already that the virus survived a close encounter with a nuclear detonation and, and the hospital's reactor has been, well, very sick."

The great light, he realized, was external as well as internal because the big, inner seal of the lock was swinging open to reveal the shape of a Telfi. Behind it there was another closed, transparent door that gave a view of the ship's interior. He decided that it must be a very healthy Telfi, because in spite of the high level of illumination, it reflected no light at all. It and the others that he could see beyond the transparent seal were like so many mobile, lizard-shaped black holes.

And every single Telfi that Hewlitt could see he recognized at once as being past, and one present, hosts of the virus creature.

There was a burst of modulated static as the one in the open lock moved closer and spoke.

"I am the part Cherxic," it said. "Please touch me, my offworld brothers and benefactors, one at a time. Our ship will be returning to Telf very soon and there is important information that must be passed to you."

CHAPTER 31

He watched as Cherxic moved between them and as the Padre, whose curiosity was greater or its cowardice less than Hewlitt's, placed one uncovered medial hand on the Telfi's head. Lioren's body trembled for a moment although it did not seem to be in any distress. No words were spoken and he had still to learn how to read a Tarlan's facial expression, so he had no idea what was going on. A few more minutes passed before the Padre lifted its hand away and it was his turn.

Unlike the body of the dead Telfi he had touched, the dense black skin of Cherxic felt cold, and there was a faint, warm tingling in his palm similar to the sensation he had felt when he had pressed his hand against Patient Morredeth's damaged fur. But this time the tingling was moving up his arm, across his shoulder and into his head. For a moment his sensorium went wild as tiny, random sensations of warmth, cold, pressure, pleasure, and pain occurred all over his body, while bursts of color that were beyond his previous experience or imagination and odors familiar and utterly strange were flooding his senses.

For some odd reason the memory picture of his cat came into his mind, and the way it had circled and stamped gently with each paw in turn as it had tried to push his lap into a more comfortable shape before it curled up to sleep. Now something was pushing and probing at his mind, trying to make itself fit more comfortably, and it was both gentle and persistent.

Suddenly there was a great, soft explosion of knowledge.

Hewlitt was still running through his bright, newly acquired memories like an excited small child exploring a new playground when the virus creature retraced its path along his shoulder, arm, and palm to return to Cherxic. Without a word the Telfi left the lock chamber and the inner seal closed behind it.

There was nothing more to be said to it, they knew, and nothing left to ask.

They maintained their silence while Hewlitt followed the Padre as it guided the gravity litter containing the two Telfi cadavers through the boarding tube and into the hospital lock chamber. The seal had closed behind them and emitted a loud, double chime accompanied by a visual warning indicating that the Telfi vessel had broken the docking seals before Lioren spoke, and then it was into its communicator.

"Braithwaite? Lioren. I must speak to Major O'Mara. It's urgent."

"O'Mara," said the voice of the chief psychologist. "Go on, Padre."

"We are calling off the search," said Lioren. "The last and only remaining host of the virus creature has been found. It is currently inhabiting a member of the Telfi gestalt whose ship is leaving as we speak. The vessel is to be given departure clearance without delay. And you can cancel the evacuation drills and disperse the waiting ships. The problem with the power-generation control systems is over and . . ."

"I don't see the connection," O'Mara broke in sharply. "Are you trying to tell me there is one?"

"Yes," said Lioren. "When two unusual events occur at the same time, the chances are that they have a common cause. I had forgotten that particular unwritten natural law and it was Hewlitt, not me, who made the connection. There is no longer any danger to anyone inside the hospital, either from a nuclear detonation or a cross-species contagion, and we will give you a full report as soon as we reach the department."

"Wait," said O'Mara, "where you are."

For what seemed a long time Hewlitt stared at Lioren, who was looking with all of its eyes at the two dead Telfi, before the chief psychologist's voice returned.

"You're right, Padre," said O'Mara, "Engineering confirms that the instability in the nuclear power and distribution systems has rectified itself, why or how they don't know, and the emergency is over. It happened within the past fifteen minutes. But that was the lesser of the two problems. There is still the matter of the multispecies virus loose in the hospital and, with respect, you two are so deeply and personally involved that your assurance that there is no danger could be, well, more an unconscious product of wishful thinking than clinical fact. Is Hewlitt fully aware of the situation?"

When it was clear that Lioren was not going to reply, he said, "Yes, I think so."

"Then let there be no doubt in your mind, Hewlitt," said O'Mara, "that you two are in serious trouble. I am personally very sorry about this, we all are, but your trouble started when you were infected by the virus creature as a child on Etla, and here it was passed to ex-Patient Morredeth, Padre Lioren, and, an idea which I find completely incredible, a

Telfi whose physiology and environment is less suited to a microbiological form of life than one of our hottest autoclaves. There are probably other hosts that we don't know about. That is why, when our power generation showed indications of increasing instability that would not respond to the fail-safe systems, we kept calling emergency evacuation drills instead of moving everyone into the ships that had been assembled for that purpose. We could not afford to take the risk of turning a multispecies disease of unknown potentiality loose in the Federation.

"Padre, I have no wish to offend you," the chief psychologist went on, "by doubting the words of a Wearer of the Blue Cloak of Tarla. But the will to survive in you two as individuals, and for the citizens of the Galactic Federation as a whole, is an evolutionary imperative that may be superseded by any ethical considerations. That is why Kelgia has been instructed to place ex-Patient Morredeth in orbital quarantine on arrival. Similar instructions will be sent to Telf regarding the ship that has just left, and to Etla regarding that cat. You two will be placed in isolation for intensive study by Pathology, and the decision is about to be taken to dismiss the evacuation vessels and replace them with a Monitor Corps sector subfleet with orders to interdict Sector General to all external contact. This could result in serious destabilization throughout the Federation, but it seems that we have no choice. Do you understand our position?"

"It sounds," said Hewlitt, with a small, uncontrollable shiver that was partly of dread as well as a reaction to well-meaning stupidity, "that you would have preferred the hospital to blow up and save everybody a lot of trouble. But please believe us, you have absolutely nothing to worry about."

"I'm sorry, Hewlitt," said O'Mara. "If the Padre has broken communicator contact with us, please ask it to speak.

Diagnosticians Conway and Thornnastor as well as Murchison, Prilicla, and Colonel Skempton are with me. You may already know that Lioren was once a highly respected senior physician in Sector General. No offense, Hewlitt, but right now we need to hear the report from a medical professional."

One of Lioren's eyes moved up to regard Hewlitt for a moment; then the Padre returned all of its attention to the Telfi dead. He could almost feel the other's present sorrow and its old, remembered pain. It did not speak.

"Lioren is unable or unwilling to speak to you right now," he said, "nor will it speak to me. But we have become very close to the Telfi and each other during the past few minutes. I understand the situation as well as the Padre does, and I am willing to speak."

"It isn't like the Padre to behave this way," said the chief psychologist, in a voice that mixed impatience with concern. "But I suppose we must settle for a bloody amateur. Talk, dammit."

Hewlitt took a firmer grip on his temper and said, "The Padre may indeed have taken offense at your suggestion that we are lying; I certainly did. But it is also gravely troubled by the thought of two dead Telfi who, if it had only known what we now know, might not have died. But in the event it decided to comfort Patient Cherxic, whose case was also terminal although the condition was not as far advanced as that of the other two. The mistake, which was not deliberate and not a reason to punish itself, was on a much smaller scale than the results of the wrong decision it made a few years ago, but its distress over the Cromsag Incident is never far from the Padre's . . ."

"Lioren spoke to you about Cromsag?" O'Mara broke in. "It never speaks of that to anyone, not even me."

"It did not speak to me," said Hewlitt. "As of a few minutes ago, after the virus creature transferred temporarily from Cherxic to Lioren and then to me, I knew everything that was in the Padre's mind. . . ."

He had to break off, because it sounded as if six voices were trying to ask six different questions at once. He looked at the Padre for help, but Lioren's eyes were still on the dead Telfi and he knew that its mind was on the terrible occurrence in its past when a planet had been all but depopulated because of a single wrong decision. Sympathy for the Tarlan made his voice sound harsher than he had intended.

"If you don't stop asking questions," he said, "I won't be able to answer any of them. Please be quiet and listen to me."

He was surprised at how quickly the voices died away until he realized that O'Mara had been giving them the same message, in much less polite language.

"Yes," he said, "the virus creature briefly reentered my body, specifically my brain. And no, the process did not render me telepathic. The effect is closer to that of the Educator-tape experience remembered by the then Senior Physician Lioren, except that the process is gentler and without the psychological disorientation associated with the sudden transfer into one's mind of the memories and personality of a completely alien donor. This was not a mind-recording, it was the transfer of memories by a thinking, sensitive entity who, because of the debt it felt it owed us, was anxious not to cause mental distress."

"Wait," O'Mara broke in, and there was a suspicious edge to his tone when he went on, "Are you saying that the memories were diluted, changed, or even edited?"

"Diluted with the passage of time," Hewlitt replied, "but not distorted. You have experience with treating telepathic species and must know that it is impossible to lie with the mind. I know everything that was in the mind of the virus creature, who, because there seems to be only one of it, does not have a name. That includes its future intentions, which in a telepath cannot be concealed or edited in any way."

"Go on," said O'Mara.

"During the recent second visitation," he continued, "I was made aware of the memories of all its previous hosts. Strongest were those of Lioren, Cherxic, and the other members of the Telfi gestalt among whom it was invited to transfer at will. When you think about it, an organized, self-aware, intelligent virus has much in common with a gestalt entity. But it was the Telfi contact telepathy that enabled it, for the very first time, to achieve perfect communication with other sapient beings. Without knowing how or why, this was the ability it had been searching for all of its life. But even more important were the Telfi radiation-based metabolism and experience in adapting their horrendous environment to their needs, together with their promise of long-term cooperation that will, hopefully, enable the virus creature to make another and most hazardous future change of hosts. That was the reason for the initial investigation and experimentation, unsettling for the hospital staff but never life-threatening, that caused the problem with the power-generation and control systems.

"I don't have the technical vocabulary, but it seems that the structure of the virus is such that it is possible for it to interpenetrate and exert a measure of control on the subatomic level."

Hewlitt paused for a moment, then moved onto more familiar ground. He said, "I was also given the Morredeth material and, strangely, the feelings of the creature from the time I first became its host as a child. That was a weird experience. Before that there was its time with Lonvellin, and before that a succession of nonsapient hosts stretching far beyond even its own recollection.

"The virus creature is old, very old. . . ."

There was no knowing what environmental influences had caused it to evolve intelligence or if there had ever been other sapient virus creatures; it could well have been a genetic accident and unique of its kind. In the beginning its hosts had been small, and rather than infecting and killing them through uncontrolled proliferation as did normal pathogens, it tried to insure its own long-term survival by maintaining the hosts in optimum physical condition for as long as possible. It transferred when, in spite of its efforts, a host grew too old or was killed by a larger predator, where-upon the predator became the new host.

A great many centuries must have elapsed before the highly intelligent and extremely long-lived explorer Lonvel-lin visited its home world and, believing that no off-world pathogen could affect it, took no precautions and acquired a most unusual and unique parasite.

Instinctively the virus realized that it had found an organism that could be made to survive for a very long time indeed, but the new host's body was so massive and strange and complex that it had extreme difficulty adapting to the new surroundings. Lonvellin, however, who must have been subject to many irritating and uncomfortable illnesses dur-ing its long life, would have deduced the virus's presence and capabilities from the fact that the incidence of its former maladies was dropping toward zero. But at that time the virus creature could not communicate with its host, nor was it aware of the reasons why certain obscure metabolic processes were taking place in that massive and confusing body. All it was able to do at the time, and then only with great difficulty, was to maintain its host in the same physio-logical condition as it had been in when found.

The virus made mistakes.

One of them, its stubborn retention of dying skin mater-ial which would normally have been discarded and replaced with new growth, brought Lonvellin to Sector General. Another was allowing the then Senior Physician Conway to trick it into leaving its host and revealing itself as a separate entity. At this stage in its continuing evolutionary development the virus creature was sapient but not very bright.

After it was reclaimed by Lonvellin, it traveled to Etla, where it had a narrow escape from the nuclear detonation that killed its host. That incident came close to killing the creature as well, but instead resulted in a structural mutation which later enabled it to enter and adapt to a radiation-eating Telfi host.

It saved the Hewlitt child's life twice, after the poisoning and potentially lethal fall from a tree and following the flyer crash, but it was still making mistakes, such as halting the blood circulation by arresting the heart so as to give it more time to negate the effect of any fast-acting foreign medication introduced, which eventually resulted in the adult Hewlitt being sent to Sector General. It was learning, however, and becoming increasingly aware of the host's mind and feelings as well as its own. The process began with Lonvellin, but the incident with the mutilated cat was more important than was realized because it was the first time that the virus had been influenced by psychological factors, specifically the emotional pressure of a child's grief for a dying pet, into changing hosts.

"The transfer was temporary," Hewlitt went on, "because it was not in the creature's interests to move from a long-lived host to a small and shorter-lived one. By then it was being driven by curiosity and the urge to experiment as well as by its need to survive into the indefinite future, but for a long time there were only Earth-humans like myself available and it had not yet fully understood the workings of my body. By the time I arrived here it was becoming intensely curious, more aware of its surroundings and hungry for the new experiences that were available in a place that is filled with very interesting and long-lived potential hosts. When it felt my sorrow and sympathy for Patient Morredeth and I accidentally touched, or perhaps was subtly influenced by it to place a bare hand on, the wound where the fur had been destroyed, it transferred to its first Kelgian. Later it moved to the Padre and then to Cherxic and, in turn, to each of the surviving members of the Telfi ship gestalt, where the latest and most significant but not, it believes, the final adaptation occurred. From the telepathic and technically highly specialized members of the ship gestalt it learned how to communicate mind-to-mind with its subsequent hosts, and to understand and control at the particle level the radiation on which the Telfi live. The covert and Telfi-guided experiments with the hospital's power system were part of its learning process.

"Now it has everything it needs to survive into the indefinite future," Hewlitt went on. "Individual Telfi will die, many with less frequency now that it is moving among them, but the gestalts replace or increase their membership and will continue to amass information and experience. It has found the perfect host species. With the willing cooperation and the radiation-absorption mechanism of the Telfi as its launching point, it will grow in size and intelligence and power, and it will continue to evolve until it is able to populate the stars or, a risk which it fully accepts, kill itself in the attempt.

"The hospital will not be troubled with the virus creature again."

In his earpiece there was a long, hissing silence that was broken by a voice that was so quiet and distorted with emotion that it could have belonged to anyone.

"So it intends to infect and populate the stars," it said. "I don't doubt that it means what it says, because we already know that it is impossible to lie with the mind. That could lead to the breakdown of the Federation, perhaps the end of free and unprotected other-species contact, perhaps of all intelligent life because of an uncontrollable, interspecies contagion sweeping the member worlds, if we don't act at

once. We're sorry, Hewlitt, but that action must include iso-
lating Lioren, Morredeth, the Telfi ship's crew, yourself, and
even your childhood pet from all future contact for the rest
of your lives."

"No!" said Hewlitt angrily. "Why don't you people listen
to me, or believe me when you do listen? Padre, will you
explain it to them, please?"

While the voice from O'Mara's office had been speaking,
the Padre had closed the Telfi caskets and returned its attention to Hewlitt. He had the feeling that Lioren's emotional
distress had eased or was at least under control again.

"I couldn't explain it any better myself," said the Padre.
"Carry on, but be quick. Our covered litters and, dear me, an
armed escort are arriving."

Hewlitt took a deep breath and chose words that were
short and simple. He said, "O'Mara, all of you are wrong,
twice. None of the virus creature's hosts are infected, or contagious, nor have we been implanted with its seed or
embryo. It doesn't work like that. The creature is an intelligent, organized collection of viruses, a single and very selfish individual who will not willingly allow parts of itself to
be detached and thereby reduce the capability and intelligence of the whole. My problems during and after puberty
were caused by the fact that, while it could understand the
need of a host to eliminate body wastes, the expulsion of
healthy living material like seminal fluid was totally foreign
to it because, at that time, it could not conceive of the possibility of any entity wanting to propagate its kind rather than
surviving for itself alone. It still has difficulty accepting the
idea of countless billions of us sacrificing ourselves so that
our various species will survive.

"On Etla, on Earth, and in the hospital," he went on,
"there was absolutely no risk of secondary infection. Perhaps in the future, if its plans work out, it may be able to
divide itself, but that time is a very long way off and even

then we would be in no danger from it. For now the virus can occupy only one entity at a time, and it does not leave its host with a disease but with a level of physical, lifelong health that is immediately obvious as a kind of organic artist's signature to all of its former hosts.

"It does this out of gratitude," Hewlitt went on, "for the knowledge and experience provided by the host. It considers itself a tenant who is obliged to pay rent."

The litters, their canopies open and ready, were accompanied by two massive Hudlar medics and eight armed Monitor Corpsmen who were large by Earth-human standards. The men's expressions showed a mixture of embarrassment and determination. Hewlitt spoke quickly.

"Believe me," he said, "neither the Federation nor its citizens have anything to fear from the virus creature. It is no longer interested in the extremely short-lived natives of any planet. Even though the project will take many of our lifetimes to complete, its ambition is to populate the stars one at a time and beginning with the Telfi's parent sun, which, in astronomical terms, is growing old and sick. While there is always the chance that it will obliterate itself in the attempt, it considers the risk well worth taking. To inhabit a sun that can be inhabited and given intelligence, stability, and control of all its internal processes is the virus creature's ultimate goal.

"An intelligent star," he ended, "would be the most long-lived entity there could ever be."

This time it was Diagnostician Conway, Prilicla, and Thornnastor who were doing most of the talking while the litter personnel and escort waited for them to decide what they were going to do. For several minutes it seemed that the Padre and himself had been forgotten as they debated the possibility of retracing Lonvellin's travels before its arrival in Sector General with a view to finding the virus creature's planet of origin and other, perhaps nonsapient members of its species who could be studied and, hopefully, helped to proliferate. If it was offered, the assistance of former virus-creature hosts would be invaluable. All necessary precautions would be taken and there would be many problems to overcome, but if they were successful they could foresee a distant future when the citizens of the Galactic Federation would carry only one virus and be otherwise completely disease-free. All that would be left for the medical profession would be the treatment of accident and surgical emergencies. It was the chief psychologist who had the last, impatient words.

O'Mara said, "Doctors, enough. Your future hypothetical problems will not be solved in the next few minutes. Padre Lioren, Hewlitt, relax. We have decided that it is safe to allow Morredeth to land on Kelgia and the Telfi crew to return home with their new friend. The armed escort is dismissed but you two will board the litters and proceed with minimum delay, not to the isolation chamber in Pathology but to this office for an immediate and detailed debriefing . . ."

Hewlitt made a small, untranslatable sound which only the Padre heard. In a loud, reassuring whisper Lioren said, "Don't distress yourself, friend. The major's office has its own food dispenser, and if we aren't allowed to eat then we won't talk."

". . . and a Hudlar-guided litter will get you here sooner than traveling on foot," O'Mara went on. "Is there anything else you need to tell me before then?"

Hewlitt was not sure whether the words were the result of fatigue, malnutrition, or sheer relief. He laughed and said, "Only that I have a psychological problem. I seem to have become an ex-hypochondriac with absolutely nothing wrong with me who wants to stay in hospital. I don't want to go back to minding Earth sheep."

TOR
BOOKS The Best in Science Fiction

MOTHER OF STORMS • John Barnes
From one of the hottest new nanes in SF: a shattering epic of global catastrophe,
virtual reality, and human courage, in the manner of *Lucifer's Hammer*,
Neuromancer, and *The Forge of God*.

BEYOND THE GATE • Dave Wolverton
The insectoid dronons threaten to enslave the human race in the sequel to
The Golden Queen.

TROUBLE AND HER FRIENDS • Melissa Scott
Lambda Award-winning cyberpunk SF adventure that the *Philadelphia Inquirer* called
"provocative, well-written and thoroughly entertaining."

**THE GATHERING FLAME • Debra Doyle and
James D. Macdonald**
The Domina of Entibor obeys no law save her own.

WILDLIFE • James Patrick Kelly
"A brilliant evocation of future possibilities that establishes Kelly as a leading shaper
of the genre."—*Booklist*

THE VOICES OF HEAVEN • Frederik Pohl
"A solid and engaging read from one of the genre's surest hands."—*Kirkus Reviews*

MOVING MARS • Greg Bear
The Nebula Award-winning novel of war between Earth and its colonists on Mars.

NEPTUNE CROSSING • Jeffrey A. Carver
"A roaring, cross-the-solar-system adventure of the first water."—*Jack McDevitt*
